M000105009

SURFMEN & SHIPWRECKS

THE LIGHTHOUSE KIDS

Spirits of Cape Hatteras Island

SURFMEN & SHIPWRECKS

Jeanette Gray Finnegan Jr.

Copyright © 2017 Jeanette Gray Finnegan Jr.

All rights reserved. No part of this book may be used, reproduced
or transmitted in any form or by any means, electronic or mechanical,
including photograph, recording, or any information storage or
retrieval system, without the express written permission
of the author, except where permitted by law.

ISBN 978-1-59715-162-7
Library of Congress Catalog Number 2017958189

First Printing

CONTENTS

PREFACE

This book presents a partial and abbreviated story of the full account of what it was like living on this island as it became its own force of protection to the mainland. Once the country came into its own, trade and wars with other nations became a part of the fabric. Travel and trade sped across the land in the form of railways and stagecoaches, later buses and trucks. The most cost-effective method proved to be transport by sea. The ports of the United States down the seacoast bordering the Atlantic Ocean were thick with all types and sizes of floating vessels. They carried weight with ease, and if the wind was right, sails were full and free. The currents became known, as did the obstacles. The shoals off the coast of Cape Hatteras were the most dangerous, as they formed at the juncture of two useful rivers flowing in opposite directions and meeting at the Point on Hatteras Island. The conflict forced up huge water sprays, sand, and as a result, inclement weather.

This book tells of the growth in solving that problem. First, the government was only concerned with loss of cargo. Later, as those undersea rivers began to carry passengers, their loss became personal, thus the Lifesaving Service.

The men who lived all their lives surrounded by water were the perfect soldiers to save both cargo and lives. There are only a few mentioned here.

The keepers were known. The surfmen, numbering from one to eight, strong of back and hands, were seldom named, even though they, too, dedicated their lives to saving strangers. They did not ask what language, what country, or what the circumstances were surrounding the peril that put them in this position. They did what they would have hoped and expected to have been done for them.

The accounts given here are as close to historical truth as could be offered. Much research went into each storm, each documented wreck, each life offered for another. An Act of Congress (18 Stat 125, 43rd Congress) authorized

> medals of honor, to be distinguished as life-saving medals of the first and second class, and bestow them upon any persons who endanger their own lives in saving, or endeavoring to save lives from perils of the sea bordering the United States, or upon any American vessel.

A note of interest: The Lifesaving Medal is unusual among U.S. medals because it is actually struck from precious metal, silver or gold, depending on the grade. Most other medals are struck from inexpensive alloys.

Since 1874, more than 600 gold and 1,900 silver medals have been awarded. There were fewer awards of Lifesaving medals than Medals of Honor.

Of those awarded who were not connected to the official Lifesaving Service the names of the following are included: Rear Admiral Richard Evelyn Byrd, Fleet Admiral Chester W. Nimitz, and General George S. Patton. Seven of the lifesaving stations on Cape Hatteras Island produced recipients.

Entire books have been written lauding the valor of the men who dedicated their lives to saving others. To hear the men tell it, yes, they were scared, and no, it did not hamper them.

Life-saving crew had spent twenty-four hours in an open
boat, without food, and with no other nourishment other
than cold water, their limbs cramped with cold and lack of
room to move about, and their bodies aching from main-
taining so long a sitting posture.

> —*taken from the log of inspector C. F. Shu-*
> *maker, after an eighteen-mile row, in the dead*
> *of winter, back to the station, the row made*
> *harder by the added weight of rescued victims*
> *and weary surfmen*

The facts are true. The fiction provides the opportunity to see the villages and the heroism through the eyes of children. The accounts retold
involved information we all wondered about but had no one to verify it.
This was the life of the island during that time in history—before the
bridge, before a paved road, before "strangers."

From the Creeds Hill Station, during an atypical winter storm of
driving snow, the men who ventured out to the schooner *A. B. Goodman*
were told, "Write your wills, boys. We're goin' to the shoals." But, as those
of us who grew up on this island know, what did they have of any value,
other than character, bravery, unselfishness, and courage under duress?

Lifesaving stations, when finally they were deemed necessary, were
located all down the Atlantic coast, around the Gulf of Mexico, on the
entire coast of the Pacific, on the Great Lakes, and on the rivers and interior lakes of the United States. They were built and manned on every
waterway connected to the country, where wind and gale could make the
waters angry enough to swallow its riders.

This book is concerned, in part, with the victims in and around the
Diamond Shoals located just off The Point of Cape Hatteras Island. The
wrecks were as much a part of the island as the early settlers. Many now
prominent families had their origin here by shipwreck. They stayed and
became a part of the weave of island men. The shoals became notorious.

On a personal note, when I was a child, walking the sandy roads to the store for my grandmother, it was not unusual for a stranger to pull along-side and ask directions to the graveyard of the Atlantic. For years I did not know what they meant.

The Diamonds deserved to become famous. For example, the *Mary Varney* rounded the capes on a run from San Francisco to New York, loaded with ten heavy redwood boxes containing bars of gold. She had been on water for one hundred days when she gained The Point off Hat-teras Island. She hit the shoal and stuck. There was only a spring gale when she drove hard into the shoal. She did not "break up." Rather, she loosed her masts, rigging, and various unattached articles on deck—those she gave to the islanders. The gold she kept. Of course, this is not the first account. Therefore, there have been numerous attempts to recover the treasure. The fact survives: when she has taken a ship for her own, no man's hand may ever again touch her. For four centuries, ships have buried on those shoals. Also, that many years for the shoals to swallow. No burps, just swallows.

The island got horses from the *Pocahontas* and the *Prince of India*, stovepipe hats from the *Flambeau*, bananas from the *Cibao*, chalk from the *Josie Troop*, a dance floor from the *Irma*, resting nearby, for the visitors at the Croatan Hotel. Lumber came for building more than a few island homes; the entire construction of a barber shop in Kinnakeet, chair and all; a boatload of ladies' millinery, plus the entirety of what was needed for building a church in Salvo. Recently, the beach at Frisco was covered in bags of Doritos. The sea has been a never ending bounty for island inhabitants.

As early as Sir Walter Raleigh, a ship under his command, *Tiger*, was lost near Chicamacomico. The Indians got a plethora of ware from the sea. Some things they did not understand. Copper pots and iron in various forms washed up on the shore, and they devised a use for it. It is the nature of an island.

There have been over 170 hurricanes to date recorded at the Weather Bureau on Hatteras Island since it was built in 1944. Only those that actually hit Hatteras make up that number.

For those islanders who marveled at the new weather predicting building, Captain Bernice Ballance asked the question, "Don't they ever look out the window? And what about the moon. Do they ever look at the moon?"

This was the island way, and it worked pretty good.

⋆ 1 ⋆

The Woman on the Beach

lue snorted and pawed at the ground, his efforts making huge divots in
the sand. On this dreary moonless night, he was impossible to see. Behind
the dune, the blond fur of a wolf was almost invisible, with the exception
of her golden eyes like tiny moons moving through the sea oats. The wolf
was visible only through the frequent flashes of light cracking open the sky,
but Ellie did not notice her friend. Ellie's concentration was settled on the
shore. Twylah's presence went unnoticed. Other than those fleeting moments
of light, the huge wolf blended into the sand. Ellie, astride Blue, strained to
see the figure on the beach. She was also unaware of the sounds of the horse,
as the roar of an impending storm drowned out all other noises. The surf was
boiling angry at what seemed to be high tide. The waves drew close as they
broke and rushed to the dunes, leaving silvery foam stretching jagged in a line
as far as she could see.

Ellie was afraid to urge Blue on. She was not sure just how high the water
would go. Not even knowing the time, she was unaware if it was a regular
high tide, a storm tide still coming in, or even if was receding? A stiff wind
accompanied the furious surf, and she leaned forward, choking up her grip

1

on the bridle of the horse to stay stable. In her haste, she had been so secretive about taking him from the barn that she did not bother with the saddle. She was practically bareback on her mount, with only a blanket between her and the slick wet back of the horse. She had never before ridden without a saddle, so this was a first. She even realized at that moment how much Blake riding behind her had steadied her. This time, she was alone.

Ellie had awakened from a deep sleep to the slapping of the shutter on the side of her window. The summer storm had come up suddenly, and she crawled across the bed to the window to lower the window against what she figured would be an onslaught of rain usually accompanying a sudden gale like this. The window did not move down easily, and she stood up on her bed to give it her full weight. As she struggled to unstick the stubborn sash, a streak of lightning crossed the horizon, and she thought she saw something silhouetted against the sky. There appeared to be someone on the beach in front of the lighthouse. Another sharp crack of lightning. This time the figure had moved. The third flash revealed the shape of a person cloaked and hooded against the storm, pacing up and down in front of the wash, always facing the sea. She watched transfixed as the rain began to come down, and still the dark figure paced in front of the rushing water, almost daring it to touch. As Ellie continued to watch, the water appeared to run under the dark form, but the person seemed not to notice. Was this someone about to step into the dangerous, raging surf? She did not see a boat, and with that heavy cloak, the person would possibly be dragged out to sea. She had to know.

Ellie quickly grabbed her slicker and put it on over her nightgown. She found her rubber boots and her rain hat with the flaps. Dressed for the storm, but still in her nightgown, she slipped quietly down the stairs and out to the barn. She wanted the comfort of a companion should this adventure turn against her. Gingerly and without any trouble at all from the animal, she moved Blue out of his stall, led him over to the fence, and motioned him to kneel for her to mount. The young stallion obliged, and with her bidding, he slowly rose and walked in the direction of her urging. He seemed to respond well to her holding his mane as she struggled to apply pressure. His back was so broad, and she so small, she was having trouble guiding him with her knees. She could not shake the feeling that she was close to sliding off. Holding tight to his mane, she entwined the thick hair around her clenched fists to hold on.

Within only a few steps, she was losing her grip. She kept slipping around on his wet back, so she nudged him back to the barn for the bridle. Once again the great horse kneeled down, and along with a bridle this time, she opened the wooden chest and grabbed another blanket for his back. She had learned the first time how slick his coat was in the rain, and she needed something between her and the horse to give her traction. Again she mounted, and for the second time they started off.

Sitting atop Blue, with the wind and rain now running sideways, Ellie wiped away the water from her eyes and peered into the light every time the sky flashed, trying to focus on the area where she first saw the man. The dark form seemed to be in the water, then on the next crack, not in the water. Ellie gave slight pressure with her knees, and Blue responded to the touch. He did exactly what she wanted him to do, only moving ahead with caution. Twylah shadowed them from behind the dunes. The wolf did not reveal herself but instead simply trailed the pair, in case she was needed. Her ears were turning in all directions listening for trouble. Ellie was one of her cubs, and as she taught her cubs to be independent, so would she treat this one the same.

The closer Ellie rode to the figure, the more curious she became. Gradually as she drew closer, she could tell from the cut of the cape and the movements of the shape that it was a woman. At this realization, she relaxed a little and reined Blue toward the dune. Ellie dismounted and led the horse to a clump of sea oats that were close to a half-buried piece of driftwood. She tied Blue to a protruding spar of the wood, knowing that he would stay. Ellie began to approach nearer the strange apparition.

"Hello?" she called out, cupping her hands to her mouth to block out the wind. "Hello?" she said again as she closed the gap between them.

The next discharge of light running through the heavy dark clouds revealed the face of the figure as the woman turned to confront her. The hood was close, covering her features, but Ellie could tell that she was young. As Ellie again moved forward, she had to blink twice to believe what she saw. Nothing! The cloaked shape was no longer there. Ellie whirled around and around, looking everywhere, even went down closer to the wash to see if the woman had indeed entered the furious surf. There was nobody, anywhere. Ellie stood long enough to satisfy herself that the lady was gone, and finally, wet and confused, she turned back toward Blue.

This time, when Christo crowed, Ellie awakened to realize that she was in her bed, in her nightgown. The window was open, and the sun was beginning its climb up from the horizon line far out to sea, over what seemed to be a typical summer day. She sat up, rubbed her eyes, pulled up to a crouch, and hugged her knees. She placed her head on her knees and concentrated hard as she tried to reconstruct the dream. Her thoughts were interrupted by Blake's knock on the doorsill of the open door.

"Whacha doin'?" he asked.

"Hey, Cuz, get ready. We got a lot of stuff to do today. We gotta get outta here!" Luke was grinning behind Blake, and they both were already dressed.

Ellie straightened up and just stared at them, seemingly looking through them. Still dazed, she was having a hard time coming back from her dream. She motioned for the guys to come sit with her on the bed.

"Hey." Ellie was slowly getting her senses back. She patted the bed and scooped aside some of the dolls that were in their place at the foot, giving the boys a cleared spot. Long ago they had accepted the special place dolls held in Ellie's heart, and even though Blake huffed and puffed about "girls!" he also accepted that dolls were as special to his cousin as his flints were to him—the exception being that dolls had no use.

"I had a dream," she said sleepily and shook her head to clear her thoughts. She thought she better spill all at that moment, because she might not remember the details if she waited, and they seemed to be clear in her memory now. She needed to tell it quickly, so as not to leave anything out.

Luke noticed the glow around Ellie, usually present when the spirit was building around her, and also a sign that this was a tap-in to the strange powers she possessed.

"Remember last night when Grandpop was telling us the story of his name? Well, it caused me to have a very strange dream, and I think it was about that." Ellie began.

Both boys were silent. She had piqued their interest, and they came into the room to hear more. With care, they further moved enough of Ellie's sleep partners to find a place on the bed to sit. Knowing how important the dolls were to their cousin, they were taking caution not to insult any of the toys she treasured.

"You look like you have seen a ghost," said Luke, grinning, sort of making reference to the rosy glow surrounding her.

"I did!" Ellie's eyes widened. It was all coming back to her now, and she looked around the room at the open window, the clear day, and the cloudless skies.

This last remark snapped the boys straighter. Maybe for them to hear that from anyone else, it might not have had the same effect, but from Ellie, it was different. Ellie did not joke about her intuitions nor her dreams. If she said she saw a ghost, she was telling the truth—or, at least, the truth as she saw it. Ellie had more powers than both of them combined, and the thoughts and dreams that came to her, they had found, were quite often a revelation that was from a deeper consciousness than normal—although they might not have phrase it that way.

Ellie was anything but normal. She was small, now almost eleven years old, with hair so long and curly it had to be contained in braids. To see her sitting here in the middle of that wild mane of sandy-colored hair was familiar, with that little face all pink and thoughtful. She had beautiful blue eyes like Grandpop, which looked so small inside all those curls. She was not, as they knew it, what one would call normal. On the outside, everything looked natural, but what went on inside of her head was anything but ordinary.

The boys had begun to notice Ellie slowly coming into her powers. They even had discussed it at night in their shared room and whispered about the things they observed about her that had changed. They had been exposed to what they had come to express as "the 'knowing,'" as it resulted in finding the pirate's chest. Ellie had "seen" where it was, just as she had "seen" the boys in the caverns when she was above them in the house. They knew to pay attention to her when she brought forth one of her "feelings." They had observed and experienced her energies, experienced her power move through them when they all concentrated their efforts. The old Indians, Weroansqua and Powwaw, had given both boys the ability to strengthen Ellie, but alone they were unable to complete tasks they managed when they all worked together.

What had started out to be a normal day was beginning to shape itself into something quite different. This was to be the first day of packing up the house to move. The world war that the boys' father left to fight was coming to them. They had begun to sit at the top of the steps at night and listen to Grandpop and his friends talking. They had also fallen asleep many nights on Ellie's bed, as her room was over the front porch. With the window open, they could clearly hear the conversations between the navy and Coast Guard men as they sat on the porch with Grandpop to share a smoke while they discussed what could or would happen should this second war take the same pattern as the previous one, known before then as the Great War. During that conflict, also with Germany, the submarines of the enemy had been successful in interrupting cargo up and down the Atlantic coast by torpedoing the merchant ships close to the coast carrying much needed supplies. The most desired position for U-boats—as the submarines were labeled by the Germans—was to submerge and lurk in waiting off the shores of Cape Hatteras, where the ships had to swing out to avoid the shoals known as the Diamonds, located twelve miles due east of the lighthouse.

The men spoke in hushed tones to Grandpop. Usually they sat for hours on the porch smoking and talking strategy out of earshot of Grandmom and Nett. These men also had families at home and were not interested in alarming the women—whose sons and husbands were either already in this mess, or destined to go—with talk of war. Captain Charlie was a respected man, and his years of watching the coast were invaluable to the newcomers. They recognized they needed his help to understand this unusual island and fortify it as the first line of defense. One thing they insisted on was that the captain and his family move away from the beach. They needed to "shore it up," as Grandpop often said. Pretty soon the sand banks outside their windows would be crawling with navy, Coast Guard, and who knows what else. The government did not want to have to worry about an old man and his curious children underfoot.

The kids were informed, and they had decided among themselves that they would not be afraid. Blake even talked of helping. Now, what could a nine-year-old do to help fight a war? Luke and Ellie smiled when he started on one of his adventures and just let him ramble on with his imaginary what-ifs, even encouraging him to see how far his imagination would go. They thought it better than to scare him. War was coming to their shore, and they had to move away to make room for those whose job was to fight it.

Going away was not an uncomfortable thought, as it meant going to the house on the hill in Trent Woods. The kids had all decided that they would come back, They never let go of the idea that they needed to be around to protect the lighthouse. After all, it had protected them for all their lives, and now it was their turn to return the favor.

"Last night Grandpop told us the story of how he got his name, and I think I had a dream about that." Ellie started again.

"The story about the portrait?" Luke asked.

"Kinda, but more than that. I dreamed there was a summer storm, with rain and lightning, and I tried to put the window down so I wouldn't get wet. It was hard to move, so I stood on the bed to push it down, and when the lightning lit up the sky, I saw someone on the beach. Each time it flashed and illuminated the sky, there appeared to be a figure, all dressed in black, in a long, dark hooded coat, like the man in the poem 'The Highwayman.' I kept standing up, and each time lightning struck and showed the beach, the thing in the long coat had moved, like it was walking back and forth, always looking at the sea. Anyway, in my dream I decided I would take a look, but I was too scared to do it by myself, so I put my clothes on and went to get Blue."

"Why not us?" Blake asked, like he was insulted.

"You know, now that I think about it, I don't know why, but I didn't. I went to the barn and got Blue, and we went down to the dune line. When we got there, the person was still there, so I tied up Blue, and walked over to it, and said, 'Hello.' When I said that, it turned around, and even though the hood was close down, I could tell it was a young girl. As I moved to stand beside her, she disappeared. Just like that! I looked to see if she went into the ocean, but she did not, and then Christo crowed, and I woke up." Ellie was flushed even as she was telling the story. "I think it was Theodosia Burr!"

"What?" both boys reacted at the same time.

"What makes you think it was her?" Luke asked. "She was in Nags Head, and the story took place more than 100 years ago. How could that be? She wouldn't be here. She would be up there. You were just having a dream about a good story." Luke didn't like for Ellie to get worked up over nothing. He sometimes tried to protect her from herself. She was so intuitive that she could be a problem to herself. He was protective, and older, and no matter what Ellie's powers were, he knew the energy was so strong that sometimes it might even be too much for her. He felt responsible for both her and Blake, and maybe he too was a little disappointed that she did not awaken them to go with her. Then he shook his head. He was so wrapped up in the story, he almost forgot it was a dream.

"Theodosia Burr! Cool!" was Blake's response. He also had taken the dream seriously.

"Well, what are you going to do about it?" asked Luke. "Are you gonna tell Grandpop?"

"I thought I would ask him some more questions about the story, but I'm not going to tell him about the dream. I don't want Grandpop to think I would get out of bed on a stormy night, go to the barn and get Blue, and strike out toward the beach by myself. He would have to lock me in my room every night!" Ellie giggled at the thought, and they all started laughing, a little too nervously, because they knew that it was just the kind of thing they all might do.

They heard Grandmom Odessa yelling upstairs for them to get down to the table. Grandpop was hungry. They hurried about, left Ellie to dress, and all rushed down the stairs like nothing strange had happened.

"Come here, girl, let me tie up that wild hair of yours. It looks like a lion's mane. Did you bring down the ribbons?" Odessa was rushing around trying to placate her Charlie, so he wouldn't get mad at the kids for keeping him from his breakfast. Grandmom was always walking a thin line between Grandpop and the kids, trying to make sure all his needs were met in a timely manner and keeping the children out of trouble. It was a dance she cherished, and to be sure, she didn't get much help from her daughter Nett, the boys' mother. Nett had already taken off to the village for some kind of community activity she and the other young girls in the village were cooking up for the church. So between servings, Odessa fussed with Ellie's hair until it was contained in all that winding ribbon.

Buxton was teeming with things to do, especially if there was a minute to spare. All the young mothers were active in some way to create a fun life on the island. Many had husbands who had already enlisted and gone off to war like Bill, and they were trying to occupy themselves in order to stave off the worry that never seemed to leave them. Visiting friends was a popular pastime in all the villages. They were all civic minded, and meetings that encompassed more than one village were common—and fun, too. Nett knew everyone. She had taught school in Trent and Kinna-keet, as well as Buxton, and had played the piano at the movie theater in Hatteras. A young man named Alvey Midgett was her contemporary and a fantastic singer, so they were usually called on to help with planning weddings. It was not uncommon for Grandpop to take her to Chicama-comico to meet with Alvey, as cars were scarce. When these weddings took place, she would sometimes take Ellie, because Nett wanted her to experience pretty venues. The boys definitely did not want to go.

The young men were usually busy working in and around the sound, or maybe they were doing nothing, but they made sure they were not around to do "women's work." Fishing pound nets required constant mending. Boats needed to be built or repaired, and that drew a crowd as they were skills to be envied. Someone was always wanting help in whatever repair work was necessary to keep a house from being eaten up by the salt that came in on the sea air. Working on cars and trucks was an exercise they all enjoyed, for on this island, sand and salt ruined even the finest and strongest machinery, and if one did not know how to correct it, it could be an expensive loss. The men prided themselves on tinkering with and reworking motors. It was a much needed skill. If one could dream it, there was always a talented person to fix it. The mail boat had to be emptied, packages to deliver, wagons and cars to fix—and nothing had a time frame. It was a leisurely life. Daily life felt like a combination of both work and play, with very vague lines defining which was which.

"Did you young-uns happen to see the rainbow this morning? It was faint, but it went over the lighthouse and disappeared in the clouds before it touched down. Curious. Usually they only come after a storm or heavy rain, and I don't recollect that happened last night." Grandpop just settled himself into his breakfast, never looking up to see the side glances the kids passed from one to the other, as they buried their faces in their plates in an attempt to hold in their emotions. For some reason, they were too busy eating to even come up with an answer.

Luke especially was pondering on Grandpop's observation. His mind was still full of the story Ellie had told. He realized he had also not heard a storm, but there was definitely one in Ellie's dream. Grandpop's remark about the rainbow prompted Luke to ask, "Pop, does a rainbow always come after the rain?"

With that question, Capt'n Charlie took a bite of his fried cornbread and thought to himself, *So much for gettin' out of the house in a hurry. These kids are on to something, and they won't get off of it till I join in with them.* After he swallowed, he looked over his glasses at his oldest grand-child. Knowing how smart Luke was, he knew he could not slough off an answer. If he did, the boy would probably leave the table and grab the encyclopedia for some more substantial information on the subject. So he gave it the full extent of his knowledge.

"Now, son, I know we see rainbows after the rain, but they are not exactly restricted to showing up only after rain. They are fractions of light that show color when the sun hits water droplets at a certain angle. Atop the lighthouse, I have seen small ones show up after a particularly tall spray from a wave breaking. You know how it sometimes sends up a spray? Standing just right, a person might see a tiny one cross the top of the mist of the spray. Usually, the big ones are seen after a hard rain, when there is a lot of mist in the air, and the sun hits the shards of light just right. Why, I've even seen a double rainbow."

"Me, too!" exclaimed Blake. Nobody even knew he was listening, but not much went on in a room that Blake did not pick up on. Maybe it was because he was little, and always afraid of being left behind, not that that had ever happened. Blake saw to that. "I saw one over the lighthouse one time, and in the puddle in front of the lighthouse. It was there, too, just like a mirror." At this point Blake was settling in his seat, like he was a satisfied man, able to contribute to any conversation. Almost nine, he sometimes thought he would never catch up, because they would always be older. So he decided that no matter what, he would always be included—not the main one, but one of the ones.

"That's right, son, there are special times when there are two rainbows, the second one maybe not as strong in color as the first." Grandpop took another bite of cornbread and motioned for the kids to eat. He had plans for the day, and all this talk was taking up precious time. If he could just get them in the truck, fed, he could continue this discussion on the way down the beach.

"Pop," asked Ellie, "do rainbows always have the same colors, and how many colors do they have?"

Wow, this was getting deep, and Grandpop's surprise trip looked like it might not happen.

"Les-see, I'm going to say seven. Things in this world seem to settle on the number seven: days of the week, sets of waves, musical notes on the scale, known objects in the solar system. Can't think of another, but it was the Greeks who first made the suggestion, and it seems to be true. Of course that is not always correct. Some people see things differently, but it is a universal truth."

"Are they always the same colors?" asked Ellie, as she at the same time saw Grandpop's small scowl, meaning, *First, you are not eating, and second, I've got something to do.*

She was right on both counts. He did have something to do, and she better stuff something in her mouth or he was going to scold her. Quickly she grabbed up her cornbread and dramatically tore into it with her little mouth, getting a bigger tear off than anticipated, and making it impossible for her to talk. Knowing this was her last question, she chewed and waited, never taking her eyes off her grandfather.

"Yes, they are always the same, in the same order, and some brighter than others, making a person think they were not all there, but they were, just faded because of the position of the sun to the droplet. Now, that is the last question, except I will say this, I know how much you kids like mythology, and I'll tell you this: the rainbow is from the goddess Iris, and inside our eyes, we call that circular color part the iris. Meaning the part that sees color."

"How—," Blake started, but Grandpop gave him the look. Grand-mom almost laughed out loud. She didn't know what she would do for smiles if that kid were not around. While she was working she could even think of funny things he did and give a little giggle. He certainly did keep things going.

"All you young-uns are going to talk yourselves right out of a trip up the beach to Kinnakeet if you don't keep quiet. I'm meeting some men from the village up there, and I won't be late, and you can't go until you eat, so make up your mind: eat or talk." Grandpop stopped short of saying that thing he said all the time: "Let your vittles stop your mouth." He felt like he had said that so much it was probably running around in their head anyway. He had to smile when he glanced around. All the kids had full mouths, choking down food as fast as possible, and totally too stuffed to get out a question.

"Get some milk in you," said Grandmom, "or I'll be the one keeping you here." She slipped a side eye to Charlie, and they both looked down and smiled. Teamwork, that's what it took. Teamwork.

★ 2 ★

Pop's Story

Looking through the penny candy at Griggs, the boys could not stop thinking about Ellie's adventure on the beach. All of the kids had eaten their breakfast silently and hardly heard Pop's invitation to go to a "vendue" down the beach north of Big Kinnakeet station, but when he yelled for them to load up, the thoughts of a dream disappeared, as another adventure was in the making. Grandpop and the boys were early getting to the vendue—the name given to selling off materials washed ashore by a ship broken up off the coast—so they accompanied their pop into the village to explore, as talk ensued among the local men about who was in need of certain salvage. The men did not want to bid against each other should it cause a needy man to pay more than he had available to spare.

In a flash storm off northern Kinnakeet, a huge three-masted schooner had spewed her cargo just before breaking up on the shore, and had driven the ship high upon the beach. All lives were saved, but the ship had come apart on the bar when she hit the breakers hard, becoming grounded and at the mercy of the pounding surf. Each wave sent more debris ashore. Luke and Blake listened to all the talking about the suddenness of the blow, giving even more evidence of Ellie's dream. The boys thought maybe she heard the storm, maybe she saw it in her mind, maybe she felt it, but there had definitely been quite a gale. However, this was in Kinnakeet, and Ellie thought she experienced her dream in Buxton. It had to have happened both places.

"But no, not here," said Blake. "Didn't she also say the lady was walking in front of the lighthouse?"

"Yeah, I guess you're right, but it could have been here, too." Luke also had a feeling, but enough said. He snapped back to reality as Pop got ready to leave and go down to the beach with the other men.

Luke and Blake climbed aboard Grandpop's old truck and leaned over the side to let the wind hit them as they rumbled along the sandy track to the area near the wreck. Grandpop had given a ride to two other men from Kinnakeet, so the boys got to sit on the rail of the truck bed. They were like dogs, straining in the wind to let it blow open their cheeks. They leaned in to avoid the occasional limb from the small scrub oaks that grew near the beach. Huge grapevines were so close to the beach road, a person literally could reach out and grab a grape from the thick vines that rested on the branches of the stand of trees near the beach. But if you stopped the car in the sand in order to pick grapes, you were *stuck!* On these sandy roads, Grandpop had to keep his wheels moving over what was a very soft track. Stick your hand out for a grape, and you were liable to lose an arm.

The truck went as far over to the side as Grandpop dared—kind of right by the two-track, so as not to get stuck. Other jalopies were also using the same tactic, some on a hard edge beside the track, and some with just a little bit of sea grass under a wheel, to get some traction. They were way ahead of the noon call, but Charlie Williams, the vendue master for this area, was already walking about, tallying what was up for auction. Men were milling around the cargo strewn across and down the beach, both ways: barrels, crates, trunks, burlap bags, wood (some with valuable roping attached), furniture, and small wares, like pots and lamps. Some mirrors were broken, but had beautiful ornate frames still intact. The shore was littered with whatever the ship had carried, and parts of the beautiful ship itself in pieces. The sail was still floating half in and half out of the water. It was truly a sight to behold. Men parked on the hard wash, as vendues always took place at low tide to allow for easy access.

On the beach also was the last of a mighty ship, the portion that had not buried itself at sea. The paint on the sides was already rubbed off from constant scraping of the ship against the sand. The curve of the piece of bow looked almost waxed. One gold letter was attached and hanging from a jagged edge. There were crates of ladies' fancy dresses and shoes. Apparently this must have been a passenger ship. But the people were long gone, taken to village homes, or to one of the surf stations nearby, to tend to wounds and have a hot meal.

On further inspection, a piece of a cannon had washed up, causing much stir among the men that it might even be a soldier of fortune who had run too close to the shore those nights ago. One could never be surprised at the character of person or the reasons one had for choosing a life at sea.

A massive anchor was resting on the beach, and several men were moving around that. It was a handsome piece. The owners of the schooner had agreed to a set price, and the bidding began. A desk went for $4.27, and a handsome rolltop desk it was. The trunks of clothing went to merchants in the villages who paid not much over $3.00 each. Wood from the vessel sold for more, as it was needed to make an extra room on someone's house. Some small things were given away, creating a bit of a scramble. Need was always the determining factor. Grandpop bought barrels of flour, salt, and the captain's trunk, whose contents were unknown. The vendue continued for the rest of the day. Men broke up the wood, making it easier to haul to its final destination. On one of these earlier vendues, held up the beach months back, a church garnered enough wood to finish its sanctuary, with all of the members pooling their resources to buy what was needed. The beach today was also full of curious children running around and playing tag through the wreckage, among shouts from the adults about being careful. More than one unruly boy was snatched up by the collar in an effort to make him compose himself. Luke and Blake were beside themselves with all the activity.

On the trip home from Kinnakeet, Luke's mind wandered back to the story his grandfather had told a couple of nights ago, the story of how he got his name. A lot was riding on the names of islanders. They were always carefully selected for the bent a parent wanted the child to take. Grandmom was named after a mountain chain in Russia, the Odessa Mountains. Her brothers Alaska and Utah were named after an area and a state, and Unaka, after another mountain chain. Another brother, Wallace Roosevelt Gray, was partly named for the popular president of the time. Ellie was named after two very prominent people: Eleanor Roosevelt and Woodrow Wilson, a first lady and a president. Luke Robert was named after Christ's physician disciple and Robert the Brave of Ireland. Blake Matthew was named after a famous Irish ruling lord and Christ's learned disciple. So, for Pop to have a story behind his name was not strange. The name, however, was.

Having begged their grandfather to tell a story other than one about a deer, they settled down to what was sure to be a tale that would put them to sleep: How Grandpop got his name.

As the story goes, he was named after an old doctor who used to visit the outer areas of the coast while on vacation. There were times when he was called upon to administer cures, if he could. Most of the time Dr. William G. Pool was on a much needed rest as he visited the shores of Nags Head, but on occasion, when he was made aware there was a need for his services, he made himself available to tend to the sick. Over the years, the young doctor from Elizabeth City vacationed at Nags Head and was known to enjoy hunting and fishing on nearby Hatteras Island.

In the later years, Dr. Pool frequently was called upon to tend to the ills of a Mrs. Polly Mann, of the Nags Head Woods. She lived alone in a run-down, graying shingled cottage deep in a tangle of oaks and dirt roads that made up one of the fishing villages nestled in the woods. These were scattered about great distances from each other, occupying space that later became a haven for tourists to build summer homes near the oceanfront.

Mrs. Mann was the widow of a fisherman who in earlier years was also considered a land pirate. These pirates operated off the Nags Head beaches before and during the war with the English in 1812. The old pirate had long ago died, leaving behind the shack and his ailing wife. Dr. Pool began to check in on Miz Polly at each visit he took to Nags Head. He seemed to be one of only a few visitors she had. One unusual part of the meager surroundings in that crumbling shanty was an obviously expensive oil painting depicting the portrait of a young woman, who, by dress, was high born. The oil was on mahogany wood, with an equally exquisite frame.

The beauty of the portrait haunted Dr. Pool, who had admired it over the years and wondered at the identity of the stately maiden—and why the painting came to be the possession of this poor old fish wife. Miz Polly told him it was a present from her husband. He was a known wrecker, both legal and illegal, and had come upon this portrait from the remains of a two-masted schooner that had come aground at Nags Head, fully sailed, rudder locked, and no people on board. There were trunks of ladies' garments and other captain's ware that either washed ashore or was salvaged from the ship. The ship wallowed in the breakers for more than a week, until it was completely stripped by hand or water and disappeared entirely. This portrait was one of the pieces of wreckage taken from the stricken vessel.

Dr. Pool was intrigued by the story, but he thought it only that—a story, probably more than fifty years old or older. He continued his practice among those he knew. One of those who knew of him was great-grandmom Elizabeth. She had occasion to benefit indirectly of Dr. Pool's expertise while he was on Hatteras Island duck hunting with one of her brothers. He was kind enough to attend to her ailing mother. Out of respect for the doctor and his generous help, great-grandmom gave her son the middle name of Pool.

Later on in his life, Dr. Pool again was to visit Miz Polly in the Nags Head Woods. This time she was dying. He tried to ease her pain, and having never taken any compensation for his visits, she offered him the portrait of the lady he so admired. She insisted that he was the only one who should have it, and she was afraid to leave it behind. Dr. Pool reluctantly took the portrait with him as he left. He never did see Ms. Polly again. On his next visit, her home was boarded up.

Dr. Pool was still curious about the portrait and began to send pictures of it through the wires, one to the *New York Sun*, to see if anyone would recognize it. Someone did: the family of Aaron Burr. The relatives contacted Dr. Pool and traveled to Elizabeth City to confirm the identity of the woman in the portrait.

Aaron Burr was a politician who was embroiled in a heated battle with another politician, Alexander Hamilton, involving the presidential elections of both 1800 and 1804. It was Burr's third time running against Jefferson for president, and Hamilton and his followers were so vicious in their attacks against Burr in 1796 that both were defeated and John Adams won. In 1800 Jefferson and Burr were running for president again. At that time in history, the winner gained the presidency and the gentleman who came in second was vice president. Burr was within one vote of defeating Thomas Jefferson for the party rule. The voting resulted in a tie, with Hamilton responsible for casting the deciding vote against Burr, thus allowing Jefferson to win. Burr became the vice president under Jefferson.

Jefferson ran again in 1804 and did not choose to include Burr. Once again, Hamilton and his colleagues disparaged Burr's reputation. Burr left Washington, and, being from New York, tried for governorship of that state. Hamilton again was the instigator, with his followers savagely attacking Burr's character. Upset, Burr challenged Hamilton to a duel. They had been political adversaries for many years, and each had politically slandered the other in previous elections.

Burr took his personal hate for Hamilton to an entirely new level. The duel ensued, and Burr shot and killed Alexander Hamilton, the then secretary of the treasury. It was legal, but still upsetting to most. Burr was tried and released, but he felt the need to leave Washington in order to avoid harsh treatment.

For a while, Burr lived in New York. His wife had died, leaving him the only parent to a young girl, Theodosia. All his attention was given to the child. She was masterful in every way. Her clothes came from Paris, her skill on the piano bordered on prodigy. She spoke several languages, had multiple teachers and coaches, and was soon the hostess of prominent social affairs.

Burr continued to yearn for political control of land, setting his sights on land west of the Mississippi, and south to Mexico. This was the early 1800s, and the whole of the United States was not yet decided. His plans became known to the officials in Washington, and as they also coveted the very land in question, they decided Burr needed to be stopped. He was captured and tried for treason. Without enough evidence to convict him, Aaron Burr was once again set free. This time he felt disgraced, and he fled to England and France to get away from his enemies.

During his trials, Burr's daughter, Theodosia, had sought direction and comfort in the company of her husband, a young politician from South Carolina named William Alston. When her father went overseas, she worked tirelessly, writing letters to prominent men in Washington to allow her father back into the United States. Her husband grew more and more prominent in the South Carolina legislature, and they lived in Georgetown, South Carolina, on his estate called Oak Hills Plantation. They had one child, a son, whom they named Aaron Burr Alston.

Years passed, and at the age of ten, the child caught malaria and died in June 1812, just before Alston became governor of the state. Theodosia was never quite the same after that. With her son dead and her father disgraced and in exile, her health declined rapidly. Aaron Burr finally was allowed to come home to New York to comfort his daughter. However, Theodosia was taken ill at the death of her son and did not recover for months, preventing her from making the trip to New York, thus denying her the consolation of her father, whom she sorely missed and needed.

Finally, on Christmas Day 1812, Theodosia informed her husband and staff that she would make the trip to New York to see her father. It was arranged for her to be accompanied by her maid. As the United States was at war with Great Britain, her husband William, being the governor, could not join the little family. Governor Alston and Aaron Burr arranged for a small schooner, the *Patriot*, a former privateer now outfitted as a passenger ship, to be the vessel on which she would sail. Along with her maid, they sent along a physician, Dr. Green. The captain of the *Patriot* carried with him notes that requested safe passage through the English blockade, as this was a case of no political importance to the Crown. They say now that an English blockade destroyer did stop and question the purpose of the *Patriot*, as revealed in the log taken from the vessel in question. The papers evidently were in order as the passengers, crew, and ship were allowed to continue their journey without incident.

That was the last known contact with the schooner *Patriot* before it was discovered stove up on a bar beyond the breakers at Nags Head beach and boarded by scavengers.

This was a time before there were lifesaving stations located every seven miles of beach from the Virginia line down the entire coast of North Carolina.

Aboard that ship, as a gift for her father, Theodosia carried as a Christmas surprise an oil painting of herself. The portrait was rendered on the finest mahogany and framed in elaborate gilt on the also mahogany carved decorative wood. It was one of the items discovered on the wreck of the ship at Nags Head beach and deemed worthless to the thieves.

For many years, numerous stories were told of the disappearance of Theodosia Burr Alston. One, that her ship was set upon by pirates, and both she and her maid were pressed to walk the plank. This account bears some weight. There were known pirates operating in the area at that time. English warships were also close to the shores of the new United States and the *Patriot* had set sail during the War of 1812, hence necessity of the papers carried for the protection of the passengers. Blackbeard had worked the same area 100 years before, and now English ships were being plundered by, among others, Dominic You, a pirate, the half-brother to Jean Lafitte, also pirating off the coast of Louisiana. Lafitte was the same pirate who helped Andrew Jackson win the Battle of New Orleans, fought just hours after the war was declared over. Lafitte and his brother Pierre were plundering ships in the Gulf of Mexico and the Caribbean, and their half-brother, You, was among the pirates operating down the coast of the Atlantic.

History documents a tremendous storm off the Carolinas during the first days of 1813, at the very time the *Patriot* embarked on its journey.

Times of war are confusing, allowing those whose interests are for neither side to steal from both sides. There were those whose imagination ran rampant with the idea of walking the plank. Walking the plank was actually not a practice of the pirates of that or any other day. The trouble it took to set up that situation was a time killer, when throwing the culprit over the side, simply to be eaten by sharks, was so much more expedient. The stormy weather also dispelled that rumor, as it would have been folly to attack a ship in high seas.

Years after the mystery of the daughter of the former vice president of the United States came knowledge of the deathbed confession of an old pirate. He claimed to have been one of the scourges who set upon the *Patriot*, thinking it carried gold hidden below. This assumption was also valid, as the *Patriot* was known to have formerly served as a privateer for the U.S. government. It was probably disguised as a private ship to carry contraband, a trick learned from the heads of Europe. The whereabouts of the ship were thoroughly investigated, and according to another old seaman interviewed, it was known to carry gold and guns in the ballast of the ship, making it ripe for plunder. These items were destined to aid the United States in its fight against the English. And he remembered the name of the woman as Odessa Burr Alston. Strange he mentioned Grandmom's name, but probably it was a more familiar name than Theodosia, and in the old sailor's mind, he could have easily been mistaken in the name.

Several broken and dying sailors took to confessing to the murder, or having witnessed such, of Theodosia Burr Alston. There were at least four stories of that kind.

One remembered a well-bred lady begging for her life at the rail of the pirates' vessel, but no quarter was given. She, with Bible in hand, leaped to her death, silently, resolved that there was no other choice. Still another pirate claimed to remember the lady's maid being thrown overboard and eaten by sharks. He said the proper damsel was given a choice to stay, as captain's lady, or suffer the same fate. She jumped willingly to her death. Even with the various stories, none could attest to the validity and ownership of the portrait.

There was yet another tale of the likeness of Theodosia Burr. The ship came ashore with all aboard, lured by the land pirates of the Nags Head coast. The dunes at Nags Head have always been there, despite the hand of man. Coastal land was never inhabited by most folk because it was prone to sand coverage and ocean overwash during a storm. It was just a wooded shore, dunes prominent in places, a piece of hunting land near the ocean used by those of the western villages. There were some fishing shacks and hunting lodges, but no connected villagers. They were a solitary lot.

The men were poor but crafty. One way they devised to make money was to take a horse to the dune, on a dark and maybe stormy night, hobble him so that he limped, tie a lantern to his neck, and lead him across the ridge of the dune. That visual, to a ship at sea and from a distance, would appear to be another ship, bobbing softly at anchor in a safe harbor. Before the unsuspecting victim realized he had been fooled into heading for shore, he was fast on the bars and shoals that made up the beaches of the Outer Banks.

With a crippled ship in the breakers, unable to right herself, the confused crew was likely to consider themselves lucky to be alive and scramble away to land in relief—or they came to harm at the hands of the land pirates. At any rate, the *Patriot* is said to have met just such a fate. Her crew was either killed or scared away, and as Theodosia watched the slaughter, her troubled mind reverted to insanity to block out the horror she saw. She was in such a state that the thieves, who were suspicious of those whose mind was in turmoil, did not bother her, lest it be a sign from God that she was innocent They, in their reverence, led her to a boat and gently took her to shore. On shore, the villagers, such as they were—those who lived in the nearby fishing shacks—took this obviously insane woman into their homes, each for monthly intervals at a time, and treated her as if caring for a child. Her portrait was prominently displayed in one of those cabins.

It was said that when the portrait disappeared from the wall, probably to be delivered to whomever was to take her in next, Theodosia was so infirmed that they thought she would not miss it, but she saw the empty wall. The story was told that she stumbled from the house through the woods to the beach, and her footsteps led to the sea.

A most unusual story was related by a Karankawa Indian chief along the Gulf Coast of Texas, who had a locket that was seen by some of the earliest settlers in that area. The locket was inscribed "Theodosia," and in the locket were two pictures, one of Aaron Burr, and the other the picture of the lady in the portrait. The old chief said he was given the piece by a woman moments before she died. He had come upon a small *piragua* (an old name for a canoe . . . usually one with a sail attached) washed up at the mouth of the San Bernard River after a storm. He thought he heard cries, and he discovered the woman chained to the bulkhead of the sailing canoe by her ankle. She gave the locket to him and told him she was the daughter of a white chief, and if he would give that locket to any government official they would track down the pirates who had done this to her. The old chief was afraid to reveal he had the locket, because he believed he would call attention to himself and possibly be blamed for her death. For those who saw the locket, the pictures were correct likenesses of both Aaron and Theodosia Burr.

Others swear that no foul play came to the *Patriot* that night, but it simply beached itself in a storm. From past experience, pirates never attacked a ship in bad weather. It would have been impossible for the vessel to have been boarded during a storm such as the one that lasted for days off Cape Hatteras.

There were many guesses and fantastic tales about the final days of Theodosia Burr Alston, but not one could be verified. They all made good yarns, and parts of them all seemed true. But the only truth throughout the entirety was that a kind doctor helped one infirmed old woman, among others, and Grandpop was named after him. Charles Pool Gray, son of Amelek Thomas and Elizabeth Hooper Gray.

That was the story that caused Ellie's dream. Hardly scary, hardly strange, and certainly not as exciting as the ones told now. There existed even more strange stories to be told by the men of the Lifesaving Service. Those men *really* had tales to tell. The children had seen evidence of what the sea coughed up.

But on that night, with Grandpop relating this fascinating story of his name, the children were all ears. Blake sat wide eyed, Luke was enthralled, and Ellie climbed down from her grandpop's lap to sit in front of him so that she could watch his face. She was caught up in the story of Theodosia Burr Alston and all the mystery that surrounded her. That night she went to bed with all of it running through her mind and troubling her sleep. And she dreamed.

When the boys got home from the vendue, Grandmom told them they could find Ellie already down on the beach. She had been there all day. At one point, she took out Blue, but they didn't stay gone long. The boys were anxious to find her, tell her about the vendue, and share the penny candy from the store, and Luke had in mind bringing up the apparition. He had a feeling, and the shipwreck sort of triggered it. As he looked at the wreckage of the fallen ship collected on the shore, he was reminded of the scene described by Grandpop several nights before, and he almost could not wait to get back home and talk to Ellie. He found her sitting on a piece of peat washed up from the sea. Come to think of it, the beach looked like it would after a storm, with seaweed and trash all meshed with trapped shells and debris tangled throughout. It was what the ocean threw away when it cleaned itself.

Quietly they sat, just staring out over the now calm ocean. The swells were steady, lightly rising, some higher than others, in sets of three and seven, just coming in, leaving a line of bubbles, and slowly taking its wonderful color out again, to form a little white-veined breaker, and go at it one more time, before retreating back to join the big boys. Waves spoke to you. Listening was fun and made the time pass. Luke picked up a stick and drew the outline of a cape in the sand.

* 3 *

The Apparition

Giovanni da Verrazano, a Florentine explorer in the employ of the king of France, in search of a way to the Far East, first came upon Cape Hatteras Island in 1524 and described it thus: "We smelled the fragrance a hundred leagues away, and even farther when they were burning the cedars and the wind was blowing from the land." He identified the shores of Cape Hatteras with such pleasing names as "Forest of Laurels" and "Fields of Cedars."

Another explorer, Arthur Barlow, who sailed with Sir Walter Raleigh, wrote, "We found shoal water which smelt so sweetly and was so strong a smell as if we had been in the midst of some delicate garden—."

Descriptions of the lure of the island did not include the most dangerous of the siren's song, the roar and clash of two of the greatest currents of the world's oceans, coming together to announce their dominance. Ten to twelve miles due east of The Point at the center of the island of Cape Hatteras, a southbound, cold, swiftly moving current made its way from Newfoundland down the East Coast of the United States, until it came to a hill of land so tall that it caused the current to collide with the bar and spew up its cold water in an attempt to crash over the obstacle. At this juncture that southbound current was challenged by another stream of rushing water, which traveled north at four miles an hour from its origin off the coast of Florida. Here the collision of the two currents, in defiance of each other, pushed up the ocean floor, creating several mountains of sand. The northern flow, named the Labrador Current because of its origin, was cold as it met the southern warm current, the Gulf Stream, with its origin in southern Florida. The battle for right of way created the underwater mountains of what are called the Diamond Shoals, thus named for the shape of the shoals and their position relative to one another in a diamond pattern. The currents of the shoals—one hot, one cold—battled off Cape Point in a masterful display of power, as they clashed constantly with the rushing tidal pull. The Gulf Stream was tracked as second only to the Antarctic current as the greatest underwater river in the world. It rushed seventy miles or more in a day, measured fifty miles wide, and reached a depth of 3,000 feet. The color was azure blue, with no traces of sand to turn even a portion of it green. The Point at Cape Hatteras was the closest land mass to the stream itself.

The island of Cape Hatteras extended off the coast of the United States thirty miles from the mainland, and at the elbow of that island, land nearly touched the flowing river under the sea. This mountain kept getting built up by both currents as they collided, bringing rushes of sand with all that water pressure to the contentious spot, until the table of the shoal reached, in some places, as high as only three feet below the surface. This rite of passage went on all day and all night, with the Gulf Stream winning the battle as it curves northeast to continue its journey across the Atlantic to Europe. The forests of the United States were cut and floated across the ocean in this manner, using the power of the current. From the forests of the islands were built the great ships of Europe.

The opposition of wind and water has created a most unusual phenomena along the coast. The mountains of Diamond Shoals have hampered ships since this land was discovered. The shoals of Frying Pan or Cape

Lookout, also located on the coast of North Carolina, though equally dangerous, do not protrude as far out as do the Diamonds, whose shoals are formed farther out and avoid the land mass of Cape Hatteras Island. The proximity of the shipping lanes has made the Diamonds dangerous. Most are not aware of a swing to either the left or the right, depending on the direction. Shipping generally wants to go straight. Positioned twelve miles off the point at Buxton, the middle village on Cape Hatteras Island, the undersea sand dunes of quicksand stand perilously close to the Gulf Stream. The river within the ocean was a popular highway, with warm currents that flowed from south to north. Riding this watery road meant smooth sailing, until the vessel met the shoals off the coast of land that also extended out thirty miles into the sea from the mainland. The Gulf Stream has always been a desirable current on which to navigate, although one needed to round those hidden mountains before the journey could continue. In the beginning, navigation was a guess, not well mapped.

Early captains were unaware of what lay below the surface should one decide to hug the shore and make a shorter route to the south, or to the north depending on the intended direction. The Diamonds, three shoals covering some thirty miles, did not take passage lightly. Not easily seen, they have been the resting place for nearly 5,000 unsuspecting vessels since the 1500s.

Only experienced seamen could access the Diamonds. There were actually two navigable channels. The first route was through the slough between The Point and the first shoal, Hatteras Shoal. The second route, Diamond Slough—harder to navigate, but possible—lay between the Inner Diamond Shoal and the Outer Diamond Shoal, which touched the Gulf Stream. The whales knew these underwater passages, as did the local fishermen. During the wreck of the *Ephraim Williams*, a trawler fishing the Diamond Slough was able to assist in the rescue.

Sailors might know of the shoals and still be unable to navigate them, especially when there was a storm. The heavy fog that accompanied each storm made the journey twice as treacherous. The fog and raging waters with their huge swells served to camouflage the shallow reefs of the shoals. Strong winds and heavy mist frequented the area. Because of the draw of tidal currents and the mixture of cold and warm air, the fog was intense. Storms drawn into its melee followed the path from the south and caused them to travel up the warm waters of the Gulf Stream, feeding on the desirable currents for strength and fury. By the time the Gulf Stream touched Hatteras Island, the tempest, fed by warm waters, was in full strength. The moisture intensified as the storm rolled in, collecting the already existing banks of fog together, blinding all vision and direction. Any vessel that wandered close was pushed by the relentless winds into the quicksand of Diamond Shoals.

Thus, because of their proximity to shipping lanes, these shoals were known to be more dangerous than their southern sisters, which were numerous and even more treacherous, but not so close as to affect commerce. The southern shoals did not reach near the Gulf Stream, they were located in a virtual cove of protection from the river highway (as the Gulf Stream was described to be) far to the east. The southern sets of shoals were not near ports, nor were they desirable for their currents. Therefore, their reputation was not to be feared. They looked more like stepping-stones than full-blown mountains.

In order to get from north to south, and get around the Diamonds, sailing ships backed up near the coast of Kinnakeet village, waiting for the winds to shift to a more favorable direction, one that would allow them to swing around the shoals and into the Gulf Stream safely. Some days there were more than 100 sails waiting in the Kinnakeet Anchorage Basin. Should the wind be south or southeast, there was no crossing over to the southern route. Bucking either current with anything but a favorable wind was treacherous. Ships waited for a wind coming down from the north or northwest to give them a boost. The basin provided protection in the lee of the land for ships to wait.

Once, according to the villagers at Kinnakeet, the wind blew from the south for forty days. By that time there were 200 to 300 vessels waiting to make the crossing into the Gulf Stream and continue south: barquentines, square riggers, two-, three-, and four-masted schooners. When the wind shifted, all sails spread and struck out in a southeasterly direction. It must have been a glorious sight to see. A local man described it as butterflies over the ocean.

Sometimes, the anchorage was deceiving to those pilots who were unaccustomed to the art of maneuvering the Diamonds, the fog alone hampering them in their effort to keep away from other ships. They waited and drifted for so long and mistrusted the shifting sand to the point they got stuck on the ever changing sandbars while seemingly stationary. Some had to be towed off the bar. Others waited, hoping that the change of tide would allow them to float free on their own.

The shoals changed with each wind and storm. The Cape Hatteras Lighthouse was erected in 1803 to warn ships of the sandbars. Unfortunately, the light was neither bright enough nor was the structure tall enough to effectively warn passing ships in foul weather of the danger they faced. The first light was only visible twelve miles out to sea. If it was observed at that point, the vessel was already on the shoals. Thus, the ship bearing Theodosia Burr was not shown its way by Mr. Hamilton's Light. This ship, the *Patriot*, had a captain who was familiar with the Diamonds and successfully rounded them ahead of a threatening storm.

Alexander Hamilton was the man who first fostered the idea of a lighthouse off the coast of Cape Hatteras. Born on the island of Nevis in the British West Indies, Hamilton, an illegitimate child, was soon abandoned by his mother. He took a job at an accounting firm in St. Croix and so outshone his employers that the company paid his way to study in New York. On that ill-fated trip north, young Hamilton, traveling to enroll in Columbia University, was a passenger aboard the *Thunderbolt*. On that unfortunate trip a storm overtook the ship and pushed it close to the shoals. The rough grinding of the vessel as it sought to avoid the grasp of the shoals caused the ship to pitch uncontrollably as heavy seas poured into the ship's galley, spilling the coals from the cooking fire and setting the ship ablaze.

The captain and some of the crew fought the storm to keep the ship afloat and to control a mast that had broken and was wildly swinging in the deadly wind. Down below, Hamilton, other passengers, and the remainder of the crew battled the fire, which was threatening to sink the ship, no matter the storm. Had they known of the dangerous passage, they would have steered a wider berth. At last the *Thunderbolt* successfully limped in to Boston Harbor. Hamilton recovered, but the brush with death stayed with him long after.

As secretary of the treasury, Alexander authorized the passage of the Lighthouse Bill, which established, under the U.S. Treasury, a series of lifesaving stations to be located along the eastern coast of the United States. The coastal armies of the government were always conscious of the need to protect merchant shipping, and the Department of the Treasury was the best protector of interstate trade. The Cape Hatteras Lighthouse, built according to Hamilton's bill in 1803, stood 105 feet tall, had lights that could be seen twelve miles away, was painted the color of sand (a mistake that was later changed), and was forever called "Mr. Hamilton's Light" by the islanders.

With a better understanding of what was required of the beacon, the light has been replaced several times, since its shortcomings failed to protect shipping in the first attempt. The 100-foot-tall sandstone-colored light was replaced in 1854 by a 150-foot structure that was painted red on the top half and white on the bottom half. This building fell into disrepair quickly, barely surviving the Civil War. With sea travel still the cheapest and fastest way to deliver goods, a new construction, placed inland and 198 feet tall, was erected in 1867. Shipping along the coast demanded a safer route.

One and a quarter million bricks were used. To accommodate the delivery of materials, the ships had to come by way of the waters of the Pamlico Sound. The sound, also riveted with shoals, was a hindrance to the ships. To solve that problem, a pier was built for offloading cargo. A railed tram was constructed from the pier to the building site, where ships unloaded materials. Another roadway was built with horses pulling carts, offloading and carrying materials to the new lighthouse location. Several cargo-laden ships trying to approach the site from the south, sank in the frequent heavy gales before they could unload the freight, dumping chunks of granite and shiploads of bricks onto the sandy ocean floor. The new lighthouse was finally lit in 1870. This was the lighthouse the kids knew.

Sitting quietly on the beach, Ellie and Luke were each deep in thought—Ellie of her dream, and Luke sensing another adventure.

"Mr. Hamilton's Light!" Ellie jumped up, and began whirling around with arms circling the air like a windmill. "Mr. Hamilton's Light!" she shouted again. Her excitement spilling into the air.

"What are you talking about?" Luke squinted his eyes together against the sun as he twisted his head up to look at Ellie. Her little head didn't block out the sun completely from his eyes, and he was struggling to see her face through the solid blaze. "What? What about Mr. Hamilton's Light? That what they used to call the lighthouse. So?" He waited for her to stop spinning. He was hoping she would fall over, which at least would calm her down. To be so quiet, and then in the next instant to go crazy on him, she needed to explain.

"That's what Theodosia was looking for: Mr. Hamilton's Light! Don'tcha see? If the light had been tall enough when Theodosia's schooner went by, they might have saved themselves. There were a lot of reasons Theodosia might have wanted to see the light. And because the night was stormy, she didn't see it. Something brought her here, to this spot. I wish I knew what it was. If I knew, I bet I could get her to come back." Ellie was thinking out loud again. She had started by telling Luke, but now she was talking to herself. She was thinking she could create a situation that would bring Theodosia Burr back just long enough to satisfy her ghost. Ellie had learned about wandering ghosts from the experience with her mother. She was thinking aloud that she could do it again. A ghost wanders in dissatisfaction, usually trying to right a wrong. A spirit only drifts and observes. It has no reason to be upset.

"But nobody ever said she wrecked on Diamond Shoals." Luke also was thinking about the ghost of Theodosia Burr. "Pop said her ship ran aground at Nags Head, not here, so she wouldn't be looking for the light-house. It was something else."

"You're right. Her ghost is uneasy for some other reason." Now Ellie was troubled. She thought she had it with the lighthouse, but it seemed that was not the case. "What would her ghost be trying to find?"

"You don't even know it was her," Luke said quietly. The game was fun to play, until it reached a dead end.

"You're wrong. I do know it was her. I just know!" Ellie was sitting down beside Luke in a reflective mood, trying to get inside the empty head of a ghost. Finally she was exhausted.

Luke was as invested in this adventure as she was. He had seen things like this develop before, and had passed it off as his cousin just having too much going on in that tiny head. But he was not going to ignore this one. This time he was going to see just how far one of Ellie's premoni-tions went. He recognized it as the prelude to an adventure. Right then and there, he decided he would hop aboard this one, if he could figure out how.

"Ellie, let's come back down to the beach tonight to see if she comes here again." That was the best he could think of. "Maybe she needs a guide, like you or me, and we could direct her to the spirit world to find peace from wandering." Luke was really trying hard to think like a ghost would think. There must be a way to get the apparition to return.

Ellie had learned a lot about ghosts when she experienced seeing her mother. She knew the difference between ghosts and spirits. Spirits were like Travis, her guardian angel. They wanted to help—they looked after their charges, sometimes putting things in the path of their wards that would make them stronger or allow them to help another. Spirits were full of good feelings. Ghosts, on the other hand, could be cranky, contentious, and unfriendly. They didn't hurt people, but they just crashed around unhappy with everything and everyone. They were unfulfilled. Usually, they were people who felt they had been called before they were ready and had left something undone. What had Theodosia left undone?

Luke knew about ghosts also, since Ellie had told him all about meeting her mother. She told him about the kids teasing her and saying her mother was a ghost, and how in meeting Ellie, her mother, Annie, had gained peace and passed to the spirit world, where she could do good. He knew the stories about the woman on the road, looking for something, and enlisting a ride from passersby trying to get to the lighthouse road. It was every child on the island's ghost story, and it was hurtful to Ellie, and Luke knew it. The taunting had never stopped, but the effect had. Ellie was no longer bothered by all those chants of "your mother is a ghost!" Before it had hurt. Now she just smiled, and her disregard was off-putting to those who wished her harm. Finally, it occurred less and less, because they could see it produced no reaction from her. Luke had previously checked out a book on spirits and ghosts from the Bookmobile and learned on his own the difference between them. This ghost needed help, and he, Blake, and Ellie were going to provide it.

Luke had a good idea of what could she do to entice the figure to return. She was sure the figure was real, or maybe not real, but an apparition, one who was not afraid—or maybe even needed—to communicate. Ellie started to feel confident she could channel that energy. She had begun to be anxious at times to try out some of her powers. She was determined to be ready for this one. During the previous months, Ellie had learned about and experienced her energies while trying them out, and now she found she was ready to test her skills to see just how powerful they were.

"Luke, let's go back to Grandpop's barn and kind of hang out with the horses. They usually give me deeper thoughts, because they listen along with me. Have you ever tried that?" Ellie asked innocently.

"No, but I will this time. I really think you saw something the other night. And, Ellie, I sometimes think I should be practicing with you more. Maybe both me and Blake. We never talk about it, and maybe we should. A lot of things are going on around here, and the grown-ups are all preoccupied, so we are left to figure things out on our own. We need to be together in the things we think. You never know, our parents might even need us. Remember when Manteo said he appreciated how we listened to the woods, and to him, instead of asking a lot of questions. He said we should be aware in our hearts of certain things. Well, I think we should start paying attention to our inside voices. Maybe everything isn't always play. What do you think? Let's study our gifts and put them to good use. Sometimes I wonder if we will have them forever. I wonder, if we just always do silly things, will they go away? Maybe if we don't use them, they will be given to somebody else. It's Grandmom's bloodline that is in us, but other kids of the same family have not had these special energies. Let's develop our talents. Want to?"

"I am always embarrassed to use what I know I can do, but if you did it with me, I wouldn't be so scared. I'd like for us to work as a team."

At that, Ellie stuck out her hand and gave Luke a hearty handshake.

Boy, she means it, he thought, *and so do I.*

They sat quietly through supper. Blake was chattering away, not even stopping long enough to know he was the only one talking. Finally, he kicked Luke's leg under the table.

When Luke looked up, Blake squinted up one eye and mouthed, "What's goin' on?"

"Tell you later, mate," Luke said, and he got a little thrill of how it would feel to tell Blake that they were all going ghost hunting. He was excited about his plan to connect with his inner world, and it would not work without Blake.

That night, long after the house had settled, the kids sat on Ellie's bed, dressed for the warm air of the summer beach. There was not a dark cloud in the sky, just stars. Even without a very full moon, the stars shone against the lumpy overhead fluff of sky, winking at them as they stepped off the porch into the night. As they headed toward the beach, Gus and Blue gave a low whinny, which the kids were sure would awaken their grandparents. They froze, clasping tight to the items they were holding. With gritted teeth, they waited, but no sound. Everyone was still asleep. Ellie turned toward the barn and, with her finger to her lips, gave a low "Ssshhhhh!" It wasn't even loud enough for a frog to hear. Luke shared her discomfort.

They felt the summer breeze coming off the ocean, smelled the salt air, and crept along to the tune of the frogs singing in the open pond behind the house. It sounded like a symphony with their *ribbitts*, the constant singing of the cicadas, and the occasional *whoop-whoop* of the loon. The kids were so anxious, they were happy not to have to hear each other breathing as they stealthily made their way to the ocean.

Blake was calmest of all, except he was creeping too low and getting sand in his pants. Luke went back and lifted him out of a crouch and popped him on the head, motioning him to walk right. What did Blake know? Had they even bothered to tell him they were looking for a ghost? He had to guess that himself. He couldn't figure out why they were looking for one, but he was game. He had conjured up an entire scenario on his own. In Blake's imagination, the ghost would look just like Blackbeard, so his crouch was that of a pirate, just in case.

At the beach, they settled down on a small hill of sea oats, near the incoming tide. They knew from the sand in front of them how high the tide would get, so with knees pulled up, they rested against the soft oats and stared at the sky. The fog crept in until the knoll was above the lift, and the children slept, under the stars. As the night thickened, so did the fog.

As Ellie awakened, she had to brush away the clouds of mist from her eyes. Standing in front of her was the lady in the long dark cape, the same lady she had seen nights before. She extended her hand to Ellie and pulled her to her feet. Ellie stepped off into a carpet of air as she strode along beside the figure. They headed out to sea.

Ellie's heart was pounding, and she blinked hard to gain her senses. The figure had continued to hold her hand, and Ellie felt a concentration of strange energy at the connection. It didn't feel real—more tingly, like the touch of a phantom.

"Hello, Ellie. Do you know who I am? We have been connecting of late, I feel." The voice of the woman was kind and not at all threatening.

"I think I know. My grandfather was telling stories, and they were so real, I wanted you to have a better life." At that, Ellie was telling the truth. She continued, "Are you Theodosia Burr Alston?"

Theodosia was stunned and flattered that anyone would have a thought of her after all these years. My, to live in someone's thoughts. That was special.

"I am led to understand, that you have a connection to the spirit world, and as I see you, I am surprised, because you are so young. That was why I disappeared the other night. I felt I had been mistaken. But my feelings persisted—that you were the one who could help me." As Theodosia spoke, Ellie had the feeling that this ghost was full of sorrow, maybe even more than the sorrow she felt her mother had. Could she help? It was true that she was young, but the connection was real, and Ellie felt it in her heart.

"I have energies that need to be put to rest," the ghost began. "I left this world in a violent, maybe voluntary way, and for that, I need to amend. One should never take one's own life. I am not sure, but I might have done that. If that proves to be true, I need to make a correction. My spirit will never let

me rest until I resolve my troubles on earth. I was drawn here by the beacon. I felt a strong draw toward that light."

"That's Mr. Hamilton's Light," said Ellie "It was placed there to help ships avoid the shoals located off our island."

"Alexander Hamilton?" asked Theodosia. "He was killed in a duel by my father. I don't think he would be willing to help me."

Ellie could feel the air getting colder as they seemed to float above the ocean and traveled away from shore. They passed the Diamonds and continued north, as they encountered the misty fog and brisk wind of the open ocean. Theodosia wrapped Ellie in her cape as they crossed the sky. The fog was so thick Ellie could no longer see the shore.

"I want you to help me find my way back. In my ghostly travels, I have met with those that believe I can cross over if I discover how I died. I have longed to see my father again, and my son, and, unless I solve my mysteries, I cannot connect with them. There are many things I need to do. I left too soon." Theodosia was sad.

"How can you do that?" asked Ellie. They were now suspended above a small, clean sailing schooner. It was so still in the water, all sails furled, just sitting there. As Ellie looked at the vessel just below her feet, she saw the fog of obscurity settling on the ocean. The ship was nestled in the silky blue swells of the sea.

As they slowly floated downward, suddenly the clouds parted and the previous serenity of the vessel at sea was a mass of bloody bodies and slashing swords, as men swiped at the crew of the Patriot in an effort to gain the cargo below deck. The weather was beginning to intensify, and rain combined with the swells of water washing over the ship, seemed to remove the blood as soon as it was shed. The pirates worked their way to the ship's hold and brought up two cannons and a chest of arms. The ragged men swore at the crew, the cargo, and the sky. The storm had been on the horizon for hours, giving the Patriot false hope that the pirates, whom they had noticed were following them, would not see fit to board them. The schooner, disguised as a passenger ship, carried gold obtained from the pillage of French ships, which stole from Spanish ships, and the ship with its arms and gold, now was headed toward the government in Washington. The country was at war with the English, and piracy had come back to take advantage of that. The high seas were crawling with unscrupulous characters. Governor Alston had placed his faith in the cunning of the American privateers to safely deliver his wife to her home in New York.

Ellie and Theodosia watched as the villains drove their prey into the sea. Cautiously she and Ellie hid behind a hatch cover storing staves for winding rope. Everything was so real, it was a question whether those on board could actually see them. They watched as the cannon were loaded into a dory, rolling and pitching at the side of the Patriot. The cannon made the boat sit lower in the unsettled sea. The ship was starting to roll in the mighty ocean so much that many of the weapons spilled out on the deck and washed over the side. The sea was beginning to curl over the rails of the ship and crash on the deck. A broken spar waved dangerously about, caught in the roping of the masts and allowing its sail to sweep the ship. A sailor tried to hack away at the obstacle with an ax that had floated out of the closet where Ellie and Theodosia hid, but the deck was so slick, he lost his balance and was last seen going overboard on his stomach, arms outstretched and clawing at anything that would stop his descent. As the interlopers struggled above deck with the chests of gold, the first thug slipped and lost hold. The chest hit the deck, cracked open, and spilled coins into the corners of the ship and the sea. Never was there such lamentation among thieves.

The second chest was handled with the utmost care and was safety lifted over the side, but dropped straight into the deep as the ocean decided at that moment to heave a sigh.

Theodosia looked at Ellie, not with a smile, but a pleasant countenance.

"I did not see all of this before," she said. "I was taken from the cabin at the beginning and chained to the lifeboat. I saw the chest drop into the sea, and I saw my friends in the ocean quickly disappear beneath. I was bound, even my mouth, lest I cry out. But the screams on the inside were of the most agonizing kind. On the horizon there were sounds of gunfire as a British man-o-war approached the two ships. The ruffians gave up and boarded the dory. Having left my ship to return to the pirate ship which was waiting yards from the Patriot, I saw the Patriot float away.

"The British ship began to chase the pirates. By that time the sea was churning and the cannon in the small dory began rolling about, finally causing the dory to overturn, dumping everyone and everything into the sea. I do not remember much after that. I was chained to the side of the boat, and when it rolled again to right itself, I was alone. I do not believe I was left with much of a mind after that. For days I begged to die, I had lost everything. I only remember begging God to let me die. That is the sin I committed. I am doomed to wander endlessly for that cowardly act. That is what I needed to see. Did I go against myself and take my own life?"

Ellie saw the hurt on Theodosia's face. How could she fix this?

"You did not take your own life, Theodosia, you gave your life. There is a difference. Remember when you said you wish you had seen Mr. Hamilton's Light? Well, because you did not, over the years, it was decided that a new, higher, brighter light needed to be there. So both you and Mr. Hamilton have been saving lives for over 100 years. You and Mr. Hamilton share a history, and though at one time tragic, it has become a stronger beacon. Your father thought the light failed you, so a bigger one was made, and all of it was because of Mr. Hamilton. My grandmom always said, "You are always the strongest in those places that are broken.""

The blue cloud laced with silver threads that circled above Ellie had never been more proud. Saint Travis began to sparkle all over. He rained down stars on the two as they drifted on a gentle sea breeze back to the beach. They sat on the ground just below the small hill were Luke and Blake slept.

Ellie gently tossed a shell, and Luke sat up. At that, Blake awakened and looked around.

"Come here. Come meet someone." Ellie motioned to the cloaked figure sitting beside her.

Slowly the boys raised up and crawled over to the two figures.

Luke sat behind the woman in the long coat, but Blake did not get near. Ellie was so anxious to introduce the boys to her apparition that she failed to see the outstretched stream of silver light extending from the heavens to encircle the newest saint and bring her to her resting place of calm. Theodosia had come home, no longer feeling the curse of never gaining the other side. Her ghostly form shed, as she nestled on the clouds above with Travis.

Ellie said, "Luke, this is—," as she motioned in the direction of thin air. There was not one soul beside her. The coat was crumbled on the ground like it had just been discarded. She gasped.

"What?" Luke could not believe his eyes.

Blake was now standing and knelt down to touch the cape. He was so cautious, his hand only hovered over the cloth for a long time. Then he finally patted it.

"Real," he said.

Ellie had her hands up over her mouth and then moved one to her heart. What had just happened was that Theodosia had finally become a spirit.

For several minutes the kids sat around the cloak and looked at it, then each other. For the first time, nobody had anything to say.

They took the cloak and walked back to the house, hardly talking at all.

They climbed the stairs in total quiet, hoping not to make squeaks on the old boards. They went to their rooms and removed their damp, sandy clothing. The boys placed theirs under the bed, thinking to take it to the wash the next day. Ellie, so tired and so content, spread out the cloak on a chair to dry, climbed into the soft bed, and was immediately asleep.

Then Grandmom was waking her. "What's this?" she asked as the sleepy head peeked from under the covers.

"Something we found on the beach. We're gonna clean it up and use it for the horses," Ellie said, and she was determined to wear that cloak every time she rode Blue out into the night.

"Oh," said Grandmom, in such a way that Ellie wondered if maybe she already knew the answer.

Bones and Ribs

Ellie, Luke, and Blake busied themselves in the barn. Ellie and Blake were making sure the gorgeous black coat of their colt, Blue, was as shiny as a dime. Luke was left to groom Pegasus.

Luke was not dismayed that he had no help in his efforts. He was happy to own a pony all on his own. This day, Blake was finding out what it was like to be the only one to brush Blue. Ellie seemed to brush, then stop and fiddle with Theodosia's cape. She had it stretched taut on the wall, void of sand and soil, drying it out from the mist of the night before.

"You kids want to ride to Kinnakeet with me?" Grandpop stuck his head around the barn door, peering down the dark stalls to the back where the three were busy with their chores. "You boys going to handle Ol' Tony and Big Roy? Don't want them to feel left out." Capt'n Charlie knew that the lifesaving crew of the Coast Guard had already approached him about leaving them at the station when the family moved to the house in Trent Woods.

He was reluctant to tell the children that the two huge surfboat horses would not be moving with them. He didn't know if even he could take the loss, as these horses had been with him for at least ten years. But they were only on loan to the light keeper, and the decision was not his. These steeds were valuable assets to assist the two other surf horses that were presently stabled at the Coast Guard station. The wagonload carrying all the lifesaving apparatus could easily weigh 1,000 pounds, and combined with strong winds and relentless rain, the dirt road became a muddy ditch. Even with eight surfmen pushing and digging out the wheels and the keeper in the lead, the mighty horses were straining both to see and move ahead. All this was taking place while people's lives were at stake. Four horses made a big difference.

There were times when the surfboat was not needed, but that decision could only come after the tragedy was being assessed, and it was not an option to turn around and go back to retrieve anything. All of it had to get to the beach on the first try. Time was a matter of life and death. It was not an option to show up at a wreck site unprepared.

At first, when it was decided that impending war would mean the family needed to move away from the beach, the officials had told the captain that he could keep Ol' Tony and Big Roy, but through several meetings, even Charlie Gray knew those horses were a necessary part of most rescues. Many a time he and the sailors had walked the huge steeds down to the beach to help launch a boat when the weather was so nasty that four horses rather than two were needed for the equipment pull. If the men discovered a ship floundering just out of reach of a breeches buoy, the thirty-foot surfboat was the only answer. He knew all this, but so far he hadn't the heart to tell the kids about the horses. Especially Blake. He was the one who usually paid the most attention to Ol' Tony. Almost as soon as his little legs were long enough, he wanted to straddle a horse by himself. Blue was kind of Ellie's horse, Gus definitely belonged to Luke, and Blake had gotten very close to Ol' Tony.

Another trip down to the Burrus ranch on the sound in Hatteras was in the front of the captain's mind, and through correspondence he had discussed the possibility of a third horse with Bill. Still on the island there were no paved roads. The dirt two tracks were the only way up and down the island, on the "inside." Of course, there was always the wash. But that discussion would be for another day. Grandpop and Nett had been looking already, and Nett had picked out a beautiful dark brown, whose rich coat picked up the rays of the sun and shimmered with a deepening mahogany color off the handsome young horse. This one was not quite two years old and had been one Grandpop had his eye on, as he was still a wobbly legged colt when the kids went for Ellie's "Black Beauty." To have been so lucky as to find Blue, since it was exactly what she imagined after reading all those books, was special, and Grandpop wasn't going to take any chances of not getting the proper horse for Blake. The little whippersnapper had waited so long and patiently, never complaining about riding behind Ellie, he deserved a horse of its own distinction—a horse that stood out in its own way as Luke's palomino and Ellie's blue-as-night beauty.

The captain had put a down payment on the horse, whose nose, mane, tail, ear edges, and lower legs were pitch black. He was saving the surprise for the time when the kids would have to part with their two old friends. Ol' Tony and Big Roy belonged to the U.S. government, they had a job to do, they loved their job, and they were good at it. With their wide hoofs and larger than normal size, they easily pulled the surfboat through the wet sand and got the nose of it into the surf before the handlers led them away. They were not afraid of the pounding breakers rushing and crashing around them. They appeared to relish the contest. Charlie loved them the most.

The kids immediately stopped what they were doing and almost knocked their grandfather over in their haste to prepare for a trip up the beach. No matter what the reason, they wanted to go, and they had already been over to the beach and knew it must be getting really low tide, so this was going to be a ride down the camelbacks of the receding wash. By the time Capt'n Charlie had a chance to turn around, they had already piled into the truck. This time Luke and Blake were sitting on the rails of the bed, ready for a wild ride. Ellie had her favorite place beside her pop, in the front seat, so that she could see the sand going by from the rusted floorboards of the old jalopy. She did not like riding in the back. The wind tangled her hair so much that Grandmom had to pull and pick to get the knots out. Besides, riding beside her pop was special for both of them.

Kinnakeet had character. It was a real village—everything built up around a harbor, with stores and houses that made a circle. Located on a flat beach, this was the most tightly knit community of the seven. It was not stretched out in a long trail down the island, but the kind of village you entered, and everything was right there. The kids didn't know the names of the boys there, but all the boys and girls knew them. They were the Lighthouse Kids. Usually Pop did business with Mr. Charlie Williams or hung around Mr. Gibb. He was friends with the Scarborough men and others who kept the village going. He felt it necessary to communicate with other villages for political and social reasons. Grandmom's maiden name was Scarborough, so Kinnakeet was a special place for her, and Grandpop had grown up near the village, as his father was the keeper at the Big Kinnakeet Lifesaving Station located between Buxton and Kinnakeet village.

Amalek Thomas Gray, the keeper at the Big Kinnakeet Lifesaving Station (the Lifesaving Service later merged with the Revenue Service to become the U.S. Coast Guard), had recognized the talents of his son and sent him away to study at Norfolk Academy in Norfolk, Virginia. Going off island was considered necessary in order for him to obtain proper credits to enter North Carolina College of Agriculture and Mechanic Arts (now known as North Carolina State University), in Raleigh, North Carolina.

Pop had a familial feeling about Kinnakeet and loved to take the kids to this perfect little village north of them. He was proud to show them off and wanted them to be familiar with all the villages. Living on such an isolated island, it was necessary for the seven villages to stick together for survival. The rough trek between villages was simply not a problem to those who were natives. The beach provided a highway at low tide, for horses and wagons and, later, cars. Most, especially those living in Kinnakeet, had small skiffs that they could hoist a sail to, or should they decide to keep to the shore, they could use their shove pole to meander down the bank on the sound side to the next village. The Indians used canoes—small, like a skiff, but a different shape.

Grandpop knew that when he got to the village, Luke and Blake would be off to make new friends, and Ellie would be stuck to his leg like glue. *Maybe girls don't make friends as easily as boys,* he thought. She definitely was her grandpop's partner.

On the way up the beach the boys were counting the remains of shipwrecks. The wind and tides uncovered a different set of ship carcasses after every storm. Some went under the sand while others revealed themselves. Islanders were used to the sight. Protruding from the sands of the beach and the dunes nearby were huge timbers that turned up like the bones of a half-hidden dinosaur. They had been there forever. It was hard to tell what kind of ships they used to be, for now all they showed were backbones and a few ribs sticking up. Sometimes there was only a long strip of huge heavy timber lying hidden near the dunes, the only distinguishing marks being equally huge iron fastening bolts sticking out in rows. The iron hulks from wrecks years past were the last to disappear. Most of anything usable had been carted away, but the beach still remained littered with the tragedies of past storms.

Even bricks, stuck together by something other than mortar, could be seen in blocks along the beach. These were obviously moved about the ocean floor and deposited on the shores all along both Hatteras and Ocracoke Islands. It was well documented that a schooner carrying a load of over 100,000 bricks, destined for the new brick lighthouse at the cape, had been caught in a gale during the winter of 1869 and wrecked south of Hatteras Inlet. Over the years, those bricks molded together and rolled up on the shore all along the island.

Parts of huge ships whose names were never known washed up along the beaches between Buxton and Kinnakeet. The bones of these unknowns finally made it to the shore that denied their human cargo a resting place. Sometimes the villagers found a bell or a desk or some heavy artifact that was tumbled and shorn down by the rolling breakers and heavy surf that washed west from Diamond Shoals. The graveyard gave up pieces of conquests, months and years after the thrashing and breaking apart of some colossal and indestructible vessel that went unrecorded on a stormy night off the coast of Cape Hatteras Island. These huge chunks of timbers and masts kept breaking off the main and wandered to the shore to rest up against the sands, only to be buried once again, far short of their destination.

The boys played I spy all the way up the beach. The foreign materials located near the beautiful shells were obviously alien to their surroundings and therefore easily discovered, even from a distance. The skeletal parts of a ship stood out against the pristine white sand, sometimes tangled up in the low-growing grapevines that almost reached the waterline. Mixed in with the carcasses of shark and dolphin that sometimes littered the beach, there was much to find along the beach between villages. The children had made so many trips up the beach, and always with a million questions, that they knew ahead of time to anticipate this wreck or that, and marvel at the condition they found them in as opposed to the last time. They were well aware of how the sea sometimes had the habit of reclaiming a treasure, or storms weathered them to a smaller size. The weather and its effects were a part of every islander's basic knowledge. Living in such an isolated place commanded a lot of respect. This was what "home" looked like.

They shouted out, "I spy," as they traveled up the beach, sometimes getting so excited they banged on the cab of the old jalopy, or Luke would lean in and yell into the window at Grandpop in an effort to get him to pull over and let them examine a piece. Capt'n Charlie was just as curious as his grandchildren, and he also wanted to stop. The only reason he ever kept going was if he was aware of a soft spot on the sand that would keep the truck from easily pulling out. This was low tide, and on this day, with the sand as hard as any asphalt highway, stopping was not a problem. He and the boys pulled over to examine almost every huge chunk of heavy wood or obvious mast located on this stretch of beach. They kicked and poked at each piece to determine which part of the vessel they were observing.

Shipwrecks littered the entire island, mostly far north of Kinnakeet. Sometimes most of the ship still sat, stuck for eternity until the tides of hurricanes and nor'easters, gales and storms beat them into submission, or uncovered even more of what was below the surface. People traveling up the beach on the Blue Bus were fascinated by what they saw when the bus moved over to the beach at low tide to ride on hard sand for a few miles. Most, even the locals, did not venture over to the ocean for any reason. They had their lives in the villages, and since all the villages had originally settled on the sound side, away from the ocean, even natives were spellbound by the gifts from the sea.

Keels and hatch covers washed up monthly, but being so desired, they did not stay long on the lonely beach. The women who ventured to the beach, usually to accompany their husbands to fish, were adept at combing the sands for colorful, unbroken shells. Sea glass was the most desirable. Bottles thrown from ships tumbled and broke into pieces that were then worn smooth by the rough sand. When they finally washed in with the shells, they caught the sun and sparkled like diamonds in the sand. Colored glass was a fortunate find and, in the hands of a talented native, was fashioned into jewelry, proudly worn by its owner.

Island yards were covered with the most perfect finds—unbroken shells, especially conchs, and strangely shaped coral. Some of the conchs were not local but from as far south as Florida or even the Caribbean, as hurricanes deposited all manner of items whenever they blew through. Even coconuts were discovered and proudly displayed as the most special. It was also quite a gift to find a sand dollar or a starfish, and all of them were kept, some inside the house for fear of damaging their delicate structure. Most prominent was the perfect conch, which circled rosebushes and lined walkways of most local houses. The children were always on the lookout for a perfect conch for Grandmom.

Island men scoured the beach for wood and building materials. Wood that washed up from ships was sturdy, of the finest quality, and usually the kind not available on the island. Many houses on the island were finished off or started from lumber that arrived by way of a ship wrecked on either the beach or the shoals. The church in Salvo was built almost entirely from timbers that arrived by way of a ship caught on the bar and broken up before the tides could carry it off. The lifesavers could save the lives, but little could be done for the vessel. That was up to the sea.

One of the more sought-after items was the roping that went on for miles on a ship. Sailing ships had rope ladders, rope holding the sails together, rope to access the many masts and spars, rope for bunks, rope stretched across the ceiling or down the sides, something to grab when the weather was having its way with a vessel in its grip. And rope was used to its fullest extent on the island. Smokestacks, anchors, ships' wheels, and storage crates also frequented the tide and disappeared into the mix of island life.

Luke and Blake were scavengers. They convinced Ellie to comb the beaches with them. They looked closely for anything that could have originated on a vessel lost at sea. Blake in particular was constantly kicking the sand for pirate treasure. He was convinced that a gold doubloon was somewhere, just waiting for him to pick it up. He thought also that if it turned out to be a gold goblet, he would take that. Beachcombing produced everything. Even Indian arrowheads could be found entangled in the grass that collected with the tide. That line of grass along the shore was a treasure full of fabulous finds.

Finally they arrived at the place to turn up for the village. Already the day had been fun. The boys were shoeless and dark-sand dirty from the beach, but so was every other island kid during the summer months. There was so much adventure to be had, it was hard to choose on which shore or which area of woods a youngster would explore.

Kinnakeet had personality. It was distinguishable from all the other villages, but the style of the people—their appearance and speech—was unique to each village. Hatteras and Rodanthe also had distinct personalities. Buxton and Trent were more mixtures and not as readily recognizable, but the boys were now in Kinnakeet, and they were excited.

The village was most bustling at the docks. Here commerce came and went, mixed with the fishermen who worked the sounds. Along the road that looped past the dock in a circle working its way back to the beach were beautiful rosebushes, climbing and wild. Wild honeysuckle caused the village to reek of fragrant smells. Luke grabbed a handful from a bush located near Gibb's store and carefully pulled on each white flower's yellow stigma to taste the sweet juice. He was in competition with the bees for that part of the flower, but this day, he and Blake had their fill.

Lester Scarborough and his cousin Georgie O'Neal connected with Luke and Blake soon after they crawled out of the back of the truck in front of Gibb's store.

"Can we go? Can we go?" Luke was dancing around like he would wet his pants if his pop said no.

"You young-uns don't get lost for time!" Grandpop scowled. "I don't intend to stay all day. Keep your eye on the sun, and stay maybe an hour or so." He knew this was one of those once-in-a-blue-moon times he would let them get away from him. Those boys being let loose in Kinnakeet? Lord only knew what mischief they would find. Those Scarborough boys would show them a thing or two. It was good for them to experience new places.

The boys were off, swapping stories and looking to get into mischief. This was the home of Mealy Mouth, a bull so named because, as a newborn calf, he fell into a trough of freshly ground corn meal from the windmill nearby. He walked around for days as the white stuff slowly wore off his face. Everyone knew of Mealy Mouth. Luke and Blake had heard the stories.

"Come on," Lester said. "Ever seen a cannonball hole? We got one here."

"Cool!" Blake was willing, this sounded fun.

Grandpop and Ellie stayed at the general store. Here Grandpop met his contemporaries gathered around the barrels and chairs scattered throughout the store, and Ellie took her place on the swing located on the spacious porch. She marveled at the serenity of the village—its birds and flowers, the huge live oaks and their sweeping limbs—and became lost in daydreaming. Her presence was almost an announcement that Capt'n Charlie from Buxton was there, leading various men to join the gathering. Included in the group was Charlie Williams, a prominent member of Kinnakeet society and the island's vendue master. But the discussions this time would not have to do with salvage or wreckage. These men would be discussing world affairs and how present developments located far from these shores would affect the tiny island of Cape Hatteras and its peaceful villagers.

The boys left on an adventure that would take them down the sandy road, past the fish docks, and around to the other side of the village. Luke and Blake took in all the sights and smells of this neat village. The odor of fish and salt met them and followed them as they stopped to watch the goings-on at the docks. Lester's dad was hauling net out of a dory, getting ready to mend it, he said. It was cool to see the life of a sound fisherman. Luke was pretty used to going out on Uncle Cyrus's boat to catch croaker and spot in the sound. If Pop dropped him and Blake off early enough, when the sun was coming up, they saw the pound net fishermen tending the sections that they had poled off in the sound, marking a spot solely farmed by each man. Their silhouettes appeared dark against a red sky as they hunched over the heavy nets they were pulling. It was the way of life in this village. Most men of Kinnakeet were connected with the sound. At one point this was the major shipping village on the island.

Kinnakeet had one of the two windmills on the island. It used to be the only landmark for boats out to sea, before the lighthouse. When the first lighthouse was built in 1803, it was so short that when citing a reference as to how close or far away from land the ship was traveling, the windmill appeared taller. There was a rather brisk mercantile trade coming and going from the natural harbor of Kinnakeet. Local men who owned boats rented out their vessels and their own expertise as pilots familiar with the shifting shoals of the Pamlico, allowing anyone who wanted to deliver trade to or away from the island a knowledgeable guide. There was a lucrative seaweed gathering business in Kinnakeet, and they sold barges full of it to the mainland for use to stuff mattresses or to be ground down for fertilizer. The seaweed was also in demand for medicinal purposes, as during one period the rich swore by seaweed baths to relieve the pain of arthritis and rheumatism. They claimed that the qualities in it detoxified the body and soaked out pain.

Even on this day, huge cargo barges were offshore. The boys walked the harbor road until it ended, and there were two ways to go. Instead of continuing along the sound, Lester and Georgie motioned for the boys to follow them to the woods to the left of the sound road. They crept their way slowly through the bushes and small yaupon trees. Nearing a house, the Kinnakeet boys knelt down, so the Buxton boys did the same.

"Okay, now," started Georgie, "Lester and I do this all the time, but ol' lady Hooper don't really like people snooping around her house. The cannonball hole is around the side over there and right on the front corner as you peek around. You can put your hand in it!" Georgie said enthusiastically.

"But you gotta know, she swears she'll shoot the next kid she finds in her yard. So, you jus' gotta know." Lester was wagging his head back and forth as he was cautioning the boys. He shifted from one foot to the other, shaking a warning finger toward the Buxton visitors.

Mighty suspicious looking, thought Luke, but Blake was up for an adventure. He was quite sure that if the boys from Kinnakeet were going to match wits with Luke, he could outthink them. His confidence in Luke made him brave. He was grinning as he looked up at Luke. Well, it was either a grin or a smirk, but his eyes were twinkling.

"You guys goin'?" Luke looked at Lester and Georgie, and their response said it all.

"You bet!" they said almost at once. "Come on!"

With Georgie leading the way, all four quietly picked their way around the back of Miz Hooper's house and stayed low. A little bit away was a chicken pound, but the chickens were outside in the yard and just pecked away at the stuff on the ground, ignoring the boys as they crept by.

If it'd been Grandmom's chickens, they wouldn't have been all over the place, Luke thought. Grandmom kept her chickens penned up. There were too many varmints near the woods of the lighthouse grounds that would gladly eat them up. There must not be so many predators here or Miz Hooper wouldn't have any chickens at all. What they did not know was that she could be seen every afternoon rounding them up and putting them in a pen. Actually, the Hooper chickens were somewhat trained.

The boys successfully rounded the back of the house to the left side, only to discover it had a side porch and a screened-in door leading into the house. That was usually not a problem, but today, as they got close, they saw that the door to the porch was open, and anyone on the inside could see through the screen—especially if maybe four boys were sneaking by. The opposite side of the house was flat, against the north wind, and didn't even have windows, allowing this house a solid wall against the cold. Luke and Lester decided they would go around and hit the north side of the house. The back side was safe, and they were determined not to get caught.

It was a farther walk to see the hole, but there wouldn't be anybody watching them. They turned and started creeping around the back, with Blake in behind them, not even stepping on a stick. Lester led the way, around the back, then along the north side, and then across the west of the house that faced the sound. This side had a long double window across the front of the house, so the boys lowered themselves to creep under, next to the hedges, and out of sight to everyone.

Just as Blake rounded the west-facing corner of the house, and about the time Luke was poised to stick his hand in the huge hole left by a Civil War cannon fired from the sound, a high-pitched shrill pierced the air. Blake jumped and ran right around Luke and Lester straight into the bushes. Luke, so close to the woods, took off running, with Lester right beside him. Ol' Lady Hooper was just hitting the door with a shotgun raised, and Georgie was standing frozen *on the steps of the porch*. Luke ran back and snatched Georgie by the collar and drug him backward to the woods, where Lester grabbed his belt loop and lifted him almost totally off the ground. They were all running, with Georgie's one foot touching to help only once in a while. Miz Hooper leveled that scatter gun toward the woods and pulled the trigger. The spray of shot was hitting the bushes behind them, but they had gained the trees and were running inland alongside the creek, seeming to be heading straight to the ocean.

Blake came out sideways from them as they ran for their lives up the creek to some other part of the village. They knew the old lady wouldn't follow them. As they slowed down, the Kinnakeet boys began to tell Blake about Miz Hooper and her shotgun.

"What were you thinking?" Lester turned toward Georgie, with his hands in the air.

"I just thought it would be fun to say hello. Maybe she would share some cookies or something. Any other lady in the village would." Georgie was actually serious, but he looked so shaken. She had really scared the stuffings out of him.

The boys continued on down the path they were making along the bank of the creek when Luke spied an large open area that looked to be a shortcut to the part of the village where Grandpop was. Luke made the suggestion that they cut across the field, just near the bank of the creek. Before any of the other boys could object, he had hopped over the huge fallen log separating the field from the canal and was on his way across the meadow, picking his way through palmetto bushes, tall grass, and huge agave plants. As he cleared his way through to the sandy patches that crisscrossed the area, Blake caught up quickly and joined him. But the two local boys did not follow. They just stood on the edge of the field with big grins on their faces.

Luke and Blake were busy making their way through some low bushes when Luke stopped short. Blake was following so close, he ran into his brother with a thud that shoved Luke forward, causing him to have to catch his balance. Blake looked up to see what had startled Luke. Right in front, several yards away, was a gigantic black bull, with huge, sharply pointed horns. Luke started walking back, just a step at a time, stepping on Blake, who quickly also got out of the way. Luke did not take his eyes off the bull, as he tried to find the moment and the room to turn around.

"Blake," he whispered, "we have to turn around and run, then split off. He can't chase but one of us at a time. Ready?"

"'Kay," Blake whispered, locking his eyes on the bull also.

As the boys began to slowly back away, the bull looked up from the tender leaves of grass on which he was munching. Maybe he thought the boys were going to eat his snack. Whatever he thought, he looked like he was coming for them.

Both turned and ran as hard as they could, but no matter what, Luke could not turn away from Blake. The plan was to separate so the bull would get confused, but Blake would not leave Luke. The bull was in hot pursuit. They could feel the ground under them shake with his gallop. They were nearing the edge of the clearing, where the log separated the pasture from the canal. Both Luke and Blake cleared the log with one leap and found themselves sliding butt-first down the bank of the canal.

Splash! They landed on their fannies in the water.

Above them on the bank, Lester and George were holding their sides and their mouths, doubled over with laughter.

"What's so funny?" Luke growled back. "You could have told us we were going to get mauled by a bull. That might have been something! You could have warned us!" He was getting riled up just thinking about it. Then he stood up and turned around to stare up at three faces: Lester, Georgie, and the bull!

"Whaaaatt?" he screamed.

Blake stood up, and wiping his soaked clothes, he turned, too, and joined in his brother's shock.

Lester and Georgie slid down the bank to give their Buxton buddies a hand. As they all clambered up the slope, the bull just watched.

"Meet Mealy Mouth, the village's pet bull. We dress him up for celebrations. Everybody feeds him. He just wanders around the village— has since he was a calf. Once there was a shipwreck off here loaded with cattle. He was born on the day his mother swam to shore, so the villagers kept him. The owner of the cattle came to pick up the stock that survived the swim, and they didn't want to be bothered with a calf. So we all just kept him. We knew he wouldn't hurt you, we were just funnin' you. Okay?" Lester and Georgie were still laughing as they wrapped their arms around the huge neck of the bull. He leaned in like he relished the attention.

"Well, we been to Kinnakeet and met Mealy Mouth," said Luke. "I don't think we have a village pet in Buxton."

"We've got wolves," burst in Blake, and as soon as he said it, he knew he was wrong and shot an apologetic look at Luke.

"That's what they say," said Luke, sort of snickering, but he was thinking something way ahead of Blake. He thought about how just the thought of wolves had kept people away from the secret of the mansion in Trent Woods. He knew he didn't want anyone snooping around there. The wolf story was a good one, and it seemed to be working. He didn't mind if someone believed it. They never would believe he had a wolf of his own. Not in a million years.

★ 5 ★

Kinnakeet

The boys walked around the village, brushing off mud and sort of hanging out while their clothes dried. They invited their new friends to visit them at the lighthouse compound. They knew they could show these guys some fun stuff to do around the woods and ponds that made up their yard, and they could walk through Buxton to let the Kinnakeet boys see what their village looked like. They knew they couldn't produce a bull, but if they put their heads together, there was an adventure to be had.

Lester and Georgie took them over near the beach to the schoolhouse. The school kinda looked like theirs. A big square building, only a few rooms, and as it was locked, they could only jump to see in the windows. The stories the Kinnakeet boys told about school were the best. They told of the time the older boys came into the building at night, or early in the morning, and filled one room with the tall tufts, called tussocks, of pampas grass. The whole time they were filling the room, they were breaking apart the tussocks and scattering them all over the room. When the class came to school the next day, they opened the door and the breeze from the air outside set those tufts a-flying, filling the air to the point they could hardly see. The tufts were so dense it looked like snow. It was even hard to breathe. Of course, school was postponed on that day until everyone could clean out the room so that class could resume.

This story made Luke's Judy-B-peeing-in-a-bucket story sound tame. But it was the only story Luke had to compete, so he told it. The boys were exploring Kinnakeet's roads for all kinds of mischief and laughing. These local fellas were fun. Along the way, a couple of other guys joined them—Harold James and Little Charlie. All were barefoot, all looking for something to get into. They wandered back down near the harbor and ended up at the windmill located near the sound. It looked like a box on stilts, and the four sails that turned on the spindle were made of old ships' sails. When the wind blew, that big box began grinding.

Another thing they noticed was the number of small skiffs or sprit-sail boats tied up near the banks of the sound. This was the preferred means of transportation, as this village was centered around the idea of the sound. It produced their living and provided their pleasure. Lester wanted them all to get in boats, but Luke knew his grandpop would kill him if he went on the water without telling him, so he told the boys they would do it next time. That would give him time to soften up Grandpop.

The kids learned a lot about life in the northern village. Every grown-up read the newspaper every single day, mostly at Gibb's store. Others sat around playing checkers, waiting their turn and discussing world affairs. Visiting was the favorite pastime. There was a ritual: visit friends and parents weekly. Everyone liked books, especially the women. Saturday night was the most fun, usually gathering at someone's house. More than half attended church regularly, and every night in August during the revival season, the building was packed. Visiting preachers frequented the island during that month with their families—(most had been invited to stay with someone in the village—and held a weeklong series of sermons at the church. During this time, those who might not have been acting right turned their lives around and vowed to change their ways, until the temptation for wrongdoing became so strong that they went back to their old habits. It was big talk around the village when someone backslid: "Oh, Lordy, somebody said that ol' man Tom done backslid and took to strong drink when he lost his catch of fish."

Actually, some had perfected the art of backsliding, as they repented their sins in front of the congregation to please a spouse or children. For the youngsters, backsliding was also an art and happened often after they had apologized for some misdeed they had performed at home. The "I'm sorry" trick didn't always work, though.

Georgie told the boys that the most favorite pastime in the village on Saturday afternoon was horse racing on the beach. Most of the boys had horses, and racing on the hard sand of the wash at low tide drew a crowd. They were careful not to race in soft sand, as it was bad for the horse's legs. At that, he took them around the back of some people's houses to see the most prized steeds of the community.

"I've got a horse," announced Luke. "His name is Pegasus, named after the horse that rode across the sky. But I call him Gus. We were thinking about racing him during the Pirates' Jamboree, but Grandpop said he had to be older. Gus is gold. With a white mane and tail, he looks like the sun. Ellie also has a horse, who is black, and we named him Blue, 'cause he shined that way when the sun hit his coat, and—"

Blake interrupted. "And my horse is still at Burrus's stable, growing up."

"But you don't have him yet," interjected Luke. "He doesn't even have a name."

"Does, too. I just haven't told *you!*" Blake never let a good argument go to waste.

Harold told them about some things the kids did at Christmastime. A couple weeks before Christmas vacation, all the schoolkids got up before the sun came up, gathered together to walk the circular road that made up the major part of the village, and sang Christmas carols for everyone. It had been going on for years. Usually the local preacher or the organist met them, and they entertained the village as they were waking up. Of course, there was a method to their madness: the cookies and milk were flowing. It seemed that on those few days before the holiday, there was never any appetite for lunch, as most had filled their pockets and jackets with sweets the local women had baked.

Kinnakeet seemed to be such a sociable village. The fact that they all lived in a cluster made it that way. Everybody knew what everybody else was doing, and nobody ever had to search for help to do anything. A group was usually close enough to lend a hand. With so much merchandise being off-loaded in the little harbor, something was always afoot on the water. It was situated kind of on a flat part of the island, so if you walked to the east, it was easy to see the ships going by on their way around Diamond Shoals.

Most drank yaupon tea, from the leaves of the yaupon holly, which were "sweated" in a hollow cypress log, put through a straining trough, and poured into casks for storage. This also became a cottage industry during both the Revolutionary War, with the rebellion against the East India Tea Company from England, and later, during World War II, when the Germans stopped the coffee trade from South America. The Kinnakeet villagers harvested salt from the ocean to salt down their fish, beef, and pork to preserve it for the winter, and had cold storage areas dug into the ground for temporary refrigeration. There were also ice houses on stilts about 1,000 yards into the sound, where ice was delivered from the mainland, usually from Elizabeth City, on the *H. P. Brown*, or from Washington North Carolina (known around these parts as "Little Washington"), on the *Carrie Bell*, both equipped for carrying ice across the Pamlico. The walls of the icehouse were thick and the cooler temperatures of the wind and water kept it solid until the boats from nearby villages hauled it ashore.

The women of the village had old-fashioned spinning wheels and would card and spin the wool into yarn and thread for knitting socks, sweaters, and gloves. Those who did not own sheep woke up early in the morning and went to the woods near the pastures to pick the wool from the twigs and branches of trees and take it back home for spinning. The industrious island fared well, off the mainland, with no thought nor need of a better existence.

There were two lifesaving stations located on either side of the village: Big Kinnakeet on the southern end and Little Kinnakeet on the northern end. The cluster of houses were directly across from the waterway of the ocean known as the Kinnakeet Anchorage Basin, and during bad weather, it was a cove of calm, or calmer, water, as the ships waited for the wind to die down, or the water to calm down, so that the vessels could continue south. This collection of ships, trying to weather storms in the bight, was what caused so much debris from wrecks to surface on the beach.

Charlie Williams, Grandpop's friend, was vendue master. As soon as there was a beached ship, Mr. Charlie would hurry to the site to keep people from scavenging the remains before someone could auction them off. Not much money changed hands, to the disdain of the ship owner. What had washed up was severely damaged and not nearly the value of the item when it was new, so even when the owner got half of some of the big items, like a huge captain's desk being sold for only $2.50 when its original cost was $1,000, they didn't make much money. For sure there wasn't much value left to a wrecked vessel. The owners complained about not getting much money from their investment, but they never thought of the unsightly debris left in the villages from a wrecked ship. Also, the owners were in no position to carry it off, so it was left to the locals to remove what could be removed, in order to maintain a safer village. Any obstruction on the beach, which the locals used often as a road, needed to be removed. Of course, while the vessel laid up on the banks, kids from everywhere were crawling all over it. Since most or all were barefoot, it presented a problem.

During one vendue, every house in the village walked away with a barrel of flour, selling for $1.25 a barrel. It was enough to last them an entire winter. Some carried away huge bags of coffee beans. There were twenty-one sacks, and they took the beans to the windmill to be ground for drinking. Bolts of linen looked all but ruined until the island women washed and brought them back to a usable form. Sailcloth was a premium, used for many things, and the huge sails of a ship tattered by a storm and almost in shreds were not any good to anyone—except a local who could stitch it well enough to power his small skiff down the back of the island to the next village. Reams of good English rag paper were restored by local women, so happy to have such a precious item. Pens were fashioned from goose quills, and the juice of the pokeberry bush was used for ink. This was the way of the island. Though seemingly ruined, most things were salvaged to make something useful. They used everything they were presented with to its fullest potential. Islanders were not scavengers. They were visionaries!

The existing stone found anywhere on the island—in someone's yard, cut and made into a useful tool, or as the foundation of a house—typically came from the ballast (heavy material, usually stone, stored below the deck in the bottom of the ship to provide desired draft and stability to the floating vessel) of a ship and had washed ashore. There was no stone originally on the island, but it came ashore in the belly of a distressed and floundering ship in a storm, and it was used. Even the Indians had stone, picked up on the beach no doubt from a ship trying to lighten its weight in an attempt to float off the shoals—by throwing over the huge stones that rested in the gut of the ship to lighten the load and allowing it to float sooner, racing against time to keep the vessel from permanently grounding. Even the stone used for grinding in the windmills came from the ship's ballasts, which were usually made from the volcanic rock regions of the West Indies and appropriately known as "ballast rock."

Kinnakeet was not on the Diamond Shoals, like Buxton was, but storms were as big a problem to Kinnakeet as to the other six villages. One storm was so bad—and the area where the village was located, being one of the lowest parts of the island, was so flat and treeless—that the community that had grown up around the Little Kinnakeet Lifesaving Station was forced to move to a higher and safer location. There had been a small harbor near the station, and it was filled in by a heavy and long-lasting nor'easter, so the people simply dismantled their houses, put the structure pieces on a barge or sometimes a raft, floated themselves south to the present-day village, and rebuilt their homes in the more desirable area. This happened before these boys were born, but the situation was not unfamiliar to the older generation. The gathering together of those two little communities into one was something the old men talked about around Gibb's store, in their remembering. The young people just listened, not really realizing what a feat that maneuver must have been.

They told of the time Gibb Gray saved the village. The locals in the village took their cash to Gibb Gray's store to be placed in his huge, brand-new steel safe, located in the back. There were no banks on the island, so they registered their cash with Mr. Gray and felt comfortable that it was cared for well. During one particularly strong storm, the sound began to wash over the island and, at its highest, was beginning to wash the Kinnakeet houses from their foundations. The wind was officially clocked at 140 miles an hour, it has now been discovered, but at the time the villagers just knew it was devastating. The holes they bored into their floors to allow the floodwaters to drain out could not keep the houses on their moorings. Gibb's store was located near the harbor, and even though a little higher than other houses, it began to show signs of being moved by the rushing water. Mr. Gray was beside himself, knowing he had the village's wealth in his store, and it looked like it might be washed away.

He fought his way from his house in the interior of the village to his store. He knew he had about $60,000 of community money in bags stored in the safe. He managed to get there, saw that he was correct in his calculating the store's fate, and waded to the back of the building to open the safe. By this time, the pressure of the water weighed heavily on the safe door, and it was with great effort that he was even able to open it. He looked around and found a heavy bag half full of coffee beans. He dumped the contents and began filling the burlap bag with the smaller bags of money belonging to his neighbors. He then lashed the bag to his back and started in the storm back to his house, thinking to take the bag to the attic and out of harm's way. The sound surge caught him and began carrying him and the bag of money away. He managed to latch on to a tree limb as he passed within only a couple of feet from the thick branch of a live oak tree. Normally, he had to look up to see the limbs of one of those trees, and now his body was passing just under the huge limb. As he caught it, he was lifted by the water, got his footing on the extension of the tree, and began to climb. He rode out the storm in the top of that tree, the money bag still lashed to his back. Of course, he was the local hero for that feat, and he remained the first choice for his neighbors to store money. They helped him get his store back on its foundation, and no one left until everything that could be salvaged and saved was—and Gibb was back in business.

During that storm, ninety-nine houses were moved anywhere from one foot to one mile from their moorings. It was an extreme accomplishment for the villagers to set things right again. But even with all that, not one household picked up and moved to the mainland.

Kinnakeet was also a village of shipbuilders, some of the best. Part of the problem, they discovered many years later, was their need of lumber for the larger vessels. Their efforts resulted in denuding the live oak forest, and since the free-roaming cattle, in their need to graze, found the young saplings in their regrowth a tender morsel, no new growth was allowed to mature. The village almost became a village of sand, and with nothing to stop the water, Kinnakeet has forever been one of the lowest parts of the island.

Kinnakeet had once been the island's capital. The richest man on the island lived there: Pharaoh Farrow, the man who introduced the windmill to Kinnakeet. B.C. Jennette had the one in Buxton. When flour was scarce, corn was ground for cornbread. Farrow was also the largest owner of timberland on the island, and he hired men from the mainland to harvest the wonderful live oak forest. He sold the timber to New England shipbuilders. Farrow was once made lighthouse keeper, at that time a political appointment. The kids at Kinnakeet were always saying that Farrow kept his gold in a chest and had buried that chest just before he died. Nobody knew where, but they said it was somewhere on one of his vast plantations of trees.

The docks were always crowded with merchandise delivered from the sound. After the 1846 storm cut an inlet between Hatteras and Ocracoke, the village was no longer the main route for commerce. Huge docks were then built on the sound at Hatteras village, with its new connection to the sea, to accommodate the traffic of vessels trading or lightering—putting merchandise on smaller ships that drew a lighter draft and would not run aground—for travel across the shoals of the Pamlico Sound. Progress always moved forward, and with the decline of the business at Kinnakeet, there was a surge of activity at Hatteras.

———

Finally the boys made their way from the windmill near the sound back to Gibb's store. The Buxton boys now carried so much of the flavor of Kinnakeet in their brains, they felt like they were part of the village.

"Where have you boys been?" scolded Grandpop, not really mad, but more worried. "Ellie and I have been waiting. Looks like a squall is brewing, and we need to get back home. We'll have to take the inside, because it is high tide now. So run, jump in the truck, and let's get going. Grandmom will have supper, and you know how she is about cold food." He shook hands all around and bid his friends good-bye.

The boys scrambled into the cab of the truck, saying good-bye to their new friends and promising them a good time under the mighty lighthouse. The boys from Kinnakeet had never been, and they seemed excited to have the opportunity. The boys were feeling mighty frisky and big in front of the Kinnakeeters, until Ellie came out to the truck and demanded they get out and let her in beside Grandpop. They gave a chagrined look of puzzlement to Lester and Georgie, who witnessed them being bossed around by a girl. So they jumped in the back again to ride in a much more manly fashion, yelling back and forth with gratitude to their hosts as they began their ramble on the sandy tracks home. When they were out of sight of the other boys, Luke banged on the truck to stop, and he and Blake climbed in. They had loads to tell both Grandpop and Ellie about their day, so many stories that they were busting to get out.

Grandpop and Ellie laughed the most at Mealy Mouth, and Ellie characteristically put her hand over her mouth as she even got scared at the telling. They told the story of the money at Gibb's store and about old lady Hooper shooting a scatter gun at Georgie. Ellie could just picture all that fuzz in the schoolroom, and when they told her that instead of presenting a play every year at school, the Kinnakeet kids had to give a speech, she was glad she did not live in that village.

Grandpop entertained the boys with stories of some of the more unusual shipwrecks. There was one where the cargo was those big, tall stovepipe hats, like President Lincoln wore. Everyone on the island had one, until they proved not so good in a stiff wind. Another vessel washed ashore with a shipment of ladies' hats, and Sunday church took on a new look. The most unusual was the time a freighter, the *Cibao*, carrying 16,000 bunches of bananas destined for up north, got caught on the bar and sent a small dory to the island to beg people to help them disperse the cargo to lighten the load. Everybody who had a boat went out to the shoal and took as many bunches of bananas as their skiff would hold and carried them back to the island. The ship was shoaled up aground between Ocracoke and Hatteras Islands, so both were in on the banana haul. People gave them to neighbors, eating bananas until they were sick of them. They tried storing the bananas in the ground to preserve them and eventually had to throw away the rotting fruit, but not until the entirety of the two islands had cooked bananas into every dish imaginable. The old people still didn't care much for the taste of bananas, but the *Cibao* was successful in becoming light enough to float off with the incoming tide.

The ship *Prince of India*, loaded with a cargo of beautiful Arabian horses, wrecked just below Ocracoke, and the horses swam ashore to the beaches of Hatteras Island in the late 1700s. Maybe that was when the Burrus family got into the horse business, as they had been around that long. Even the Burrus family started from a man who stayed after being shipwrecked on the island. Grandpop said a minister was so distraught over the lack of meat on the island that he prayed for a ship to throw over a barrel of pork. Not too long after, there was a wreck, the *Mary Varney*. She broke up offshore, and pieces of the wreck began to wash in on the tide. Lo and behold, big ol' pork barrels started coming ashore, but instead of the pork the preacher had prayed for, the barrels were stuffed with bodies trying to escape the wreck. Some were already drowned, and some not. They say that the first Oden to arrive came to shore in one of those barrels. He married a native, and that family has been a pillar of the Hatteras community ever since.

Riding home from Kinnakeet, the wind began to pick up, and that squall that Grandpop had sensed began looming dark in the sky. As they rushed to get home, they passed the Big Kinnakeet Lifesaving Station, and Grandpop promised the boys he would take them there on the first nice day. This was where Pop grew up, and the boys were anxious to see inside. They had been in the one near the lighthouse, and it was full of pictures of men they knew from church. The boys wanted to see who operated out of this one. They were curious to see if Great-Grandpop's picture was there.

Grandpop told them there used to be a tall broken ridge running down the middle of the island, from Hatteras to almost Kinnakeet, but the wind and weather had worn it down. The Indians used to hunker down in the lee of the ridge to avoid the storms that have hit this island since time eternal. He told of the grapevines covering the top of the ridge on the trees, so thick the children would swing on them. They reached almost to the ocean, and during the season where they ripened, the ocean ran purple with their juice. He said the vegetation was so dense around Kinnakeet that one could travel on the Indian trails to within fifty feet of the ocean and never see the sea.

"What's the Smithsonian?" asked Blake.

"Oh yeah, Grandpop. Lester said that a model of the Kinnakeet windmill is in the Smithsonian. He said it was a big place in Washington." Luke also wanted a better explanation than Lester and Georgie had provided.

"Why, that's true, son. The Smithsonian is the largest museum in the world, with almost twenty buildings that keep pieces of American history for people to see. And there is a model of one of our windmills. Everything that the country doesn't want to forget, they place in one of those buildings. After all this war stuff has passed us by, we might take a trip there for you to see. I want my grandchildren to know what there is to know about the world, and that's as good a place to start as any." Capt'n Charlie was dead serious when he said that. He had never thought of it before, but it was a wonderful idea. He wanted to take Grandmom and Nett also, and he was praying that Finnegan came home safe from the war, so he could go, too. "Finnegan would be interested because General Billy Mitchell's plane is there, and if your dad ever had a hero, Billy Mitchell was the one." Everyone called the navy men by their last name. Even Nett called her husband "Finnegan," because that was how he was introduced to her. The navy men who settled on the island and married local girls were always referred to by their last names.

"They have a plane in a building?" Blake was shocked.

"Sure do, son. Lots more, too. We'll just have to pay those boys a visit!" Capt'n Charlie laughed at the stir he caused. Traveling around with these young-uns kept him young. He almost was willing to eat a cold supper, but he also didn't want to keep Odessa from hearing their stories. He knew that there would be more chatter than eating tonight. Oh, well, more for him to eat. He smiled at the thought of them all talking at the same time about this day.

My goodness! he thought. *Who would have thought a visit to Kinnakeet would provide such entertainment?*

He almost laughed out loud thinking of what a reaction he would see if the kids were ever to go to the Smithsonian. What a wonder life was through the eyes of a child.

Spirit

Supper that night was full of stories. All the boys were wound up, including Grandpop. Grandmom laughed so hard at the story of Mealy Mouth that she actually sat down at the table, something she seldom did. Usually Grandmom walked between the table and the stove, waiting on everyone and making sure her culinary creations were enjoyed. Ellie laughed again, even though she had heard the stories on the way home. What she found so funny was the change in the stories—more dramatic, scarier, more dangerous. Usually all the embellishments came from Blake, who loved to entertain. In his efforts to make sure everyone laughed, he usually exaggerated—a lot!

When Luke mentioned that Lester, Georgie, Harold, and Little Charlie had taken them around to look at horses, he was proud to tell Grandpop that their own horses were much prettier than the ones seen in the northern village. As he was elaborating on the style of horse, Blake interrupted him.

"Pop, when do I get my horse?" As usual, as soon as Blake said that, he wished he could take it back. He realized that he only knew about the horse because he, Luke, and Ellie had overheard Grandpop and Nett as they sat in the rocking chairs on the front porch talking, not remembering the porch was located below Ellie's bedroom window. The two adults were discussing getting another horse. Since the government horses were to be returned, they felt Blake needed his own mount. That night, Ellie was staring out the window and overheard Nett and Grandpop talking on the porch below her window. Quickly, she hopped out of bed and alerted the boys that Pop and Aunt Nett were getting something for Blake.

Both boys hurried to Ellie's bed, and with three little heads pressed against the screened window, they listened as Grandpop told Nett that when the family moved to the mansion in Trent Woods, the Coast Guard would be keeping Ol' Tony and Big Roy. He was explaining that they were the type of horse, oversized and with wide hoofs, needed to pull the heavily loaded surfboat through soft sand to the beach in anticipation of a launch to save the lives of those about to perish as a ship was floundering off shore in distress. With war on the way, and the government in suspect that it would again affect the island, those horses began to be more and more valuable. Straining to hear, the children also overheard Nett talking about another horse, like it was something she had already seen. They looked at each other gap-mouthed and wide-eyed, as their minds raced to a conclusion. Another horse? But, in all of this, they were eavesdropping, listening to a conversation they were never meant to hear, and now Blake had blabbed it all out.

The looks snapped between Grandpop and Nett. Grandmom stood ready to defend the children and was waiting until the top blew off the kettle before she jumped in and rescued her precious grandchildren.

"What are you talking about, son?" Grandpop cast a quizzical eye at Blake, whose guilt was in full display across his face as he sat in his chair with his head lowered, resting on his chest. He began to tear up.

Luke spoke. "Grandpop, Blake and I were in Ellie's room the other night, looking at the stars, and we could hear you and Mom talking on the porch. We heard you talking about Blake's horse, and we thought maybe you wanted to surprise us, so we kept quiet about it, until now, when ol' Big Mouth spilled the beans. We're sorry. We didn't mean do any harm. It was just too exciting to keep to ourselves, and we have been ready and waiting for you to tell us ever since. Don't be mad at Blake, Pop. It was all my fault."

"No, Pop, it was mine!" Ellie slid her chair back and walked over to stand by her beloved grandfather. Tears in her eyes, she leaned down and gave the captain a hug. "I was the one who heard the word 'horse,' and I was the one who told the boys to look at the stars, because I knew they could hear, and I wanted Blake to know he was getting a horse."

"Well, you three better hold up and stop trying to get your story straight, because you are digging a hole you can't crawl out of. I know now that the porch is the wrong place to talk, since you three little pitchers have big ears. Blake, you are getting a horse—" But before he could finish his sentence, Blake rolled out of his chair onto the floor and lay there like he was dead.

The whole crowd erupted in belly laughs. Nett was choking, Grandmom was sitting, Luke was snorting his food, and Ellie was down on the floor trying to lift up Blake.

When things calmed down, Blake jumped up and grabbed Grandpop around the neck and almost made him choke on his cornbread.

"What about me?" asked his mother. "Don't I get any credit for this? I'm in on it, too."

Blake rushed around the table, almost knocking Grandmom off her perch on the edge of the chair, and shimmied between the sideboard and chairs to get to his mother. She braced for a big hug.

Finally everyone settled back into their regular places and quickly did as Grandmom suggested.

"All right, now, we can continue this conversation once you young-uns finish your supper. You are letting everything get cold, and there is lemon meringue pie for dessert, so get to eating before any more talk!" Grandmom didn't say much, but when she did, the room got quiet and everyone did as they were told.

Blake began shoveling in food like he was never going to get another bite, and Grandpop gave him a scowl and a cocked head, a sign of disapproval. Blake settled down.

When supper was over, Grandmom delivered pie all around. This was a signal that conversation could start again. Nett began.

"Blake, son, yes, you are going to get a horse. Pop and I have been down to Mr. Burrus's corral and picked out one you might like. You know, from all the packing we've been doing, we are soon going to be living in the Trent Woods. It is quite a way from the village, school, and the lighthouse. We thought that the government was going to let us keep Ol' Tony and Big Roy, but that's not the case. Seems they think they'll need them to be close to the Coast Guard station for use in an emergency. It makes me sad, because I have been around them, seems like all my life, and I wanted to take care of them, too. But even though we don't like to talk about it, this country is at war, and they are expecting it to reach this beach, so we cannot stay here. I don't like that you three listened in on a conversation that you knew you were not supposed to hear, but I'll have to think of how to deal with that. Don't think you will get off scot-free! There *will* be a consequence to your actions. You need to keep yourselves from doing things you know you shouldn't do, no matter how tempting it might be. And, Miss Ellie, just how often *do* you listen from your window? And what else have you heard? We need to know." Nett was scowling.

"Honest, Aunt Nett, it was just that one time. When I heard the word 'horse,' I just couldn't keep it to myself, but I promise I won't do it again." Tears involuntarily rolled down Ellie's cheeks. She could take her grandparents' scolding, as the three of them were tight as ticks. But for her Aunt Nett to be angry at her was unusual. Ellie so admired her.

Ellie's confession called for another hug, and this time it was Nett shimmying around the chairs to get to Ellie. She and her father had often discussed how lucky they were that the children were just exactly like they were. Once in a while, and only once in a while, did they ever do anything that either of them disapproved of, but they did have to have rules, and those rules needed to be obeyed, so they did not let them get away with much. That these three were exceptional was a fact. Nett couldn't put her finger on it, but they were different from other kids their age. Nett had taught and been around enough island children to know that there was a spirit around these three that did not exist with the other children. She thought it was just because they belonged to her, and maybe all parents thought that. But whatever it was, they needed to be guided, and no matter how much it hurt those in control to punish them, they needed to be taught certain things.

All this drama was getting to Pop, plus Grandmom had stopped him from getting his second piece of pie. She did not let him eat too many sweets, as she was worried about his heart.

"Okay, back to the subject of the horse," he said.

Blake was bouncing up and down in his chair and clutching Luke's arm. Grandpop went on.

"Your mother and I have been down to Mr. Burrus's corral, and we have paid for another colt, this one for Blake. Now that the cat is out of the bag, we might take a trip down there tomorrow afternoon, after you three make a place in the barn for the new guy. We'll let the Coast Guard boys know they can come take the older horses. Then we will bring the new one home. But you kids need to prepare a place for him, and decide which stall he'll take. Remember, it won't be for long, because the boys at the station are helping us move, and they'll need the big horses to pull the wagon to the woods. Uncle Baxter has also volunteered his side-railed truck to help. So, we can look at the new boy, but maybe not bring him home until things get more settled. We'll try to take you as many times as possible, and maybe, Blake, we can let you spend some afternoons with him, like we did with Luke when we got Gus. So don't push too hard. After all, we wouldn't have a problem if you hadn't been listening when you weren't supposed to, so you are just going to have to keep your pants on and let me do what I need to do in my own time. Understand?"

"Understand!" they all echoed, and Blake threw his hand to his forehead and looked like he would faint again.

Grandpop continued, "Miss Ellie, about you and your window—from now on I'll go over to the assistant keeper's porch to talk privately. I don't want you to suffocate in a room with the windows closed. But you three are too curious for your own good. Don't think I don't know about your little escapades, so don't get too smart for your breeches. We grown-ups might be slow, but we win the race." At that he gave a hearty laugh and a wink to the kids as he stole a bite of pie from Grandmom's plate when she went around to the kitchen.

It was the perfect crime, and the children got a kick out of it, as the mood was definitely back to normal.

There wasn't much sleep that night, and once again the boys crept over to Ellie's room and crawled into bed with her. They stretched out on their bellies and stared out the window at the mighty lighthouse. They talked horse, about how much they would miss the two bigger horses, and how much attention they would now pay to them, and how they would visit them after they moved. Their plan was to ride their horses back to the Coast Guard station and sort of hang out with Ol' Tony and Big Roy. They talked about tomorrow, about the wolves, as they could see them now, asleep curled up in the middle of a huge clump of pampas grass near the lighthouse. They talked about their dolphin, and now their horses.

"What are you going to name him, Blake?" Ellie needed a picture.

"I've been thinking about that," said Blake. "I think I'll name him Charlie, after Grandpop."

Both Luke and Ellie cocked their heads toward each other and rolled their eyes. This was a Blake-ism.

Finally the three simply passed out from all that had happened that day. The roar of the ocean was in their heads, the wind had picked up, and Grandpop's squall was coming in fast. Sometime during the night, the rain started pelting the window sill, and as the children awakened to pull it shut, the boys went back to their rooms, leaving Ellie to fall back asleep to the patter of raindrops.

By the morning, the squall had passed, and by the reflection of the lighthouse in the pool that had formed on the level ground in front of it, it must have been quite a heavy rain. It almost looked like two lighthouses because the rain had made a reflecting pool on the ground, creating a mirror for the mighty tower. They had stayed awake so long, they were late getting up for breakfast. Neither Grandmom or Nett had awakened them. It was summer, and letting them sleep sort of gave everyone else time to get some work done. The three kids were definitely a handful.

When the children came downstairs, Grandmom had their breakfast on the table. She was good at that. Hearing them shuffling around upstairs, she smiled and did what she did best: had a hot meal waiting. On this morning, Nett was packing and stacking some of Grandpop's saved boxes, so Grandmom sat down at the table with the kids.

"So, what do you think?" she asked. "You know you are going to get some kind of correction to make up for eavesdropping." She really wanted to soften the blow, which she already knew was not going to be too harsh, but she also needed to drive the lesson home.

"Grandmom, I don't care what they do to punish me. I can take it. All I have to do is think of my new horse," Blake bravely declared.

"Why, son, you act like you are going to get whipped or something. You know your grandpop better than that. He's liable to take something away from you, or not let you leave the yard, but you know it won't be much." Grandmom couldn't bear for them to be unhappy.

Luke also was contrite. "I want him to do something. I want to be punished. I know when I'm wrong."

"Me, too," chimed in Ellie. "We are ready!"

With that declaration, Grandmom just smiled and cleared the table.

Off they went to the barn, to first brush and feed the older horses, then take care of their own. Ellie, of course, had to finger her cloak, still stretched on the wall. As she felt that it had recovered from the moisture, she carefully folded it up and put it in her special crate, along with the items she treasured from Weroansqua.

The Coast Guard boys were around all the time now, as well as the new sailors who were housed in the assistant keeper's quarters until the navy could make better arrangements. The compound was never as empty and personal as it had been. There was a lot of activity. It felt a little like everyone was anxious to move the keeper and his family inland before something happened and they would get caught up in it.

By the time the barn was as organized as the kids could make it, they went on a hunt for Grandpop. The last place they checked was the house. Having learned at an early age to tell time by the sun, they knew it was dinnertime, and with a laugh they realized that was exactly where Grandpop would be. With that in mind, they raced to the house, trying to see who could get there first. Blake won, but was so tired from the effort he sat on the steps of the porch, heaving big breaths to calm his racing heart. Luke leaped over Blake on the porch and made it to the front door first, declaring himself the winner. Blake was still gasping for breath and could not protest, although anyone could see from the downcast look he gave his brother that he was disappointed with Luke and his strut as he slammed the screen door behind him.

Ellie had given it her all, but she didn't have Luke's speed or Blake's single-ness of purpose. Blake's mind was on the trip to see the horse, and he had expended everything he had to be the first to ask Grandpop. As Blake and Ellie caught their breath on the steps, Luke realized his win had been hollow, as he really didn't like being left to celebrate the victory by himself. He turned around on his heel, came to the screen door, held it open, and waited.

"C'mon, y'all, Grandpop's going to finish before you get to talk to him."
He continued to hold the door open.

Blake slowly got up, head hung, shoulders slumped, looking for all the
world like a man defeated, but as he passed Luke in the doorway, he took
off in a sprint through the house to stand beside Grandpop at the table,
giving the others the widest grin he could muster. First!

Still all out of breath, the three intended to hold poor Capt'n Charlie
to his promise to take them to see the horses at Mr. Burrus's corral.
Grandmom, once again, stepped in to save the day. They were informed
that they had to stop pestering Grandpop and sit down to dinner, which
was their favorite: fried cornbread and navy bean soup. There was not
much digesting going on at the table, as they were slopping down their
soup before they even chewed the beans. Grandpop, meanwhile, was
taking his time—carefully buttering his cornbread, folding the pancake
in half like bread, dipping the edge in the bean soup, and trying to have
himself a leisurely meal. Two days in a row with that crew in the truck
might be more than he could handle. Working around the compound
didn't look so bad, knowing the momicking he was getting ready to go
through over his little secret, which had turned out not to be so secret.
No sense planning anything around here. Too much room for drama!

The problem was, if they didn't discover a surprise by their own
snoopy little methods, than by golly, it came to those young-uns by way
of some vision or dream. Grandmom had prepared him for all of this,
and he was fascinated, but he should have never thought that he could
keep a secret from that crew. Not one as big as this.

Dinner finished, the three antsy kids rushed out the door to the old
jalopy and jumped in, ready and waiting for Grandpop, who was again
taking his time. He rounded up Nett and they climbed in the government car, pulling up beside the truck, just sitting there grinning as the
kids realized they were in the wrong vehicle. Faster than fast, they all
rushed to get in the backseat, and off they went to Hatteras.

The rainstorm the night before had caused the inside road to be firm, with very few places to worry about. There were more puddles than soft sand, and the kids had a great time leaning this way or that, acting like they were going to tip over. Grandpop and Nett ignored them as best they could and just smiled.

As they rode through Hatteras village and came to the fork in the road before the sound, they took a right and headed to the corral. With the end of the road in sight, the three were leaning over the front seat, breathing on Nett and Grandpop and straining to see the first sight of the fence where the horses were kept. Grandpop would not let them get out of the car until he found out whether Mr. Burrus was home. He was, and he seemed quite pleased to see the kids again.

At the horse pen, the kids stood on one of the rails of the fence, leaning over to see all the herd as they were roaming around and trying to pick out the horse that Grandpop and Nett had chosen. Willis Burrus invited them to come in the gate and walk around the pasture. This was a vast stretch, sort of a wide rectangle of grass and low foliage, fenced in with a rustic wooden split-rail fence. The east side was next to the shallow sand edge of the Pamlico Sound. The sandbank must have gone 500 feet out before the ground sloped down and the water got deeper. It was a great place for the horses to wallow around in the wash and ward off flies and mosquitoes. It also was fenced to keep the horses from swimming away.

The corral was so long, there were pens separate from the main, plus a huge barn down at the end. It was bordered on two sides by water, allowing the horses to enjoy a breeze on a sweltering day. They tossed back their heads, took in the salt air, and snorted it out with gusto, all while shaking their beautiful manes. There were all kinds of wonderful horses in front of them. They ranged from young to old, some just born and still hanging close to their mothers. They just stood there, each in its own thought, some nuzzling each other and others solitary. There must have been thirty horses. Many clustered under the grand live oaks that covered the south and west ends of the ranch, providing shade. These horses were well cared for.

Even Grandpop was fascinated as he, Nett, and Mr. Burrus walked through the sand and grass admiring the steeds. Finally, Nett pointed out the horse they had chosen, and Mr. Burrus culled it out of the herd and walked the animal over to the group—that is, the group minus one. Blake was slowly roaming around, eyeing all the animals. When called, he came back to where Mr. Burrus was with the beautiful horse. It truly was handsome, rich brown with black mane and tail. The mane was shorter in length than either Gus's or Blue's, but he also had a brown face with black markings. His chest had a large white spread, and he seemed very gentle.

Blake stood with his back to the other horses and was rubbing the new horse's nose as the deal was being made near the section of the corral closest to the house. Curiously he left the horse and walked across the pasture next to the gate, to where his mother and grandfather were discussing the terms of the deal. Blake, still with his back to the rest of the herd, stared at his new horse from a distance, getting the full view and imagining himself with a ride of his own.

While the group was standing in a circle, Blake felt something push him hard on his back, almost sending him to the ground. Had it not been for bumping into his mother, he would have fallen. He turned around sharply and stared face-to-face at the nose of a horse he had not seen before. The horse had come out of the herd, sauntered over to Blake, and nudged him with his nose to get his attention. Everybody abruptly turned to the horse and Blake. This handsome animal was what they called a bay, all dark red, sort of burnt orange or dark red, with long black mane and tail, and black hair also from his knees to his hoof. On closer scrutiny, this bay's mane was a deep red, but only when the sun hit it. His long mane appeared to be black against that red coat. He and Blake just stood looking at each other.

"Pop! He loves me!" Blake said almost in an embarrassed whisper, as he tugged on his grandfather's sleeve. "Can I have this one?"

Capt'n Charlie turned to look closer at the horse who would not leave Blake's side. "Well now, son, we bought this other horse, and possibly this horse is not for sale, or not ready, or belongs to someone else. You just can't have any horse you see. Mr. Burrus runs a business, and your mom and I have already paid for the first horse." Capt'n Charlie was embarrassed as he looked back at his friend Willis, trying to make up for the outburst.

"As a matter of fact, Charlie, this horse is new, just now moved to this pasture. He was a colt when you and your daughter were here, so he was separated from the others along with his mother, so's he could be kept away from the older horses. But, tell you the truth, his momma has been sold. 'Course we haven't delivered her because we were trying to acclimate this young one to the herd before she left. Your boy wants this young horse, he can have him. Same deal." Mr. Burrus was smiling down at the cute look on the face of the mischievous youngster.

Blake never took his eyes off the new horse, and the horse nudged him again with his nose, this time sending him up against his grandfather. The whole circle of adults and children were beginning to marvel at what they were seeing. Luke and Ellie left their petting of the younger horses to come over and see what all the fuss was about. This was the sweetest bonding moment any of them had ever seen. They came to pick out a horse, and the horse had picked them.

"You sure?" Grandpop said. "Now, I don't want to take advantage of our friendship. If this horse is going to somebody else, you let me know. This young-un would be satisfied with a mule at this point, so don't think you have to give in to him. He's going to be just fine. The horse we already picked out is a beauty, and I know," he said as he ruffled Blake's hair, "this one would love him." The horse trading had begun, and Blake was winning.

"Lordy Be! Don't think I'd ever forgive myself if these two didn't get together. Just look at them. That horse walked away from his mother all the way across the field to touch this kid, and by Jiminy, he's gonna have him if I have to pay for him myself." Mr. Burrus reached down and held out his hand for Blake to shake.

Blake responded by extending his own. They gave one strong shake, and Mr. Burrus said, "Done!"

Blake reached up and rubbed the horse's nose and exclaimed, "Look! He has a white spot all down his nose. It's the only white spot on him!" Sure enough, right between his eyes, the young colt had a white streak, starting right under his forelock and going partway down his nose. It was curved like an Arab scarf, wide in the middle and tapered on both ends. Blake stood on his tiptoes and reached out his hand to touch the white of the horse's nose. He couldn't quite get to the top, and the others were shocked to see the horse lower his head to accommodate the hand of this little boy.

"We call that a blaze," said Mr. Burrus.

Blake looked squarely into Mr. Burrus's eyes, held out his hand for a shake, and as Mr. Burrus grasped on to his hand, Blake said, "Mr. Burrus, I think that is his spirit, and to me, he is my spirit, so that's what I am going to name him: Spirit. Look at him. When the sun hits squarely on his eyes, they look blue." Blake gently turned the horse's head. Sure enough, the light on those amber eyes looked blue, just for a flash. Again the company of onlookers seemed shocked. This was a drama playing out like none any of them had ever seen. Luke's horse was just drop-dead gorgeous, and Ellie had had her mind set on a black horse like the ones in the book. Blake, he just dreamed of a horse of his own. To the other two children, in their developing paranormal minds, this was how things should go. Blake had waited patiently for his turn at a special friend, and somehow, Brendan, his spirit guide, had presented him with the perfect companion. With his adventurous personality, Blake was going to need heavenly protection to keep him safe, and now he had Spirit.

Mr. Burrus winked and pulled the smart, engaging young fellow in for a hug.

Blake had a horse, and his name was Spirit, and he was a different color from Luke's or Ellie's, and for some reason, Blake and Spirit had bonded.

All during the negotiations, Blake and his new horse stood together. Everywhere Blake went, Spirit followed. He had actually left his mother already. Nett kept shaking her head at the spectacle taking place in front of her. She had never shown any interest in horses. She saw no need to go exploring, or riding from one place to another. She and her sister, Iva, usually played house. They gathered boxes from the grocery store Pop had during her childhood to make their "house." Nett had five brothers, and she and Iva were not invited into their world. This connection between Ellie and the boys was something she envied. Usually friends came to see Nett, not the other way around. Even one of her boyfriends came to see her from Hatteras, down the back side on the sound, and parked his boat behind her house for a visit. She grew up with lots of friends. These kids were growing up with lots of animals.

Sometimes animals proved to be the best friends.

⋆ *1* ⋆

Ship Ashore!

On she came with a cloud of canvas,
Right against the wind that blew,
Until the eye could distinguish
The faces of the crew

Then fell her straining topmasts,
Hanging tangled in the shrouds,
And her sails were loosened and lifted,
And blown away like clouds.

—Henry Wadsworth Longfellow,
"The Phantom Ship"

Grandpop's was the happiest car on the road. Blake could hardly contain himself. Ellie was also excited, knowing Blue now belonged only to her. She couldn't wait to get home to tell him. Luke was daydreaming of the adventures ahead. The three at this time were of one mind. The saints had sprinkled an extra flurry of silver flakes on the car, making Grandpop feel that he had just missed the rain. Brendan, Blake's saintly overseer, had been hovering over Mr. Burrus's corral for a while. He knew the horse that Grandpop and Nett had chosen. It was a beauty, but Brendan had other plans. He had watched the red horse being born. He knew that the mare was of fine Irish stock, and that the little colt would be perfect for Blake.

The mare had come to Mr. Burrus in a very unusual way. A fine steamer had delivered the mare to Hatteras Island on a barge. The pilot from Hatteras was one who was trained as a captain who lightens the load of a vessel that cannot get through the shoals of the Pamlico Sound. He operated a lightering business and boarded any vessel that could draw a small enough draft for the experienced pilot to avoid grounding the barge. On this trip, cargo from the large ship was met just offshore. It carried stock horses for inland, but it rode too low in the water to navigate the unpredictable bottom of the Pamlico. These were horses from all over Europe—stately Spanish horses to be bred in the United States, horses from Ireland, even a few from across the Mediterranean, which were bred for speed. Mr. Burrus was contacted by the owner of the cargo that one of the mares was ready to foal, and he feared it would not make the treacherous journey through the sound and then the long stock drive to its destination. Mr. Burrus agreed to take the horse and care for the foal. As payment for his service, the owner would return to pick up the mare, and Mr. Burrus could have the foal. That way both parties were satisfied that payment was made.

Brendan was on watch over the chosen horse. When the mare was delivered to the corral, from that moment on he carefully hovered over both mother and foal. The saint had been in control of this situation since the colt was born. He knew this was the steed for his earthly charge. As the foal grew out of his spindly legs, he exhibited a vibrant red color, which pleased the saint's Irish heart. Saint Brendan had ridden the horse at night and found him to have a fearless heart. It was a fine horse Blake was to have, a fine horse.

Nett talked her dad into taking a detour to Trent Woods to visit the old house. She had been visiting frequently since she found out it was to be her new home. As soon as they pulled up to the yard, the kids jumped out and went straight to the barn. Grandpop found the key, and the large double doors were swung wide open to let in a little fresh air. The day was crisp, dark clouds still hung overhead, and a strong southerly breeze immediately whipped through the house. Nett hurried through the dining room down the kitchen stairs and flung open the door to the yard. The kids had already gained the barn. She went to the opposite end of the kitchen and opened that door also. This made a good draft through the musty old house. Everything was going to need to be taken outside and beaten. She might do that this week, she thought. The children could clean all the outer buildings. She needed to get started.

Nett went to the foyer and opened the French doors leading to the main sitting room, which took up most of the entire right side of the first floor. Behind the bookcase at the back of the spacious room were long narrow rooms, separated only by archways, that extended the entire length of the main floor. The bookcase doubled as a hidden door to access this area. Luke had found the rooms accidentally when they were trying to find ways to travel between the walls. He had played with the books until he found one that served as a latch, and the heavy door opened to a small pine-paneled set of rooms, long and narrow, with a vaulted ceiling. He took pride in showing it to Grandpop, who in turn revealed it to Nett.

This was to be exclusively for Grandpop and Grandmom's private area. The series of rooms extended across the back of the house, only narrowing to a hall as it ran under the stairs. At the archway just past the stairs, the area widened again, and there was a rather large section behind the formal dining room on the opposite end of the house. Here there was a door, not hidden, but obviously one that had been crafted for some fancy house in the Caribbean, which allowed entrance to both the dining room to the left and the four stair steps that led down to the kitchen on the right. Grandmom chose this space as her sewing room, and it allowed her to move freely and without detection to either the dining room or the kitchen, or, should she fancy, she could go the back way through Charlie's study and be in the sitting room.

Capt'n Charlie had chosen the suite of rooms just behind the formal sitting room for his study. He could move from the sitting room to his private papers, or have meetings there, should he so desire. Even though he was no longer the keeper, as the Coast Guard had taken over the compound for use of the lighthouse as security, the time was fast approaching when he would no longer be needed, so he had accepted the job of principal for the school in Buxton village. He was also elected as the county commissioner and was still working to bring electricity and paved roads to the island. From that suite, he could also, without detection, access the kitchen, which to him was a plus.

After opening the doors to her parents' quarters, Nett went down the hallway to the opposite end to check out her living quarters and the rooms for the kids. On the second floor, there were two huge apartments, with sleeping rooms attached, which anchored either end of the hallway. When ascending the stairs, either to the left at the middle landing, or the right, the stairs separated and led to the rooms and foyer upstairs. Between both apartments were three more large bedrooms, just right for the kids, although Luke wanted to live on the third and fourth floors, in Uncle Jabez's office and sleeping room.

In the barn, the children were staking out their respective stalls, as they were organizing for three, rather than four or five horses. They separated Twinkle's stall, cleaned it first, and each began rearranging their respective spaces.

Nett called to them to come inside and go over their bedroom situation with her. Grandpop was busy in his new imagined office. They left Grandmom's kitchen alone. Reluctantly the kids came in from the barn, only to get excited all over again looking at their potential rooms. Ellie took the one on the end, near her grandparents' apartment. Luke got the room on the other end—that is, until he could convince them that he was old enough for the top floor. He put forth the argument that he needed to be near Uncle Jabez's personal library. Of course, he also was keen on how close he would be to the attic, with all the trunks and journals. It was loaded with information about the past, and he intended to study the whole of it, and maybe start a journal of his own. He imagined sometime in the future, some other kid would be fascinated by his memories and thoughts. He was too young to realize that the little kid in his imagination could easily turn out to be his own child. His room was larger than the other two. He was satisfied.

Blake got the room in the middle. Looking out his bedroom window, he noticed the widow's walk that went across the second floor for decoration, and he saw it as his own special porch. There was also a way to shimmy down the lower porch posts to get to the yard without going through the house. His mind was clicking away. He couldn't wait to tell the others. They had already figured it out and were planning their escape!

Summer hours being deceiving as to time, and rain coming in under darkening skies, caused the group to close up the house and try to get to the car before they got soaked. Another squall was upon them. It had been playing with them for a couple of days. Grandpop was seldom wrong when anticipating a storm, and the slow buildup of this one surely meant it would deliver a mighty blow. All the warning signs were there. For several days Grandpop expected the storm. He and Burrus had discussed it, and preparations were being made to take care of the horses.

At home, Grandmom had a hot dinner ready for the mountain of news that came her way. Stewed chicken and, Ellie's favorite, dumplings. More lemon meringue pie and Pop's radio tuned in to the news made everyone drowsy. Blake went to sleep in Nett's lap while she was reading and had to be carried up the stairs. He was worn out physically and emotionally, he was OUT!

The wind and rain put the rest to sleep. The storm raged, and the waves tuned up their volume in their steady crashing sound on the shore. Sometimes the rain was strong, then it would lighten up. There was definitely an orchestra playing out there. The room where the boys were had to be closed up, as their window faced the sea. Luke was awakened by the loudest clap of thunder followed by a lightning strike that lit up his closed eyes. He opened them, but all was dark. He could hear the rumbling of incoming thunder on the way for another blast. As the rain pounded on the screen, Luke—the head of his bed against one window, Blake's against the other—raised up to see if he could catch the activity of the waves as the light from the lighthouse flashed every seven and one-half seconds, lighting up the beach for a second. He was met with another more robust crack, this one more violent than the other. This tremendous round of thunder lasted for several strikes, and the lightning that followed was more magnificent than anything Luke had ever seen. The line of heavy silver led from the sky to the ocean, and it ran along the top of the ocean until it reached the shore. At that point it lit up the breakers, making what looked like a wall of fire down the beach. For sure, no ship could see the lighthouse tonight. The sheets of rain even blocked out the surf, leaving only the sound of the breakers as they pounded the beach, which appeared to be only yards away. He strained to see how large the breakers were getting, the white water was already on the shore.

COSTON LIGHT! SHIP ASHORE! flashed like a dream in Luke's head. A Coston light is a flare of sorts that, when lit, allows a stricken vessel to know that someone has seen it, and gives the distressed victims knowledge that help is on the way.

Yes, there was a light! He could almost make out a figure standing high atop a tall dune north of both he and the lighthouse. He quickly bounded out of bed and began rummaging around for his clothes and his boots. His slicker overalls and jacket were on the back porch. He grabbed Blake's arm and shook him quickly but gently. Blake moaned and rolled over. He was exhausted after all the excitement of the day. A horse and an escape corridor? What more could a kid ask for?

Luke took boots in hand and raced down the stairs, lightly, but two or more at a time, balancing his gymnastics with the railing, as he sailed down the stairs to Pop's room. Time was everything, and he knew it would take too much to awaken Blake and get him dressed. He worried men might die while he dithered around doing kid things.

He stuck his head in. "Pop!" and softly again, "Pop!"

"What is it, son?" his grandfather turned his head to look at the door. He rolled over. "What is it, son?" he asked again.

"Ship ashore, Pop! I saw the Coston light from my window, just north of here. Should we call the Coast Guard?" Luke was careful to relay the message and its urgency without waking Grandmom.

Grandpop was out of the bed, putting on his pants and looking for a shirt.

"Pop, can I go? I won't be in the way. I only want to watch, and I'm the one who saw it. Oh, please, Pop. Please let me go with you. I can handle Ol' Tony, I can—"

"Yes, yes, yes, now quiet, and go get your foul-weather gear on, and bring me mine. Don't forget the hats, the most important. I got to find my boots. Hurry up, son. I'm calling the Coast Guard." When his grand-father came in to the kitchen where the big black wall phone was, Luke handed his grandfather his set of yellow slicker foul-weather outerwear. He had overalls, like Luke, and a jacket, with that, Capt'n Charlie hopped around, one boot half on, and carrying the other. He had pulled up his overalls, but they were not yet buttoned up. He began to wind up the ring on the old telephone, two long, for the Coast Guard, Buxton.

"Boys, this is Charlie Gray, over at the lighthouse," he announced. "Somebody's burning a Coston light up yonder north on the ridge. You boys know anything about it?" There was a pause. "Good! I'll get 'em ! Comin' to ya!

"Okay, son, let's get goin'. I told them boys we would bring our horses to help them pull the equipment cart. Ready?"

"Yessir!" Luke was dressed and out the back door, his heart pounding with the quickness of the situation. He opened the back door while Grandpop was putting on that last boot. He shrugged on his jacket and followed his grandson out the door. The smell of storm was in the air. It was different from a simple rain, thick and strong and fresh all at the same time.

Rain pounded Luke's face and eyes as he struggled to hitch a bridle to the large horse. It took him several tries, and finally he led Ol' Tony to the fence and was able to wrap the straps around his head that way. While he was busy hitching a bridle on Ol' Tony, Capt'n Charlie got to the barn and did the same for Big Roy. Luke handed his grandfather a set of blinders for Big Roy, and he took a set.

"Get us a couple of blankets, son. Don't know which ones you kids use."

"Grandpop, you gonna ride Big Roy?" Luke was dumbstruck right in his tracks, amazed. He was surprised to see Grandpop sit atop a horse.

"Who do you think taught you?" Grandpop tossed the blanket over the huge animal's back, put his foot on the lower railing of the fence, and threw himself on the horse. He then turned around with a satisfied look on his face and tipped his yellow slicker bill at his astonished grandson.

Luke copied his pop, put his foot on the first rung of the fence, and hauled himself aboard the broad back of Ol' Tony.

They gently nudged the two plow horses forward, while Gus registered his objection, and into the storm they went.

Capt'n Charlie and Luke headed toward the road that led to the Coast Guard station. They put blinders on the two horses to protect them from any blowing sand or stinging rain they would encounter. Down the soft and now muddy road, they encountered the surfmen struggling to pull the 1,000-pound loaded equipment cart. Behind them through the heavy rain, they could see the lights of the men and horses pulling the surfboat. They reached the first group and dismounted to help hook up the cart, thus freeing the weary seamen to help with the weight of the boat.

Capt'n Charlie and Luke grabbed the reins of Ol' Tony and Big Roy and began leading them in the direction of the ocean. The second Coston light was lit to assure the floundering ship that it was still in view of the lifesavers. The helpers, now leading with the cart, headed toward the light as the sand turned to mire and the horses labored under the heavily loaded equipment cart.

The cart carried the cannonlike Lyle gun, used to fire off the line attached to the gun over to the ship in distress. There was also a faking box, a square box fitted with tall spikes around which to wind the rope, keeping it straight, so that as the projectile carrying the eye bolt would not tangle or knot, but would shoot and unwind in an orderly fashion, using the full measure of the line. It also included a pick, shovels, bucket, projectiles, shot lines, haversack containing black powder charges and firing mechanisms. heaving stick and line, two tally boards, whip line, whip line block, hawser, traveling block, breeches buoy, fall, straps, sand anchor, crotch poles, hawser cutter, and lanterns.

The cart itself was especially built, with iron wheels that supported the weight. These had wide bands outside the wheel base to keep them from sinking in soft sand. Supposedly, the victims would catch the line, made of woven waterproof linen, and secure it up high to one of the ship's masts. This line was tied to a heavier line, carrying the tally board, which had instructions in English on one side and French on the other. The instructions told the stranded passengers how to tie off the whip line tail block and secure the hawser, which anchored the line to the ship. The board was followed by a tail block designed to support another apparatus called a breeches buoy.

The 200-pound Lyle gun could fire a twenty-point metal projectile with a line attached to it up to 500 yards. The equipment cart also was loaded with extra line, shovels, and poles used for hoisting and securing the crotch pole. It also carried the block and tackle, and emergency supplies for whatever condition in which they found survivors.

The breeches buoy lines were assembled with a crotch pole (an A-frame) to hold it high, and once they were sent out, survivors could be removed from the vessel by hand, hauling in the rescue apparatus. The breeches buoy looked exactly like it sounded. It was a lifesaving apparatus consisting of canvas breeches attachable at the waist to a ring-shaped lifebuoy, to be slung and run upon a rope stretched from ship to shore to and from a wrecked vessel. The buoy was fixed to the life line by three ropes, making a triangle to the traveling block overhead, allowing the breeches buoy to slide down the rope to the shore. The rope shot from the Lyle gun needed to be fastened high up the mast of the vessel, so that the weight of a human, sitting in the life ring—in "breeches"—would carry the cargo down to the ground.

On the beach, the breeches buoy line or hawser was secured to a wooden anchor buried in the sand deep enough to sustain weight. Using block and tackle to keep the line taut, it was caught up and threaded through the crotch pole to keep it above the sand and sea. Once the line was hooked up in the crotch pole, they could begin to bring survivors from the ship to the shore.

One of the most frustrating parts of a rescue from the shore was trying to communicate with the victims on the sinking vessel. The surfmen were prepared to use anything to relay messages to the stricken ship. In the past they had used signal flags, speaking trumpets, hand signals, anything they could, to convey to the ship where to fasten the line from the Lyle gun and make it secure, high enough and strong enough to survive the wind, waves, and pitching of the ship, and tight enough to support the weight of a man. Many rescues would have been more successful had the crew known how to help save themselves. Some vessels had practice drills on the knowledge of how to participate in a rescue, but most thought it would never be needed.

Thankfully the crew of the vessel was not desperate enough to try to swim for it. Being within sight of the beach sometimes made victims think that they could make it to shore on their own. Most drowned trying. It was common knowledge to stay with the ship, especially when help was that close.

This style of lifesaving was more complicated than it appeared, as much depended on the victims, the pitch and roll of the vessel, and the ferocity of the sea. The survivor was dangled over a violent sea, attached to a line, for as much time as the lifesavers needed to haul in the line, hand over hand. This type of rescue was only used when the ship settled within 500 yards of the shore. Otherwise, the lifesavers went out to the vessel in the surfboat. Not until the crew of the lifesaving station arrived would they know which method to use. Therefore, it was necessary to come to the sea with everything one might think to need, because returning to the station to retrieve something otherwise required meant too much time, and sure death for the victims.

There was a third method of rescue, an enclosed life car. It looked like a huge bullet, totally enclosed against the sea, and could carry more than one body. The surfmen always included this on the cart, which added tremendous weight on its own. This was heavy and hard to handle—and even harder to distribute to the ship—but no matter what station came to the rescue, those men practiced their skills every day of their duty. The most stressful practices were held at night, and during a storm. As they practiced, their shot improved, and their bodies became familiar with the weight and the wind—all this in order to be ready and capable on the day they were needed.

Capt'n Charlie kept watch on the surfmen following him with the boat. He was only there to lend a hand. He was not trained as they were, and he worried that he would hinder them, so he pulled the cart to the point near the waiting surfman who had first seen the ship. His Coston light was no longer burning, but the noise coming through the wind and roar of the ocean indicated the survivors knew that help was on the beach ready to rescue them.

The ship was aground on an outer bar. It was not out as far as the Diamonds, but they had still either steered, or were pushed by the wind, onto a reef located out past the breakers. Luke and Grandpop unhooked the cart and horses and led the horses to the lee of a dune, out of most of the weather. It appeared that the surfboat would not be needed, so the boat and the horses pulling it were left with the lighthouse horses, and the men began to dig a six-foot-deep hole to secure the anchor and set up the faking box for the length of rope needed to fire a shot using a breeches buoy. The rope had been carefully wound so that there would be no glitches once it began uncoiling from the frame. The surfmen were comfortable with their decision to use that form of rescue. In 1899 the entire crew of a three-masted schooner, *Minnie Bergen*, was saved with a breeches buoy. They were just hoping the crew, in their desperation, would not decide to set to the sea on their own. Those who were familiar with shipwrecks, as the islanders were, knew that trying the sea on your own usually did not have the desired result. The surfmen knew they had to hurry.

Luke and Grandpop left the horses and stood nearby watching as the surfmen feverishly worked to set up the Lyle gun for the shot. The first line shot out, went wide of the stricken vessel, and had to be hauled back for another try. The first try was studied as to reason for failure—wind, rolling ship—whatever they saw, they corrected and fired again. This time, on board the ship, two of the crew members maintained hold of the line, and one began climbing the shaky structure to secure it high enough for a transition to the lower shore of the beach. Most of the crew was already lashed to parts of the ship, trying not to get dumped into the sea or washed overboard.

It was not uncommon to find the passengers and crew entangling themselves in the mast, bow sprit, spars, anything that a rope would wind around. Anyone having been tossed around by the sea knew the possibilities of a slick deck from breaker wash taking the feet right out from under a man.

The ship was rolling heavily. Sometimes its upper structures touched the water as it pitched from side to side. There appeared to be fewer than ten men aboard, or at least that was what each lightning strike revealed. The light from the lighthouse was unable to penetrate the curtain of water being dumped from an angry sky. The surfmen did not know how many others were below deck, if any. The dark night, the distance from shore, and the blinding rain prevented the surfmen from determining even the kind of ship they were dealing with. Sporadic flashes of lightning did not last long enough to see all of the danger. The vicious strikes were also a danger to victims and saviors as they came vicariously close to protrusions of the ship and apparatus being assembled. Lightning striking a ship was another possible danger. The position of the ship was more forward the beach, and the middle and stern were caught over the back of the bar, creating a structural strain for the ship to stay together. Each breaker crashed over the stern and washed forward, and that thrust buried the vessel deeper into its grave. That hold was beginning to come apart as the thrust of the mighty water moved the ship around. The groaning of the vessel was deafening as it lurched forward, twisting boards and apparently beginning to break apart.

Debris began to come ashore as the waves washed clean the unprotected deck. It was dark, and it was impossible to determine what they were looking at, but they knew they also had to contend with keeping their survivors free of being hit by something caught in the wind and acting as an airborne projectile of destruction.

Luke could hear the timbers breaking and scraping against something not yet loosed. The sounds were the sounds of devastation. Mixed with the sounds of the storm and the coming apart of the ship, there were the cries of the humans on board. He and his pop stood close as they watched the first man being delivered to the shore by the relentless pulling on that connecting rope by the eight men of the Lifesaving Service. Hand over hand they gripped—no gloves, just skin on wet, unforgiving rope. They brought the first man to shore, and Pop took off over the sand to help the weary man gain his feet as he hit the beach. It was most important to get him quickly out of that gear and send it out for the next man. The men manning the rope began to pull hard again, this time to get the wet rope to respond and to deliver the breeches buoy to the rails of the vessel again.

He knew he was too young to help, but Luke felt a lump in his throat knowing he could not. This was supposed to be exciting, as least that was what he had thought before this night. He always imagined what saving lives might look and feel like, but this was not at all what he had imagined. He had heard the statistics—ships by the thousands, some unknown as to where they came from or where they were going. This was the most dangerous shore in the United States. He began to think about the bones and ribs of ships he had seen on his ride up the beach to Kinnakeet. This vision in front of him was what they had experienced. That huge ship meant nothing to the fury of the storm and the strength of the sea. It looked like one of the boats Pop had given him for Christmas—like a toy. The weight and strength of the ship paled with the elements it had encountered.

Another crewman was reaching the beach, and Luke watched as his grandfather and the other men tried to untangle him from the buoy and get him to dry land. Luke thought of the horses and ran back to check on them. All four were surfmen. They stood, their heads turned away from the blinding rain and wind, with their position protected by the location of the surfboat. They did not move, just stood there against the wind, heads down, waiting. He ran back up the bank to watch the continuing rescue operation. He was by now soaking wet, but so was his grandfather, and so were all the other men, and he was proud to be the same.

He watched as the rope stripped the skin from the hands of the surfmen handling it, and still they steadily hauled in more and more survivors. The ship was in bad shape now. A portion of some of the cargo was floating toward the beach—crates, all shapes and sizes. Decking had been torn loose and was washing up in single boards and sections of boards, making everything the surfmen did even more dangerous. He saw an instance where he could help. He rushed down to the men working the breeches buoy and began trying to pull aside anything coming out of the angry ocean that would hit them on their feet or legs. He worked rigorously to keep the rescuers from getting banged up by incoming wood, pieces of iron railing, and anything small that could become a missile to hurt the men. He could not get over how their hands bled.

When the last man was pulled ashore, the men sat down on the wet sand, just out of reach of the ocean's fists thrusting out through the tide to gain another conquest, and rested. Grandpop seemed at that time to be in charge of the survivors. Everyone rested, including Luke. He almost crawled over to his grandfather, just to be near him. They both had done well tonight. This was a night he would never forget. His admiration for his grandfather, from the time he mounted a horse to the take-charge manner he displayed as he found a way to help, was overwhelming. Luke needed to be near him. Capt'n Charlie put his arm around Luke, and they both collapsed flat on the ground, rain beating down on them, and them not caring. After all, there was water everywhere.

Almost at daybreak, the ship now making louder and louder noises as it struggled to stay intact in the relentless ocean. Its crew took a last look, glad not to be on it. They struggled to get to their feet for whatever was next for them. The surfmen began gathering up their equipment, with the help of Luke and his grandfather, and replaced it neatly, to Luke's surprise, back in the equipment wagon. Luke and Capt'n Charlie, without being asked, went over to the surfboat and gathered up Ol' Tony and Big Roy, brought them back to the cart, and hooked them up. The surfmen were most appreciative that they did not have to push that heavy cart back to the station through all that mud and strong wind.

Luke was also impressed that men he had known all his life were so brave, and so caring, as they directed the survivors to get into the surfboat so that they did not have to walk back to the station. The weary surfmen, with their hands raw from the rope, gathered up their supplies, thanked both Luke and his grandfather, patted them on the back—there would be no handshakes this night—and started back to the station with the help of the two lighthouse horses. Back at the station, the survivors would be clothed, fed, and given a bed, until other arrangements were made.

By morning, the village would be on the beach, collecting what they could from the mess of wood, boxes, barrels, pieces of ship, equipment, and foodstuffs. News traveled fast on the island. By breakfast, the news of the shipwreck would be common knowledge. Grandpop and Luke slowly walked back to the house. Blake, Ellie, and Nett were still asleep. Grandmom was standing in the front door, wiping her hands on her apron, ready to give her husband and grandson a hug and all her attention. This was not the first time for either her or her Charlie, but for Luke, he could hardly believe what he had just seen. He was so tired, and hot oatmeal was just what would take the chill off.

He could not get the sight of raw hands from his mind as he collapsed on his warm, dry bed.

Surfman

Ellie listened intently to the early morning chatter below her. She had been at the window most of the night, listening to the noises coming from the beach. Her position faced the lighthouse, not the sea. She could only hear the things that were happening—not see them—and from the time Luke awakened, her eyes opened and she stared at the ceiling. When Pegasus had objected to being left behind, she moved to the window and opened it just enough to hear and have a place to lay her head without getting wet. She put a barrier between her head and the storm, and the water from the gusts of rain simply ran down and out over the outside sash. Sometimes she listened and sometimes she dozed off. It was a long night. As she dreamed, *Saint Travis lifted her above the fray, and they watched through a foggy portal.*

Blake awakened with the realization that the storm was still raging, although there seemed to be less slapping shingles in his head than he had experienced the night before. His first thoughts were, *I have a horse. I wonder when I will see him again.* He was trying to hold those thoughts in, but it was worse than Christmas. He knew about it but had to wait. Waiting was not Blake's strong point.

"Luke?" he whispered, turning his head to see his brother heavily stretched out on his bed. It was not like Luke to sleep late. Usually he was the one trying to awaken Blake.

"Luke?" he whispered lightly.

Luke just waved him off, and it was just with his fingers, not his hand.

Blake was anxious to talk about Spirit, so he dressed, not bothering to care about noise, and got himself together for the morning, not even being careful to shut the door quietly. He didn't slam it, but he just didn't sympathize. He knocked quietly on Ellie's door. Even she did not answer.

"Ellie?" he said softly. No answer. *Nothing to do but go find Grandpop. I know he's awake,* Blake thought. Down the stairs he went, only to find Ellie in the kitchen sitting on a stool next to the big white porcelain stove talking to Grandmom and watching as she made breakfast. What was going on? He guessed he was just tired from all the excitement, and probably Ellie was telling Grandmom about the house.

"Where's Pop?" he said. "Boy! Luke is sure asleep, he wouldn't even turn over."

"They were out all night long helping with the ship that wrecked on the beach during the storm, and I've been waiting for you to get up and go down to the shore with me to check it out," Ellie said matter-of-factly, not thinking about what a shock her revelation would be to Blake.

"What! Who?" he said, with a confused look on his face. "Who is 'they,' and what are you talking about?" He was more confused than ever. Luke would not go anywhere without him, and he knew that! Ellie must have been telling some dream. She had such an imagination, but maybe she saw something, and maybe they were getting ready for one of their adventures. All these things were flying around in his noggin when Ellie began to tell him what had happened.

When she finished, he was crushed. She had no way of knowing that

Luke had tried to awaken Blake. That part made the story horrible for Blake, and he would continue to feel that way until Luke could get up to tell him differently. But both Grandpop and Luke were still asleep.

"Not a step until you two get some oatmeal in you. I made it this morning, so you don't have to wait."

Grandmom was spooning in the hot cereal as Ellie told Blake what she had heard. Grandmom filled in what she knew, as she lay awake waiting for her husband and grandson to return. Even though Luke had tried not to awaken her, she had heard every word, and from experience, she saw in her mind the scene and watched as her husband readied himself for the storm. She knew he would take Luke because it was time for him to see some real men do the things they did out of compassion for another human being. She had seen it before, when she was younger. She had followed Charlie to the beach to see the rescue. It quickened her heart to think that there were good and bad outcomes, and both lay imprinted on the soul of every man who lived it.

Ellie and Blake rushed to gulp down sustenance and get dressed in their anticipated walk down to the scene on the shore. It was beginning to clear up even more as the morning went by. Grandmom made them promise that they would look, but come right back. She didn't want them to get sick, so she oversaw the clothing they wore as she let them out in the rain. Even Grandmom knew when a storm was going away, hearing the wind die to only occasional gusts with fewer bursts of solid rain. The signs were there, and it was safe for the children.

"Fifteen minutes!" she cautioned.

They knew she meant it, because they knew how lucky they were to get to run in the rain and experience the wind. They were really island children—tough, curious, and in tune with the nature around them. That included storms and weather patterns that went with an island existence. They, too, could smell a shift of wind.

Luke did not awaken until after dinner. On the island, the hot meal of the day was served around noon, as everyone arose early, sometimes before daybreak, and there was still a full afternoon of work to be done that required energy. The nighttime meal was supper, usually a combination of the dinner and other foodstuffs that Grandmom made to make every meal special. The only time there was a reference to "lunch" was when people referred to a "school lunch."

Grandpop was eating when his surf buddy slipped in beside him at the table. The other two kids were already there, listening to his tale of the shipwreck.

Blake looked squarely into Luke's face. "Why didn't you take me with you?" His mouth turned down, and his eyes were glassy. It had truly hurt his feelings.

Luke could see the effect his leaving had on his little brother. "I tried to wake you, I tried! You were so tired from yesterday that even when I shook your arm, you just moved away with your eyes closed. I had to hurry downstairs to tell Grandpop, 'cause I thought I was the first to see the Coston light burning. I was afraid somebody was going to drown. I didn't know I would get to go, and I was so concerned with time, I just ran out. Then things went so fast. I wished I could come get you, but there wasn't any time. I promise! I wanted you there, I kept hoping you would hear the noise. Then it got going so fast, I couldn't leave. Don't be mad at me. I missed having you there." At that he got out of his chair and hugged his brother's head and sat back down.

"What about me?" Ellie said.

"Shoot! You wouldn't want to get in all that. You would be sick today!" Luke smiled big, knowing she would never have ventured out in a storm if she didn't have to.

Ellie knew he was right and shot him a half-cocked smile, letting him know she was just poking fun with him.

"Well, I guess it's okay, but now you have to tell everything!" Blake demanded.

"Let's go to Ellie's room. Her bed is bigger. C'mon, we can wait for the storm to go and then I'll show you, but now, let's go watch things until the rain stops."

They sat cross-legged in the middle of the big bed, enthralled, as Luke told of his emotional adventure the previous night. He even choked up when he talked of his grandpop taking care of the survivors, and they all laughed at his description of Grandpop astride a horse. Luke was struck with a fit of giggles when he said they rode bareback on those two humongous horses.

By late afternoon, the storm had passed fully, and word had spread about the night before. The kids were not the only ones standing on the dunes peering out to sea at a huge ship still floundering as the breakers washed over its crippled form. It was located about 500 yards out, absolutely headed straight for the beach, stuck solid on the bottom. Her bow appeared to be broken, as it looked so much lower than the rest of the ship. From the shore, the angle allowed a view of the decking of the forward bow. Its masts and yardarms were either gone or snapped. The beach was littered with cargo in containers, and other separate parts of a ship. Huge pieces of wood were everywhere, as was roping, barrels, crates, metal parts, brass fixtures, and burlap bags bulging and soggy with something. Also washing up were foodstuffs, cooking utensils, cordage, books, clothing—so many items, it probably was enough to help a lot of families who did without. Whole pieces of the deck were strewn among the hatch covers, interior ornate wood railings, hardware, beams, and furniture. Each big breaker carried with it some part of the ship or its cargo. The beach was littered with the innards of the ship as it began to break apart.

The ocean plunder kept families housed, heated, clothed, and fed, as the islanders recovered and used every item. Villagers arrived with their carts and trucks to rummage through the remains of a once mighty vessel to see if something of value could be saved from the ocean. Early in the afternoon, a vendue master arrived and began to organize the salvage according to the new rules set by the state. There would be an auction of goods that had not already been carted off, and a portion of the sale would go to the owner of the ship, 5 percent; a portion to the wreck commissioner, 5 percent; and should there be salvagers, they would get 90 percent. The salvagers were the ones whose job it became to get the ship off the beach or out of the breakers, which would not willingly let go of the struggling vessel. These men, mostly locals who owned a boat, went out to the stricken ship and steadily broke it up, and hauled it away. Many times the parts of the ship were towed to Elizabeth City to be sold again to ship's chandlers. Chandlers were men who furnished trappings for boats.

In addition to the local people coming from all seven communities, others traveled down from Manteo or villages inland to bid on portions that were difficult to remove. Eventually the ship, piece by piece, slowly disappeared. It was common practice to place a guard at night near the ship to keep people from stealing valuable articles before they could be auctioned off. Most of the men went to the vendue for business. Families rarely went.

Traveling the wash at low tide, which most villagers did when traveling from one location to another, the evidence of past shipwrecks was commonplace. Some could name the heavy pieces of wood as they approached them. This was the *Edwin Farrow*, or that was the *Robert W. Dasie*, or the barquentine *Altoona*, and then there were those whose names were never known. The remains of wrecks were well known by the locals. Shipwrecks were common and there were remnants scattered all down the entire island. They were natural to avoid, and travelers on the beach just rode around them with hardly a glance.

There were over 1,000 documented shipwrecks, and an untold number never recorded. Those were referred to as having "been lost off the coast of Cape Hatteras."

Before the Civil War, rescue was spontaneous and improvised. Most shipwrecks happened during a storm and were not discovered until debris began washing up on the beach. The tragedy was that bodies were also thrown up on the lonely sands, drowned trying to gain the shore. All those years, the villagers of Cape Hatteras buried the dead in unmarked graves behind the dune lines. Most were blessed as they were wrapped and given a "Christian" burial. The beach was cleared until the next wreck was discovered. The villages were not located on the ocean side of the island. All were back from the ocean, located on the sound. Thus, help from the shore was a folly that could be dismissed, as no one was near enough to know that a ship was in distress. Not until 1787 was there an effort by anyone in the United States to address the rescue of drowning men escaping a ship going down. Then the only help was the building of small shacks along a treacherous coast, to be stocked with food, candles, firewood, a tinderbox to start a fire, and shelter from the elements until they could find a town. These small shacks were called humane houses.

Not until 1803 was there an investigation into lifesaving by using lifeboats to gain a stricken ship. And not until 1870 was there an effort to establish a proper system for saving lives as well as cargo previously claimed by the sea. In 1878 an official bill provided for the Lifesaving Service and placed that service under the governmental branch of the Treasury Department. Still, the government was only concerned with the monetary rather than the humane side of a shipwreck.

Nine lifesaving stations eventually were built on the island. These were manned by local men familiar with the sea. A great deal of pride accompanied the job, and even though the government attempted to reward a man with a "political" appointment, it proved to be a grave mistake. Eventually the Service evolved as having *standards*, rather than giving the job to those who were not qualified.

"Historically, the first lifesaving stations erected on the island were in 1874, at both Chicamacomico and Little Kinnakeet. They were plain, barnlike buildings and not entirely organized. Not until the official Lifesaving Bill was passed in 1878 were seven more added. From 1871 to 1915, the lifesavers of the island assisted with 28,121 shipwrecks and rescued 174,682 lives, more than were lost during several wars combined.

"With the lifesaving stations in operation every minute of a twenty-four-hour cycle in stormy weather, a surfman was somewhere within a five-mile radius of his station, watching for vessels in distress. It was his job. Some patrolled the beach on foot, some on horse. They would meet another surfman from a neighboring station halfway and exchange tokens to verify each had walked his beat. Also at each halfway mark between stations there was a small box, or sometimes a small four-by-four shack with supplies, off the beach, where a man could check in to indicate he had completed his shift.

"From the south of the island, the stations were Hatteras Inlet, 1883; Creeds Hill, near Trent village, 1878; Durants, called the Hatteras Station, 1878; Cape Hatteras, located at Buxton, 1882; Big Kinnakeet, south of the village, 1874; Little Kinnakeet, north of the village, 1874; Gull Shoal, located south of Salvo, 1878; Chicamacomico, Rodanthe, 1874; New Inlet, north of Rodanthe, at the opening of an inlet cut by a storm, only in operation two years as it was destroyed by fire; Pea Island, 1878; and Oregon Inlet, 1874; completed the scope of vision provided to detect ships in distress."

The man Luke saw that night holding up the Coston flare was just beginning his patrol when he saw the ship in distress. The lookout at the station had also seen the light of the flare and readied his crew for a rescue.

Luke stood away from all the commotion of the arriving salvagers. He was silent, still remembering the events of the night before—the harried victims, those whose faces said it all, the fear of death, and the relief of the rescuers. He did not look at the scene as the others did. He had experienced the horror of men struggling to live and other men struggling to help them. His admiration for his grandfather had grown, and his admiration for the surfmen was more than he could explain. He wanted Blake to have the same knowledge as he had gained. It would serve to make him a better man, as it had done for Luke. He made up his mind that he would retell the story to his brother and cousin, this time emphasizing the bravery of the men who came to help. His excitement had been overtaken with the urgency to help. It was not exciting. It was necessary.

That evening, Uncle Baxter came to sit on the porch and talk with his brother-in-law about the rescue. News traveled fast on the island, and the heroics of Capt'n Charlie and his grandson were being discussed. Baxter had retired only a few years before as keeper of the Cape Hatteras Lifesaving Station and had been credited with saving over 300 lives during his distinguished career. He was anxious to hear of his close friend's encounter with a beach rescue. He occupied one of the rocking chairs on the front porch and Capt'n Charlie the other.

"You young-uns come on out here and talk to your Uncle Baxter," Pop called into the house.

He didn't have to call very loudly, as the children were doing their best to stay away from the window in Ellie's room so as not to eavesdrop, but they were not far from the door. They all burst out of the screen door and climbed on the porch swing with eager looks on their faces. Luke had a thousand questions. He always knew that Uncle Baxter (they called him Uncle Backie) was a former surfman, but it did not have as much meaning as it had now. He stared at the huge man sitting calmly in the rocker, smoking a pipe, next to Grandpop, who was smoking a cigarette.

"Son, you got some questions for your uncle?" It didn't take a mind reader to see that, and it was the reason that Grandpop had invited the children. They needed to hear what a surfman had to endure to be in that position.

"Uncle Backie," Luke began, "what was it like to be a surfman?"

"Well, son, that's a big question." Baxter paused as his mind went to some of the things he had seen and experienced. He was trying to get back to the root of the question, to lend some continuity to the story. He didn't want to just jump in on the actual shipwreck of it. He wanted to talk about what one needed to do to be able to render assistance to a vessel in distress.

"Surfmen are chosen for many reasons: strength, ability to read the weather and water, the inner strength to be away from family, and the ability to be composed facing great danger. That don't mean 'no fear.' There's fear, but a man needs to work through it. There's a life at stake here. Most, a man also needs pride. Wouldn't want a man who takes no pride in his work. There's a certain amount of preparedness to the job. There is a need to practice drills every day. Each day had its drill. One day, breeches buoy, like you saw last night. How to wind the rope in the faking box so's it don't get tangled as the gun fires it off. Wouldn't do no good to have that thing tangle up on the shore. Why, a man could drown, or be thrown into the sea, waiting for somebody to untangle the line onshore. They need to be strong enough to haul the rescue equipment from the station to the shore. There's a need to know your signal flags. Sometimes, if the weather is clear enough, a surfman is able to 'talk' to the ship using flags. Handling the Lyle gun, getting enough depth in the hole to support the heavy poles that hold up the lifeline. We don't just be sittin' 'round the station playing cards. Nope, it's drill during the day and patrol at night.

"Used to be, they only worked a four-month season, because that was when most storms come, but then, counting nor'easters and other winter blows, the need to be year-round changed that. There's men on who spell other men, so's they can go home. The surfboat needs nine men: the keeper, who steers the boat from the back, and eight men to row, with their back to where they are going. They depend on the keeper to tell them when to row and when to stall. He faces the breakers and ocean, and he sees when there needs to be a heavy pull to mount an oncoming wave. He sees a stall in the breakers and shouts to 'put your back into it, boys!' and they know there's a break. If'n I shout, 'Back water, boys,' they know to back up. It is really up to the keeper to make sure the boat don't get swamped before it gains the open sea.

"The keeper sees the breakers and shouts for his men to put their backs into it in order to go up the side and over the crest of the wave, without it breaking into the middle of the boat and capsizing it. Broken many a pole trying to steer my men out of harm's way, and keep several in the bottom of the boat. The surfmen are given numbers—like Surfman #1, now he's a hearty fellow and has proved his worth. Surfman #4 is a good man, but even a Surfman #6 can move up if he proves to be a good man with an oar. Nobody takes it personal, cause it's always for the good of saving a life. I used to tell my men to 'look me in the eye, boys, just look me in my eye.' They could concentrate on the job at hand, if'n they didn't look to the sea. Worst thing can be said about a man is that 'you wouldn't want to be in a boat with him.' You don't want a man with you who don't stand to the sea.

"There's scuppers, or drains, built into the surfboat, then decked over, with the water outlet areas above the waterline, so when large waves broke over the boat, the water could run out the scupper areas. There's been times when men and horses slept on the beach, waiting for the weather to allow them another try at saving a life. Yessir, seen men with mountains of courage in a small body. Took muscle power and courage to man that wooden boat and set her on the boiling sea. Those wooden boats carry iron men. Yessir, iron men."

With that, Uncle Baxter got a 'thinking' look in his eye, remembering some of the things he had seen. He continued. "They's two six-hour watches during the day, and four at night. Our job was to face the beast and fight the surf. We also know, the more we train, the less we bleed."

Luke thought of the bleeding hands of the men, but he knew that the same amount of rope burn that made these men bleed would have ripped apart the hands of a lesser man. His eyes teared up just thinking about it. He couldn't help glancing at the mighty hands of the man telling the story.

"When a ship is aground, we use flags to communicate in the day, and signal flares at night. No surfman ever refused the sea, and no regular trained crewman was ever lost. Why, I seen men on a sinking ship so scared, they wouldn't get in the surfboat. Thought it was too small. Can't make a man save himself. Nope, can't force him. Why, one time, we couldn't get the line to the ship, so the crew anchored a line, secured the other end in a dog's mouth, and threw him overboard. He swam to shore, and we was able to get them off. Why, we been known to throw a drowned man over the back of a horse and let the horse trot the water outta him. We'll try anything to bring a man back. Dead ain't dead till all of us know it."

"Uncle Baxter, tell us about your most famous shipwreck." Luke was fascinated. So were the other two, but they didn't know enough to ask a question, and they smiled when Luke did.

"Oh, son, that's a tale. Yessir, that's a tale." Baxter smiled and looked at Charlie, who was also smiling. Why, if Luke hadn't asked that question, Charlie thought that he would have.

"Go on, Baxter, let's hear it." He smiled, knowing what was coming, and happy to hear the tale again.

The Ghost Ship of Diamond Shoals

axter Miller was born in Avon, to Christopher Columbus Miller and Emma Dolly Fulcher Miller. He entered the Lifesaving Service at age seventeen, and three years later he married Capt'n Charlie's sister, Josephine Drinkwater Gray, eventually having nine children. He had no more than a grammar school education, as the island did not provide much more. Most were sent away for their high school diploma, usually staying with family off island. Baxter did not have the funds for more formal studies, and he worked as a fisherman until he was old enough to join the Lifesaving Service. He worked as a surfman through to its evolution to the Coast Guard in 1915 and eventually spent thirty years at sea.

As a man of the sea, he was one of the most decorated men in the country. He was the recipient of a Gold Lifesaving Medal of Honor from the U.S. government, and later a Silver Medal, for saving the life of a fellow surfman—Josh Dailey, son of B.B. Dailey, who was swept overboard by a shifting boom. The others on the thirteen-ton sloop *Defender* were unaware of the man overboard and would have left him behind. Someone on the boat saw Josh's derby floating in the water and sounded the alarm. Baxter heard the screams and rushed to launch the skiff onboard. This action was inhibited as the small boat was full of the lumber they were transporting across the Pamlico Sound from Elizabeth City to the island. Baxter had to unload the lumber before he could launch, but meanwhile, the semiconscious Dailey had gone down for the third time. Baxter reached the scene and saw the boy on the bottom, about ten feet down. He thrust the oar to the weakened young man and hauled him aboard the boat. The boat had been filled with lumber because it was rendered useless due to holes in the bottom, The leaking boat was hard to maneuver, but it limped back to the schooner, almost full of sound water by the time they returned. It took a mighty strong back to row a boat full of water. Over the years Baxter earned numerous ribbons and bars for courage above and beyond the call of duty. For the *Brewster* rescue he received a silver watch from Germany, inscribed with the Imperial Eagle.

During storms he had been known to get up in the middle of the night for fear of a shipwreck. He knew he had men on watch, but storms were deadly, and would throw a ship into the grinding shoals without any notice. With the noise of both wind and rain, sometimes it was only a flash from a lightning strike that revealed a ship in distress.

Most women were reluctant to marry a man of the sea, and Josephine Gray was among those. Had she known that her tall, handsome husband would eventually end up as a man who tested himself against the raging ocean on a regular basis, she might have had second thoughts. There were times when she was so stricken with fear during a storm that she took her oldest child at first light and drove the two-wheeled cart to the ocean's shore to see for herself that he, on this night, had not fallen in harm's way. To her, the sea had the look of death, but as a devoted wife she kept a good home and did not complain. When Baxter and her brother, Charlie, decided to build a shrimp boat in the backyard after he had retired, she refused to allow him to name the boat for her, which was a common practice with fishermen. Instead, the boat was named for Charlie's wife,

Odessa, and the wife of one of his sons, Thomas, hence, the "W," for Winnie. The boat that Baxter tooled around in after retirement was the *Odessa W*, and Josephine was just fine with that.

Surfmen made a steady income: forty dollars a month during the working months. The keeper made $400 a year. All were provided uniforms and keep. Most lived as close as possible to their assigned stations. They were allowed to go home one night in every nine. Women were not welcomed at the station. The surfmen took their duties seriously, especially if they had witnessed or participated in saving a life. That experience changed them, and knowing their worth, the work almost became a calling. The most horrible sight seen by these men of the sea was a beach strewn with bodies from some ship that had broken up before help could arrive. The sea was the highway of the world, and the surfmen were the rescue squad that showed up when a person's life was in the balance.

"Young'uns, how'd you like to hear about a ghost ship?" Baxter had a huge grin as he observed the wide-eyed children, who literally stopped the swing, as if the swinging of the bench was the same as their hearts, which had stopped as well.

"The last shipwreck I went out to is considered to be one of the mysteries of the sea. Lessee now. . . ." Uncle Baxter paused to get the sequence of his story right. It was an important one, and there were details to remember.

"I was keeper here in Buxton, at Cape Hatteras Station, #183. I was serving my last duty, waiting for my retirement papers. This was to be the final assignment. It was the last day of January, and the weather was brutal. With the storm full on, I went to get some shut-eye. This kind of weather was the perfect time for a ship to be blown off course, and all the surfmen in every station knew it. The winds were comin' from the southwest, the sea was rough and tides were running high. Seen this kinda thing before, but when my man took his watch, there was no sign of a ship to be seen.

"I was asleep with the night watch covered, when Clarence Brady awakened me with the alert, 'Ship Ashore.' He had been on watch, and through the telescope, which had a range of twelve miles—plus she was a seventy-one-incher, one of the best—he thought he had seen a ship stalled on the shoals of the Diamond. The fog was thick that night, and the ship appeared to be under no distress, as she was low in the water. The fog and waves were relentless, the breakers high up on the shore. It appeared the vessel was a five-masted schooner. All masts seemed to be in place, and all sails unfurled with davits swung out. As Brady continued to observe the ship, he noticed that it did not move forward, nor did she fire off a signal. At least in watching he did not see one. He was trying to track the ship's progress with each lightning strike, and when several minutes passed and the ship was still stationary, he reckoned it was stuck on the Diamonds.

"Brady awakened me with this knowledge, and I went to the tower to have a look-see for myself. I stood for long enough to see that he was indeed correct. The ship was in trouble. I gave the alarm, awakened my team, and gave the order to suit up. We prepared for a rescue at sea using the surfboat. No need to burden the boat with breeches. One of the men hitched up the two huge government horses. These horses, you know, are different. Why, you seen Ol' Tony and Big Roy at work. Well, my two was just as strong, and I do believe they favor bad weather. He led them to the caisson pulling that big ol' thirty-five-footer. We readied the surfboat. No need to bother with the equipment cart, as this ship was miles out. All men were reminded to wear their cork vests and prepare for a long haul at sea. I put in an alert to both stations on either side of Buxton. I telephoned Creeds Hill, Station 184, south of the point; Big Kinnakeet, Station 182, north of the point; and for good measure, Hatteras Inlet, Station 186, also south of the point. That big a ship was gonna need several boats to unload her, and there would not be time to come back twice. Actually, it was too far to row for more than one trip. A man's hands can only take to the oar for so long. Creeds and Big Kinnakeet came to help, and Hatteras launched their big motorized surfboat from down there.

"We had a pretty good bead on things, because the Coast Guard station at Buxton has the second tallest point, outside the lighthouse, for watching the sea. Top of our two-story building there's a tall square cupola running the ridge of the roof, with windows fore and aft." Baxter paused and leaned forward, then slipped back into the rocker and thought, as he proceeded to have a rock.

"Yessir men, she was a five-master, with sails fully rigged, showing a full set. The schooner was on the shoal, *riding high* on the shoal. She was a sight, like a picture, but she was 'bout to get beat up! When I came downstairs, Brady had already poured coffee in my special good-luck cup, a tin one, with blue and white speckles on it. Your aunt Josephine gave it to me, and the boys always teased me. But this time they wanted me to be alert, and they thought maybe we might need a little luck. We all knew that only a few men stood between life and death for these poor fellows. This night was cold, and those poor souls were likely to freeze to death if somebody didn't come for them. That's the job. . . .

" Mine were the mightiest of men, had pride in their work, and were fearless against the sea. We got all slickered up in sou'wester gear, and I met the men as they stood, waiting beside the long, white, clinker planking surfboat. She was a beaut, a fine boat. Each board in her was overlapping to produce strength and power against the sea she needed to face. I crawled up into her, and my men stood with their hands on the gunwales as those huge horses pulled her out of the boathouse and down the ramp to the sandy trail leading to the ocean. We all braced forward to the wind, including the horses. Right off, the rain pelted us to the point the horses had to find the road. I stood in the bow with their reins in my hands, and I was glad they had blinders on, so's not to be spooked by the wailing wind and driving rain. The boys urged the horses to the sea.

"We were the only ones who could render assistance, and we were ready. Our drills had been perfect, my men were strong on the oars, and all I needed was a break in the water to get her over the bar. The sea was raging, and it was foolish to strike out until I saw an opening in the sets of waves. The men from south and north of us showed up on horses, also dressed for a long haul. The keeper who spots the wreck becomes the one who runs the show, even if there are other keepers there. There were two others. I picked the two biggest men from each station to join my crew of eight for the attempt. This called for men to row and men to spell. It was not going to be easy. We had, along with keepers C. R. Hooper from Big Kinnakeet and J. C. Gaskill from Creeds, twelve rowers.

"We tried launching from both cricks of the point, but on the north side, the sea was even higher, so we tried again to the south. Here we stayed, determined to gain the sea. The first two attempts to get past the breakers failed. They were mor'n a two-story building, and as you got to them, looking straight up that wall, even my boys couldn't pull it. Finally I saw an opening and yelled for the boys to put their backs into it, and they started up the side. 'Pull, boys! Pull!' and by jiminy, those boys did it. They went straight up that wave, crested her, and pitched head fo'most down the back side of her! Again, the breakers came, these even higher than the first, but we had momentum by that time, and maybe just a little bit of sand, making us determined at beating that ocean.

"Waves come in sets of three and seven, so we knew what was in store, and I could see it all. My boys had their backs to it, and I was facing the crew with the rudder steer pole in my hand trying to guide her through that set of waves. Sometimes I do believe we went sideways, but we finally gained the sea.

"Me, Hooper, and Gaskill knew what was comin'. It was a long row out to the Diamonds. Took us every bit of two hours to get to her. Motor don't do no good in heavy sea. We used manpower. Pat Etheridge, the keeper from the Hatteras Inlet station, showed up soon after. The sea was running higher, waves crashing against us, pushing us back, both boats bandied around like toys. There she sat, but we couldn't get nearer than half a mile. She was just sitting there, stretched out, sails full out, beautiful, not moving, like a picture of a ship posing for the artist. We tried to get near her, but the chop was high and we couldn't see how to get close without us getting washed over. We saw nary a soul on board. Neither surfboat could get close enough to her. The breakers were running higher on the shallow shoals, building up the sand along the shoal, then tearing it down. The colliding of currents into each other, spewing up walls of water, made it folly to get involved with that angry meeting. The water crashed into our boats, and along with the fog, rain, lightning licking the ocean, and distance, all that prevented us from seeing the ship's name. We was all so wet, we couldn't keep the salt spray outen our eyes. The breakers were hitting her high, and no letup in sight. They were comin' from all sides. Dangerous to get in the middle of all that, and she was just takin' it. Strong, big schooner, she was, just a slight pitch, but buried.

"Seemed to be no life on board, and it didn't appear we was gonna get any closer. We were using both power and oars, and couldn't conquer that sea. So we decided to come about, as we say, and headed back to shore. We thought to let the sea lay down for a day, and the next day we were all right back at it. This time, we were joined by the Coast Guard cutter *Seminole* from Wilmington, and then the cutter *Manning* and wrecking tug *Rescue* from Norfolk. I had alerted the Seventh District superintendent and division commander of the situation the night before and requested the larger craft for assistance.

"My telegraph read,

COAST GUARD WASHINGTON D.C.
Unknown five masted schooner stranded Diamond Shoals
sails set boats gone no signs of life sea rough stations number
182 183 184 186 unable to board schooner

"The *Seminole* stood off the point and signaled us to send a boat. We rowed out to her and boarded her for a trip to the wreck. They said they passed only one ship heading north near the Diamonds, but didn't see a wreck. They had gone right past her, but because her sails were set, they thought she was under way. Still, the sea wouldn't let us nearer than a mile, so we all spent the night on the cutter.

"All of us had attempted getting close enough to board, even the navy, but it weren't happ'nin'! So nothing to do but keep going back. Since there were no signs of life, it was just a ship we were lookin' at, and weren't no sense in risking any lives to save wood and sail. It wasn't till four days later did the sea lay down enough for all of us to get to her. By that time, the waves breaking over her had filled her hold and ripped apart her seams. She still stood upright, listing only a few degrees. All sails on her were unfurled, slapping in the wind, making a fierce noise, made it hard to hear each other, even side by side. We could see there were no lifeboats attached to her, and we finally saw her stern. *Carroll A. Deering*, out of Bath, in Maine. We saw the rope ladder dangling loose over the side. We tried a couple of times to board her and could not.

"The navy let 'em have it with the bullhorn, but no answer. All we could hear was the slapping of the sail, and we knew that they was gonna shred any time now. It was not going to happen this day. With any luck, the weather would slack up, and we could come after her again.

"She was a beauty! Looked new, shiny white paint, fancy nameplate. She had three decks—oak frame, with trimming visible of mahogany and cypress. Her masts were 100 feet aloft, and I'll bet there was 6,000 square meters of sail on her. One of the pertiest ships I ever saw. There she was, 'bout fourteen feet buried in sand, waves pounded her to be 'bout six feet above water in places as she broke up. Water coming through windows on all decks.

"We finally got to board her. I was the first one on deck. Still those sails were flapping, so loud now you couldn't hear yourself think. Those hundred-foot masts were steady in the wind. We went through her. She musta been over 2,000 ton, long as three houses, wide as two. Coulda loaded tons of coal or lumber. Almost a barge. 'Twas a fine merchant ship. Not a soul on board. Her steering gear was ruined, the wheel broken, boxes of instruments bashed in. There was a sledgehammer on the deck. Things on board were either missing, or in the wrong place, we could tell the ship had been ransacked. Whatever cargo there was, weren't no more. Left only the ballast.

"The capt'n's cabin was as fine as any settin' room. Fine wood panels, brass lanterns on the walls, rope bed, handsome desk, but no personal belongings. Capt'n's sea chest gone, and all his log books and journals, charts scattered all over the floor. The wheelhouse had been stripped of navigation equipment. Whoever went through her took all her instruments, and from the few we found, they were of the finest made. No clue where she was going or where she had been. But, kids, the strangest thing: We went to the lower deck, and in the galley, the table was set for a meal, spareribs on the stove, there was a pot of coffee, full, on a burner. Pea soup on the stove in a pot, table was set for eight. Looked like somebody was called away unexpectedly. Otherwise the galley was squared away. No struggle. Not a glimmer of what had happened. We searched around until the ship gave a jerk, as one of the masts toppled, sending her a little sideways. No need staying till the weather calmed itself. Nothing to do but go back home. Darndest thing I ever saw. By this time, four days in a row and already hours of rowing, we was too tired to do anything but go back and get some sleep.

"Word got around, and when the weather cleared, the ship was still there, but by now, she was totally the property of the Diamonds. High and buried, nobody was gonna get her out. Men from the villages rowed out in four small boats, with fifteen men, for salvage. There was a vendue on Buxton beach, and people got foodstuffs, dishes, desks, tables, chairs, rope, sail, lots of the mahogany and cedar trappings, anything that looked to be of value. Somebody got a Bible, and somebody else got the ship's bell. From that day on, debris brought a little of the ship to shore each day. Some of her even washed up on Ocracoke. Oh! forgot to tell you, there was a survivor!"

Blake could not contain himself. He had been mesmerized by Uncle Backie's story, and he blurted out, "Who was it?"

"It was the ship's cat, and it had six toes!" Uncle Baxter had saved the best for last.

"Noooooo!" they all said, almost in unison.

"You're making that up! Serious?" said Luke. He thought Uncle Baxter was funnin' them.

"Hand to God," said Uncle Baxter. "One of the men took him home."

There was a long silence. The kids were thinking. Baxter lit his pipe, Charlie lit a cigarette, and they both waited.

"Now that's a story!" said Capt'n Charlie. "Best I ever heard, and it was true!"

Grandmom showed up at the screen door with two cups and a kettle of coffee, some biscuits, and of course a plate full of hot cookies. She poured for her husband and brother-in-law. The children reached out, and each took two cookies and settled back in the swing, satisfied. Grandmom set the dish on the side table between Uncle Baxter's rocker and the swing. Once again, they pushed off on the swing.

Finally, Luke, munching around the very edge of his cookie, taking rabbit bites as his mind began to fill in a mystery, asked quietly, "What do you think happened, Uncle Backie? Did anybody ever find out?"

"Well, son, there was a lot of talk around here for quite a long time. Maybe still is, but there were detectives looking into it, and the police from Maine. There was a lot of strangers poking around the island for about a year. It was in all the papers, up north, everywhere. Seems they tracked that ship from Norfolk, when the regular captain got sick and a new one took over. She was headed all the way down to Rio de Janeiro,

Brazil, with a load of over 3,000 pounds of coal, then to Buenos Aires, and was supposed to return to New York with over 3,000 pounds of Argentine corn, with one stop off at Puerto Rico.

"Since we were just out of war at the time, some people thought it was Russian pirates. There was unrest in Russia, and they were all over the seas, robbing and sinking ships. And there was another ship missing, around the same time, the *Hewitt*. Tell you the truth, that fueled it, but then a local man—name of Christopher Columbus Gray, no kin—said he found a bottle with a note saying they had been captured by a Russian vessel and needed help, and it was signed by the captain of the *Deering*. The FBI checked it out and found the handwriting to be Gray's. That set people talking about Russians, and they were amight disappointed when they found out it was a hoax.

"Seems it had something to do with that captain begging off sick and new people taking over. Reports were—there was talk when she was in the Caribbean of men smuggling rum onto vessels that were heading north. This was the time of Prohibition. Then, there was an unsavory redheaded character who had an argument with the new captain, witnessed by a few people, and some others thought mutiny. No lifeboats and such, and that ladder overboard. Also, seems a vessel passed her, south of here, and a crew member was trying to hail them, saying they had lost their anchors and needed assistance. but the Deering just sailed on. When they inquired, they couldn't say for sure, but they might have seen the redheaded man on the deck. Some thought the captain had been murdered, as he had complained about the redheaded man being hard to handle.

"I think they finally decided it was a smuggling operation. The thieves needed an empty ship with a large cargo storage. They boarded her in the Caribbean, pretending to be crewmen. There must have been another ship, come alongside, and took the cargo and crew, got rid of whoever didn't agree, and just let her drift. When that storm struck, the wind and water had their way, and she ended up on the Diamonds. She finally had to be dynamited, and sent to the bottom to keep her from being a shipping hazard. She was determined to ride the top of that shoal. She must have been a ghost ship to any who saw her in the fog before she was destroyed, riding the top of that shoal, with those tall masts and tattered sails. Enough to make a man a land lubber. She was missed around here. We got used to her, and some of the boys fished her. Why, Wheeler Balance still has her capstan in front of his Texaco station. Maybe your grandfather will take you to Hatteras to take a look."

"Pop has to go to Hatteras pretty soon, Uncle Backie. He bought me a horse, and we got to go pick him up, don't we, Pop?" Blake's mind was never far from his horse. He was hatching a plan to get the horse as soon as he could manage it. This looked like a chance.

There had been hardly a pause before Blake's mind clicked from ghost ships, to the word "Hatteras." Both Luke and Ellie tipped forward to glance at him as his butt started wiggling on the swing.

"Yes, I believe we do, and Baxter, on that subject, I was going to ask if I could borrow your side-railed truck. I'm gonna need to stock the new barn with hay, and I could load up a bunch if I had your truck. Got any day in mind you can loan it out?" Charlie was killing two birds with one stone. When he looked at Blake, he had to laugh out loud. Blake looked like he had been struck by lightning. His eyes were closed, and his face was turned toward heaven.

Both Capt'n Charlie and Baxter looked at each other and grinned. He was so energetic—all boy, that one. He never could hold in an emotion. Even Baxter was wishing he had some young-uns at home. All his kids were grown, and their children were babies, not yet showing personality.

"Well, Charlie," Baxter gave him a wink the children couldn't see, "I might be using my truck for a couple of weeks, but after that we'll see."

Blake's face fell immediately—so fast, in fact, that he stopped wiggling. Uncle Baxter saw immediately the anxiety in the young-un and didn't want to be the cause of it. He smiled and cocked an eye over at

Blake. Then he slowly leaned over in his rocker, put his elbows on his knees, hands together, and turned his head to look at the dejected face.

"But you son, if you want to borrow my truck, I believe I can wait on my chores until you finish with it. How 'bout tomorrow?"

Blake jumped off the swing so fast, he almost dumped the other two. He was hopping around, giving his best impression of an Indian war dance—or, make that a Happy Dance.

The two older men rared back in their rockers and had a good chuckle. It was one of relief, and expelled a sign of happiness to replace the gloom they had been feeling. Times of shipwrecks and tragedies were not easy pictures to remove once the mind had a hold on them. They began looking forward to a trip to Hatteras. Both had friends there, and there was much news to exchange. Austin's Store would be one of the stops. Then Burrus's store, and finally, the ranch near the sound.

★ 10 ★

Progress

The kids rushed around that morning after an early breakfast, busying themselves and waiting until they could hear the rumble of Uncle Baxter's side-railed truck as it clanked and rattled over the sand tracks leading to the lighthouse compound. They sat on the fence and tearfully said good-bye to Ol' Tony and Big Roy. When the Coast Guard boys came to fetch them, Luke decided that he would like the opportunity to ride Ol' Tony one more time. He jumped on and rode him to the fork in the road—where it turned right to either go into the village or left to the Coast Guard station. When he looked back, he was surprised to see both Ellie and Blake on Big Roy for their one last ride. The Coast Guard boys sent to retrieve the pair of surf horses were walking down the sandy road behind the horses and children. When the riders got to the Coast Guard turnoff, they hopped off and each gave their ride a piece of apple and a big hug. They were all teary eyed, including the horses. The children knew this was not the last of it. They would make it a point to visit often.

The pain of this parting was not lost on the sailors. They wanted to fix it. They had gotten close to the family and knew the kids well. The kids were substitutes who reminded them of their own brothers and sisters or children, left behind when they were assigned to this faraway place. Urged on by the Coast Guard boys, who held out cupped hands for a leg up, the three again mounted their beloved first pets and proceeded to ride them all the way to the new stable.

What they could not see was Nett and Grandmom standing in the doorway with tears in their eyes also. Grandpop watched the scene from the top of the lighthouse and struggled to swallow the lump in his throat. He made up his mind that if he could buy them back, he would. It had not hit him just how close he had grown to these two huge animals. He was thinking about all the help they could do—pulling his wagon, hauling things, and for he and Grandmom to take a buggy ride, should the notion hit them. He didn't think he could let them go. With all these things racing through his mind, he began his descent down the stairs to catch up with the departing sailors to tell them what he had decided. After all, in some manner, the horses were his. For more than ten years he had had them. He was fuzzy on the particulars of the deal, it was so long ago, but he thought maybe he had only loaned them to the government. He knew he could keep Ol' Tony, but he was not sure about Big Roy. Ol' Tony had been with him before the lifesaving keeper's job, but Big Roy came after. Surely he could make that point. Another point he decided to put in his argument was the horses' age and their service to the government. Everybody, he thought, ought to be able to retire. They were old and didn't need to be pulling that heavy surfboat. In his head, he compiled a list of all the reasons for not letting those horses go, as he turned the key to the jalopy and started down the road to the station.

Charlie met Baxter almost at the fork. Baxter had already made the turn, and Charlie pulled to the side of the road. Window to window, the two talked about Charlie's decision. Baxter saw the emotion in Charlie's face, left his truck sitting in the tracks, and crawled into the jalopy beside his friend. Here they went, two old men trying not to let go of the past and willing to buck the U.S. government to keep a hold on their own. They reached the sailors, stopped, and offered them a ride. The sailors jumped onto the back of the old car, which had long ago been cut down to make a small truck.

"Get in, boys. No sense in getting all dusty. We'll take you to the station. That's where we're going. It's a big mistake to let those horses go. I'm gonna get them back!" Charlie said.

At the station the sailors began to talk about how much they did not want to take the horses away from the kids. They knew each had their own horse at home, but this kind of animal loved a herd, and the seamen didn't think that this separation was going to work. Both of the Coast Guard boys were familiar with horses, as they had much experience with them back home. They had been chosen to handle this duty because of their knowledge of horses. They offered to help Capt'n Charlie with his quest. But both older men refused any assistance. They were determined to win the day on their own.

"Good Capt'n, I can't see separating up a family like that. We were even sad to see the kids' reaction. Seems like those horses wouldn't know what to do in a strange place. We'll help you get them settled at your place in the woods. Besides, I think I overheard some of the fellows talking about using your barn at the compound for a while to house them, putting them out of everybody's way. I was thinking those horses were gonna get awfully lonely, so I'm glad you are planning to take them," said Paul, one of the sailors. He was familiar with the house in the Trent Woods, as he had been helping Nett move some of her things over the last couple of weeks.

"Thanks, Paul, I'll be needing that information to help make my point." Charlie looked at Baxter, and they knew this was not going to be as hard as they had imagined. The government didn't want these horses anyway. The Hatteras lifesaving station had the first motorized surfboat on the island, and as technology goes, it would appear that eventually, with the Coast Guard phasing out the Lifesaving Service, the new boys would be using motorized boats to launch, and only two horses to pull the boat to the ocean. Using four horses was necessary in bad weather to get a boat into the breakers, but things were changing with the addition of motorized craft being put in place. The old surfboats and all horses would be replaced. They reckoned they would take the position of doing the government a favor. That way, everybody would retain their authority, and the station captain could claim he was doing the Coast Guard a favor. Besides, it was Baxter Miller who was doing the asking. The Medal of Honor hero would not be denied.

The compound was looking a little bare, as most of the big things had already been moved. The last thing to go would be the horses and other livestock, pigs, chickens, and Twinkle the cow. They only had a couple of weeks before the government was scheduled to take over the light. The war was beginning to fill the front page of the paper every day, and they could not afford to get caught up in it. The admiral had already begun to ready the complex for surveillance. The bunker that the kids had found when playing pirate had been outfitted, and the path leading to it had been planted over with bushes to further hide it from prying eyes—plus the compound around the lighthouse was already off limits to anyone not approved to be in the area. Yep, they were expecting the U-boat to make a return visit, and this time, with a lookout on top of the lighthouse and a bunker for keeping a watch on landings by night, this family had to get out of the way—and fast.

Merchant ships were using this sea lane, from New York to South America, to ferry needed supplies up the coast. The Germans had discovered that sea highway toward the end of World War I and had found it to be a chink in the armor of the allies. Intelligence about the supply route that crept up the coast, to the shipyards of Hampton Roads and New York, would prove invaluable, especially since the merchant ships were not protected by military accompaniment. Goods from South

America—platinum from Colombia, cotton from Peru, petroleum from Mexico and Venezuela, and more—all were being shipped up the coast to the ports of the New York area for distribution across the Atlantic to Europe, now in dire need of supplies to fight the Germans. The war in Europe was no longer isolated overseas. The United States had also joined, making the opportunity for supplies to the front endless. With the Americans as an ally to Europe, the Germans had to stop the flow of goods to the battlefront, and the unprotected sea lanes seemed the least risky place to do it.

War in the past proved to be an endless pit of need. U.S. armed forces found their own supplies diminishing, as the demand grew to furnish the countries whose farms and factories were overrun by the destruction of cities and towns in the path of war. These supply lines ran from as far south as Argentina, Chile, and Brazil. From Brazil came coffee and much needed latex. The forests of the Amazon kept the trucks and planes in rubber for tires. From Argentina came industrial manufactured items, plus corn, wheat, beef, and wool. Chile probably provided one of the most important ingredients for the effort: copper and nitrates used in explosives.

Huge merchant ships from Europe were also traveling unprotected on the sea rivers of the Gulf Stream and the Labrador Currents. The men of the merchant marines were vulnerable as their ships were loaded with supplies more than weapons, and at times were also transporting troops to the war front. These ships were outfitted with very few defense mechanisms as they mostly had room for the items they were hauling. Military convoys to protect them were not available at the beginning of the war. Countries were racing to turn their factories from peacetime products to the necessities for war. There were not enough ships yet to spare destroyers to protect the massive supply vessels traveling up the coast. Fatio, the oldest of Capt'n Charlie's sons, had joined the merchant marines and seemed to be in more danger than those sons who had joined the Coast Guard, navy, or army. The Atlantic Coast was like a candy store to the hungry Third Reich. Their plan was to destroy Europe's ability to fight by cutting off their supply source. They simply had to cross the Atlantic and stop the ships before they ever reached their intended destination.

The kids were surprised to see Grandpop and Uncle Backie driving up right behind them as they urged the horses to the back of the Coast Guard station. Luke thought they had done something wrong and rushed up to his grandfather, ready to take the blame.

"Son, you children stay here. I'll be right back. Your Uncle Baxter and I have business at the captain's office. We won't be long." With that, Charlie and Baxter squared their shoulders and disappeared into the station.

About thirty minutes later, both men emerged from the station, each wearing a satisfied smirk.

"Boys," said Grandpop, "get back on those horses. We're taking them right back home. We might be able to keep them a while longer, but at any rate, they won't be leaving us today."

You never saw such happy faces as those kids displayed.

"Really, Pop?" Luke seemed so excited. "I know we can take care of them, I just know we can!"

Blake went into one of his happy dances, and Ellie joined him. It turned into a swinging contest as they grabbed hands and skipped around in a circle till Ellie fell down. She jumped up, brushed off her clothes, and gave Blake a look of disgust.

"Not so fast, Blake!" she chided. "You swing too hard."

"Sorry, are you hurt?" Blake never wanted to harm Ellie. She was not a child who could take a bruise. Born with a trait that caused her to bleed easily, the boys were always careful to protect her.

"Nah."

By then, Luke was on Ol' Tony again, and the other two forgot their slight disagreement and rushed to mount Big Roy. A bunch of happy children pulled on the reins to head the horses home.

The captain had made a deal, not so much the one he wanted, but better than the one he had. The two horses would go with them to the house in the Trent Woods. But since it was so near the Creeds Hill Lifesaving Station, and they did not have horses, Charlie had agreed to stable his two at Creeds Hill during the stormy season only, so he got them half the year, and Creeds Hill got them the rest. Also, the Lifesaving Service would pay for their keep. He had made a deal to rent them out. He and Baxter were both satisfied with the terms, as it allowed them access to the animals whenever they needed them. And, most of all, if the horses were at Creeds Hill, knowing those sailors were in need of them, then the family knew Ol' Tony and Big Roy would get the special attention they had become accustomed to—more so than if they went to the Cape Hatteras station, where there were already two, and two more might present a burden. Captain Charlie wanted his animals to be loved, like they were around him, not to be playing second fiddle to some other critters.

When the horses were finally settled into their own stalls, after having had a nice stretch of exercise, there was another matter to be tended to: Blake's very own horse.

The trip to Hatteras was under way. The kids thought it was a treat to ride in the back of Uncle Backie's side-rail truck. The chance to stand up and look around, and to move around safely, was something different. Luke and Blake made the most of it. Ellie mostly just watched, sitting on her knees hanging on to the slats of the truck. Uncle Baxter and Capt'n Charlie were in the front seat talking politics while the three kids were hanging over the rails, peeking through the slats, and taking in the three villages as they meandered down the inside road to the village at the end. They stopped for gas at Mr. Eph's store and watched intently as the gas pump's pretty orange fluid was transferred into the truck. They passed Mr. Ike's store and the Assembly of God church. Across the street was where Grandmom's brother Unaka lived. Charlie blew the horn in passing. There were lots of yards and houses they didn't get a chance to check out very often. Then Mr. Hollivey's store, where they purchased comic books. They passed Aunt Beck's house where Uncle Jack and Lindy went for pull candy parties with other young people. Then to the end of Buxton and their church. The ride through the village was a head turner, with each child pointing at various landmarks along the way. The kids never tired of getting out of the compound.

The sand got a little soft nearing the houses at the end of the village, before the deep, dark woods of the village of Trent. Boards had been placed on all the soft spots and were replaced frequently by almost everybody. Eliminating the soft spots, where cars got stuck, was an island effort, and they kept it up. Buxton Woods began to form, and the road became the best, as the pine needles from the canopy of trees provided a solid trail over the soft sand.

Going over Peter's Bridge signaled the end of Buxton and the beginning of Trent. There were fingers of several canals reaching into the land from the sound, and the locals had built makeshift bridges to allow a buggy or car to safely cross over without having to find a way around. The kids stared up at the pieces of sunshine punching through the heavy canopy of trees leading to the village of Trent. It was called Buxton Woods, and this was where the men went to hunt deer, turkey, rabbit, and the occasional wild hog. It was also where the wolves lived. In the woods, the children encountered hawks and falcons—birds that did not live at the shore. They looked for the peregrine falcon, who could swoop down at the rate of 200 miles an hour. Since they ate smaller birds, as well as small rodents, the hunt was fascinating to watch. The kids had been introduced to the birds that frequented the ocean shore, the sound area, and now the woods. The I spy game was fun, as they challenged each other to find the various nests in the trees from the larger birds. They were quite fascinated that their raven, Rook, was flying overhead, which meant the wolves were also on the trip, although it was impossible to see them.

In Trent they passed the house of a man who made the most elaborate martin boxes. The martin is a bird that eats more than 1,000 mosquitoes a day. Mr. Farrow's small houses were especially appealing to this type of bird, and he made some of them like a hotel, with several little holes and perches to house lots of bird families, which hopefully ate lots of mosquitoes. The "boxes" were put atop very tall poles, usually two pine trees stripped of limbs and bark, and nailed to each other end to end with braces on either side to hold them aloft, extending the length. This construction was necessary to keep the cats from climbing the pole and feasting on a mess of martins. Mr. Farrow had a booming business, as everyone in all the villages had more than one of the houses in their yard. It was a good business for a talented carver, and this island had an abundance of carvers and whittlers. Their specialties included martin boxes, carved ducks, and goose decoys, for the hunting season. Capt'n Charlie and Baxter favored men whose hand was talented enough to whittle out even the feathers of particular fowl, thus making the decoy so real looking it was truly an accurate depiction of the desired bird. Men took pride in their decoys. Many decoys were so treasured they were passed down to family members in their wills.

"Luke, think Pop will buy more martin boxes?" Blake was especially prone to mosquito bites, and Grandmom kept his exposed limbs lathered up with her special mosquito deterrent.

"I like that one with the blue roof." Ellie was already picking out the biggest one. She also was not looking forward to the mosquitoes that seemed to rule the woods. They were not bad on the ocean, but these kids had spent enough time in the woods to know the difference. They were now moving to the woods, and there would be a need for many martin boxes. The mosquitoes needed to get ready as the enemy was coming in the form of a tiny, hungry bird. Looked like everybody was getting ready for an invasion.

They passed the churches, houses, and store that made up Trent, and then the sand began again. Thankfully, recent rain caused it on this day to be packed down solid. The stretch between Trent and Hatteras villages was treacherous, as the island narrowed, the trees thinned out, and the sand took over. They went by the Creeds Hill Lifesaving Station, where Ol' Tony and Big Roy would summer. The kids were critical of this thing or that, vowing to make it a better place for their animals.

They saw Tandy's, a tavern where Uncle Jack, Lindy, and their friends went to drink beer and dance. Tandy's was also a place that was sort of infamous for its Saturday night fights. Seems the boys would occasionally challenge other boys from different villages to rumbles. Tandy's was where the Gray and Miller boys met Bill, Nett's husband. Bill Finnegan—the Irishman, they called him—could wipe the floor with all comers. Jack and Lindy were so impressed they were determined to add him to the family. Both introduced their sisters to him, but he was stuck on Nett, because he saw her playing the piano at the movie theater. That wedding was a proud day for more than Nett. Jack thought himself quite the matchmaker, and a lucky one at that. Little did Jack know at the time just how special Finnegan would be to his life. He would eventually train both Lindy and Jack in boxing. Jack would even end up winning the Golden Gloves in Texas. Tandy's tavern took as much credit as anyone, and it became known as the home of a famous boxer. He was one of their own.

There were other bars and taverns on the island, usually located on a desolate beach road just outside the villages. The community would not allow such a thing to be built inside the village, so the beach road it was. The Beacon was the one for Hatteras, and the Bucket of Blood was outside Kinnakeet. Buxton and Chicamacomico did not have a bar. Those who wished that kind of entertainment traveled to get it. Their goal was to find a champion to compete in boxing matches with the off-islanders who frequented the Casino in Nags Head.

Blake's favorite place appeared in the distance: Durant's lifesaving station. Here, in 1923, Billy Mitchell parked British-designed, American-built DeHavilland DH 4 plane to make ready for his grand experiment to introduce the capability of air power in war. He was Blake's hero. Mitchell was a frequent visitor to the island before and after World War I. An avid hunter, he was a member of the Gooseville Hunt Club in Hatteras. He stayed at the Atlantic View Hotel, and night after night he and locals, friends and hunting guides, sat around and played cards and told stories. Mitchell proved in 1923, at the cost of his career in the army, that a plane armed with bombs could sink a ship. His experiment took place off the coast of Cape Hatteras Island and settled a dispute. Sometimes losers in a wager are often disgruntled rather than gracious, and Mitchell was hounded for going against the top brass to prove a point. He was court-martialed for his efforts, which would eventually prove to win the next world war. Mitchell was much revered on the island, as they knew the man, not the general. Ever since he could read, Blake did his best to study all things "Billy Mitchell" and became quite the expert on the subject. Seeing any ground where his hero had walked was a thrill to the kid.

(Later, in World War II, most pilots flew the B-25 Mitchell aircraft. Exonerated at last.)

Many of the more expensive buildings were built and donated to Hatteras by men of great wealth, who appreciated the sport available on the island to hunt and fish. The Girls Club of Hatteras was also one of those endeavors. Albert Lyons, of Detroit, Michigan, gave this as a gift to the young girls of Hatteras. It was a large building housing shuffleboard, Ping-Pong tables, a tap dance studio, and access to magazines and books. The club required a small membership fee, which everyone gladly paid. It became a haven for all the girls of the island. They even put on plays for the community.

Besides the kindness of lovers of the island, the participation of the U.S. government had a lot to do with amenities that islanders enjoyed, especially during and after the Great Depression. Right after the First World War, the United States and its allies entered a financial recession that became particularly severe in 1920 and 1921, becoming a full-blown depression in some areas, with businesses failing and people in bread lines trying to live until jobs could be found. The war had employed everyone, and in some way every company, so when it was over, there was a huge scramble to make up what they lost. Most in the United States were severely affected by the crash of financial houses. They had been living on worthless money for a while, and when the war ended, countries all over the world were faced with starting over. They all needed to switch their factories from producing materials for war, no longer in demand, to supplying for the peace.

The effect of the Great Depression that began at the end of the 1920s was probably felt the least on the island. People here were used to little money and bartering for what they needed. The islanders did experience hardships, but strangely enough, they were not devastating. They were used to providing for themselves and their neighbors. Women took in ironing and washing, boys dropped out of school and joined some of the work camps set up by the government in order to add to the family income. Most helped each other. Grocery stores ran credits for people, as the owners just put the supplies on account and allowed people whom they knew could not pay to stock up with essentials anyway. Normally fishermen and carpenters always found a way. Fishermen suffered as prices dipped so low that they had to endure the consequences (one pound of fish sold for one-half cent). It was impossible to make a living. Carpenters were not able to find jobs, as there was no money for lumber.

Food prices were low, but there was no money to buy. Three cans of milk sold for twenty-five cents. Potatoes normally sold for three to five dollars a bushel, and during the Depression the price dropped to twelve cents a bushel. Twelve pounds of flour, twenty-five cents. One pound of beans, one penny. One hundred clams or oysters, a dime. Six pounds of ham, sixty cents. Beef, fourteen cents a pound. Butter was only nineteen cents, and one pound of corned beef was four cents. Sugar was impossible to get, so a substitute called penman was used.

It did not take long after experiencing these anomalies that the island went back to the life they had known. They ate more fish, rather than suffer the indignity of giving it away—also crabs, clams, oysters, and waterfowl. They grew their own gardens and ate from them. They tilled the ground using scraps of seafood, making their garden soils rich in nutrients. Lye and grease were used for soap. Since there was little flour, they ground corn from the garden for cornbread. The locals fared better than the rest of the country by living off the land, something they were quite used to doing.

Most joined the camps set up by the government to improve the communities, and that small paycheck provided money to start again. The efforts to bring the country back also reached Cape Hatteras. Used to living hand to mouth, this island began to experience something very unusual. While others were losing their jobs, the island began to experience an influx of jobs.

In order to put people back to work, the federal government chose programs that improved the infrastructure of the island, thus providing a paycheck to circulate through the community. Two government programs were initiated across the country. They were the Works Progress Administration (WPA) and the Civilian Conservation Corps (CCC), designed to put people back on their feet. The WPA shored up the schools and built community and government buildings, just perfect for island carpenters. The new work included erecting community buildings and improving schools. They funded and built the dipping vats on the island to run the cattle and horses through, thus ridding them of deadly ticks. They planted seedlings for replenishing the trees deforested in the late 1800s by off-island men who purchased large chunks of the island's forestland to cut for profit in supplying wood for building ships and also for sale to those whose voracious appetite for wood for whatever reason needed quenching. Cedar, which was plentiful on the island, was the desired wood for shipbuilding because of its deterrence to insects.

The CCC built sand fences and dunes to hold back the sea and made the island bridges more sturdy. They improved the sandy roads snaking through the villages. They planted trees on the north side of the island. Many men who came to work in the camps fell in love with and married local girls and stayed to become valuable members of all the communities. Most of all, both organizations provided a paycheck to those who did not have one, putting money in the businesses of the island and bringing new wealth to the people. The results of the Great Depression advanced the island's economy. No longer were they separated from the mainland. The newcomers began to devise plans to bring electricity, roads, and other creature comforts to those who saw no need for change. But change came anyway.

As Grandpop and the crew rode into the village of Hatteras, they passed the Atlantic View Hotel, the only hotel on the island, and across the road was the Beacon, named for the single light over the door. Then they drove over the slash creek bridge, which crossed an inland creek running the whole of the village. There were two stores rather close to each other, Austin's movie theater, the Girls Club, the docks, the porpoise factory, and fish houses for packing and shipping across the sound. This was the personality of Hatteras village. It offered a busy hub of activity that did not exist in Buxton or Trent, but had once existed in Kinnakeet. Hatteras village profited from the storm of 1846, which opened an inlet, taking the fish trade from the treacherous shoals of the Pamlico Sound and the inner village of Kinnakeet to Hatteras village and easier access to both sound and ocean.

The children knew that Blackbeard had walked this village, had traded on these docks, and hid from his pursuers with the help of the villagers. Luke knew that this was the place where Uncle Jabez and his niece Sabra had operated a shipping trade. Flashes of Uncle Jabez, Charles Jr., and Capt'n Johns crossed his mind, with the adventures he experienced on the docks, in one of his daydreams at the old house. His mind saw the docks now, and there was a faint recollection of the docks then, when he and Nathan had been kidnapped by the pirates. He knew it was only a dream, brought on by the magic book, but to him it was still a memory he could bring back as he daydreamed of times past.

Luke banged on the cab of the big truck to get his grandfather's attention.

"Pop, can we ride by the docks? We can't do it when we have Blake's horse attached, and the truck will be loaded."

At that, Capt'n Charlie made a left at Burrus's store and went down the sandy road running parallel to the sound, until they encountered huge fish houses, lots of boats, and the docks of Hatteras. Grandpop had heard of the new ferry Frazier Peele provided across the inlet to the island of Ocracoke. This was funded by Thomas Spurgeon Eaton, the son of a Reynolds Tobacco executive from New Bern, who wanted to become a part of the growing interest in the island. In 1935 he saw the economic need for both Hatteras and Ocracoke, and he also saw a profit for himself. Eaton, like most others of wealth who partook in the bounty that was Hatteras Island wildlife, also cared enough about the place to give back. They saw a need, realized they could help, and did. The ice plant and the electricity allowed the fishing community to widen their opportunities. Instead of being dependent on hauling to market only the oily fish, such as menhaden and spot, which would not spoil in transit and required no refrigeration, now they could set their nets for fresh fish of all kinds: croaker, mullet, Spanish mackerel, sturgeon, speckled and gray trout, cobia, and many other more profitable fish. Pop and Baxter remarked about Hatteras being the only village having electricity, and even though there was no wealthy benefactor for Buxton, they had found a way to rig electricity to their own homes. They felt they were just as powerful in purpose to get the job done for the whole island, if some of the local men interested in politics whose visions matched their own would pool their efforts to petition the government to join in the effort. With insight enough to fashion a ferry for Ocracoke, Frazier Peele was one of the innovators in Hatteras village. He also built a restaurant and ran a fish business transporting cargo to the mainland, giving the fishermen of the village a market for their catches.

The islanders were the kind of people who would work another man's nets if he was sick and needed the money for his family. The communities were tightly knit, caring for their sick, poor, handicapped, and mentally challenged and expected nothing in return. It was no surprise that outsiders coming on to this island fell into the same kind of community involvement. The kindnesses displayed by the islanders to strangers usually was returned manyfold.

The kids walked the docks and waited within earshot of Grandpop and Uncle Backie, who seemed to enjoy talking to the fishermen even more than Luke wanted to see the docks. He, Blake, and Ellie nosed around all the boats tied up, got on one that seemed to be the largest, and even went up in the wheelhouse. They had only seen a wheelhouse on wrecked ships washed ashore, so this was their first time seeing one intact. They saw the ice and electric plants that powered the fish houses, wandered around the tackle and hardware store, and explored as much as they could within sight of their grandfather. There was no end to the wonders of Hatteras village.

Grandpop decided the kids needed to go into at least one general store for candy before they got to Mr. Burrus's corral. The general stores in every village were mostly the same. Before the ferries, everything came from the mailboat. If someone wanted to get to the mainland, they had to book a seat on that bargelike boat. Usually that seat was a bag of mail. All strangers came to the island by way of the mailboat. This did not leave a very good impression to some, especially young teachers just out of college who imagined a wonderful paradise on an island off the coast of the United States. Hawaii, it was not. Once they crossed the sound sitting on a bag of mail, their expectations took on a more realistic view. In spite of first impressions, they went on to become islanders, and most never wanted to leave. Interested strangers brought culture and the arts to the children in the form of plays, which all, including the adults, participated in. They even wrote away and enlisted the services of musical groups and not-yet-discovered singers to perform on the stage of the Austin Movie House.

Progress came hard, but when it did, it was welcomed with open arms. The new ideas of the mainland became a jumping-off point to the innovators of the island. The new people—the WPA and boys, and those who came from parts west—brought to the island a new way of looking at things. They changed the island forever. People opened their homes to visiting teachers, preachers, entertainers, and families who, by way of the new government programs, had lost forever their son or daughter who came to work there and never left.

The trip to the general store was like looking at a three-dimensional catalog, like walking around the pages of Sears and Roebuck. General stores on the island carried everything. A man could even get a shave and a haircut in the general store. In Buxton, at Mr. Eph's, there was a red-and-white-striped barber pole in the back of the store, indicating the room where haircuts were available. There was also another general store that gave haircuts, and a person could tell which store a family patronized by the style of haircut they sported. Luke, Blake, and their family displayed the "Mr. Eph cut." There was a public phone, and the entire time they were there it was being used by one person or another. Besides foodstuffs, the walls of the store had shelves and hangers bulging with parts for cars, belts and hats, medicines, cosmetics, ribbon, gloves, and bobby pins, for women's hair. Ellie saw the prettiest compact she had ever seen. It was round, silver, and had small gemstones on it. She asked what it was, and the clerk, the daughter of the owner, opened it. Inside, it had a mirror. She wondered if she would ever have a thing like that. Seeing her admire it, Uncle Baxter bought it for her. There was no talking to Ellie after that. Constantly gazing into the mirror she ran into things, and even ignored things that might have also fascinated her. The mirror was a special item she couldn't wait to show Grandmom. It was like she had never seen herself before. She also noticed something else about the mirror. There were sparkles above her hair. She swished her hand over her head, and they moved but came back. Strange. Saint Travis was having a belly laugh in the clouds.

There were huge fishing nets and twine to mend them. Paint cans were stacked up to the ceiling in a corner, rope curled up in another, nails and hammers, wading boots that covered the body, and strange-looking hats with green plastic in the brim. And there was candy—a penny apiece, rows and rows of it, all kinds. Soft drinks were in a tub of ice, and Luke picked one. Instead of candy, he bought a sleeve of peanuts and dumped those nuts in his RC Cola, and drank and ate at the same time. He had seen Georgie Tolsen do that at Mr. Eph's store, and he had been wanting to try it ever since. He had a little trouble with drinking and chewing at the same time, but he finally got the hang of it and couldn't wait to show off for Uncle Jack. Ellie and Blake shared a bag full of assorted candy and intended to share it with Luke, who was not sharing his peanuts. Satisfied, the group got back in the truck to finally take the road to Mr. Burrus's ranch.

⋆ 11 ⋆

The Horse Whisperer

inally they were on their way to the other half of Hatteras village.
They reached the fork in the road, this time going straight across to
the other side. They passed the weather station where Ellie was born, as
the road continued running parallel to the sound, then to the canal that
extended past the porpoise factory and more fish houses.

This side of the village was home to the sound fishermen, whose nets
were visible on stakes stretching them out to be mended. More things
to see: different-looking houses, plus other docks that they had not
seen. This road went down a canal that ran through the inner village
and emptied at the end into the Pamlico Sound. The boats anchored
here were smaller, community fishing boats, belonging to those who got
up before dawn and set nets to catch salable fish, and smaller boats that
fished for themselves. It was more of a community dock than a commercial one. On this small canal fish houses were located, and the porpoise
factory was owned by Joseph K. Nye from New Bedford, Massachusetts,
and operated by a local man, William Rollinson. Here they harvested jaw
oil, body blubber, and skin to be used in various ways. The jaw oil was

used for watches, clocks, and similar delicate lubrication. A gallon of that kind of oil sold for twenty dollars.

There were not many houses on that road, but at the end, the whole area was the Burrus ranch. Baxter drove up to the house, and Mr. Burrus's wife came to the porch and indicated that her husband was in the back, dealing with some problem he was having there. Neither Baxter nor Charlie quite understood what exactly Mrs. Burrus had said and mistakenly thought she meant for the kids to find him at the end of the property in the barn. Charlie had already informed Willis Burrus that he would be needing a load of feed, and to pick up the horse, so they let the children out with the message they would return for their feed and animal, figuring to let Willis finish what he was doing. They felt they were doing him a favor by not interrupting his chores to fill their need. They were not in a hurry.

"Be back later," Capt'n Charlie yelled to Burrus's wife, and the men turned the truck around and headed back to the store for some local gossip. They always said, "You could sneeze in Hatteras, and somebody in Rodanthe would offer a tissue." That was how closely the villages kept up with what was happening on the island. Here would be two very important men of Buxton, visiting the general store, ready to trade Buxton news and ideas for Hatteras news and ideas. The two older men were as anxious to sit around the pickle barrel at Austin's General Merchandise and Dry Goods Store and pick up the flavor of the minds in Hatteras as the children were to help out Mr. Burrus. The war was on everyone's mind, and the men of Hatteras wanted to discuss things with Charlie Gray and Baxter Miller also, two men who were in on the ground floor of the activities going on around the lighthouse and Coast Guard complexes.

The men at the store earlier had passed the word of the bull session about to take place, and by the time Charlie and Baxter got back to the store, several men were waiting to hear what the Buxton men had to say. There was quite a collection of fishermen and business owners of Hatteras waiting for them when they returned.

The kids rushed to the back of the house where the fence held the herd of horses Mr. Burrus stabled. They were surprised at what they found. Evidently, unbeknownst to Mrs. Burrus, her husband was out in the sound, way out, up to his waist trying to coax at least a dozen of his prize horses out of the water and back to the corral. Somehow, the tall posts that were positioned out in the water and served to fence in a watery area used for the horses to swim and get relief from flies and mosquitoes had been blown down, and several of the horses had waded out to a part of the sound that had no fence. This was dangerous, as the horses were in danger of getting farther out than need be and not coming back. Mr. Burrus was not making progress. He was too far out to be heeded by the horses, and they continued to play and get deeper and deeper out into the sound, where they could not be corralled back to the shore. It did not look good.

The children stood for a minute to allow what they were watching to sink in. Luke started forward to help Mr. Burrus. He was familiar with the horses, as he had spent so much time on his weekends helping the rancher during the time he was waiting for Pegasus to be old enough to leave his mother. Mr. Burrus waved him back. It was too deep, and even though Luke was a good swimmer, there was no guarantee he could get to the correct horse to mount. The lead horse for the herd was the farthest out. Mr. Burrus began to wade back to shore. He passed a sandbar where some of the horses rested in only ankle-deep water, but try as he could, they would not leave the area where the lead horse was, and all his pulling and yanking was for nothing.

"I got to get the skiff and go after that horse. I ain't gonna get them back without him," he said to the kids.

"I'll go with you, sir," said Luke. "I've been around him before, and he knows me. If I stand up on the boat, I can hop on and ride him past the others, and hopefully they will follow."

The grown-up way he handled the request gave Mr. Burrus a start. With this, his admiration for Charlie Gray's grandchildren reached a level above the high esteem he already had from dealing with all of them—Luke with Pegasus, Ellie with Blue, and the antics of Blake as he became overwhelmed with the attention of a horse, one who displayed the unusual trait of picking out its owner.

When Mr. Burrus went to the long, narrow dock leading out into the sound where he kept his skiff, Luke pulled Ellie aside, and of course, Blake followed. His horse was also wading in the water, and he was determined to be in on all the plans to retrieve him. Luke kneeled down to remove his shoes and got next to Ellie's ear. Quietly and quickly he whispered, "Ellie, think you can get their attention? Think you can talk to them? We need for you to talk to that lead horse, the big brown one, out there, see it? Then, if you are successful, and I get on, switch your talking to one of the other horses, or all of them, however you do it, and make them come back." Luke had great confidence in Ellie's power to communicate with animals, and he figured with her giving it her full power, and holding hands with Blake, adding his power, he would also be on the same wave length, and the three of them could get those horses back to the corral.

"I'll try, and Luke," she looked straight at him, her blue-green eyes steady in his, and with a twinkle, she said, "I got this. I feel it already!"

Luke climbed into the boat with Mr. Burrus.

"Sir, we can do this. Don't worry."

Mr. Burrus looked very worried. He looked flushed and out of breath. He also didn't have any faith in a favorable outcome. He held these kids in high esteem, but he did not *really* know them. He had no hope this was going to be okay. He was looking at losing half his herd, and only had a twelve-year-old boy to fall back on. His feelings showed on his face, even though he was trying to hide his sinking heart from these kids.

Ellie and Blake held hands, and so did Saint Travis, Saint Brendan, and Saint Micah. This was the first time in a long time the kids had asked for their help. It was a challenge they were up to, and they were happy to be back in service. The deities had not anticipated this. They were primed to help the kids during the upcoming war, when they knew they would be needed, but this was a fun experience, one where nobody was in danger, and it would allow the kids to have the faith to practice more. They threw their colors in the sky, and as Ellie looked into the water at the horses, overhead she saw the blue and silver clouds forming, and she smiled.

"Look, Blake, at the clouds," she said.

Blake looked where she was pointing.

"I don't see anything," he said.

But she did, just like she had seen the sparkles in the mirror over her head. She saw clearly several puffs of clouds moving slowly across the sky, and she could have sworn one of them was shaped like a horse's head. She was all in now, and she squeezed Blake's hand and closed her eyes.

In her mind's eye, she saw a scattered herd of horses, wading around in sunlit gray-green water, with trails of sunlight stretching out from their feet. Then she saw a dark golden, almost brown horse ahead of them, and she concentrated on that one.

As Ellie and Blake were sending signals for the horses to come to them, Mr. Burrus and Luke neared the horse who was half walking and half swimming in the murky, sun-kissed waters of the sound.

She pictured Luke on the back of that horse. She concentrated hard.

The boat got close to the horse, and Mr. Burrus was talking softly to the animal the whole time. Luke stood up in the back of the boat, and with the horse's back almost even with the rise of the boat, he too started gently talking to the horse, reminding him that they had met before, and would he mind if he got on him for a little ride?

"Just a little ride, not too long, don't be afraid, we'll have fun," he kept whispering in a quiet voice.

The horse's eyes widened when he saw Luke, and he snorted several times and shook his majestic head. His tail was straight out now, floating on the water. Luke reached over, grabbed a handful of mane, and swiftly hopped over onto his back, almost falling over to the other side. The horse was so wet, Luke had to scramble to right himself before he fell off completely. The horse was not spooked. He hardly felt it at all. Any weight was countered by the buoyancy of the water. He had been calmed by forces unknown and accepted the rider as if it was meant to be.

Luke gently guided the horse with his knees away from the boat, and out in the open water. He felt if he gave this fine animal the swim he wanted, he would be better able to coax him toward the sandbar where the others were wading.

Ellie's eyes were still closed. She sat down, dragging Blake with her. The little guy plopped to the ground without opening his eyes. He was determined to use Ellie's power, and he did not want to break concentration, so he just kept to the plan. The squeeze of Ellie's grip told him the task had not yet been completed. After a bit, Ellie's grip lightened, and she moved her shoulder to him.

"We did it!" she said. "Now we have to get Spirit back. Ready?"

"Ready!" Blake's heart was racing. This was the most important part to him. He didn't yet realize the power one horse had over the herd, but he was learning. In his mind, they should have started on Spirit, but he was outnumbered on some things, and this was one of them.

Ellie began to picture the brown horse, with his golden halo, walking in front of all the other horses, back to the area of the corral. Blake just sent the message, *Spirit, come to me.* He was beginning to gain confidence in his power and was relaxed by Ellie, just touching, not squeezing her hand. The touch was all he needed.

Luke and the lead horse swam a little ways back, Luke hugging his mighty neck and patting him as they rose from the deep water to a place where the horse could touch the bottom. With his knees, he began to guide the horse to the sandbar. Mr. Burrus poled around away from the horse and rider, amazed at what he was watching. By this time, Mrs. Burrus had glanced out the kitchen window and seen the theater playing out in the sound. She wiped her hands on her apron and slipped out of her shoes. She stuck her feet in the white rubber fishing boots she used when she went to the barn or into the chicken yard for eggs. She rushed out the kitchen's screened door, being careful not to let it slam so as not to spook the animals who were left still grazing in the pasture by the shore. She took her position standing in the shallow of the sound, shielding her eyes, as she strained to see what was happening. The horses on the sandbar were her worry, and why did Willis let that child ride the lead horse around in the sound? She didn't yell out anything. She just stood there anxiously.

He'd better not lose one of Mr. Charlie's kids, she thought.

To Mr. Burrus's surprise, the horses stepped off the sandbar into knee-deep water and started toward the horse they loved to follow. Luke whistled and clicked his tongue to the roof of his mouth as he beckoned the horses to follow him. Slowly, the train of horses with their engine clicking them forward fell in line behind the brown horse. Mr. Burrus was left where he was, with his hand frozen on the tall shove pole in amazement. He had no thoughts. He snapped out of it as the horses moved ever steadily toward the shore. If he didn't get to shoving that thing in the soft sandy bottom of the shallow sound, he was going to be left out there in the water.

The clouds drifted away, and the one that was the horse's head began to re-form with the drift of wind to resemble more of a unicorn than a horse. As Ellie stared at the clouds changing formation, she smiled. She loved unicorns. As she continued to drift with the cloud, the silver thread now led her to a trail of fluff that resembled a wolf, Then another gust erased the wolf to achieve a more rounded shape as clouds collected up until she could see the white form of her dolphin. All of this, and from the corner of her eye, she could see the horses walking toward them on the shore, led by the brown horse, with Luke as its rider.

Mr. Burrus poled the boat around toward the dock and tied it to one of the posts and crawled out of it. He was unsteady as he walked the planks of the pier and stepped cautiously to the ground. His legs were weak. He had been in the water for a long time, and at his age, he was tired of dragging his feet forward and pulling heavily against his own weight as he chased the horse out to deeper and deeper water. He needed to sit down. Mrs. Burrus hurried over to her husband and hooked her arm under his, grabbed hold of his waist, and they both leaned on each other as they approached the kids.

Luke climbed down from the brown horse and patted him on the neck. He went over to the feed bucket hanging by its handle on one of the posts of the enclosure and gave a handful to his new friend.

"I can do better than that!" said Mr. Burrus as he came closer. "Alice, go get some carrots. You will not believe what has just happened." He grabbed a nearby wooden bucket, turned it over, and sat down, wiping his forehead with the forearm of the sleeve of his shirt.

"Young-uns, how can I thank you? You've just saved my life and my livelihood. Reckon Charlie Gray would sell you to me? I got room in my house for all of you." At that he gave Luke a big grin and held out his hand. When Luke extended his, he had to brace back, as Mr. Burrus used it as a "pull up" and almost pulled the child over. Luke tugged hard, using the bulk of what weight he had, and got Mr. Burrus to his feet.

"Son, I ain't never seen such a thing. That horse don't go to nobody, and here's something for your thinking cap: he's never been ridden!" At that Willis grabbed the boy and put him in the biggest hug, strong and tight. Luke thought that Mr. Willis was crying, as he could feel his body shaking slightly against his.

As the grip was loosened, Luke pulled back. "You okay, sir?" he asked. "That was fun, and sorry I scared you, but I thought maybe the horse wanted to get that swim in, and I was thinking he needed to do that in order to do something for me. I'm sorry if I frightened you, honest, I didn't mean to. It just felt like the right thing to do."

"Son, don't you apologize to me for nothing! No sir, nothing! I don't know what would have happened to me or those horses if you hadn't come along."

"Mr. Willis, you might not believe this, but Ellie and Blake helped, too." He couldn't tell him the truth, and he couldn't take all the credit.

Mrs. Willis appeared with a handful of carrots, and the three began breaking off pieces for the horses. Blake gave Spirit the biggest piece, and they shared a gaze at each other. It was as if Spirit knew he was leaving with this kid.

"Well, whatever you think, son, but I'm telling you, for a minute there, I thought I was a goner. Thought for sure I was cashing in my chips, till you came along. The wind blew down that part of the fence, and I hadn't noticed till I saw the horses so far out. Nothing to do but go out after them. Seemed the farther I went, the farther they went. 'T'wer'n't lookin' so good till you came. Come sit on the veranda with me for a while. I need to sit down. Wait, let me put this pole across that broken part so's they don't get past to the open sound again till I can get it fixed." Mr. Willis started toward the water again.

"Wait, Mr. Willis. Me and Blake can do it. Blake's been wanting to get wet since he got here, haven't you, Blake?" He smiled at the grinning face looking back at him.

Blake knelt down to untie his shoes and threw them over to the side.

"Race you!" challenged Blake, and he took off toward the sound, with Luke right behind him.

"Grab that pole!" Mr. Burrus yelled behind them. He turned to see the pretty face of Ellie right under his gaze, holding out her arm to steady him. He put his hand on her shoulder, and they walked to the front porch. Mr. Burrus sat down in one of the many rockers there, and Ellie took another. Mrs. Burrus joined them, but only for a minute. She looked at the two new friends and got up and went into the house. When she returned she had a tray with a carton of milk, four glasses, and a plateful of ginger snap cookies. These cookies did not require huge amounts of sugar, as the island was beginning to feel the effects of what would later become a ration of certain foods.

When Ellie looked out at the clouds, she saw the fluffs of hundreds of little balls, all bordered in light blue and gray edges, not moving, not connected, not making any faces. Just quietly drifting clouds. She could smell the salt of the sound, the aroma of horses, and the familiar tinge of ginger. Grandmom's gingerbread was one of her favorites. This was a happy day.

The boys came back wet and laughing. It was so much fun to go swimming in their clothes. The weather was still hot, and they would dry quickly, but they didn't care. Cookies! Swimming in the sound and cookies. Doesn't get better than that.

There was an unspoken look between Luke and Blake. Luke was reminded of the day he and Manteo had raced against the others out in the sound, and when he won, Wematin and Blake had jumped from their boat where they were watching, and all four frolicked in the sound. It was on a day just like this one.

⋆ 12 ⋆

A New Guy in Town

Charlie and Baxter heard the big grandfather clock in the corner of the store as it chimed one note for the half hour. Charlie looked up, and his heart sank.

"Baxter, it's gettin' late, and the kids are with poor Willis, probably driving him crazy. And," he whispered, "we haven't given them anything to eat. Dessa will kill me! Let's wrap this up and get on the road. With all the loading, it'll be dark by the time we get to the woods."

Then to the group of friends sitting around the store he said, "Boys, got to go. . . . Just realized the time, and the kids are running Willis ragged, I'm sure. He'll probably add to the price of the horse. Got a lot on my mind, but let's do this again. I'm goin' down to see Capt'n Levene sometime this week, and I'll get the feel of Chicamacomico. They're right in the middle of this thing, being on that stretch of beach. Levene can usually judge the wind of things. Been a pleasure, boys! Might be back dragging a horse, forgot to feed the kids, so I'll probably let them run in for ice cream."

When Mrs. Austin heard that, she jumped right in, they hadn't heard a peep from her till then. "No, sir, you will not send those little young-uns in for ice cream. That's not food. By the time you get back, I'll have a box lunch for all of you. Why, Odessa would never forgive me if she knew I let her children go hungry. And, Youahhh! Men! sat right here and let those young-uns starve so's you could talk! I'm gonna fix you both one also, but not because you deserve it but I don't want you eating theirs. Now, go on, get those kids, and send in the oldest." She gave them a wink. "Give Odessa my regards, tell her the churches are planning an end-of-summer gathering, and I'll be in touch." With that she spun on her heel and disappeared to a kitchen located somewhere, probably upstairs or out back, wherever, but her instructions were clear and heeded by the two abashed men. The island women were strong and not to be messed with. They were not wilting flowers hovering in the background, but were beautiful sunflowers who had sturdy backbones.

Baxter also bid his farewells and shook hands all around. "Good talking with you, boys. Look me up when you get to the village. Things are happening fast now."

Both men rushed out the door, with Capt'n Charlie leading the way. The captain was a fast walker, which is why Ellie stood at the door of the keeper's quarters whenever he had a business meeting in town or in Manteo. She was his "hat girl," and her job was to hand him his hat as he headed out the door. She was so trained in his ways, she would peep around the corners to see what he was wearing so that she could select the right hat. All, except the uniform hat, were brown fedoras, but there was a difference in each, and she knew which hat went with which destination. The county commissioner hat was special, his Sunday hat was special, his everyday hat was particular. Each had a purpose, and they were all brown.

The side-railed truck pulled up in the yard in front of the Burrus house. The two men got out and walked to the front porch where Willis was sitting in an old rocker looking plumb tuckered out.

"Willis, looks like they ran you a new one," said Charlie. "They weren't too much trouble, were they? Me 'n' Baxter lost track of time. Ready for us to load that hay?"

He extended his hand as he got to the steps, and Baxter did the same. Both sat down in the rockers beside Willis, and Mrs. Burrus came to the door.

"You men want a cool drink?" she said.

"Much obliged, Miss Alice, kind of you to ask, but we got to get going. After we leave here we have to haul that hay up to the Trent Woods. My family and I are moving over there, I guess you heard." Charlie knew everyone knew the circumstances of his move. As news raced around the island, he knew that would be a choice piece. "Ready, Willis?"

Willis Burrus rocked one more time, till he had to lift his weary body off that chair and get back to work. "I got a tale to tell you boys. Yessir, a tale to tell."

Baxter said, "Uh-oh," and looked at Charlie. "Kids aren't in trouble, are they? I'll take responsibility along with Charlie to make it right."

As they descended the several steps needed to hoist the house above the tide line, he put his hand on Charlie's shoulder and smiled at Baxter.

"Capt'n, you got some special kids there—special, they definitely are. Hard to tell where to begin, might even let them tell it. I'd like to hear what they thought of what just happened."

"Don't sound good. You sure they didn't cause you bother?" Charlie looked puzzled.

"Don't suppose we can do anything to help fix things?" Baxter was all for taking up for these young-uns. He had spent enough time with the little wigglers, he didn't want them to cause problems for anyone.

"Just you wait, hold on. There's a tale here." Willis couldn't stop smiling, and it was confusing to both Charlie and Baxter.

They rounded the corner of the house and looked at the corral. Blake was bareback on his new treasure, Spirit. Luke was bareback on some huge brown horse, and Ellie was over in the herd petting a pretty and very young colt. The colt's legs were still wobbly, but the mother just turned her head and lowered down to nudge and nuzzle both Ellie and the colt. Quite a scene, one that added to the puzzlement. Both boys immediately swung their legs over their mounts and dropped down to hit the ground running when they saw their grandfather.

"Pop!" Luke yelled. "Did you see me riding that big brown? He's never been ridden before, Mr. Willis said."

"Pop!" Blake yelled out right after, hardly waiting for his brother to finish "Did you see me on Spirit? He's my bestest friend already." The three men just started laughing, for as Blake ran to his grandpop, the red horse lumbered along right behind him, without so much as an encouragement.

"Ever seen anything like that?" Willis Burrus said. "Charlie, you ain't heard nothin' yet!"

"You kids behave yourselves?" This was all bewildering to both Charlie and Baxter. "Mr. Willis says you got a tale to tell."

Ellie walked over to her grandfather and hugged his waist. "We were all good, Pop. Luke saved Mr. Willis's herd." She blurted it out so fast, Luke turned quickly.

"Let me tell it," he said. "I know all the good parts."

With that, as they all walked to the truck to back it up to the area where they would load the hay, Luke began his story of the "rescue." He would tell a little, and Willis Burrus would throw in a better version, giving much favor to the acts Luke had committed. They both talked and told the tale, while Blake and Ellie nodded. The events of the day were so interesting, the group had stopped before they reached the truck. They all stood in a circle quite a ways from their destination, listening intently to the yarn spun by the tall young boy. Ellie and Blake gave it weight by nodding in agreement during the most exciting parts.

"He almost fell off," interjected Blake, when Luke reached the part where he mounted the brown horse in the water.

When everyone seemed to have gotten the story out, and the two who were listening had a good understanding of it, Capt'n Charlie said, "Sounds like this was quite the day. No wonder you were tuckered out, Willis. Good thing it turned out okay."

"I helped, too!" Blake interjected.

Uncle Baxter reached over and ruffled his hair. "And just how was that?" he said to his favorite dancer.

"What did you do, son?" Capt'n Charlie asked.

That question threw Blake, and he saw Luke shoot him a look, and Ellie punched him.

"We thought," Blake answered sheepishly and in that small voice that told his grandfather that Blake was wishing he had never spoken up, because he was thinking maybe he had gotten himself in trouble.

Pop reached over and pulled Blake to his side, gave him a hip hug, and said, "You probably did help, little man. You always do."

Blake smiled as he felt that his grandfather understood what he was talking about, even though neither Uncle Baxter nor Mr. Willis did. His grandfather supported him, and that was all that mattered.

As they once again began walking to the truck, Capt'n Charlie sent the two boys to stand over by the waiting bundles of hay and told Ellie to bid farewell to her new friend, the newborn colt.

When the children were out of the way, Willis Burrus told Charlie the truth of all that had transpired that day, from before the kids got there to the cookies and milk on the porch. "Ain't never seen kids like yourn. No sir, never in my born days have I seen a kid that young tackle a task like that without a single hesitation. He showed no fear. And those other two, yes, they did help. I don't know how, but they were calm and stayed out of the way, and just waited for it all to right itself, never once were a problem. Looked to me like they were praying, don't know, but looked to me they was in prayer. Now I know that ain't true, but it looked like that." When he finished, he had the look of a man who had just been relieved of a huge burden.

Charlie Gray knew his children. No, it wasn't prayer that Willis observed. It was akin to it, but it was something different. He puffed up with pride and put his arm around Willis Burrus's shoulder.

"Willis, my man, I live and learn with those young-uns every day. Don't nobody quite understand them 'cept Dessa. I'm sort of an outsider, too. They are more Jennette than Gray, and it is something to live with, I tell you. They amaze me every day." He was counting on Willis knowing the gossip surrounding the Jennette women, and hopefully he was putting two and two together.

"I'd be proud to have them ride down here when they get a little older and visit me and Alice sometime. I think I'm smitten. and I could use some good help with these horses. Any day they want. Don't even have to alert me. I'd be happy to see them anytime." Willis Burrus really did wish they would spend time with him and his horses. That was no empty compliment.

Charlie went in the back of the truck to stack, and with Willis, Baxter, and Luke working the hay, they got the truck loaded. Then they tackled the question of the horse.

The horse had been walking around behind Blake since they arrived, following him like a dog would follow his master, just staying close. Finally Uncle Baxter cupped his hands and gave Blake a leg up, and later they looked at the two and almost doubled over with laughter. Blake was so relaxed, he had draped himself over the horse with his head turned sideways resting on the black mane and turned toward the ones talking, with his arms dangling down over the horse's neck, and his legs loose on either side. He looked for all the world like a blanket. But the horse! The horse was accepting that unconventional rider and seemed to take care not to drop him.

Pop and Mr. Willis began bargaining over a saddle for Blake. Burrus's ranch also was like a livery stable and saddlery, with all the trappings. There was even a corner where he acted most like a blacksmith, shoeing horses. Willis wanted to throw the saddle in for free, but Charlie was having none of that. They dickered over the price of each piece. Willis went low, and Charlie would refuse the lower price for a higher one, more in line with what he considered to be fair.

Baxter laughed on the way home, talking to Charlie about how funny it was to stand there and have a man keep raising the price—not the seller, but the buyer. It was the most fandangled discussion he had witnessed in all his years of haggling. Blake got the horse and all the trimmings, at a good price—not free, but a decent, fair price.

Saying their good-byes, the group piled into and onto the truck. Ellie got in front with her grandfather and uncle, with Luke and Blake riding the hay in the back. Spirit was tied behind. He and Blake were eye to eye on the return trip, just what Blake wanted.

They stopped back by Austin's store, picked up the five small brown bags from Mrs. Austin, and each ate their delicious food, like it was the best they had ever had. They were all hungry, and Mrs. Austin had put in fried chicken, potato salad in a small Dixie cup with a little ice cream spoon from the store, and a huge piece of coconut cake, which was Baxter's favorite. Inside paper bags for the children, she had placed several pieces of penny candy. Baxter vowed to get Josephine to make him a coconut cake soon as he got home.

They left Hatteras village on the way to Trent Woods. On the way home, they got Ellie's version of the story. They expressed worry to each other about all the stress and energy their friend Willis Burrus had been through that day. A man's heart can only take so much, but they were glad Luke had reacted just like he did. Uncle Baxter thought he might be president one day.

The big clattering truck lumbered up the two-track road in the woods leading up to the house on the hill. The boys in the back were dodging tree limbs and bushes as they rumbled through the thick forest. Grandpop and Luke both knew they had to clear some brush to widen the sides of the road if they were going to be living here. Capt'n Charlie was thinking about the car he was bound to buy, as he needed to relinquish the one the government had loaned him. He would be using the jalopy until he could make up his mind what to purchase. He had seen several of the newer ones and was anxious to try one of those. It was exciting, but not necessary. It could wait until some other things were taken care of. Then he smiled as he thought about how many horses they were going to have, so transportation would not be a problem. Of course, he had to think of the women, so his thoughts went back again to the car.

They reached the house, and Blake hopped off his perch on the hay to unloose his horse, and he immediately pulled him over to the steps of the front veranda and mounted him. No saddle, no bridle, no blanket, just Blake, and he walked him around to the barn, ducked his head as they went inside, and, still atop his prized possession, he began to pick out the stall he wanted. Meanwhile, Baxter maneuvered the truck around to back up to the barn. Charlie got out and climbed the ladder to the hayloft. He readied the pulley connected to the block-and-tackle piece, with a huge hook at the end of the rope, to bring up the hay. Luke stayed on the hay to hook it up, and Baxter was the guide. They took most of the afternoon getting that hay put away, out of the rain and off the ground, in a place where it would not rot. While Blake and Spirit walked around, Ellie had disappeared inside.

Theo, Blake's wolf, stood in the shadow of the woods at the edge of the yard and observed. Blake spotted him and slowly led the horse in that direction. When he got close, within speaking distance, he talked quietly to both the horse and the wolf about being friends. He had a new buddy, but he never wanted his grand wolf to feel left out, as if they had feelings like that. What Blake did not know was that the wolf had visited the colt before the end of its first year and had prepared him for his charge. Those nighttime meetings had been the reason the horse was so attached at the sight of the boy when he first visited the ranch. The introduction was good, but not necessary.

When the men were finishing up, hoisting the hay into the second-story hayloft, the jalopy showed up with Nett and Grandmom and a load of stuff. They had a couple of the Coast Guard boys in the back to help with the unloading.

"Shoulda been here a little bit ago," yelled out Capt'n Charlie from the loft. "We could have used you."

"Yes, sir," said one of the boys as he began to unload some of the boxes Nett had packed. She and Grandmom began directing them where to go. Charlie was familiar with that drill and actually felt sorry for them. He was glad they didn't have to deal with the hay and the boxes. That might have been too much. But the sailors would have rather been loading hay than listening to these women. However, they were happy to be the ones chosen to help, as the Coast Guard had volunteered to assist Keeper Gray in the move. They liked the old house. It was magical to them, it gave them a good feeling, and they had never seen anything quite like it. Blake rode up to the steps to greet his mother and grandmom, and to show off his new horse to the two seamen. They took some time to admire the beautiful red steed, then went back to work.

Watching Blake, Grandpop thought that the kid would never again let his feet touch the ground, as long as he had that horse. The novelty of a new ride had sort of worn off the other two, but this new one would start things up again, and Charlie imagined there would begin to be more excursions now that all three had a horse. He thought to himself that maybe he better have a talk with them tonight, before he lost them to the beach, the sound, or the woods. He'd better set some ground rules. These were adventurous kids, and he needed to keep a tight line on them.

Baxter walked around the old house for the first time in a while. He hadn't been there since he, his boys, and Bill had hooked up the generator. It was magnificent but had its drawbacks. It was a little ways from the sound, a little too far from the village, and he'd heard of the wolves. The wolves were legendary. There had even been stories of the Civil War, when the federal soldiers occupying the island had chosen that house to commandeer for a headquarters, and how they had to leave because of the wolves. Heard tell they even tried to shoot them, even sent a group of troops to clean them out. But they never saw them, only heard them, and the horses began to refuse to climb the hill to the house and bolted when they were put in the barn, so the idea was abandoned. There was even talk of burning it down, but they couldn't even get close enough for that, so they let it be. Burning, though a harsh retaliation against the house, would have taken too many blue coats to keep the fire from consuming the entire woods. The idea was canceled as an abundance of caution.

Baxter was fascinated with the indoor-outdoor toilet and vowed to make one for himself. He thought it was the wave of the future. He and Charlie took time to talk about a shower on the back porch. Seemed water was easily drawn from the ground, and the generator was so big, it could run a pump as well as a house. After all, Charlie now had two, as the Coast Guard was now responsible for the keeper's quarters and didn't need the generator Finnegan had installed, thus giving another to the house in Trent Woods. If those two monster engines could run a ship, they could certainly run Charlie's operation. These island men were becoming all in on progress.

Baxter and Charlie also walked over to the boathouse and examined the skiff that had been left there, probably by Sabra's twin boys. They observed the shove poles and oars still in fair condition, and looked at the now-rotten net and threw some of it into the back of Baxter's truck to be taken to the trash pile down back of the hill behind Baxter's house. Everybody had a trash heap behind their house, in an area obscured from their house, and when it got tall, they either burned it, or buried it. Charlie needed to find a place here for trash. Burning was going to be a problem, as he had to be careful not to burn down the woods.

Nett and Grandmom were in the house, telling the sailors what to do, and Ellie was in there exploring. She was in her room, punching on everything to see if there was a secret passage she might have overlooked before. So far, nothing. She opened the windows to let in fresh air and get rid of the moldy smell of the heavy curtains and chairs. She just knew there was something special about this room, *her* room, but she just hadn't found it yet. But she would.

Luke was in the barn, scoping out the stall for Gus and the other big surf horses, for whom he now felt a new connection and a responsibility on their behalf. Blake wandered in, still astride Spirit, and they began trying to sort things out. As they talked, Blake assumed his blanket position on the horse, with his head turned toward Luke. Even Luke had to laugh at how ridiculous his little brother looked. And how did the horse tolerate it? They came to an agreement, one that left Ellie's horse down at the end. She was not there to put a word in, so she had to take what was left. Neither one of the boys thought it would work out the way they had planned. They knew it all depended on Ellie and her choice. It always did. But, for now, they could be satisfied they had pulled one over on her, even if it was only for a day.

Grandmom was walking around the yard with one of the seamen, pointing out the chicken coop and giving instructions on shoring it up. She also showed where she wanted a pigpen constructed, and where she wanted a ditch dug to throw the trash for burning. Grandmom was as savvy a woman as existed on the island. She was a Jennette, and she had a willful mind of her own. She also pointed out a space to be cleared for pasture. With five horses and a cow, they could not be cooped up in the barn all day long, no matter if the barn was a big one.

As the sun began to hover over the sound, they all decided it was time to wrap it up. Everybody needed to get out of here before it got dark. They could see the path of the sun through the thick overhead, and as the sun moved, the area it left behind became dark, as the canopy of trees took over. They had to clear the road if they wanted to be there late in the evening. There was much to be done, and they certainly couldn't do it all today. Also, everybody was getting hungry. So, Baxter and Charlie, in the cab of the big truck, and the sailors in the back bed of the truck with the boys, left for the village, Spirit tied to the back. Finally, Blake was using his own two feet. Nett, Ellie, and Grandmom Odessa climbed into the jalopy and followed the strange caravan in front.

Theo was joined by Twylah and Rafe, stretched out on the ground, guarding the house till the family returned. They would eventually wander back and forth from the mansion on the hill to the lighthouse complex checking on everything. Wherever the children were, there they were also. They might have been guarding this house forever, protecting it for these kids. Who knew? What the kids knew was that they were comfortable that the wolves would always be around.

An old hoot owl in the dark of the trees, somewhere up above, gave out a burst—maybe a good-bye, maybe a hello. The trees had golden tips as the sun began to sink toward the sound, giving out shards of light as they neared the tall pines. Their needles had made a good solid road to the house, but the bushes and palmetto plants were moving closer and closer to the road. Once in a while they spotted delicate circles of white belonging to the tall dogwood trees that grew naturally in the woods, sprinkled along with the delicate pink flowers that popped out on the lacy leaves of the mimosa tree. There were lots of things they would all be finding out once they moved.

It had been a long day. At the keeper's quarters, Grandmom sent everybody to get cleaned up and ready for the fried chicken she was about to make. Not a single soul objected. Nobody protested at having already had fried chicken from somebody else's kitchen. To the person, they all knew better. They just smiled, went their separate ways, and prepared to sit down to the table. They were all looking forward to relating the events of the day to Grandmom and Nett. Even Charlie was anxious to get in on the story. He knew he would need to calm the women down when they heard of Luke's part out in the sound. It was a manly task that the young feller had performed, and his grandfather was not about to have it ruined by a bunch of female objections. In his mind, his grandson might have saved his friend's life. Willis had not looked good when they found him resting on the porch of his home. Both Charlie and Baxter had been worried. Heart attacks were familiar to the islanders. Many of the men worked far beyond their capabilities. This was a good life, but not an easy one.

Blake was the last to be cleaned up. He went straightaway with Spirit to the barn and settled the beautiful red horse in the stall. He had already spent days cleaning the spot for his horse and making it comfortable for the new resident. All the trappings Pop had bought him were put in their place, alongside the gear belonging to the other horses. Luke's horse, Pegasus, had the least, as Luke was a blanket-and-bareback kind of guy. Eventually he would also need a saddle, but right now, he didn't want one. Blake lined up his brushes, curry combs, hoof pick, and mane comb. He hung the bridle inside the stall, collected up his old saddle pack and filled it with things Blake, straightened out the reins, gave the saddle a wipe, and not until Luke came to pry him out of the barn to get cleaned up for supper did he leave. When he finally did come to the table, he asked if he might have his supper in the barn. That brought about a chorus of laughter. He gave them one of his one-sided smiles and bowed his head for grace.

★ 13 ★

Storm!

Lord of the winds! I feel thee nigh,
I know thy breath in the burning sky!
And I wait, with a thrill in every vein,
For the coming of the hurricane!
And lo! On the wing of the heavy gales,
Through the boundless arch of heaven he sails.
Silent and slow, and terribly strong,
The mighty shadow is borne along,
Like the dark eternity to come;
While the world below, dismayed and dumb
Through the calm of the thick hot atmosphere
Looks up at its gloomy folds with fear.

—*William Cullen Bryant,*
"The Hurricane"

"They say on Pawley's Island, in South Carolina, that there walks a gray man who shows himself on the shore days before a storm to warn of impending destruction." This was the story Grandpop began with, as he attempted to calm the children and put them to bed. They almost were lost to the family, as each day, right after breakfast, they went to the barn, cleaned the area, brushed Ol' Tony and Big Roy, fed them, and after completing all the chores expected of them, they saddled up and rode down the beach to the mansion on the hill in the woods. This day had been long.

Also that day, they had cleaned yet another barn at the new house and here they organized their stalls—Ellie getting the first one, Blake the one in the middle, and Luke getting the last stall. According to Ellie, Luke's horse was the lightest, being golden with pure white mane and tail, allowing him to be seen better in the dark barn. Blake, having the next lightest horse, the red, got the middle, and Ellie, whose horse was black and the hardest to see, was nearer the door. It took them quite a while to come to Ellie's conclusion, but as expected, they finally agreed the horses would be placed in order of color.

On the right side of the huge barn, nearest the doors, was the tack room, housing all equipment: shovels, pitchforks, buckets, tubs, chests with blankets, and everything Grandpop. Located farther into the structure were the three smaller units housing the children's horses. These stalls also had room for hanging personal items for each horse, in addition to their saddles. Also, because of Capt'n Charlie's penchant for being a pack rat, they each secured one of the many wooden chests their grandfather saved from the equipment sent to him. Ellie got the most special one, a wardrobe chest, which had washed up on the beach during one of the wrecks. It was the first thing she spied at the vendue with Grandpop, and she had begged for it. She then worked the wood of the unsightly piece of furniture until it looked almost like new.

Ellie's fascination with chests was a familiar one to her grandparents. Here at the old house in the woods she discovered yet another one in the boat barn, and claimed it. It was so unsightly that the others deemed it trash, and the plan was to throw it "down back of the hill", but Ellie wanted to restore it to house her treasures, and she began scraping it with the old pieces of sandpaper her grandfather had discarded. She intended for the piece to eventually store her Indian treasures and the special quilt Grandmom's friend Miss Blanch had crafted of dark squares, accented with red. This was her own special horse blanket. When she used her saddle, it went between the saddle and the horse. When she got the notion to ride bareback, it was the cloth she sat on. This beautiful quilt looked striking on the back of her black horse. When her grandmother walked into the garage and saw the dome-top chest sitting in the middle of the barn and the tools Ellie was using to restore its luster, she and Nett joined in to help. The group effort paid off. Grandmom convinced Charlie to load it on the back of the jalopy and take it to Mr. Conn, one of the woodworking artists Odessa favored, and he painted some small accents on it. It turned out to be something that could have been placed in the house, but it was Ellie's work, and they were bound to honor her wishes.

On the left side, the three stalls were much larger. Housed in the first stall was Twinkle the cow. This made it convenient for Grandmom when she needed milk. The other two large stalls were reserved for the big Vermont plow horses that had been in the family forever. Here, they had company, which all horses need, plus an enclosed pasture cut through the woods, and a small wooded area for their curiosity. They were content with the occasional ride.

The kids continued to roam the house, readying their rooms and watching the sailors build small sheds for Grandmom's chickens and enclose a pen for the pigs. There were others making a yard for Grandmom's flowers. This clearing around the house was the only area not shaded by trees, as the woods around them were so dense. This spot allowed the sun to warm the house also, keeping away the damp. Grandpop also had a group of men removing the underbrush blocking the road leading up to the house. Time was drawing near for the move. Grandmom was a strict taskmaster, but the rewards of eating her cooking all day was worth the energy spent to make her happy.

The women had heavy drapery pieces on clotheslines, also newly constructed, and were busy beating the dust from them with a wide, flower-shaped wire extension on a broom handle. They would eventually air out the blankets and linens of all kinds, and drag the upholstered chairs and mattresses out in the sun to rid them of the must of age.

Ellie found her secret hideaway. Luke knew of his, as they had used it before, and that knowledge was the reason he chose that particular room. It seemed Blake had not discovered any hidden access to either the walls or to the attic room between the second and third floors. Ellie had found her hatch to the attic in her closet. Luke's was also in a closet, and Blake practically tore apart the walls and closet in his room looking for any secret egress.

What he did not discover was a door at the back of his closet, covered by old clothing left hanging from some previous occupant. But that door was an entry into Ellie's room. The passageway accessed the huge bookcase in Ellie's room, whose shelves hid a door matching up to the opening in Blake's closet, and the same configuration was in place in a rather grand bookcase on the wall in Luke's room. Blake's bookcase on the wall next to Luke's room had a special book, *Knights of the Roundtable*, which, when pulled out, opened the left side of the bookcase, revealing the back of Luke's bookcase. Blake's bedroom dressers were designed with pull-out drawers on one side, and on the other side, a door obscuring shelves for storage. It was a double-sided wardrobe with drawers on one side and shelves on the other. He had two of these dressers on the wall in front of his closet.

When Blake tapped on that inside wall of his closet, Ellie knew to open her side. Or Luke, whenever he was trying to access his brother's room, pulled out a book located on a section of his bookcase, *Moby Dick*, which resulted in that side swinging open, revealing a space to enter the other room through the bookcase in Blake's room. It would take awhile for them to discover these passages. It appeared that all three rooms were connected, and it would turn out Blake's room was the best room of all. Later, it would become their meeting room. Their obvious means of escape was out the window and across the roof of the porch. But this was too easily detected. Blake began to research other ways.

Pop continued his storm story.

"Here we have villagers who also think they have seen a gray man. Their gray man was not dressed in a riding coat and hat with shiny black boots, like the apparition on Pawley's Island. Our gray man appeared as a surfman, dressed in the typical foul-weather hat, brimmed with flaps down the side, and a long slicker, not yellow like the surfmen, but gray, to match the darkening sky of imminent bad weather. Our gray man had on knee-length fishing boots. He was also said to be one of the omens of an impending storm. People have claimed that when seeing the figure walking toward them on the beach, he disappeared upon reaching them. In their fear, knowing the legend, they rushed home and prepared for a storm. Inevitably the storm appeared, quite on time, as within twenty-four hours they began to recognize signs that usually accompanied a severe storm beginning to appear.

"Can you tell when we are going to have a storm?" Blake asked. In his mind, there was absolutely nothing his grandfather could not do.

"Well, son, I believe I can. You know, I've been through many of these things. My father, Amelick Thomas Gray, was the keeper of the Big Kinnakeet station, and he was out in every storm that appeared to threaten ships at sea. And as a surfman, he looked for the signs, just like Uncle Backie did when he was a surfman. I believe your Uncle Backie can also tell when a storm is coming. Now, these signs are subtle, and they only show up when the weather is going to become particularly vicious. There is also another man who knows the sea better'n most, and that's Captain Bernice. He is the most savvy man of the weather I have ever met. I think all those years as a captain in the Coast Guard—plus all the time he's spent on the water, both in the sound, hauling freight for the island, and fishing with rod and reel on the surf—has made him as much of a predictor of weather as one human can be. He constantly watches the skies, and to him, they are like a book. He *reads* the weather. Now, Bernice is not looking for storms. He's reading the signs that tell him when the fish are running. He's always looking for good fishing weather, and he even knows what kind of fish are on the run, as he knows the habits of all the fish that pass The Point. If he detects a storm, it is not because he is looking for it, but because he recognizes it.

"Now, all of us men know one sure sign, but it's not always detected. So far, if that indicator shows up, at least one of us can identify it." Charlie smiled at a thought.

"Well, bet you young-uns thought we old men were always sittin' round Mr. Eph's store gossiping. Didn't know we were discussing the weather, did you?" At that, he slapped his knee in jest and continued on.

"The sea itself tells us she is coming. A day before the sea invades and the swirl of a storm is ready to hit land, it sends out through the atmosphere a sound wave—like a shot, a crack, a loud onetime noise—that sounds like a loud gun discharge. It originates from the source and travels through the air waves from the direction of the incoming storm, over the atmosphere until it reaches the beach with a heavy and loud crack! I've heard it. Seems to be just one hit, but it is so loud and so singular, and leaves such a feeling in your ears and chest, you know what it is. It is like the sea is saying, 'Look out, here I come. Heed my warning.'

"The animals warn us by disappearing. The birds are gone, the turtles also find a place to hide. Sometimes you can tell by the seagulls, who cluster and become confused, gathering into the shore trees, making it look like the trees are white. That particular sign also indicates impending snow. Both times the birds sitting in the trees even look like snow from afar. But I've heard that crack from the top of the lighthouse, and boy, do I take notice.

"Now, my brother Cyrus can tell by looking at the sound. He calls that body of water 'swollen.' Because he spends his days fishing the sound, and he knows how it is supposed to look every day, on those days when it seems swelled up, or full, he comes home to prepare."

"Can you tell us when you know you've seen a sign?" Ellie asked. "We want to be good islanders, and we want to read nature, so will you teach us what you know?"

"I surely will begin to train you. I will train you in lots of things that relate to weather."

"What's ever been the worst storm?" Luke asked.

"Now, son, that's a hard one. All the storms seem bad at the time they are happening. But there have been at least two that wrecked multiple ships, not just one. And we know this because of the survivors who lived to tell the tale."

"Tell us one," Luke asked again.

"Well, one of the first we have in history, when they first started documenting them, was one called the Racer's Storm. That monster first hit near the island of Jamaica, in the Caribbean." Capt'n Charlie took a drag off his Camel cigarette and blew a smoke ring, then another, then another, till the smoke trickled slowly up and lost itself in the air. The children were fascinated with the smoke, and it set the tone for the story to come.

"That thing left Jamaica, crossed the water to the west, and hit the area of the Central American peninsula called the Yucatán. Still working and growing, it went up that line of land till it slammed into the Gulf Coast of Texas. It tore that up, Galveston Island and such. Then, not yet finished, it went east again, traveled back across the Gulf of Mexico and wreaked havoc with the state of Louisiana, with Lake Pontchartrain there filled to overflowing, and then went to Mississippi, Alabama, and Georgia, and here it started barreling up the coast to South Carolina and finally on to North Carolina, picking up strength as it was feeding from the warm waters of the Gulf Stream. When it neared the coastal states of South Carolina and North Carolina, it started tearing up the sea. Throwing ships around, maybe losing some we don't even know about, but we know it struck land below Portsmouth Island, and off there it began to get nasty. She took a four-masted schooner, the *Cumberland*, and rammed it right into to Core Banks, close to Portsmouth Island. It scattered huge bags of coffee, crates of hides, and cigars on their way to New York from South America. Lost more than ninety lives.

"Then she destroyed two more ships, as they and it rushed up the east coast of the waters of North Carolina. This time a brig, the *Enterprise*, got caught in it. This was a huge vessel, and the storm beat it up pretty good. First it loosened the deck load, and freight started sliding all over the deck of the ship, causing damage everywhere the cargo boxes struck. The storm also was battering the ship itself, so the crew began to throw everything that was loose overboard. Lives were more important than merchandise. They lasted all night, fighting the storm, with breakers near to mast high. The tremendous wind of that monster swept everything by the boards. They could not control the ship, and it started toward shore, just north of here. She started going through the breakers and hit an inshore reef, hard. Sailors jumped into the sea, for fear of broken masts and spars threatening to knock them out, and thus leave them in the sea to drown. Only one man was lost in this one.

"But the Racer's Storm was not done. She was so wide and so powerful in wind and wave that two more ships, not even near each other, got caught. The steam packet *Charleston*, going south trying to reach home, was not near shore, but right out in the middle of the destructive tempest. A steam packet carries a particular cargo, passengers, mail, and other things on a fixed route and a regular schedule. Anyway, the waves broke over the deck with regularity. The ship rose with each breaker, only to be dropped down maybe two stories, to land flat in the trough left by the buildup of the huge wave, and again it was lifted by another wall of water, and dropped. The Charleston began to break apart. The sailors said they thought the sea would swallow them up."

"It's like it had a big open mouth, like a sea monster!" Blake was into this story. He had the pictures of it running around in his head.

"You are right, son. That storm began to roll the ship. They kept upright into the night, and then about two o'clock in the morning, pitch dark, the sea broke over the stern like an avalanche, breaking the bulkheads and shattering the windows—glass everywhere, and water pouring in through the holes left gaping open. Then the skylights blew out and water came in from the top, and the onslaught of water then took a clean sweep across the deck, filling the ship with four feet of water. The captain ordered everybody to set to bailing—even the women, everybody had a bucket or anything that would hold water. It was a useless attempt. The next day, they were about twenty miles off Hatteras. By this time, everything was loose: settees floating around on the second deck, bonnet boxes. With the skylights out, water poured in from the top, as passengers stuffed mattresses and pillows into any hole they could reach.

"The captain told them all to get ready as he was going to try to beach the ship. He began heading toward the direction of the shore, hoping to ground her. They all switched from bailing water to getting wood for the engines to keep the ship running against the weather for the shore. If the engine went down, the ship was at the mercy of the sea. They burned the torn-off doors, floating hatches, everything they could get their hands on to keep the ship heading into the shore. With everybody bedraggled and most near dead, the ship ran aground south of here.

"The storm's next victim was the most famous. It was so devastating and loss of life so dramatic, it prompted the government to take notice of the tremendous peril to human life attributed to shipwrecks off the shores of the United States.

"The ship was the steamboat *Home*, said to be the fastest passenger vessel afloat. She was more'n 200 feet long, and 500 ton. Shipped out of New York, carrying over 100 souls. She was considered one of the finest steam packets afloat, but some say that she was never meant to challenge the Atlantic. Her early successful voyages were on rivers and sounds. She was built fast, but not sturdy enough for the sea. They said she was an elegant 'floating palace.' She had handsome staterooms and well-appointed berths, with custom finishes on every turn. Paneled with mahogany and cherry wood, the salons offered every plush amenity known in that era. Her maiden sea trial proved the fastest voyage on record between New York and *Charleston*, and everyone wanted to board. This voyage was a prized ticket for the wealthy and prominent citizens of the day. The company of owners was also advertising for future trips across the Atlantic.

"The *Home* left New York without knowledge of the track of the storm, since last they heard, it was somewhere in the Gulf of Mexico. The passenger list included women, children, families, their servants, businessmen, and crew. The trip down the coast was always a dangerous one, but these travelers were looking for a pleasure cruise. They encountered a heavy gale just after departure, which they deemed manageable, but as they continued on, the vessel, riding low in the water anyway, found that any ocean chop sent water sloshing into the boiler room.

"The ship felt the full impact of the storm near Cape Hatteras. One boiler sprang a leak north of the island, and even though they commenced to bailing and pumping out the water, the leak began to widen, causing them to scuttle the cabin floor. The ship was tossed so violently in the tumultuous seas that her paddle wheels rose completely out of the water. As the ship obviously began to falter, the captain ordered full steam ahead, and unbeknownst to him, he ran the ship right into the center of the oncoming Racer's Storm. At this point, a more serious attitude took over, and all who were capable began to assist in the bailing, including the women and children. The rolling ocean doused the fires of the furnaces operating the side-wheeled steam packet and forced the crew to run her under sails.

The wind began to push the huge vessel to the shore, with the sea breakers pounding the deck and masts, in a furious attempt to stove her in.

"The passengers, anticipating the ship to be beached, carried their belongings to the deck, thinking they would board lifeboats and be carried to safety. The raging surf had smashed one of the three lifeboats the ship carried. Two able-bodied men grabbed the only two lifejackets and jumped into the sea, thus making it to shore. The rest of the passengers were left to fend for themselves as the raging surf washed over the deck, sweeping many of the passengers into the angry, boiling water. One lifeboat, with women and children, capsized as it hit the raging sea; the other, also filled with women and children, sank within a few seconds of landing upright. Each wave carried away more passengers.

"She hit the outer bar off Ocracoke, where she stuck, and was then at the mercy of the sets of waves exploding over the deck, eventually destroying the finely trimmed cabins and taking parts of them to shore ahead of the ship. There was panic on deck as men, women, children, and crew watched the destruction of the lifeboats. The crew and some of the men lashed themselves to masts and spars, some floating half dead, half alive to shore. The captain and some of the crew lashed themselves to the forecastle, which also broke apart, sending them and others into the rabid ocean. As the boat began to quickly break apart on the shoal, parts of it washed ashore with the furious currents created by the storm. Maybe only eight or ten people came ashore alive on those masts. The constant pounding of the relentless storm breakers eventually beat the *Home* to pieces, leaving it in three parts. The shore and water were full of the debris from the ship as it broke apart, and washed ashore to strow a line of carnage that went on for miles. Human bodies, ship's parts, sail, boilers, anything that the Racer's Storm could tear off that vessel washed ashore on Ocracoke Island."

"Pop, even the children? Even the ones in the lifeboats?" asked a concerned Ellie.

"Yes, honey, even the women and children. After the storm, they say, there were all manner of bodies, well dressed, sporting jewelry and finery, stretched out on the banks, tangled in disconnected ropes and sail and covered in sand, having been tumbled mercilessly through the violent breakers as they were thrown up on the shore. One woman had lashed herself to a settee, and, waterlogged, she came ashore alive.

"Now, this changed the direction of sailing ships forever. Newspapers in New York took up the cry, as the *Home's* passenger list read like a who's who of the aristocracy of New York."

"What's a 'who's who'? asked Blake.

"It means everybody knew who they were. They were famous people," Grandpop explained with a grin.

"Am I a 'who's who'? Blake grinned back.

"Oh, I think someday you will be, but to me and Grandmom, you are now."

"*Blake!*" Luke was anxious for the story to continue.

"Of the 130 occupants, only forty survived. Ninety people lost their lives that night. The people from Ocracoke, south, scoured the beaches picking up bodies and taking them to a safe quiet place, to give them a Christian burial. They cared for the survivors, mostly men, and took them to Portsmouth Island to gain passage on outgoing ships. Captain White remained on Ocracoke to supervise the burials and then returned to New York to face charges of negligence and drunkenness.

"The next year, Congress passed the Steamboat Act, which required all ships to carry one life preserver for each person aboard."

"Wow, Pop, that was a terrible storm. Hope we don't ever have one like that. Man, I don't want to be at sea when there is a monster barreling down on me. I guess we need to pay attention to the weather, even when we are on the sound." Luke looked at his cousin and brother and imagined how it would be to be trapped, knowing the next wave would take them under. He also wondered if their dolphin would be around to help them.

"Well, son, that won't happen to you guys. Your parents and grand-mother and I will make sure you are smart about the nature around you. You need to respect the ocean, sky, and wind, because that is what we live with all the time. You saw yesterday all the men who live on this island and make their living from the sea. They know the currents, the winds, the shoals, and the creatures who live beneath them. There's a lot to be said about respect for your surroundings. Yessir, you need to respect the ocean. She's a mighty creature, all on her own. And when old Mr. Wind gets involved, it is a fight to the finish, and you don't want to get in the middle of one of their brawls and have it be your finish."

Luke's mind drifted to the mighty Poseidon, his massive frame rising up from the deep, dripping in electric eels, his frosty brow knit in a scowl, as he began throwing huge torrents of water and dastardly foam, sending fog and mist into the battle with the wind. The wind fielded the massive water barrage and swirled the onrush into dangerous tides and currents that whipped up the waves to heights that few saw and lived to retell. Poseidon answered with more water, which towered skyward and rained back down as it encountered the wind, the action sending it swirling until it reached out for hundreds of miles, tightening the circle created by the wind. The wind let out a tremendous howl and fought back, but when Poseidon threw the electric eels into the mix, the sparks sent bolts of lightning piercing the atmosphere. What the earth heard and saw was thunder and lightning, and they struggled to protect themselves. He wondered what the name of the God of the wind was. Guess he could look it up in his mythology book. That would be a good spirit to know, the God of the wind.

"Now, get ready for bed. Tomorrow brings its own surprises, and you want to be looking forward to them." Capt'n Charlie had worn himself out.

"Was that the very *worst* storm *ever?*" Blake was ready for more.

"There was one more, maybe even more destructive, happened about fifty years later, but we'll get to that some other time. Too much talk of sad, and not enough happy. Didn't forget about your horse, did you?" Grandpop laughed as he tried to switch to a less energetic subject. He was afraid he would give them nightmares. Knowing these kids, they'd be sailing a ship in their dreams. Capt'n Charlie knew these children better than even *he* knew.

On his way upstairs Luke slipped over to the area where Grandpop's precious set of Encyclopedia Britannica stood with their majestic leather-bound covers lined uniformly along the bookcase. He pulled out two volumes, the "W" and the "M." Wind and mythology. In bed, when all was quiet and he was sure Blake was asleep, he found his flashlight and began leafing through them, looking for the name of the wind. He found the name of the Greek god and ruler of the winds. It was the main god, Aeolus, who was Poseidon's opponent. Then each of the compass points had a lesser god. They all had names. The East Wind was Eurus. The north wind was Boreas, who was also the god of winter. Notus was god of the south wind, and Zephyrus god of the west wind. However, most important of all was Kitchi Manitou, the Algonquin god of the wind. He had heard that name before.

He fell asleep with the flashlight burning and his cheek resting beside one of the magnificent volumes.

⋆ 14 ⋆

Pea Island

The Lifesaving Service began operating off the coast of North Carolina in 1874 and eventually boasted twenty-nine outlets, from Wash Woods to Oak Island. Ten of those stations were ultimately located on Cape Hatteras Island. The configuration of this strip of land, extending, unattached to the mainland, thirty miles out to sea, put the island close to two very dangerous shoals offshore: Wimble Shoals, located at sea, close to the northern part of the island, and Diamond Shoals, located off The Point of the farthest extension on the island, which marked the center of the island. These stations, from north to south, were Oregon Inlet, Pea Island, New Inlet, Chicamacomico, Gull Shoal, Little Kinnakeet, Big Kinnakeet, Cape Hatteras (located at The Point of the island), and down the southern shore, Creeds Hill, Durant's, and Hatteras Inlet, guarding the Ocracoke Inlet also.

They were built as needed, and each was constructed according to the architectural plans of the government. They were barnlike in appearance, with king post ornamentation. Each measured twenty feet by forty feet and were two storied. They employed one keeper, who was in charge, and eight surfmen, all living at the station during the peak seasons for storms. As need demanded, the stations were occupied year round. The surfmen were chosen usually from the residents nearby and were experienced with knowledge of the sea, the weather, the tides, and currents off the coast. Most had been fishermen who possessed personal knowledge of the area and its strength.

Listed among the keeper's duties was training and disciplining the crew. He also manned the steering oar on rescues and gave all commands. The keeper was also accountable to his superiors for keeping a journal or log of daily activities and the names of, or at least the number and time of, ships passing their position. The top of the two-story building had an open watch tower that was manned during the daylight hours. The man who held the position of surfman #1 was second in command, and rank went down from that. Rank was usually determined by the strength of a man with an oar. If a surfman was particularly good on an oar, he could advance up the ladder to higher positions (lower numbers). As the surfmen operated always with backs to the sea, the keeper, facing forward and looking into the eyes of his men, also had to display knowledge of water habits, as it was up to him to maneuver between wave sets and breakers to gain the sea. On the return, the keeper had to make sure the boat was not swamped by incoming breakers and strong undertows as they sought to gain the shore. All of this after having rowed miles to exact a rescue.

In good weather, ships were so far out, nobody noticed, but in weather that whipped up the sea, they were likely inshore, either by design to avoid heavy seas, or unavoidably blown in that dangerous direction.

Before the advent of modern technology, most ships hugged the shore and did not take their chances in the open sea during inclement weather. Those wrecked usually grounded within 100 yards of shore. The Diamond Shoals were the exception. The shoals were like landing on the shore. In some places, not seen with the naked eye, one could stand on the shoal and have water only up to his neck. This natural disaster lying in wait was uncharted for years and resulted in wrecks that went unrecorded in history.

The surfmen assisted in refloating vessels after having been beached, taking custody of cargo, and sometimes recovering bodies washed up on the beach. Fishermen sometimes found bodies, and the lifesaving stations would recover and bury the victims. The surfmen were also schooled in first aid and would give it in an attempt to save a man picked from the sea. They were even known to put the man belly down across a horse to walk the water out of him. Their training, dedication, and talent were unmatched, and as a result they were well-respected members of their community.

The keeper of the station was in complete control of a rescue, even over the captain of the vessel he was trying to save. He had the authority to throw overboard any personal possessions carried aboard the surf-boat. He had to be of a dynamic stature and nature to run his operation. Because the men hired were locals, any evidence of cowardice or lack of ability was common knowledge. Men chosen were of the highest skill and character. During the early years of the service, political favoritism was something the locals had to combat, and finally the requirements rested on skill, rather than politics. Inspectors investigated every shipwreck, and should any dereliction of duty be uncovered, that individual was relieved of his position. Usually political appointees were obvious, as their inability to perform tasks was immediately obvious, and upon return to the station, they were sent home.

The stations worked in tandem with each other on most rescues. Always a keeper would request stand-by or assistance on a particularly dangerous endeavor. Keepers and surfmen were sometimes stretched to their mental and physical limits in their attempts to save lives that would otherwise have perished without their aid. The most famous quote relating to the Lifesaving Service was attributed to Captain Patrick H. Etheridge, keeper of the Creeds Hill station and later the Cape Hatteras station: "The book says we have to go. It don't say nothin' about coming back." The Service adopted that epigram as their creed, and it became a motto for the men who served.

Capt'n Charlie, having been the son of a keeper at Big Kinnakeet station, was determined to honor his father, his friends, and family who served as surfmen, and was bound to introduce his grandchildren to as many of the stations as he could. The surfmen were such honorable men. He needed for his grandkids, especially Luke and Blake, to see that kind of bravery and unselfishness. What they must be thinking as they wore out their hands and bodies in an attempt to save another man was hard to tell. Capt'n Charlie could only imagine the struggle it took to face the open ocean in its most dangerous form.

The children came to know the men and they them. Ellie, Luke, and Blake even ate meals and once spent the night at the Pea Island station, located nearest the ferry leading to the mainland. This was the only lifesaving station that was manned by an all-black crew. One of Capt'n Charlie's friends was the man in charge, the chief boatswain's mate, Maxie Berry. Charlie enjoyed the stopover to visit, either coming or going to the ferry. This station had endured much discrimination in its earlier existence, was even destroyed by fire and later rebuilt. There was speculation that the fire was not accidental, which might have been easily true, but with respect for their bravery, strength of purpose, and standing in the community, documentation existed, as it did with other stations that experienced fires, that the station was equipped with a faulty chimney, and that could conceivably have been the cause. That argument was made as the New Inlet station nearby also burned down, not at the same time as Pea Island, but later, and the fault proved to be the chimney. Also, in 1908 the chimney ignited at the Chicamacomico station and burned down the cookhouse. Yes, there was a problem throughout with faulty chimneys, and Charlie Gray, as a licensed architect, chose to believe that both were accidents, a result of faulty construction. He respected both his community of islanders and the men who served. The New Inlet station was never rebuilt. Both Chicamacomico and Pea Island were replaced. The Pea Island station fire was always questioned. It made a good story, for those inclined to bend that way. However, in an attempt to make the stations safer, the kitchen houses were constructed as a separate building, away from the main quarters, to keep fires, should they start, from burning down the entire station.

The men of Pea Island walked the route together with the men of Oregon Inlet and New Inlet, when it was operational. Many traveled their patrol on horseback, or with a dog, to take advantage of the more acute instincts of the animals. They listened to the breakers crashing both onshore and with an ear turned to the ocean's sound, the offshore break as well. If they could hear, it was the same as sight.

The shipwrecks littering the shore were hazardous at night, but each man became accustomed to their position on the beach, anticipated the structures, and walked around them. The men of Pea Island were determined to be a part of saving the lives of those hapless souls whose timbers testified of their fate.

Richard Etheridge, a black man, was the second man to occupy the keeper's position at the Pea Island station. The station was not an all-black crew by decree, but because Richard Etheridge had made it a point to choose black Outer Bankers. As long as he had that authority, he was determined that African Americans would have the chance to serve. He was resolved to create a legacy of excellence in the black communities of the South. This was the only station of its kind. Therefore, promotions came with difficulty. Either someone had to quit or be fired. There were no transfers. Theodore Meekins, who joined the crew in 1890, served twenty-seven years as surfman #1 and never got the opportunity to run a station. Said William Simmons, a surfman at Pea Island, "We knew we were colored and, if you know what I mean, felt we had to do better whether anybody said so or not." They more than accomplished that goal.

The Pea Island station protected both sea and sound. Because of its proximity to Oregon Inlet and swift currents moving through from the sound to sea and vice versa, many times they were needed to rescue those on particularly turbulent seas racing through that area. Between 1895 and 1896, the surfmen did not even have time to replace shingles on the roofs of their stations. Rescue operations—the salvage of humans, cargo, and ships—took precedence.

More than twenty entrances in the keeper's log detailed occasions when the surfmen were able to warn off a ship heading too close, in fog or gale, and those warnings served to avoid what could have been a catastrophe. Lifesaving was not all about helping a ship after it found itself in trouble. They used their skills also to avoid trouble. The station was successful in rescues involving 400-ton steamships and the occasional fishing or rowboat. They even raised the mailboat when it sank in rough waters of a sudden gale that had whipped up in the sound. They rescued and housed the postmaster until he could return to his home base. On that occasion they also went back and recovered a majority of the mailbags. Because of its location, within sight of both waterways, the station served as a haven for fishermen, hunters, and stranded souls who wandered into the station from various accidents at sea or sound and found welcomed shelter.

In one especially vicious storm, with the Atlantic Ocean on the front porch of the Pea Island station, and the Pamlico Sound on the back porch, the station master wondered if his men on patrol would get disoriented. Those waters were meeting, and the patrol was still operating. Familiar fishing shacks had disappeared, old wrecks that had been covered by nature had resurfaced, and Theodore Meekins, on the watchtower, was in search of a signal fire he imagined he had seen from a distressed ship.

A faint light had been seen, so more than one man was summoned to verify. Finally, the station sent up a flare, and it was answered. Thus the journey began. Etheridge marked the proximity of the flare and saw no need for a surfboat, especially with no solid sand in sight. He marked in cadence the movement of the equipment cart as his men trudged forward in the direction of the stricken ship. The walls of wind-driven rain came up the beach, passed the men, and continued on toward the north. The ship in distress was the 393-ton *E. S. Newman*, which had been fighting the storm for ten hours. The fury had caused the Oregon Inlet Station crew to seek higher ground inland, as the wind lifted the station off its moorings. The stations south of Pea Island were in as much trouble, the storm surge being "crotch deep" in all directions at Chicamacomico, prompting the station master to call it the worst storm he had ever experienced. As others sought shelter, the men of Pea Island went out.

After what seemed like a lifetime, the crew of the ship saw nine shadows and two carts, one dragged by mules, and one by men. It was impossible! The sea washed over the beach and met the sound, knocked some of the surfmen to their knees, and still they moved forward. The shouts and cries of the crew echoed through the resounding wind and reached the exhausted ears of the surfmen, strengthening their resolve.

The men from Pea Island saw the dark shape of a schooner perched high on an inner sandbar. They could hear the men aboard her but saw that it was beginning to break apart. It was a three-master no more than fifty yards out, on her side, deck facing the shore, every mast and spar damaged and threatening to loosen and float to the beach. Before the keeper could issue an order, the surfmen began what they knew to be each man's job, and holding onto the cart and each other, they resisted the waist-deep water to stay upright and operate the equipment. There was no beach or solid sand on which to anchor the Lyle gun.

The search for solid ground was fruitless, and as the ship's crew waited for the loud sound of the gun, shooting them a line, they too realized that it was going to be impossible. Hearts on both sides of the dilemma sank as minutes passed in death-gripping silence. Only the fury of the wind, tides, breakers, and rain prevailed.

The captain's wife saw it first. Two men, in the surf, attempting to swim to the ship. Etheridge had asked for volunteers. It was not a command. Meekins and Stanley Wise, half waded, half swam forward, in water past their armpits, to accept the challenge. They were then tied together eight feet apart, with a heavy line attached to the heaving stick, which, if possible, they would toss aboard the ship, thus anchoring the line of safety to the shore. The heaving stick was a heavy dowel about two inches thick with a weighted ball on the end. It was attached to the rope that served to connect the ship to the shore. The rescuers wore only their clothes and cork belts, no rain gear, allowing them more freedom of movement. The brave men struggled with their belts, whose buoyancy prevented them from diving under to avoid the trash and projectiles from the battered ship as it was driven like missiles through the sea seeking them out as they struggled toward it. When they reached the trough that came before the bar, each anticipated the expected pull of an undertow. There is always a swift current running before a sandbar. Most of the time it is an undercurrent or undertow.

Once, Meekins could not find Wise in his sight and felt the dead weight pulling on his rope as it tugged heavily on his body. He feared the worst. As the next breaker rolled past, he saw his comrade still there, fighting to gain the surface. Satisfied, he moved forward. At that surge, Meekins felt the sandbar under his feet, and he drug his friend out of the surge of the ocean to the bar, nearer to where the ship floundered in its attempt to evade the sea.

Fighting the pieces of iron tackle and lumber driving forward in the sea, Meekins flung the heaving stick over his head to the waiting crew aboard the ship. The rope ladder toppled down the side of the ship and the surfmen edged toward it, dodging the heavy obstacles that came their way in the surf. The groans of the ship as it broke apart were deafening to the men as they gained the ship and tied the line, thus giving a lifeline to shore. The rescue commenced. Meekins carried a young child, the captain's son, and he and Wise began the struggle back.

Etheridge, on shore, kept watch over the line, keeping it taut, and instead of a breeches buoy, this was a human rescue. They finally reached the beach, or where the beach should have been, and now someone had to return for the other victims. Meekins volunteered to return, and from the look on his face, Etheridge did not refuse. Once again Meekins, along with Benjamin Bowser, stepped into the raging surf to save another man. Nine times this was repeated. The captain was the last to leave his battered ship.

The trip back to the station was as difficult as anything the participants had thus far experienced. The sea tides continued to wash over the island, and footing was tenuous, but in the silence, the saviors and the saved trudged forward. The child was placed on the cart, along with his mother and an elderly man, which added to the weight. All was born by the surfmen in silence.

Nine black surfmen knew the magnitude of what they had done on that night.

Richard Etheridge spent the night at the station with the medicine at his side tending to the wounds of both his men and the thankful voyagers of the *Newman*, treating cuts with alcohol, bandaging more severe lacerations, and providing the weary a place to rest.

Mrs. Gardiner was given a proper dress without complaint to replace the one she wore, which was in shreds. Each was given shirts and trousers, most belonging to the surfmen, and coffee was made. Eventually the survivors were fed, and the group settled in for a longer stay at the station to ride out the rest of the storm.

Keeper Etheridge offered his quarters to the family, as he went about his tasks entering in the journal, adding to the log, and directing one of his men to the lookout, in case another ship appeared to be in distress.

He wrote in his journal, "Although it seemed impossible to render assistance in such conditions, the ship wreck crew was all safely landed."

In surveying the remains of the ship, days after the storm passed and when the men had recovered from their ordeal, Captain Gardiner went down to the site of the wreck, searching for anything he might recover from the ship. He found only lumber, a few bundles of clothes, ruined sea charts, much tangled rope, and, still nailed to a part of the wreckage, the ship's nameplate. He wrenched it free and dragged it to the Pea Island station. Here he presented it to Captain Etheridge. Unanimously, the crew voted to give that significant piece of salvage to Theodore Meekins, who had been paramount in the saving of all who survived.

Theodore Meekins continued to serve for twenty-one more years. In 1917, while boating home on leave, a squall came up at Oregon Inlet*, capsizing his small boat, he drowned while trying to swim to shore.

*Oregon Inlet has three currents running through it at all times. The mighty Atlantic, trying to push it's way into the opening, where it meets the waters of the Pamlico Sound, trying to get out to the Ocean. The Sound, has the rivers running down stream and emptying into it, the larger body of water, thus adding current to that onslaught from the Ocean. Theodore Meekins was a hero, because along with his courage, he also had strength, as he was the finest and strongest swimmer at the station. Apparently he could beat back one angry body of water, the Ocean, but he could not beat back the three currents running through the inlet.

⋆15⋆

Chicamacomico

As the children watched the keeper's quarters empty out, they enjoyed their trips down the beach to the house in the woods. There they muddled around, continuing to explore, cleaning their rooms, and helping the workers who did the heavy lifting—and there was a lot of it, since both Grandmom and Nett could not seem to decide what should go where. To the chagrin of the workers, they moved the same piece of furniture more than once, trying to get the perfect feel. The kids were careful not to get in the way. The last thing to move would be their clothes, so they sneaked through the walls, trying not to be detected. In the grotto, they met their wolves and waded in the cool underground spring, poled down to the sound in the small canoe, and generally did what kids were bound to do.

If anyone questioned their whereabouts, they simply said they were exploring. That was true, and it settled the question. Always they went on rides to the beach to dry out from their adventures underground. They were in constant lookout for their dolphins, as they were anxious to let them know their new location. They were hoping the dolphins did not prefer the cooler waters of the north side of the island to the south side, which was warmed by the passing Gulf Stream.

At supper one night, Grandpop presented the family with some good news. An admiral of the navy, temporarily housed at the Coast Guard station while helping to organize for the defense of the island, was in need of transportation, and even though he did not relish the idea, he knew he had to take the car, which was property of the government presently being used by the keeper's family. Capt'n Charlie assured him the transfer would not be a problem. He had expected the loss of the car long before this and had in mind a trip to Manteo to obtain another, newer car for his brood.

"Young-uns, how'd you like to ride the ferry tomorrow—"

Before he could finish, he was deafened by the response loudly given in unison by all three.

"I haven't finished there, speedy!" Grandpop chuckled at the energy these kids possessed. "Admiral Cullpepper needs his car back. You know that black car does not belong to us, but the government. Well, they need it back."

A big collective sigh rose from the previously slap-happy kids, and of course Blake showed his disappointment on his face.

"Now, don't get your shorts in a bunch. We are going to get a new one. That's why we need to go."

Another deafening cheer rose from the three, and Charlie could have sworn that both Grandmom and Nett in the kitchen joined in as they prepared dessert.

"The trip will be fun, and Uncle Backie is going with us, since someone needs to drive one of the vehicles back—"

"The jalopy!" Ellie said with a definitive voice.

"Well, now, that wouldn't be very nice, since he has volunteered to go with us," Charlie responded, "but he also suggested the jalopy, and it was because he wanted you three to be able to ride back in the new car."

"I'll ride back with Uncle Backie," Ellie said quickly. "I forgot how much I like to watch the road under the truck," and with that, she had redeemed her initial rather selfish remark.

"Oh, we'll see," Grandpop said, so proud of her he could burst. "But there is something else to add to this trip. Captain Levene Midgett, of the Chicamacomico Station, has just been given a new navy vehicle, a truck, and Baxter and I want to take a look at it. It is called a DUC, but that is not the real name. The letters of the thing are 'D-U-C-W,' but everybody just calls it a DUC. It is a truck that can carry cargo from land into the sea, where it becomes a boat. It is half truck, half boat. We want to go north and check it out."

"Charlie, do you think you will have time for all of that?" Grandmom said, knowing how much time it took to go up the beach and back in the same day. Even if conditions were perfect, it seemed like a rather time-consuming adventure.

"Well, Dessa, if we think we won't make it to Chicamacomico, we'll just spend the night with Maxie at the Pea Island Station. He and Baxter should have a lot to talk about, and I think Maxie would enjoy having some time with him." Charlie had already thought about the trip to the mainland, with all that it entailed. Only using low tide, so as not to get stuck, possible lines at the ferry, and even if he was not the one stuck in the sand up to his axle, he knew they weren't going to get the trip done without having to help somebody else dig out.

"How 'bout it, kids? Up for an adventure? You can take a small bag with your pajamas, just in case we have to spend the night." He already knew the answers.

"Yes, yes, yeah-h-h!" they shot back.

"Now, it means getting to bed early. We'll be up before daybreak, got to catch low tide, and we don't want Uncle Backie to have to wait for us to crawl out of bed." Even hearing the rules about going to bed on time, still the children were enthusiastic.

Charlie purposefully neglected to tell them that Captain Levene was going to give them all a ride in that new vehicle. He wanted them to sleep, not stay up all night talking and imagining no *telling what!*

"If it's all the same with you, I'll sleep in," smiled Nett. The thought of all the things she needed to do and arising before day was not something she cherished.

"I'll get up and have breakfast ready. Charlie, call Baxter and tell him he will be eating his breakfast over here. No sense getting Josephine up when there's no need." Odessa was not about to miss the table talk with the children before they went.

Next morning, still dark, Odessa crept into each room and snuggled the three sleepy-heads out of their dreams. She had their clothes already laid out, with their small bags of extra pajamas on the end of the bed. She hustled them downstairs, where Baxter and Charlie scurried around packing the jalopy and waiting for their breakfast. There were endless questions, as expected: *What color car? What does the DUC look like? Will we get to ride? Into the sea? Are we going to eat with Mr. Maxie? Do they still have mules?* (Mules fascinated them: they were so cute, they thought, and so small, to be so strong.) *Can we feed the birds on the ferry?* An exhausting amount of chatter for so early in the morning. Baxter was thinking maybe the little ones might be too much for him. He was beginning to take back wanting them around all the time. But the longer they were around, the more he cherished them and settled in with the realization this was going to be two days of laughing, and maybe hoping the rhythm of the camel-backs on the wash would put them all back to sleep.

They were off. The men let the air out of the tires and headed toward the dark of the ocean shore, turning left to the no'therd. They soon realized they had company, as always, since villagers chose to go up the beach together. Word got around of who was going north, usually through the gab sessions the men held at the various general stores. The caravan of cars headed up together, riding easily on the hard sand of low tide. Just below Rodanthe, they crossed over from the beach to avoid the "red sand" (minute broken shells—pea gravel, the official name—which seemed to settle in certain spots and was impossible to travel over. A place where vehicles went down, and because of the stretch of it, most stayed there until, with the effort of several heavy trucks, they were pulled out—or not). Day was just beginning to break, and the jostling of the crossover awakened the kids. The adventure *really* began.

Grandpop smiled at Baxter, who returned the grin.

"Kids," Grandpop said, "Look in that brown satchel in the back and pull out what's in there."

The children did as told, giving the bag to Luke, who looked in, and said, "Wow! Lookie here," as he pulled out three sets of binoculars, one set smaller than the others. He handed that one to Ellie, he and Blake taking the other two.

"Thanks, Pop," Ellie said.

"Yeah, thanks!" echoed Blake and Luke.

"Thank Uncle Backie, too. One of them belongs to him. We thought you would enjoy them."

Ellie crawled over the seat and planted a small kiss on his cheek and slid back to enjoy the show.

From that moment on, Uncle Baxter did not have to worry about the chatter, so he thought, but both were sucked into the action in the back and could not help paying attention to what was being observed by the kids, as they called out an "Ooooh," or a "Look at *that!*"

"Look, there's a bunch of red-winged blackbirds over there, on top the hill eating those sea oats."

Pop wondered how in the world Luke knew that. What he could not know was that it was one of that type of bird's feathers chosen by Manteo for the hem of his great cape. Instead, he just looked at Baxter and shrugged his shoulders. Baxter answered by cocking his eyes in Charlie's direction. This was going to be an interesting trip. There was so much activity in the back, they finally had to tune it out, unless asked to identify something, which seemed often.

The line of cars hit the flats running side by side, with the inevitable race commencing. Capt'n Charlie was not as good at this as was Uncle Jack, and the children relaxed as they knew they would not be the winners. But when Jack or Lindy drove, they had a chance—unless they were racing against one of the Kinnakeeters.

At any rate, it was okay today. The slower they went, the more they saw. In abundance were swan and snowbirds, with Uncle Baxter pointing out the difference. In spite of himself, he had gotten into this I spy game, and was thoroughly enjoying giving the names of the fowl he knew they were seeing: the ducks, geese, and a one-legged snowy egret, standing on one foot, lifting his left wing to shade the water as he searched for food. The birds were standing in the marshes, just watching as the cars sped by.

Once in a while the sky was almost black with flocks of birds going somewhere. There were too many to look at. The island was alive on the sound side.

Birds on the back side of the island were not the same as beach birds, and the children saw types soaring above the marshes and pools next to the sounds they did not recognize: the beautiful white ibis, with its orange legs, and the occasional handsome Canadian geese.

"Love to have my shotgun with me. How 'bout it, Charlie?" Baxter said in a quiet voice, careful not to alarm the children, when he saw the Canadian goose. "It's early for them yet, so this one must be a scout."

"Look!" said Ellie behind her binoculars. She was sharing a window with Blake, as Luke used them all. There was a lot of wiggling going on in the backseat of the jalopy.

"It's a raven. I know it is!"

"Where?"

"See that one just floating along, not flapping his wings? The black one," she said.

"Reckon that's the one that steals Grandmom's buttons?" Blake asked.

Ellie, inside her head, decided to ask, and with her binoculars trained on the bird moving easily above the truck, she tried to connect. She smiled, he had heard her, and one sound came from his throat. Not several, like a crow or blackbird, but one. It was the same. He was having fun with them. Ravens were notorious for being tricksters by nature, and this one was acting true to norm.

"It's not a raven," said Blake. "It's a crow."

"No, it's not!" said Luke. "Its tail is not fanned out, it is pointed, and see how wet and separated his feathers are? And it is larger. Also, it isn't flapping and cawing like the crow. It is a raven. I know it is!"

Ellie knew it was also. And she knew his name. Yes, she knew him, and his name was Rook.

They passed "the bridge to nowhere," broken and actually going nowhere, as it remained unfinished after having been built to go around an inlet previously cut by a storm and threatening to isolate that part from the rest of the island. Before the bridge was finished, the inlet filled in, and life went on as usual, causing strangers seeing the structure, and not knowing the history, to scratch their heads. *Those crazy islanders!* they must have thought.

They reached the two grassed-over dunes and knew they were approaching the ferry docks. The kids stored the binoculars away and rummaged around for the sacks of bread Grandmom had packed to feed the seagulls that followed the ferry, in anticipation of the engines working up small fish. Those wily gulls were familiar with the bread tossed by the occupants. They were referred to as "laughing gulls," stemming from the *ha ha ha* they let out as they soared behind the boat, catching and fighting over the white morsels.

They were in luck. Not one car got stuck on the way up, and nobody was full of sand.

Sitting on the ferry dock pole was a true-life pelican. They didn't recognize him at first. His face looked skinny, and they had only seen pictures of a pelican with a gullet full of fish. Uncle Baxter pointed it out to them.

Toby Tillett and his partner, Pam, greeted the group. These men knew everyone by name, even though they were from the mainland, not the island. All the men got out and commenced to gather in groups or by a neighbor's car windows to talk and relay the reason for their trip to the mainland. Meanwhile, the lighthouse kids and other children from the cars on the ferry settled in, feeding the screeching seagulls, which dipped and snatched the pieces of bread from the air as it was thrown high above their heads. It was fun for the younger ones to meet others from the different villages, as the schools were not yet consolidated. There were introductions all around and the sharing of bread crumbs for the trip through the sound to Bodie Island, and on to Manteo.

Not one child went up the stairs to the visitors' lounge near the pilot house. Evidently they also knew about the vicious bite of the green flies lurking in the enclosed little room. It had a concession of boxes with small nab packages, and one with small sleeves of peanuts, plus slightly warm drinks. People sat on long leather benches along the windows that wrapped around the cabin. However, nobody used it. It only took one time to suffer those awful flies to know you didn't want to do it again. The wind blowing and salt spray were welcomed alternatives. Plus, who could resist watching the gulls as they fought over a crumb of bread? Gulls never seemed to tire of their place behind the boat, and they soared along, wings out, hardly flapping, just carried on by the breeze coming off the sound.

The latest model cars at Meekins Auto were slightly different from the previous "new" car they were using from the government. Mostly the body was the same, but inside was different. There was a special smell, a good one, and the seats seemed better. In addition, across the top of the backseat of the four-door models, there was a shelf, just in front of the back window, allowing lots of stuff to be stowed back there. All the cars Pop looked at were black, but the kids didn't care. It was a new car!

Charlie sealed the deal as fast as he could, but it still was a little past time for "lunch," so Ellie took the first leg of the ride home with Uncle Backie in the jalopy and was still enthusiastic when they got to the small restaurant in Nags Head, located near the turnoff to the long ferry road. They all loved the sandwiches at Sam & Omie's, across from the new Jennette's Pier.

At the table, Grandpop finally told the kids that Capt'n Levene had invited all of them to take a ride in the new contraption, even going into the sea, but they were to keep their mouths shut about it. No matter what, they were not to mention it to him again, or they would ride right by the station and not stop. Charlie had no intention of allowing these kids to mommick Baxter and him all the way to Chicamacomico.

Grandpop and Uncle Backie chatted with the owners before they left.

Ellie gave Uncle Backie a hug as she finally got to climb into the new car for the trip to the ferry. When they arrived, they caught the waiting boat without having to sit in a long line, otherwise they would have had to cool their heels until it came back. More seagulls, more bread from the waitress—a pretty young girl who knew both Jack and Lindy—and they started back to the island. The smell of the sound was so different from the ocean. It had character, while the ocean was just fresh. It was almost four o'clock by the time the ferry docked, and they knew they would not be able to stop at the Chicamacomico station for a ride on the DUC. Plus, somebody got stuck almost as soon as they left the ferry, and more time was eaten up digging and pushing him out. Pop said they would not go home until they looked at the newfangled vehicle, which the navy wanted Capt'n Levene to put through its paces on the sands and beach of the mighty Atlantic. It needed to pass some tests before it was shipped over to help load cargo on the beaches of the islands of the Pacific.

Luke jumped into the jalopy to ride from Sam & Omie's to the ferry and on to the Pea Island station with Uncle Backie. They liked to talk, and Luke was an impressive young man to his great uncle. He quizzed the big man all about rescues, his feelings surrounding them, the excitement and danger of it all. Luke's understandings about surfmen was formed by his experience the night he spotted the red glow of the Coston light right outside his window. The things he saw that night would never leave him, and his admiration for Baxter Miller, the Congressional Gold Medal winner, was embedded in his mind, especially after the story about the ghost ship.

Reaching the Pea Island station, number 177, the kids exited the cars in a rush to the small kitchen shack in back of the station. They had been here before, and especially remembered the cook and the concoctions he made, which were so different from Grandmom's. His name was Buster McCoy. He always told them they were his Irish friends, since Luke and Blake's last name was Finnegan. He told them he was "Black Irish," and he would throw back his head and give a laugh that made his chest, stomach, and shoulders move. It was loud and friendly. He always made something special for them, with whatever ingredients he had at the station. Each sweet surprise was something they had never had. They could not wait. When Buster saw who was there, he quickly put his mind to working on what to dazzle them with this time. They dragged him out of the kitchen house to look at their new car, his hands full of flour, as he protested the entire way. These kids would not take no for an answer.

He was quite impressed with both the kids and the car. They even made him sit inside to get the full effect, which he did after wiping his hands on his apron. He let them go up in the lookout tower before dark, watching as they turned around and around, marveling how close the station was to the ocean in the front and the sound in the back. Pea Island station was on one of the flattest beaches on the entire strip. There were no trees, and no vegetation to speak of. It was obvious the wind and weather had affected the land around the station. It was also obvious the sound and the ocean had met here, more than once. The destruction caused by salt water is distinctive in its look. These barren beaches had that look. Finally they all settled down. Charlie and Baxter sat around the station with Maxie and the surfmen and sent up smoke rings, talking politics and the war. The children were given the keeper's room for sleeping and dreaming of the next day's introduction to the truck that could ride in the water.

Luke could not help but look at the hands of the surfmen. And he couldn't help but notice that all these black surfmen also sported beards. He was too shy to ask, but all the surfmen he knew had beards. Pop didn't, but they did. Uncle Baxter didn't also, but then again, he was not a surfman anymore, so maybe he sported one when he was in active service. Luke intended to ask. He had kinda noticed it before, but seeing it here, too? He was tired of wondering, so he would ask Uncle Baxter.

Buster fixed them all a heavy breakfast, much more than the kids could eat, but after they tasted one of his biscuits, they didn't want anything else except biscuits. Grandpop just gave a slight indication with his eyes toward the eggs and ham on their plate. They hesitated about the ham. It looked like it came from a different kind of pig—all reddish—and not being accustomed to anything but Grandmom's cooking, and loving those biscuits so much, they thought they could get away without eating anything but those delicious biscuits. They got the point, and they ate the eggs. Still, they left the ham. Grandpop, knowing it was going to be a busy day, gave another look toward the meat left on each child's plate. Actually, Buster was looking at them also. He took pride in his concoctions.

Luke tried his first. His eyes lit up, and he cut another, larger piece and flashed a big smile. Blake dived in and really grinned wide, with ham bits in the corners of his grin that made everybody laugh. Eventually, Ellie closed one eye and tried it. She also came up grinning. The kids had finally eaten ham with red-eyed gravy. *Yum!* They grabbed a biscuit for the road, but they needn't have, as Buster gave them a bag full. He didn't get much company, so this was a good day for him.

They arrived at the Chicamacomico station right before noon, and Levene Midgett was waiting for them. He was outside with Fonzie, the surf-dog. Fonzie was considered one of the crew, taking part in all activities, including standing at attention when the flag was raised. He was invaluable during storms, as his senses of direction and smell were unmatched by any of the surfmen at the station. They used to borrow him when walking their beat. Capt'n Levene was standing beside something the children could only describe as a tank. It was up high, with a grill or bumper that looked like the ramp on the ferry when it was raised, angled up to be the front, a square front. It did not have a roof, but it did have a high windshield coming up from that ramplike front. The six huge wheels were the biggest the kids had ever seen. It did look like a boat on wheels. How in the world did a person ride in it? The back looked like the front, but it looked like a broken ramp, half angled out, and half straight up the back. In the middle of the back, was an arched cavity place that housed a propeller. It was high up off the ground, under the boat/truck. An iron ladder hung down from the railing that hooked over the side and rested against the vehicle. It was pulled up when the craft was moving.

Capt'n Levene was grinning when he extended his hand to his two friends.

"And these must be your famous grandchildren," he said with a smile. His son, Levene Jr., was a good friend of Jack and Lindy, and as babysitters, they probably had recounted some of the funny stuff.

Luke reached out to shake his hand, Blake stood there with his arm extended for the same reason, and Ellie glanced at them and stuck hers out, too.

"Let's go for a ride!" He couldn't have been more popular than he was at that moment. Truth be known, the old men, including the decorated Capt'n Levene Midgett and Baxter, who had ridden the waves to save hundreds of men, were as anxious to get in that vehicle as any of the kids. Everyone headed for the ladder. The seamen of Capt'n Levene's Coast

Guard helped the kids up first, then Charlie, then Baxter, and they all, to a man, stopped before they lent help on the ladder, saluted the older men, and shook their hands.

"Proud to meet you, sir," was the greeting all around.

Off they went, circling around the station in that big boat, so far off the ground that the kids had to be helped up to see over the side. Then the seamen scooted over some crates and a huge rolled-up green canvas, allowing them to stand and see over the side. It was still awfully high off the ground. It was like if they rode on top of the Blue Bus that took people off the island. They did not know that, within the year, they would be just that far up, riding in a war-era Commando-type truck up the beach to the ferry—bigger than any the island had seen.

When the truck hit the water, it was the most excited the kids could remember being. It was the most excited both Charlie Gray and Baxter Miller remembered being. This was remarkable!

The pilot, or driver, shifted some gears, and when the tires got to the breakers, he switched the lever to "prop," and they heard the whirl of the propeller they had seen earlier. It was choppy getting past the breakers, but when they gained the open sea, the children hung over the side, as the mighty ocean rushed by their eyes. They were so far over, each had a seaman's hand on them, not to inhibit or scold, but to protect. They also should have looked out for Charlie and Baxter. Ellie's sharp eye saw them first—maybe she connected with them in her mind—but up on either side of the craft popped a school of dolphin, sometimes breaching, sometimes head down racing, but whatever they were doing, they were surely having a good time. Everybody on board was enthralled, especially when the dolphins started doing tricks over to one side. What a beautiful day it was.

They rode around, they rode straight, and all the time, Capt'n Levene was explaining to his two colleagues what this new navy acquisition was capable of doing and how it would help in the war. He was given one to put through the paces, as the Coast Guard had spelled it out to him.

"See what she can do!" the commandant had said in his letter.

They needed to know the capabilities and the negatives, before they put it in the War in the Pacific and it became responsible for young American boys' lives. They had picked the most unsatisfactory conditions they could find: the soft sand and shifting shoals of Cape Hatteras Island. If this strange vehicle could master this place, they were in business. These had to be the worst conditions in the world they could find for a proper trial.

The DUC was a winner. The children felt so lucky to even see one, much less enjoy a ride. Most everybody was wet as they reached the beach. The speed of the vehicle kicked up a lot of spray, but after all, it was not made for comfort. In order for it to again run on the sand, the lever was shifted, and the wheels turned before they ever gained the shore. Once the wheels were down, the propeller was turned off, and the monster became a land transport vehicle once more. The man at the wheel could raise and lower the pressure of the tires from the cab. The rig rumbled back to the several buildings that made up the old lifesaving station, presently being remodeled to house the new Coast Guard station. Lifesaving was now only one part of the responsibilities of the Coast Guard. All the sailors were also trained for combat. The men of the Lifesaving Service already felt like combatants as they fought the sea each time they were called into action. The wet and happy travelers climbed down out of the mighty truck and went inside.

The three men sat on the porch of the station, and Uncle Baxter and Capt'n Levene smoked a pipe, and Charlie a cigarette, as they talked seriously about what they thought was going to happen to their tranquil island. There was much speculation. They knew that the Germans had found the sweet spot for destroying shipping in World War I, right here off these banks. Of course, they would do it again. Question was, were their submarines already here, watching them, studying them, getting ready to "let loose"? Baxter thought there was a possibility they might have even seen the trial today, but it wouldn't do them much good. However, the Japanese would certainly like to have seen it.

As the men talked about serious things, the children wandered around the station. They went out to the barn, stuck their heads in the kitchen house off to the side, and marveled at the big water tanks and cisterns the Chicamacomico Station had. They looked at the huge tracks made by the DUC, and back at the station they began to study the walls. Luke noticed that all the men in those faded pictures on the wall had the last name of Midgett. *Capt'n Levene Midgett, he thought, are these his brothers and father? Is everybody in Chicamacomico named Midgett? They were all in uniform and had lots of medals on their jackets. Who were they?*

Out on the porch, Charlie and Baxter continued talking. Luke joined them. Ellie and Blake busied themselves playing with Capt'n Levene's pride and joy, his curly haired black lab, Fonzie. He looked like a cross between a lab and a Chesapeake Bay retriever. He had the jet-black hair of a Labrador retriever and the curly hair of a Bay retriever. They called him a "surf-dog," as he loved the water almost as much as he loved the captain. When there was a lull in the conversation, Capt'n Levene asked Luke how he liked the new cargo barge. Luke answered quickly and saw his opening. Since someone had spoken to him, he figured he was included in the conversation, so he asked a question.

"Captain Levene," he said, "how come everybody's name on those pictures is 'Midgett'? Who are they? They have so many medals on their jackets. Are they your relatives?"

He had so many questions. Levene smiled and answered, "Well, son, yes, they are my relatives, and the medals they earned just like your uncle Baxter did, and some of the things they accomplished were quite remarkable. My family has been in this business for several generations. This is what we do. We are Coast Guard and former lifesaving surfmen. When the service switched from just lifesaving to guarding the coast in 1915, we all switched with them. You know, down this end of the island, to the no'thard of you, we are mostly fishermen. Pretty much all of us have a job on the water. It sits both sides of us. Everything that happens in these villages has to do with the sound or the sea. My family has been in the business of saving lives off the water for as long as I can remember. Yep, that's what we do. We honor and fear the sea, as a result. We know it, yes we do, we know and respect the sea. We watch her, we listen and know her voice, we hear what she has to say, so we have been good at our jobs. Most of us started young, watching our uncles, cousins, grandfathers, and fathers.

"Maybe your grandfather will tell you sometime about some of those men in the pictures. What say, Charlie? You got some stories about the Midgett family. I can certainly tell your boy about the Gray boys, past and present." At that he let out a chuckle.

"I'll do better than that, Levene," said Baxter. "If the boy will give up his ride in the new car and change to riding with me back to Kinnakeet, I'll tell him some stories. I know them by heart. They inspired me the whole time I served in the service. I know some of those Midgett men stories. How 'bout I tell him?"

Luke felt like he had stumbled into the best contest ever: who could tell the best lifesaving story? And they knew all the people. He could hardly wait for the day to wrap up among the old friends. He was anxious to get in the truck with Uncle Backie for the trip home. Here he would hear heroic stores, talk about healing hands, find out why everybody had a beard. The questions ran around in his mind so fast, he was afraid he would forget them.

Grandpop realized from the look on Blake's face that he wanted to ride back with Luke and Uncle Baxter. He also wanted to hear the stories, but he didn't want to hurt his grandfather's feelings.

"Son," Pop asked Blake, "want to ride back with Uncle Baxter? I don't want you to miss the stories. I'm sure you have some questions of your own. Ellie, you, too. I'm just fine."

"Oh, Pop, can I?" Blake was so excited at being considered.

"Of course you can. There will be lots of rides in the new car. Don't you worry about that."

"Pop, I want to go with you. I'm not really interested in those things. They scare me." Ellie was not about to let her grandfather ride alone. If anything was said of interest to her, she was sure the boys would talk about it. She was going to be in the front seat of the new car with her binoculars and a full observation of everything that was the beach.

BUSTER'S RED-EYED GRAVY
Fry up a pan-sized piece of ham.
Take it from the pan and put it aside.
Pour brewed coffee in the grease the ham was cooked in.
Let it cooks for a while, until it blends together.
Pour over the ham and serve hot.

BUSTER'S BISCUITS
Cooks in oven at 475 degrees for 11 to 15 minutes
2 cups All Purpose Flour
2½ tsp. Clabber Girl Baking Powder
½ tsp. salt
⅓ cup lard (shortening)
¾ cup milk
1 Tbsp. soft butter or margarine

In modern mixing bowl, stir together flour, Clabber Girl Baking Powder, and salt. Using a knife (pastry blender), cut in lard until mixture resembles coarse crumbs.

Make a well in the center of the flour mixture. Add the milk all at once. Using a fork, stir just until moistened and dough pulls away from sides of bowl (bowl will be sticky).

On a floured surface, lightly knead dough with floured hands for 30 seconds or until nearly smooth.

Lightly roll dough to ¾-inch thickness. Cut dough with a 2½-inch biscuit cutter, dipping cutter into flour between cuts. Place close together on greased baking sheet. Brush with butter.

SOME NOTABLE WRECKS RESPONDED TO BY THE CHICAMACOMICO STATION

February 24, 1897: *Samuel W. Wall;* Schooner rig; 306 ton; crew 7; 7 saved; beach apparatus used.

February 17, 1898: *Samuel W. Tilton;* 4 mast; 890 ton; crew 9; 9 saved; boat used.

April 27, 1898: *George L. Fessenden;* 3 mast; 393 ton; crew 7; 4 saved; beach apparatus used.

August 18, 1899: *Minnie Bergen;* 3 mast; "tonnage unknown"; crew 7; 7 saved.

March 26, 1904: *Benjamin M. Wallace;* Schooner rig; 57 ton; crew 16; 16 saved; boat used.

April 11, 1905: *Blanche Hopkins;* 3 mast; 505 ton; crew 8; 8 + 1 passenger saved.

March 21, 1908: *Raymond T. Manill;* 3 mast; 511 ton; crew 7; 7 saved; boat used.

August 17, 1911: *Willie H. Child;* 3 mast; 595 ton; crew 8; 8 saved.

November 2, 1912: *John Maxwell;* Schooner rig; 532 ton; crew 7; 1 saved.

February 27, 1913: *Jaccheus Sherman;* Schooner; 635 ton; crew 8; 8 saved.

September 2, 1913: *Richard F. C. Hartley;* 3 mast; 398 ton; crew 7; 5 saved.

April 3, 1915: *Loring C. Ballard;* 3 mast; 627 ton; crew 7; 7 saved.

★ 16 ★

Heroes

As we delve into Coast Guard history, one name continually appears. The name is Midgett. The Midgetts have been labeled; they have been catalogued; they have been described as legendary, heroic, loyal, proud and, above all, American! The Midgett family has had a profound influence on the Coast Guard's history and is an inspiration to the young boot and the old salt alike. We could spend hours talking of the heroics of the Midgett family. The traditions of this legendary family can serve as a guide for the officers and men of this ship—the *Midgett*——as they chart their own destinies.

—Vice Admiral T. R. Sargent
at the dedication of the Coast
Guard cutter bearing the name

The group waited until the evening low tide in order to travel home on the hard highway of the wash. They were provided a box of savory treats from Capt'n Levene's wife, Miss Lucretia, to stave off hunger until they reached their destination. Capt'n Charlie had refused the invitation for supper, needing to pay attention to the tide. Miss Lucretia was certainly not offended, as she had lived her life as the wife of a man of the sea, and knew just what a fickle mistress she was, having played second fiddle to the sea since her marriage to a surfman. She was a local who married a local and knew the ways of the island. Miss Lucretia knew Miss Odessa from island church activities, and she was not about to let her friend's family go hungry. On the island, the women were always concerned with taking care. Miss Lucretia was no different.

At low tide, Capt'n Charlie in his new car, along with his granddaughter and sidekick Ellie, started out on a two-car caravan down the beach, south to Buxton village. They would pull up and over to the land at the sight of the Cape Hatteras Lighthouse. The second car was an old jalopy, no telling what year, so rusted out that the sand could be seen rushing by through the salt-ravaged floorboards under the passenger's side. In this car were three men, actually—one man and two boys who wished to be men. Baxter Miller, brother-in-law to Charlie, and Charlie's two grandsons, Luke, twelve, and Blake, eight. In Blake's mind, he was a twelve year old, trapped in an eight year old body. His admiration of his brother knew no bounds, and he was forever attempting to be "just like Luke".

Baxter had promised the children to tell them stories of the surfmen from the Chicamacomico area whose pictures lined the lifesaving station in Rodanthe, historically known by the tri-village name of Chicamacomico. Their names were Midgett. Their pictures proudly showed them stoic on the wall, all with a chest full of medals. The Midgetts were famous for their heroism and bravery over the years as men who went into the raging sea when no others would, and plucked out people who would otherwise have perished.

"First story I recollect was the exploits of Bannister Midgett. They called him 'Little Bannister.' Only reason I can account for that would be his size. He wer'n't high, he was wide, and all that wide was muscle. The funny thing about Lil Ban was his refusal to kowtow to the people who thought they had rank over him. Oh, this was in the late 1800s, 'round 1880 or such, but Bannister got around his government superiors by 'lowing that he couldn't read or write. He blamed that condition on the 'damned Yankees' who invaded the island during the Civil War. When the occasion presented itself, he also blamed the 'treasonable neglect of the Confederacy to maintain schools during the Rebellion.' Any answer that would set a man back, he was bound to give, depending on who he wanted to insult. One of his answers was, 'The hawgs et up the schoolteacher!'"

Luke and Blake were laughing so hard at the way Uncle Baxter told a story, they wondered if all the old men on the island prided themselves in storytelling. Surely Grandpop did, and he could tell some good ones. Grandpop loved to tell stories, and evidently Uncle Backie did, too.

"He was the first Midgett to hold the top post at the Chicamacomico station, number 179. Now when you hold that position, part of the job is keeping a journal and a log of the ships passing your area. Not just the ones in trouble, but the ones you can identify that travel past the station, either goin' north or south. So ol' Bannister, saying he had no learning, just refused, and passed that job on to one of his other surfmen.

"After his death, there was plenty of evidence that this was a fib, as he wrote well enough when he wanted to. But all that expensive rag paper sent to the station by the government just sat there unused. His log of ships was being kept, and if needed, produced, but not by him.

"Once the top brass sent him one of the first gas engines to try out on his surfboat. It was a naphtha engine, one of the first—simple, no gears, single cylinder, and would go both forward and in reverse. But Banister had a grave mistrust of anything he couldn't figure out, so he refused to use it. It just sat in that crate brand-new, taking up space. On several occasions the younger boys attempted to convince him to *just try it*. The paperwork, which Bannister read in private, said that the keeper was to install the engine in a particular boat and send the results of its success or failure back to the company in *writing*. Now this was not gonna happen. No sir, this weren't happenin'.

"Bannister was a mighty man with an oar, and the oar had served him well. He saved many a life with that oar. He used to keep three or four of those big things in the bottom of the surfboat. In case the surf was so rough he broke one, then he could reach down and get another one and continue on. He told of the time the Yankees ran out of steam in the sound and lay dead in the water. The Confederates surrounded the steamboat in sailboats and took every man jack prisoner, probably down to the deepest part and drowned them—at least that's what they shoulda done, said Bannister. The boys at the station said they thought ol' Bannister was going to dump that crate in the ocean just as soon as nobody was looking. They wanted to see the new engine in action, and secretly they discussed just how to get around their stubborn leader. They talked quietly for several days thinking they would install it in the skiff and then show it to him. Ol' Bannister overheard them talking and realized it was gonna happen anyway. To their surprise one morning he burst in where they were eating and demanded they put down their vittles, gather up that cussed crate, and meet him down at the sound.

"The crew sat on the bank of the sound and read the directions to him, and as they read, he followed the instructions, and kept saying, 'What next?' as they went step by step through the installation of that 'foul-smelling' contraption. Finally the last step was accomplished. With a loud belch, the engine started, and lo and behold, ol' Ban had put her on backwards, and the engine started in reverse instead of forward, sending the skiff, ol' Ban, and that engine out in the sound, stern first. It ran out in the sound, to the amazement of the crew, who were worried and feeling responsible for losing their skipper. They ran up and down the beach, yelling and screaming, stifling anything that looked like a laugh or even a smile. They watched as the skiff went farther and farther offshore, with Bannister standing up in the boat looking at the contraption fixed to the back. Both they and him thought he was headed across the sound to the mainland. But that didn't happen. Ol' Ban picked up the heavy poling oar in the bottom of the boat and beat that piece of machinery to pieces. Then he took the shove pole, shoved his way back to the bank, got off the skiff, and walked away. Neither he ner nobody else said a word about the new engine, not ever again, leastwise not around the *old man*.

"Yes, sir, he was a proud man, and they teach you in church that pride is a terrible trait for a man to have. But Bannister Midgett had more pride than most. He knew it, he knew what the church said about it, but Bannister said that pride was the basis of all true courage. He 'lowed that there'd never been a hero without it, and, 'By gollies there ain't never been a danged coward yet who could ever boast of having any pride at all.'"

"What's 'pride'?" Blake asked. He couldn't decide if he didn't want it, 'cause the church said it was bad, or he did want it, because he wanted to grow up to be a hero.

"Pride, I guess, is when a person has a high opinion of himself or of his importance."

"Is that bad?" asked Luke, also stuck on whether he should have it or avoid it.

"I more think a man has to have pride in himself in order to do a good job. I think maybe the church is talking about *false pride*, acting like you're something when you really aren't. For a man to have true pride is to never quit a job halfway, or to make everything you do as excellent as it can be, something to be proud of. Maybe it can be described as self-confidence. You know you're gonna do a good job, or you hand it to somebody who can. I imagine Bannister didn't tackle a thing he knew he couldn't do." Baxter struggled with the right answers to these questions, because he wanted them to grow into fine men.

"You mean that engine?" Blake quickly observed.

"Yes, maybe that engine." And Baxter had to laugh out loud.

"Yes, ol' Ban was keeper for thirty years, and because of that position, and his attitude, he was the most respected man in the tiny community of fishermen. He doctored them, settled their disputes, preached to them, taught school if the school found itself without, and was the object of more humorous stories than I can recount. We even got some of his wisdom filtered down to my station. Boys would be transferred to the Cape Hatteras Lifesaving Station from Chicamacomico, full of Lil Bannister's wisdom. As a result of his iron will, he was investigated thirty-two times, but headquarters was never able to interfere with him. Once they said he had an 'unkempt' station. His response: "I'm a surfman. It is my business to save lives. If you want a housekeeper, get one of the old women in the neighborhood to keep house here for ten dollars a month.'"

"But you said he couldn't read or write. How could he teach the schoolchildren?" Blake was listening behind his binoculars as he sat in the backseat, every once in a while leaning in between his brother and uncle, then sitting back to observe whatever his little head swiveled around to see as the stories continued.

"I said he *told* them he couldn't read or write, I didn't say he *couldn't.*" Uncle Baxter had to chuckle at the thought of it all.

"He was a pistol, that great man—a pistol. He weathered hundreds of storms during the fifty or so years he was a surfman. He attended, himself, mor'n a hundred wrecks, and assisted in saving over a thousand lives—"

"But, Uncle Backie, that's more than you!" said Luke in amazement.

"Son, I told you these were men I admired all my life. I don't hold a candle to them. One of his younger surfmen once told Lil Ban that one day he would become a legend. Bannister thought, and said, 'Well, I reckon a legend ain't nothing but a lie that takes on the dignity of age.' I reckon he's reached that point. It's been many a year since he served, and his accomplishments and character have survived the dignity of age," Baxter said, sort of in a reflective voice.

Then he got more serious. "He was a proud and humble man, God-fearing, not afraid of anything in the sea or out'n it. He had some spectacular rescues during his fifty years. One of the most famous was the *Thomas J. Lancaster*, stranded on the shoals offshore of Chicamacomico. She was breaking up bad by the time the keeper got to the wash. Winds 'bout seventy-five mile an hour, men and the captain's wife lashed themselves to the port fore-rigging, his children were swept overboard and drowned. Capt'n Ban and his men worked all night long trying to breach those breakers to get to the schooner. When they finally gained the sea, they held on like snapping turtles to the sides of the ship until they could loose those people from the rigging. The ocean beat against them in rage as they were bent on denying it these poor people. Finally they got 'em all in the surfboat. It was most the same each time they went out.

"You know, after all that, and all those lives, Bannister Midgett, with his pride, in the end was not treated well by the government. Every paper he signed, or had someone sign for him, on over a hundred accounts of shipwrecks, was labeled 'Keeper, Chicamacomico Lifesaving Station.' But ol' Ban stayed in the service too long. A year before he retired, 1916, the Coast Guard took over the Lifesaving Service, and when they sent him his retirement papers, they labeled him 'Chief Boatswain Mate,' because they had no rank in the new outfit for a keeper, so they gave him a rank as high as they could below a captain. There never was a man so insulted as he was, to be called a 'mate.' He would have no one think he was a 'mate.' He declared he was not a sailor and resented being called one. He was a keeper, a surfman, and he was determined to be remembered that way. In his pride and embarrassment, he left the island and retired to the Bodie Island area, where his son was also a keeper, and settled his final years there. Now there's an example of pride, but maybe he was just too old to change."

"You know, Uncle Baxter, our men are strong on this island, aren't they? I see Pop's friends, you, Mr. Bernice, Mr. White, and they are all mighty men. And Mr. Williams in Kinnakeet—all our villages have strong men. I want to be like them. When I saw the shipwreck a while back—and watched the things the men did and saw how their hands bled and they carried on anyway—I was scared, but after a while, I wanted to be them, so I stopped being scared and started helping. Think I'll be a prideful man when I grow up, like Keeper Bannister?" Luke's words gave Baxter a warm feeling in his chest. He had succeeded in his mission and was forming a fine young man. He would have to tell Charlie.

"Me, too!" added Blake. His little, brave heart was also working, and even though he seemed not to be listening as he crawled around in the backseat looking through his binoculars at every sanderling, shorebird, seagull, or flight of cormorants that blackened the sky over the ocean, he was still listening and taking in everything.

There were a few minutes of silence as all three paid attention to the beautiful sunset that was getting ready to disappear over toward the sound. The sun was still high, but the colors were starting to build.

"Uncle Baxter, can you tell some more? I'll never get this chance again, and when Capt'n Levene comes to see Pop, I want to already know about him." Luke could not forget about the other men looking down from the wall, sporting a chestful of medals. Maybe they were even more courageous, maybe not as funny as the first one. He was interested in *all* of them.

Poor Baxter, he asked for this assignment. Now he was gonna know what Charlie had to deal with. Thank goodness he spent his time away from home and Josephine was left to raise his children. He took pride in having the handsomest boys and the prettiest girls, but he was beginning to think all that was his wife's doing. His respect for Josephine Drinkwater Gray rose. He would give her a compliment on her supper tonight. Baxter, his idea of a gift was a fat goose!

"Now, the second man, after Bannister, to take over Chicamacomico was John Allen Midgett Jr. His father, John Allen Midgett Sr., was the keeper at the New Inlet Lifesaving Station north of Rodanthe and south of Pea Island. Capt'n Johnny, as his peers called him, started his career as a surfman at the Little Kinnakeet station, then the Gull Shoal station near the village of Clarks—it's now Salvo—then on to the head position at Chicamacomico. Now remember, boys, being keeper is not automatically given to a man because of his name. He had to earn it with an oar.

"Now, many a story was told about Bannister. Most were humorous, some absolutely death defying, and all with respect. But now John Allen Midgett Jr.—there's a man they told a tale or two about common sense, helping the sick, putting the hand of the surfmen to work saving those on land as well as sea. Why, once, there was a terrific hurricane, washed over Rodanthe, took homes from their moorings, washed them away, water circling the station, and Capt'n Johnny on the lookout tower, looking seaward. Lo and behold, he spied the house of an elderly woman of the community slowing riding toward the sea on the backwash. He yelled to his men, "Suit up, we're going to sea!" And instead of grabbing the equipment cart or the surfboat, he hitched up the horses and grabbed some heavy line, and his men waded out, strapped that house all round with hawser lines, hooked those up to horses, and pulled it back to safety.

"Not just because of that one act, but many, they said he would see for those who could not, he carried the weak, and he stood between life and death to those who could not help themselves. The entire community depended on him for even small things, and Capt'n Johnny never disappointed—from pulling a cow out of the mire to counseling his children to never worry about their enemies, but to beware of false friends. He was a man to be respected, and maybe feared. That cow he pulled out—he told his men to get ready, they were going to save someone's cow. One of his young surfmen, frisky in his attitude, told Capt'n Johnny he weren't gonna do it, he 'lowed he joined to be a surfman, not to rescue an old woman's cow. Johnny just looked at him and said, "Be ready in thirty seconds." That young squirt was the first to be ready and the one who tightened the straps under the cow, slowly sinking by that time, in the mud. Why, Capt'n Johnny even breathed life back into a child who was pulled from the water and thought drowned.

"His men said of him that he was a man who stood erect by bending over the fallen, and a man whose stature rose by lifting others.

"'Course, he did his duty, saved every soul ever floundering off the sea on his watch. Nearly got burnt up saving a British ship, *Mirlo*, during World War I. Got his Gold Medal for Lifesaving on that occasion, and that silver cup he holds in the picture was given to him from England. That crew he saved in that burning ocean was all British. They say Capt'n Johnny was the greatest. And boys, I do believe Capt'n Levene will be even the most distinguished of all the Midgetts. He is already a great man.

"Levene served in lots of lifesaving stations before they let him come back home. Some of them off island, places he'd never heard of. He was a keeper at Hatteras Inlet station before he came back to Chicamacomico. One Christmas, I think in about '31, he got a radio message from a fishing boat breaking up in the wintery winds of the Diamonds. It was one of our famous winter storms, and the ship was aground. Levene told his crew of the message, and I'm sure they didn't think it would be their responsibility, because other stations were closer, and surely they too had gotten the wire. Capt'n Levene never asked a man to volunteer. He just looked at them and said, "Boys, I'm going!" He then proceeded to suit up. Turned out, he was the last one to the boathouse and found his men had hooked up the horses to the surfboat and were awaiting orders. There were even boys there who weren't on duty.

"Knowing the job ahead, having seen the seas in all their anger crashing and roaring toward the shore, where he was, he knew it would be worse on the Diamonds. So he radioed Cape Hatteras Coast Guard Station, Creeds Hill, and Big Kinnakeet to be ready. We all cooperated. It was never a job for a glory hound. It was a job for a bloodhound. She was the trawler *Anna May* outta Hampton, Virginia. Hatteras Inlet rowed out fighting the oars and the sea. Engines didn't do much good in heavy seas, just couldn't handle it. A man had to depend on his oar. Launching on the south side, they both rowed and used the engine for five miles till they got to the shoals. They couldn't get to her from the south, seas so high they couldn't even get near enough to see the name of the boat, so they had to come back. Then they hauled the boat to the north shore. Once again they tried, as they launched from the north side. Still, they couldn't get close. They returned to the shore. Next morning, daybreak, all stations were ready on the north shore.

"The surfboat from Cape Hatteras, captained by Bernice Ballance, spotted the trawler. By then she had been swamped, buried deep in the shoal. The fishermen were strapped to the mast, shouting and waving as the storm tossed the mast around, sending gushes of sand and shell-filled water 100 feet into the air. They tried to reach her. About an hour and one-half later, the boys from Hatteras Inlet arrived. Now there were two boats. As the men watched, the mast toppled with the weight and dumped the five men into the sea. Instantly the two stations put their lifeboats into the dangerous breakers. After several attempts the Cape Hatteras crew picked up two men, then the Hatteras Inlet boys got the other three. The two boats returned to the waiting crews from both Creeds and Big Kinnakeet. Took four stations to get five men, but we did it 'cause, 'twer'n't no need to not let those men see their kin at Christmas."

Luke saw the look on Uncle Baxter's face. He wondered if he was one of those men, even though he took no credit. He wanted to ask, but he was stopped by his grandfather's warning: "One question opens the door, the second question slams it shut." It was the manner of privacy a man kept who was born on this island. All the things he had said about the other heroes were things Luke saw in his uncle. He couldn't have been more proud. At that, they all rested, and Luke thought, and tried to remember who he had seen on that wall he wanted to know about.

"Did Capt'n Johnny die in the war?" asked Blake.

"No, son, 'bout a year before he was going to retire, he was killed in a car crash up in Currituck. He was up there Christmas shopping for his family and neighbors. Now ain't that something!" Baxter wondered about the twist of things. "You know, a man needs to do all he can when he can. You never know."

"I know who I want to hear about," said Luke. "It's that man on the wall who wears a surfman's uniform but he didn't have a keeper's hat. He had a funny name. Remember, Uncle Backie? That man? Do you know who I'm talking about?"

"Sure do, yep, sure do, and son, it is the most remarkable story of all. His name was Rasmus Midgett."

"Uncle Baxter, if you're tired, you can tell it another time. I don't want to be a bother," Luke said.

"Son, this is the most famous man of all. I like telling this one. Lessee, now, it was in '99 during the worst storm to ever hit in the history of keeping storms. They called it the San Ciriaco storm. It lifted the Chicamacomico station near off her moorings. Circled around the coast of the United States and the islands for twenty-eight days. Stayed here for four, but it just kept coming back alive. Just when they thought it blew itself out, here it would come again. When it hit here, it was mighty! Winds a-blowing, sea raging—we all knew somebody was gonna get it, and we were all ready.

"Well, Rasmus Midgett was a surfman at the Gull Shoal station, taking his nightly patrol down the beach. It was August, right when the worst ones come, and Rasmus had had a dream the night before that his station was gonna have to save somebody. So he didn't balk at having to take the night watch. He took it on his horse, Gilbert, because he knew his horse could see through the storm, had better hearing, and could smell things a human could not. And Rasmus was tuned in to his premonitions. He believed in them. He felt like, on this night, he would be needed. So he struck out on his own, south to meet, or not, the other surfman, from Little Kinnakeet, the station below him.

"There was a northeast wind, pushing toward the shore. The hurricane San Ciriaco had turned again, and the ship *Priscilla* was caught in her fury, keeping count of the fathoms, hoping not to be pushed into the Diamonds. They measured thirty fathoms, twenty fathoms, ten fathoms—they feared the worst. They missed the Diamonds but were blown even closer to the shore, and finally they felt the inner bar, as she fired into it so hard it broke the hull, midship. The captain's wife, eldest son, and a cabin boy were swept out to sea. The captain scooped up his youngest son, only to have him torn from his arms and washed down a hole into one of the cabins, where they later found him.

The survivors couldn't see through the surf, and on shore, Rasmus couldn't see either. He began to encounter articles on the beach. The horse had to walk around them—boxes, barrels, equipment, rigging, large pieces of wood, crates, and more that was undistinguishable. Water began covering the island from the sound. It was up to the girth of Rasmus's horse. He wanted to turn around, but he had been walking two hours and that meant twice that long to get help. Still it was getting bad, but he hadn't finished his watch. He could see debris swirling around his horse's feet. A little farther and he could hear cries for help—voices—and then he dismounted and struggled as far as he dared into the vicious sea, in the direction of the voices. Then he saw her—the *Priscilla*, broken up and with shadows of several persons clinging to her, about 100 yards offshore.

"Best thing to do was get back to the station and get help. He knew they couldn't see in the raging storm, which was sending sheets of rain to cover a man's eyes. He pondered the situation. By the time he got back to the station, those boys out there would drown, especially if they tried to make shore on their own. There was no time to get help. What had to happen was clear to him: he needed to do it on his own.

"Like all of us, he knew the habits of the sea, even at her most furious. He waited for the sets to regulate, and when the largest wave receded, he managed to get close enough to holler to the crew, ordering them to jump overboard, only one at a time. He told them to wait for another backwash and jump to him. He took his opportunity to get back, with the thrust of another wave, and waited on the shore for another dangerous entrance to the sea as it held the ship tight. The men heeded his instructions, and one by one they jumped and waited for Rasmus to come back for another to jump again. Rasmus drug each soul from the raging water to the bank, watched for another chance, and returned for another. This he did seven times. The three men left were too far gone to heed his instructions, so he got right down into the sea, close to the wreck, dragged himself up a rope to the deck, picked up the weakest, and carried him to shore. He returned two more times, boarded the ship, and carried each, one by one, all the way to the beach. Ten lives he saved that day, all by himself. He and Gilbert got them all back to the station, where they were bandaged, stripped of their torn clothing, and given the surfmen's garments, an offer of food, and a clean bed."

"Gosh, Uncle Backie, he should have gotten a medal for that. That sounds impossible. He must have been a good swimmer." Luke sat wide-eyed beside his uncle.

"Did they find the other people?" asked an equally impressed Blake.

"Well, son, unfortunately, the sea sometimes gives up her dead, and some bodies did wash ashore, but none that belonged to the poor captain. His family was lost. They did find the boy drowned in the cabin when the sea finally died down. But there's no accounting for how life turns out. And yes, he was awarded the Gold Lifesaving Medal by the secretary of the treasury, who also wrote the brave man a personal letter. You know, these men in Washington probably can't imagine why a man would risk his own life for another. But maybe they have just not been in that position. At the time, it is your pleasure."

Luke looked up at his uncle and turned his head away so as not to disturb the thoughts of the elderly hero. He imagined Uncle Backie was thinking back on all the things he had seen and survived to see again. Maybe he even wondered why he did it. A man is fortunate who is selfless, but how does he get that way? Luke also now knew the meaning of pride. Anyone would be proud to save a life, but what makes a man pass from fear to bravery? That would be something he would have to find out for himself. He neglected to count himself as being brave for saving Mr. Burrus's herd. He had not felt afraid. He had felt inspired.

They were almost to the lighthouse by that time. The sunset over the sound was so red, orange, and purple that it was comforting to look at. It reminded the children of God. They were amazed by the colors that man could not duplicate. Luke remembered the feathers collected by Powwaw, and it was the same. No paint could duplicate what nature set her brush to.

> More than 150 living members of the Midgett family have made the Coast Guard a career, including more than thirty still on active duty.
>
> Seven men of the Midgett family have been awarded the nation's highest award for saving a life, the Gold Lifesaving Medal. "Extreme and Heroic Daring in an Attempt to Save a Life" is required for this high honor. Three Midgetts have received the Silver Lifesaving Medal, the next highest award.
>
> —The Coast Guard News

Midgett Family Recipients of Gold Medal Lifesaving Awards

Name	Position/Station	Date
John H. Midgett	Cape Hatteras	April 24, 1885
Rasmus S. Midgett	Gull Shoal	October 18, 1889
John A. Midgett	Bos'n (L), USCG	August 20, 1924
Zion S. Midgett	Bos'n (M), 1c., USCG	August 20, 1924
Arthur V. Midgett	Surfman, USCG	August 20, 1924
Leroy S. Midgett	Surfman, USCG	August 20, 1924
Clarence E. Midgett	Surfman, USCG	August 20, 1924

Midgett Family Recipients of Silver Medal Lifesaving Awards

Name	Position/Station	Date
O. O. Midgett	Surfman, Cape Hatteras	December 6, 1911
E. J. Midgett	Surfman, Cape Hatteras	December 6, 1911
Levene W. Midgett	CBM (L), Rodanthe, USCG	December 17, 1935

Other Island Recipients of Gold Medal Lifesaving Awards

Name	Station/Ship	Date
Benjamin B. Daily	Keeper, Cape Hatteras/ *Ephraim Williams*	December 1884
Patrick H. Etheridge	Keeper, Creeds Hill / *Ephraim Williams*	December 1884
Isaac L. Jennette	Creeds Hill / *Ephraim Williams*	December 1884
Amalek T. Gray	Big Kinnakeet / *Ephraim Williams*	December 1884
Jabez B. Jennette	Creeds Hill / *Ephraim Williams*	December 1884
Charles E. Fulcher	Cape Hatteras / *Ephraim Williams*	December 1884
E. H. Peele	Keeper, Creeds Hill / *Brewster*	November 1909
Baxter B. Miller	Acting Keeper, Cape Hatteras / *Brewster*	November 1909
Prochorus L. O'Neal	Chicamacomico / *Mirlo*	August 16, 1918

Island Recipients of Second-Class (Silver)—Above and Beyond

H. S. Miller	Cape Hatteras / *Brewster*	November 1909
Isaac L. Jennette	Cape Hatteras / *Brewster*	November 1909
V. B. Williams	Cape Hatteras / *Brewster*	November 1909
W. L. Barnett	Cape Hatteras / *Brewster*	November 1909
D. E. Fulcher	Creeds Hill / *Brewster*	November 1909
W. H. Austin	Creeds Hill / *Brewster*	November 1909
Baxter B. Miller	Cape Hatteras / Rescue man overboard	June 1911
Bernice B. Ballance	Keeper, Cape Hatteras / *Anna May*	June 1911
Frank W. Miller	Cape Hatteras / *Anna May*	June 1911
Baxter Jennette	Cape Hatteras / *Anna May*	June 1911
James M. Ketcham	Cape Hatteras / *Anna May*	June 1911
Thomas Barnett	Hatteras Inlet / *Anna May*	June 1911
Dallas Williams	Hatteras Inlet / *Anna May*	June 1911
R. J. Scarborough	Hatteras Inlet / *Anna May*	June 1911
Guy G. Quidley	Hatteras Inlet / *Anna May*	June 1911
Tommie G. Meekins	Hatteras Inlet / *Anna May*	June 1911
Sumner Scarborough	Hatteras Inlet / *Anna May*	June 1911

★ 17 ★

The Hungry Sea

I do not believe that a greater act of heroism is recorded than that of Daily and his crew on this momentous occasion, These poor men, dwellers upon the lonely sands of Hatteras, took their lives in their hands and, at the most imminent risk, crossed the most tumultuous sea that any boat within the memory of living men had ever attempted on that bleak coast, and all for what. That others might live to see home and friends. The thought of reward or mercenary appeal never once entered their minds. Duty, their sense of obligation and the credit of the Service impelled them to do their mighty best.

—From the report on the wreck
of the Ephraim Williams

Grandpop and Ellie climbed into the new car and smiled at the smell that had lingered from the first time they'd crawled in. Pop asked her about the stories.

235

"Pop", said Ellie, "I really wanted to hear the stories, but I didn't want to interrupt Luke and Uncle Baxter. I know the boys want to be together and I want to be with you." The Captain smiled at the generosity of his little girl.

"Well", I guess I know those stories also, so I'll tell you the good ones." Pop began, and she settled to listen. It had been a long ride down the beach, and eventually, Ellie crawled into the backseat of the car and went to sleep. The fresh air from the ocean was too much to ignore. It smelled salty and had a bite that almost tickled her nose. Breathing in deep was the best, and she did that before she drifted off.

Ellie smelled the crisp air as the sailing vessel headed for the inside. She was dressed head to toe in sou'weather gear, as were the other passengers and members of the crew. Everybody was holding on to something nearby, all half wrapped in rope, with more at the ready. This weather change was sudden, and they were too far out, heading north, when the squall went from a blue-black cloud to the east coming in fast to a terrible storm whipping the ocean into a frenzy as it rolled in. Breakers were beginning to hit the side of the schooner, driving it farther in to the shore, and inevitably the shoals that preceded them. The crew worked frantically to recover from the incoming surge. A wave crested over the masts and crashed into the middle of the ship, sending it under on the port side, showing the entire deck to the shore. Anything loose slid across the deck to the shore side, and only the railing held the larger chests from dumping into the sea. The sliding heavy boxes hit one of the crew and for sure broke his legs. He doubled over the container, obviously unconscious, as his upper body, only held by the rope around his arm, washed about with each following wave.

The craft never really recovered as it was driven closer to the shore. Ellie fought the spray with pursed lips and head turned away as she tried to think clearly. She figured they were close to the newly cut inlet, and if that happened, they could run down the back side of the island south toward home. The sound would be choppy, but not above the mast, like this. She was staring at a white-veined blue wall moving their way. When it hit now, all she could see was a gully, and she knew there was another crash coming. She steeled herself, took as many tucks in the ropes as possible, and waited, practicing holding her breath, and then taking big breaths of the clean salt air, trying not to drown standing up.

When it hit, she felt and heard the beautiful three-masted schooner breaking apart somewhere, and as she tumbled over with the ship, there were pockets of air as she hung from the roping. Then her portion of the broken vessel rose above the whitewater of the oncoming breakers and crashed again against the hard water. She was still attached to this side of the ship, which was being beaten into smaller pieces. Wrapped into the railing, the ropes had come detached from the mast as it cracked in half, taking the other half of the rigging with it—her half. Then it broke, dragging with it a portion of the railing that remained tightly knotted to the mast. Ellie once again entered the sea. She tried not to swallow, kept her head toward light, and hoped the wood floated. Breaths came at intervals as she traveled through the ripping water. She felt she was going through a tunnel. Everything underwater was quiet. The few times she broke the surface, she could hear the mighty roar and then silence once more.

She awakened at the top of the dune. As she tried to sit up, she couldn't stop coughing. The water poured out of her, salty and sandy. She looked around and saw she was alone. She did not drown, but her stomach hurt. The storm's winds had died down, but still she heard the angry waves beating against the dune line. Getting slowly to her feet, she looked around. No signs of the ship or crew anywhere, just the loosened ropes attached to the broken mast. The railing was askew somewhere below them, dug into the dune still with a section of rope around it. She looked toward the sound. It was high and also lapped up to the top of the dune, the breakers going farther up the peninsula than normal. With breakers in the sound, she was trapped between two angry walls of water. The sea had not lost power. It was coming in high, now reaching up to find her again. Abnormally huge waves continued to beat at the shoreline and race up the dunes. She brushed off the sand and looked down the island to the south. This part of the island was narrow, with much more tide, and she could be trapped. She needed to move. She would walk home.

Ellie began her journey down the ridge of dunes between the ocean waves lapping below her on the left, to the rising tide of the Pamlico Sound on the right. There were times when she felt she could make better time down the right side of the dune, but on that side, nearer the sound shore, the waters lapped up so hard that the sand gave way and allowed the beach to disappear right under her foot, causing her to slip slightly into the water, filling her shoe and sock with mud. She quickly pulled back and climbed with hands and feet up to the top of the dune again. She managed to keep moving forward. As the waves threatened, she feared what had happened to the sound. She felt as though she was walking on the top ledge of a mountain of sand, with water just below her on both sides. Should her foot falter on either side, she would drown.

At one point, near what she estimated to be time for her to be just north of Chicamacomico, and safety, she stopped and looked over at the ocean, still sending up high waves, washing out crescents of the dune, revealing amazing objects from the past that had been lost at sea. The water slipped back into the sea to gather another monster wave, taking all its volume with it and leaving the beach exposed. As she watched the backwash of the ocean, with its receding tide, she saw chests of gold sitting on the bottom floor of the ocean exposed by the wave as it rushed to form again, ready to muster a huge wall of water. She stood there mesmerized, unable to move her feet. With the next receding wave she saw a small pirogue, with eight oars, four on each side, extended in their locks and dragging behind. Some of the chests were open, their rounded tops hinged upright showing jewels spewing out, large gold goblets extended up to catch the sun, before the wave crashed over them and they disappeared. Pirate gold! She almost thought their ghosts were there, and she began to run south along the shrinking dune line of solid ground.

Finally she passed the area of shelter she anticipated. It was not there, just more of the same, except the land widened and filled in. There were small scattered scrub oaks, yucca trees in bloom, bushes and sea oats revealing a wider grassy area, and a two-track road down the middle of the land. The rain had stopped, the wind took a moment also, the storm was passing. She began to walk south, and for some reason she remembered the small sandy road, long abandoned, hidden between the main road and the dune line, known only by the locals, as it ran between the inside road of the villages, and the dune line. It was concealed from the main road and obscured from the sea by grassy hills. She felt safe walking in that trench, and only once did she imagine she heard activity on the main road. For some reason nothing felt safe, and she did not try to contact help. She had a feeling of fearful anticipation, and she clutched her heart as she neared the lighthouse keeper's lodge where she lived. She was tired, thirsty, and chilled. It was such a long way home, but she had to keep walking.

As she got closer to the lighthouse, she could see it looming in the distance. The storm had gone, and she was finally away from the water. Wet and exhausted, she crawled up an unfamiliar sandy hill. Laying on her belly, she surveyed the compound in the distance. Something was strange. A black sedan pulled up to the lodge, and four men in khaki uniforms with unusual hats advanced toward the building. She saw Luke and Blake go out the back door to the barn and leave on their horses, dragging Blue. But they did not come in her direction. She wanted to call out, but was afraid of the wrong person hearing her. The men went into the house.

Ellie awakened. Grandpop was just starting the tale of the San Ciriaco storm. She had dozed off listening to his relating the exploits of the men whose pictures lined the wall. She heard Grandpop say, "That's how they got all those medals, sacrificing their own lives for that of strangers. But there were so many other storm victims who were not lucky enough to be near one of our boys. That hurricane that Rasmus faced. The San Ciriaco, she was a beaut! Knocked out every single bridge on this island. Winds 104 miles per hour, and upwards of six inches of water. Rodanthe was under water, ninety-nine houses washed off their moorings. Water covered the whole island as the Pamlico Sound met the Atlantic Ocean. Ciriaco sank ten ships and stayed a threat for more than a month, destroyed property, took lives, and sank ships that were unlucky enough to encounter it. It was all over the Atlantic, going and coming back. Three lifesaving stations worked together those four days and nights. Chicamacomico, Gull Shoal, and Little Kinnakeet went from shipwreck to shipwreck as vessels ran ashore and were destroyed in the fury of the offshore breakers. One ship, the first one, they could only save three. They were coming so fast, the victims got pounded to death on the ship or drowned when they tried to reach the shore. Pea Island and New Inlet were busy working the north end.

"Two miles south of Big Kinnakeet, fifteen miles south of where the northern three stations were patrolling the shore, there was little beach to be seen. The water was over the land. They saved the living with the breeches buoy but lost cargo and ship. The devastation was more than all of them could handle. On this island there weren't mor'n four houses without water in 'em. Beach so dangerous the lifesavers couldn't walk their beat. Most of the vessels that wrecked on the coast during those four days couldn't be reached. Everything was water. Three ships— *Robert W. Dasey*, *Fred Walton*, and schooner *Lydia Willis*—laid high on the beach till they all broke up and were washed away or hauled away.

"The strangest was that the wind was so strong it broke loose the anchor of the *Diamond Shoals Lightship*, *number 69*, and floated her to shore around the Creeds Hill station. The crew was saved by breeches buoy. They stayed at the station till the storm finally blew itself out, and they towed the lightship back to be fitted with a new anchor and put in place on the shoals. That's how strong that one was.

"Here on the island, people went to any house that had upper floors, sometimes two, three family groups in an attic, trying to escape the water. The livestock drowned—cows, chickens. The wind recorders at the Weather Bureau were blown away. Every lifesaver was in it, saving men and watching men die. It was a terrible time. The villagers could hear the wind and waves beat their houses. We were caught in the eye, the wind kept changing and coming at us from another side.

"Saw pictures of some of the prettiest vessels ever crafted by talented boathouses left on the beach and wallowing in the breakers after she was done with us. Same wrecks we drive around today. Looks like burnt logs now, grand ships before. All in all, the *Minnie Bergen, John C. Haynes, M. B. Millen, Albert Schultz, Elwood H. Smith, Henry B. Cleaves,* and *Chas. M. Patterson* . . . all lost. The Pea Island station got out to the *E. L. F. Hardcastle,* but all five of her crew were lost and the lumber she carried slid overboard. That was on the Pamlico Sound. Same time as Rasmus Midgett was saving the men of the *Priscilla,* all that was happening."

"Grandpop, do you think the island will wash over again?" She was remembering her dream, and it was all like this, except she saw chests that had been described in The Book, and she saw all her family leaving the lighthouse, just before the men came wearing hats like the pictures of the enemy forces she knew were attempting to come to bomb the island. They were taking over, and her family was gone from the lighthouse. Maybe the dream meant they were moving, because they were.

"We haven't had one like that since. Had some bad ones. Remember that one where we walked in the sound? But it didn't wash over the island. Besides, sweetie, we will be so high up on the hill in the woods that the water won't ever reach us. And that's pretty soon, so there isn't enough time for the old ocean to get us. Don't think of it as a dangerous thing. We owe most everything to the ocean around us. It has destroyed, but it has also given back."

"How did Uncle Baxter get his medal?" Ellie didn't know she would be the only one to know, as Uncle Baxter probably would never tell the boys.

"As I recall, it was close to Thanksgiving. Baxter, married to my sister Josephine, well, we gave thanks together that year. The weather was cold, and Baxter, surfman #1 at the Cape Hatteras station, discovered her at daybreak on the shoals, the *Brewster*. She had broken up the night before. Three stations went out: the Cape and Creeds Hill and the powerboat from Hatteras Inlet. Creeds Hill got in trouble on the way out and was picked up by the Hatteras Inlet boat, so both crews were in that one. The captain of Creeds Hill boarded the boat from the Cape station, with Baxter as the acting captain. Then both loaded, attempting to get close to the ship on the shoals. A huge private boat, fishing in the storm about a mile away from the area, saw the whole thing and offered to tow the Cape Hatteras surfboat closer. Thus, with both motor and oars, it allowed them to make better time in getting to the stricken vessel. The ship was coming apart fast, with breakers crashing over, both fore and aft. The crew of the *Brewster* were thirty-three, and with both lifeboats loaded carrying the men of the Creeds station, plus their own, the boats were overloaded before they could even pick up survivors. It made it look impossible to take on more. No, sir, things didn't look good. The private powerboat waited nearby, not venturing near the violent breakers. It idled, handling the pitch and roll, but staying away from the Diamonds. It waited for the return trip as the lifeboats attempted to get near.

"The seas were so high, they couldn't get near the ship, so the men of the *Brewster* began to try and drift a line from her attached to a buoy, trying for the boats below. Finally the connection was made, and the lifeboats started taking in the men. When ten or so were on the surfboat, they were transferred to the bigger powerboats: the one from the Hatteras station and the commercial fishing boat waiting in the area. That repeated until all three boats were full. The trawler hooked up again to the surfboat and they all made it to shore. At one time the Hatteras Inlet boat had over forty men aboard.

"Five of the men were picked up by the lifeboat from the *Diamond Shoals Lightship*, so Uncle Backie went back for them. His hands bled for a week. The owner of the powerboat, *Gaskill*, said he was fishing and did what he could, not getting close up, like the lifeboats. He 'lowed that the rescue was impossible, as he lay off to the lee and watched. It was him that wrote to the government."

"Gosh, Pop, how many times do you think Uncle Backie did that?" Ellie just could not imagine. They were crossing over to the compound now, and the sun was making blue and purplish-orange stripes across the sky. She was hungry, and she knew Grandmom was waiting for them with a hot meal. They never had their biggest meal in the evening but always during the middle of the day, but she could smell something good coming from the kitchen, out the front screened door. She leaped from the car, then turned and ran back to hug her grandpop, and rushed again to the kitchen. She had forgotten all about her question to her grandfather, and it didn't matter. He didn't know the answer.

Everybody eventually settled in around the dining room table, Nett and Grandmom anxious to hear about the adventure. Unfortunately, the hungry travelers had to wait for the two women to run out to see the car. Supper on the stove, Luke saw Grandmom slap Grandpop's hand as he reached for a cookie, hot, still on the baking sheet, and obviously intended for a nighttime snack. Pop licked his wound and gladly showed his sweetie their new car. Nett immediately got into the driver's seat, with Blake beside her, and Luke inspected the trunk.

At long last, the group was allowed to sit at the table. Uncle Baxter had transferred to his truck, anxious to get home and to his Josephine. Everybody was hungry for a home-cooked meal.

Grandmom had stewed chicken, with Ellie's favorite, dumplings. Of course, they all had to remind her of the time she asked Grandpop to grow them, but it was the price she had to pay for being able to eat them, so she just laughed it off, with a mouthful, and being careful not to let the butter drip. It was the best meal they ever had, they all agreed. And maybe Grandmom's biscuits were as good as Buster's, and maybe they weren't. Anyway, they said they were and knew enough to stick to it.

"What was the most famous shipwreck?" Luke was putting his fork into another piece of chicken from the pot.

"You young-uns not tired of shipwrecks yet?" Capt'n Charlie had two in mind. "Well, I can think of only two that we know of that were worse."

"Pop, tell us one. Mom and I are tired of talking to each other. We missed all of you," Nett said, leaning forward for another spoonful of Mom's gravy. There were things she had never heard her father speak of. Maybe she had been too busy with all of her social projects, moving, and worrying about Bill to even ask.

"The *Ephraim Williams* comes to mind. It wasn't so much the ship as the rescue that made that one special. And it was near Christmas, so it was a bad time for everybody. The *Williams* started taking on water in a gale south of here, fighting their condition for three days, almost drifting out of control. They were attempting to round the Diamonds and had all been worked out by that time. They were weak, but alive. They say it was the roughest Atlantic they had seen in a lifetime. Here, the winds groaned through the boards of the houses, as everybody hunkered down for a Christmas storm. Lookouts at Durants, Creeds Hill, and the Cape all saw the floundering ship, but it gave no distress signal, so they kept watch, hoping it would work itself out of trouble. By morning it had moved past the Diamonds down toward Big Kinnakeet. It was obvious she was gonna go to ground. Benjamin B. Dailey from the Cape lived right here in Buxton. He called on the Creeds Hill station keeper to meet them, bringing with him their best oars, as he began to follow it down the beach behind his horses pulling the lifeboat. Four hours it took him. He was eventually joined by Keeper Pat Etheridge from the Creeds Hill station, who agreed to fill in for a man whose wife was dying. Both keepers watched as the ship disappeared below the waves, showing only her masts. They watched as the walls of ocean washed over her, and the breakers on the shore became so high it was impossible to see beyond them.

"Watching from shore, a flag went up, indicating life on board. Five times it showed. Five men. Dailey gave the order to go. He was the main keeper, and as he looked over the crew of the three stations, he picked the strongest oars and gave the orders. The chosen surfmen quietly took their places along with Pat Etheridge, buckled their cork belts, and got her into the breakers. The men on shore grabbed hold of the horses as Big Kinnakeet watched, ready to go.

"The walls of the breakers were cresting about twenty to thirty feet, and equally as deep troughs behind. The men had their backs to it, but they had seen as they pushed out the boat what was in store. Dailey, facing the obstacle, was ready with several rudder oars, as he faced the solid blue face of the wave as its lip, foaming across the top, building to crest, waited to bite down on the crew. Dailey gave the order, 'PULL!' and the men put their backs into it. The boat went straight up. From the shore, the watchers could see the deck and all the equipment stowed under the seats. The boat was on its stern climbing that mountain. She crested and dropped out of sight, only to repeat again and again, until the sea beyond was gained. The drop caused every man's jaw to jar as he hit the bottom, stunning them for a second, until Keeper Dailey ordered, 'PULL!' again. Dailey studied the waves for the best path. They rowed on for five miles to reach the stricken ship.

"Meanwhile, the surfboat from Big Kinnakeet set out on the same path, only to be overturned and dumped on the second try. It was up to Dailey to make the save. Dailey and his men fought the ocean all the way to the sailors, who were trying to make rafts from the broken ship, lashing wood together with rope. The rescue boat got close enough to pick the men from the water, where they would have surely drowned, and return safely. Anxious men on the shore watched as the boat was thrown up on the beach and Dailey tried to steady her against the oncoming wave behind them. Overloaded as it was, everyone was saved. The surfmen on that boat did not sit or hold a fork for two weeks, their hands and bodies were so beat up."

The meal continued, with everybody asking questions and eating, and Luke again thinking about a man's hands. But he finally remembered to ask the question that had been on his mind. "Pop, why do all the surfmen have beards?"

"Son, it gets mighty cold on the water, makes a man's face freeze against his teeth. Can't take it, all that wind and salt water. Every other part of him is covered. He can't cover his eyes, but he can cover his face. Kinda like an animal is covered with fur to protect him from the harsh weather, not just salt wind and biting cold, but also the sun. The elements play harsh on the tender skin of the face. So the men grow fur to protect themselves." Grandmom was getting up for dessert as Blake burst out laughing so hard, his head was almost in his plate.

"Fur! Everybody's got fur!" and his laughing got Luke going, and Ellie, too. Even Nett had to giggle at fur!

As they all enjoyed the lemon meringue pie, Blake couldn't let it go.

"Grandpop, you said two. What was the other one?" he asked.

"Oh, this was the most famous, but it wasn't made by the surfmen. This shipwreck didn't happen here, but it could have been saved here. This story should be the most famous story of a shipwreck there is. She was the *Titanic*, and she was unsinkable."

Capt'n Charlie had a fine piece of pie in front of him. Odessa had just filled the three coffee cups, and milk and a plate of cookies appeared in the middle of the flowered tablecloth Grandmom had placed there ahead of their arrival. This was going to be another of those special times, when the family of the Grays got to sit at the table, looking square at each other, one and all, and with comfort food at the ready, they would discuss their day. They had all been working hard over the last few weeks. Moving was to be a final thing in two days, as the crew had finished packing their belongings. The furniture, with few exceptions, they left for the Naval Officials who were to take over that outpost. There was stress all around—on the family, the sailors who were their friends, and the newly acquired strangers who needed a friend on this island. They found one in Captain Charles Pool Gray, who fit that bill to a fare-the-well. He was the perfect man to explain the workings of the island to men who needed to know. All were on alert, the children sensed it. Nett was always quiet, either stunned or scared or in denial. The time was now.

Tonight, they would, as a tightly knit family, relax to breathe and cement their bond, making a stressful time comfortable in the knowledge of togetherness. To the man, at that table, they were one—listening, wondering, laughing, sharing their lives and knowledge. There was much to know and time to teach. Grandpop was getting ready to tell of a time like the one they were facing and almost ready to experience. The anticipation of war could be as stressful as the war itself.

Grandpop began, "Three men met on this island, stayed over at the boardinghouse. They were inventors in electricity, all of them—greatest minds on that subject ever, here because of their knowledge of the airwaves that crisscross this piece of land called Hatteras Island. The air and ocean currents cause this. Strong ocean currents converging connect to this air above us. Right here the air is rich in conductors, and those men had figured it out. They intended to make their experiments right here: Edison, Marconi, and Fessenden. They had finished testing this place. They thought, to the man, that they could send sound through the air, using electricity in the atmosphere as the vehicle on which it traveled. When they were all in agreement, Fessenden made his trial and telegraphed across the ocean a human voice. Marconi, of the same mind, constructed a tower on the Cape, Fessenden, another tower over in Trent. They proved successful, and radio waves were invented. Finally the human voice could be heard around the world. Men took advantage, and the government and private companies began operating the wireless, connecting faraway places.

"Years later, using a combination of those things that were perfected in experiments that took place on this island, Richard Dailey, whose family has been on this island long as us, worked the wireless down at the weather station. On this particular night he started his shift by relaying an SOS from a ship in Panama, his fingers moving along the keys with the message for New York. He then began to pick up another signal. This time it was a communication from the ship *Titanic*, midway the Atlantic, clicking out a transmission of distress. It clicked again, 'URGENT!' Dailey took down the dispatch and relayed it to New York and was immediately reprimanded for sending a hoax. The *Titanic* was unsinkable, they clicked back, warning him of the consequences of 'cluttering up the airwaves.'

"The ship was a passenger liner, the most luxurious one ever put on the seas. She had ten decks and the most extravagant suites ever placed aboard a ship. She had closures built in, so if one level failed, the other compartments were sealed off from incoming water. She was thought to be unsinkable. She was traveling from England to New York, and her passenger list included some of the richest families in the world: bankers, department store owners, movie stars, politicians, and financiers. She had lifeboats for about half of these, but it seemed not to be a concern, until she hit an iceberg. There were sufficient lifejackets on board, one for everybody, but things happened so fast, most panicked and failed to go back to their cabins to retrieve them. When they did try to return to their berths, the onrush of frightened passengers prevented access to decks below. Even with a lifejacket, the water was so cold, most froze within fifteen to thirty minutes. She went nose down, broke in half, and took about 1,500 people with her.

"Later on that night, radios all over the nation reported having picked up the message from a nearby ship the *Carpathia*, that she was going to the aid of the *Titanic*, sinking twenty miles away. The young man David Sarnoff had ignored the relay that would have given notice hours earlier, before the ship slipped below the ocean with all those people. Sarnoff is the man who owns RCA and radio stations like the one we listen to now.

"So, that's my second most important shipwreck story. Now, young-uns, we got lots to do tomorrow, and I'm plumb tuckered out. Let's all hit it. Whaddya say?" Charlie had told the most intriguing story. Too bad it was true.

★ 18 ★

Good-Bye, Old Friend

The day began early. The children were awakened by noise, banging, voices, Grandmom and Nett giving directions—there was no sleep to be had. Ellie jumped out of bed and dressed quickly. They were moving today! She put on sturdy leggings, an old dress, and a full apron, covering the entirety of the garment, except for sleeves. She bound up her hair, as she knew there would not be anyone else to take the time. So she did her best pigtails, a little messy for sure, but out of her face. She hurriedly made her bed and looked around at the piles of boxes in her room. She started for the door, and with a second thought, she jumped, full bodied across the bed, to look out her window at the most beautiful sight she had ever seen: the mighty Cape Hatteras Lighthouse. She blew it a kiss and silently promised to never allow anyone to hurt it. She pledged to that stack of bricks and stone that she was here to protect it, and she would be back.

The door to the boys' bedroom was closed, and she tapped lightly and heard a sleepy, "Yeah?"

She then heard lots of commotion as the boys realized, as had she, that this was a day they had been planning for, and here they were still asleep. It was early, just light, and they usually slept maybe an hour more, but everything had already begun. She waited outside the door till it opened, revealing two boys, sleepy faced and sloppily dressed, who rushed out so fast they almost knocked her over.

"Let's go!" she said. "I think they are going to leave us!"

"Let 'em," said Blake. "I got my horse!"

They all smiled at each other and took the steps down two at a time, balancing their leaps with the railing. Grandmom was at the stove as usual, and did not appear to be in any hurry.

"What are you three doing up so early?" she said. "Noise wake you up? Now sit down at the table, I'll get breakfast for you. Your grandfather and mother have already eaten, but I wasn't expecting you to be up this early. Not a problem, I've got cornbread fried and dripping with butter. All I have to do is cook the eggs. How would you like a slab of fish." The resounding answer was *no!*

The children took their place at the table, but they were turned around in their chairs watching what was going on in the yard in front of the house. They could see through the screened door the trucks stacked behind each other, and the men loading boxes, mirrors, the radio, and that was all they could see, even though they strained to gather it all in.

They woofed down their breakfast, and each grabbed some fried cornbread for their pockets. No telling when they would eat again.

They raced to the front yard, greeted everyone, surveyed the loading, and—satisfied they knew all that was going on—headed toward the barn. The two government horses were already attached to the cart, with Grandpop on the buggy seat. He would go first because it would take some time for him to get through the village. Attached to the cart was the skiff mounted on a two-wheel dolly, loaded down with boxes, all belonging to the family and making the move.

This weird caravan would hopefully go through the village before anyone else was stirring. He would leave it all and come back on the next truck returning for a second haul.

The seamen had the big Coast Guard truck, Uncle Baxter was there with his side-railed truck, and Mr. Rocky, who designed and helped build the *Odessa W*, was there with a flatbed truck he used when hauling wood. Everything was loaded and moving. What time did everybody get up? It was only seven o'clock. Maybe they had all stayed up and worked all night? No use thinking about it now. They had avoided lifting heavy boxes, and it was probably a good thing they were out of the way.

Even the barn looked empty. Twinkle was at the new house already, and the three horses looked like they were ready to go. The chests for each horse, tack on the wall, chest loaded with blankets, most all the hay, water buckets, and grooming utensils were already at the new barn. Today, the only items left were one blanket for each horse, two saddles, bridals, and saddle bags—very unconventional saddle bags, as each child had his own invention. Blake had the most, he had lots of things he felt the need to carry with him. He and Spirit were just getting to know each other. The hours Blake spent draped over the horse's back, like a human blanket, resting his head on the red horse's neck, made them fast friends. During all conversations in the barn, that was Blake's "riding" position. The horse walked around gingerly, so as not to dump his cargo.

They mounted their rides and walked out of the barn almost for the last time. They headed over to the lighthouse. It was being readied to shut off the light, so as to deny a signal to the enemy. It was crawling with navy men, who were up and down the steps, securing every tiny thing. The lens was already covered with thick material resistant to breaking glass. The thought of hurricanes without any supervision was paramount to the navy. All working parts of the huge light were protected and secured from any larceny. They had polished, wiped down, painted, and generally readied the light to be lit again, maybe years from now.

The kids put their horses near the base, tied to a fence picket, and walked over to one of the sailors they knew.

"Can we go up, one more time?" Luke asked, and could not avoid the huge lump in his throat.

The young man, dressed in denim shirt and dungarees, his sailor hat cocked to one side, gave them a broad grin and answered with his Yankee accent, "You betcha!" He dropped what he was doing, and with a bow and a sweep of his hand, he motioned them up the steps.

The children started up the steps leading inside. At the bottom, in the round hall, they touched the wall and ran their hand along the inside to the iron stairway circling up and toward the tower. They began to count each step out loud, as they took their time pausing at each small window to look out at the ocean, on both sides. Luke lifted Blake each time to see what he and Ellie were seeing. They never let their hands leave a solid structure of the lighthouse. They were saying good-bye, and they wanted to feel their protector one more time. They were not worried about its destruction. They were just going to miss it.

On the top, one of the sailors allowed them to go out to the portico, and they walked all the way around. At the position where they could see the south side, they saw what Grandpop saw, and they smiled at how naive they were. They realized that Grandpop had known of their trips to the house on the hill every time they went. They wondered why he allowed it and decided it was his trust. They vowed to continue to feed that. It was a great man, a good Grandfather, a fine friend, who gave them their lead. How lucky they were to have him in their lives. They had recently met other great men, different occupations, but in their own way, they made up an island of men who would make anyone proud. What they did not realize was how talented they all were to do what they did, with the little they had to work with. Material things were overrated.

They sat with their feet through the spokes of the railing, wrapped their arms through the spikes, and watched the activity playing out in front of their former home. Nett was calling the shots. They could tell by her tone, she was giving directions—just her voice, not even what she said.

The workers moved to her tune, as Pop was on his way into the village and beyond, with Ol' Tony and Big Roy. Everything they had imagined was happening today. The sea looked calm. It was hard to believe everyone was expecting such horrible things to happen. Once again, they had gathered most of their knowledge from the window in Ellie's room. They were not afraid. Ellie, with her cheek on the railing, felt sad. This was her lighthouse. She knew it better than most. She said good night to it every night. She talked to it. The tower made her feel better with its silence. Others were in charge now, and what if they did not respect it? She was worried—and sorry to not be around to protect this wonderful friend, whom she had seen fight and win against so many storms.

Finally, Luke started making his way inside, and the others followed. Their actions on the way down mirrored the actions on the way up. This was the final good-bye, but secretly, in each child's mind, this was not good-bye, but "see you later." They were going to come back on every ride down the beach.

They mounted their horses. Blake and Ellie got a help up from one of the eight cornice circling the bottom, and Luke took a few quick steps and leaped firmly on Gus's back, pulled the reins to the right, and headed south down the beach to the house on the hill. They had planned to go to the house and organize their rooms, help Grandmom, and especially Grandpop, then, tomorrow, they would take their morning ride and revisit their beach, just to sit in front of the lighthouse. After all, they had not yet contacted their dolphins, and they needed to tell them where they went.

The kids turned up at their usual path and reached the scrub oaks and tall grass leading to the woods and the cleared footpath they had opened for their horses. Still, it was obscured from the beach, but now their horses would signal their directions, because now they were three, and they had learned from Manteo how to track. They remembered his checking tracks on the ground whenever he looked for an animal. Their animals were leaving a clear trail. Hopefully it would not be followed by random travelers on the beach. Spirit was the last, Pegasus the first, it would be that way forever. Blake hugged and patted his buddy's neck. It was his companion, just like his wolf, Theo. They made up a team, and it was not lost on him that he was now an independent man!

"We need to get some tools and chop down some of these limbs." Luke noticed the summer had caused much growth since they first removed the underbrush for a path.

"Let's do it tomorrow on our way back to the lighthouse. We can store the tools in the woods and pick them up when we get back," Ellie said.

"I've got a knife and a hatchet in my pack now," Blake volunteered.

And who was not surprised at that! Luke and Ellie leaned over, laughing as they turned around, and finally noticed just how much baggage Spirit was carrying. Poor horse. Blake needed to have a horse like Ol' Tony, because his horse was going to be packed with all things Blake. It was okay, Spirit was strong. As they turned around, eyes not looking straight ahead, they saw, lurking around in the thick bushes and trees, two of the wolves. Theo and Rafe sat together. Rafe, being black, was the first sighting, then the gray Theo behind, and into the thick brush, there was a white solid mass, obvious in all that foliage. Twylah was watching all of it, horses, children, and her pack. They were all together. The horses moved ahead. They smelled the wolves, but it was a familiar and nonthreatening nearness.

The nine companions, animal and human, reached the back of the house, walking up to the yard behind the barn between it and the little cottage. Grandpop was loosening the cart, and Luke jumped down to help him unhitch the skiff. They rolled the cart into the boathouse, leaving the boat in the yard. They were not ready to store it, as the boathouse needed to be organized to fit everything in a proper place. Thrown in the middle were poles, nets, crab traps, and various things to be used on the water. Grandpop missed the canoe. They informed him it was in the sound, *not... at the sound, as it enters a cave, as they had not yet revealed the cave's entrance.* They were determined to show Grandpop the cave, but it was not the time. There was lots to do, everywhere, the outbuildings and the big house.

Wow, here they were. They would spend their first night here. New bed, new sheets, different food, all kinds of unfamiliar life faced them. Books, hundreds of books, and the attic, the interior walls, the caves—so much, so different. The children wondered if they were the only ones who felt a little overwhelmed. Probably that person would be Grandpop, who had a new job. Not only was he in a new house, but a new job. He was already working on that. He was to be the principal and math teacher at the school. Now that he was a civilian, there were many other opportunities for him. He had been thinking of taking a more active part in the governing of the island—petitions to the U.S. government for roads, electricity, schools, and they needed a doctor. If the islands were to fight back an enemy on their shores, they would like to be rewarded with the same amenities the government afforded to the mainland they were protecting.

Grandpop had already been studying at the keeper's quarters, where he was often seen sitting on the porch, or at the dining room table, bent over state math books that he researched in order to better teach the topic to the high school students.

The children let the horses loose in the split-railed pasture area the workers had cleared when they made the chicken coops, and fashioned a fenced-in garden. The garden enclosure was complete with chicken wire to keep out varmints. This was not necessary. The wolves had taken care of the property over the years, and there was not a possum or a deer that came near the grand mansion. Nett and Grandmom, when talking about bringing in cats, had thought about the fact that they had not seen any signs of mice, rats, or rabbits. It was a strange thing for the house to be left unattended and not taken over by the woodland inhabitants.

Ellie was happy to see the many beautiful martin boxes already reaching the sky, most around the porches. They had at least four. They were beautiful, and someone had painted them. They looked like little houses up in the sky. They were little houses up in the sky, and the families of martins had already settled in. She looked at the horses, which finally could move around in a corral. They, too, having been locked away in a dark barn, were now out in the open for a few hours of the day. They must have been happy as they stood together, freely watching the goings-on at the new compound.

The trucks arrived, and things were carried to the veranda, then directed to the proper room. The unloading continued all day. Nett and Grandmom arrived in the new car, also loaded down, and they retired into the house. Grandmom went straight to the kitchen, lit the new stove, and began to make a substantial meal for at least a dozen people. The huge dining room table could take it all, but Grandmom sort of set the long butcher-block counter stretching the length of the kitchen, with all kinds of dishes, and she invited all to hang around the table and take their plates wherever they chose to sit. Some were on the front porch, some on the back, and others walking around in the barn and yard. Grandmom made fried chicken and flat fried cornbread, finger food that was easy to feed everyone. The smell alone was exceptional. The odor was even strange to the horses as their noses searched the air. Fried chicken christened the house, and life began to become normal. Grandmom had even ferried in a box full of all kinds of cookies. Now, it was official. The Grays had moved to Trent Woods.

The wolves settled down in their spot behind the small cottage to watch the activity. The kids ate and separated in order to unpack the boxes that had been deposited in their respective rooms. Grandmom settled in to make the kitchen her own. Grandpop stood on the porch, watching as Nett, her girlfriends, and sisters-in-law directed traffic. There were too many women in charge.

"Grandpop, I'll help you move your stuff." Luke stood on the covered veranda, with the wooden porch blinds pulled all the way up, probably to stay that way for a long time. His grandfather was not as young as he used to be, and those boxes of books destined for his new study were small, but heavy. He meant to help his grandfather settle in. Everyone else was busy with their own rooms, and Grandpop was probably totally out of his comfort zone, trying to organize a room. Grandmom would normally take care of all of that, but she had her hands full with the rest of the house, and Grandpop needed a place to hide and to study. Luke's help was the very thing the new "Mr. Charlie" needed, and he gladly accepted the offer.

Together they slipped, carried, and slid the items destined for Grand-pop's study into place. The room, though narrow, was perfect. It was equally as large as anything he had at the keeper's quarters, but this was such a massive house. Up high, probably where the kitchen had been added to the main house, there were windows that peeked out over the roof of the kitchen. They could only be propped open, as they were long and narrow—about two feet high by four feet long. They had been screened in, and there was a long pole to hook under the latch allowing the window to open a crack at the bottom. They provided both light and air to the room.

Luke directed the men to place Grandpop's rolltop desk in a proper place and began unpacking books for the walls of empty shelves, as Capt'n Charlie stacked his private papers in needed storage. He would stay in that area all day, away from the women, purposefully not available to make decisions, yet close to the action. Just down the hallway between the rooms, through Grandmom's section, he could get to the kitchen, unseen by anyone in the family. Especially Grandmom. He smiled as he thought of all the cookies he would steal over the next few years.

Charlie walked leisurely through the downstairs rooms and selected a large plush chair with a matching ottoman. He directed it to be moved to his study. Of course he had to test it out, so he sat down, put his feet up, and rested his head on the back. He was in a perfect position to be aware of the main sitting room, just on the other side of his door/bookcase.

He could hear anyone on the stairs and was just on the other side of the lower floor. Uncle Jabez had it all figured out. His clandestine deals with the pirates gave him cause to be aware of all things around him. With these thoughts, Grandpop took a long-earned nap.

When Luke once again ascended the stairs, he was met with a stupid grin on the face of his little brother. It was one of those looks that said, "I know something you don't know." Blake had been at the top of the steps on the right stairway that split from the landing, one set going right, one set of steps leading left. He was patiently waiting for Luke to come up to his room.

"What's that look for?" Luke asked, and Blake, silent, motioned him to his room, between Luke's and Ellie's. Ellie stuck her head out of her room and quickly ducked back, as Blake, showing an obvious scowl, motioned with a quick slap at the air to get back! She drew her head back in and disappeared.

"What is it? I haven't had a chance to unpack cause *somebody* had to help Grandpop, and neither of you were around."

Inside Blake's room, he positioned Luke to stand in the middle, facing the door leading to the hall. As they stood there, Ellie suddenly appeared, behind Blake. Luke whipped around with a puzzled look.

"How'd you get here?" he looked toward the window. It was closed, the curtains undisturbed.

"Look," and Blake opened the door to his closet, motioning for Luke to come in.

"You found a ladder!" Luke said excitedly.

"Nope, something better," and he moved aside the clothes on the back wall of his closet. There was a door with a latch, and when Blake pulled the latch the door slid aside, and there was Ellie's room with the back side of her bookcase open, like a door.

"Wow! How'd you find that?"

"I was looking for a ladder and ran my hand up and down the wall till I felt this crack. Then I saw a place to put my fingers, so I did, and slid it over. The whole door moved. I saw another crack on the other side, so I went into Ellie's room. We started looking and found a book, *Gulliver's Travels*, on her bookcase, which would open a section, like a door. Then, when we closed it, it looked just like a bookcase. You can see the crack a little bit, but nobody is going to get that close." Blake and Ellie could not wait to show Luke.

"Ellie and I started trying to find a special book in my bookcase, on the wall near your room. We tried all the books, but nothing worked. So we started unpacking our rooms again. I just knew my bookcase worked, I looked closely, and I could see the crack, so we started again with the books. On the left end, just like Ellie's, we pulled out *The Last of the Mohicans*, and it worked. I didn't think it was that book, cause it wasn't thick, but it worked. When the door opened, we could see the back of your bookcase. Want to go see?"

All three went into Luke's room, found the crack between the sections, and began pulling the books that might trigger an opening. When they pulled *The Complete Works of Shakespeare*, the bookcase swung open, and they walked through. Back in Blake's room they sat on his bed and just laughed. Blake was the happiest of all. He might not have a secret ladder to the attic, but he had access to everybody else, and he knew that from now on, all meetings would be in his room. He had finally achieved being the center of attention!

The bookcases worked just like the one leading to Grandpop's study. *Plutarch's Lives* was Grandpop's book. Each opened in the middle and swung open to the left of the double cases and revealed an opening.

Each room was big, bigger than the apartment Nett had at the keeper's quarters. Each had a double bed. The head of the bed was just below the window, allowing a draft with the open door for summer days. They each had a desk with a bookcase making up the top part. There was a kneehole on one side, with deep drawers on the other. The three rooms had a comfortable chair that matched the desk. Blake had two rather large dressers on one wall and a tall bookcase on the opposite wall, the wall he shared with his brother. Luke had a closet on the wall, next to the wall he shared with his mother. His closet went the entire length of his room, and his dresser and writing desk were up against that wall. Also in that closet was a ladder leading to the attic with all the old trunks. Ellie also had a huge closet, next to the wall she shared with her grandparent's apartment/ bedroom, with dressers on either side of the closet door. On the opposite side, next to Blake, she had a long, tall bookcase, in her mind, for both books and dolls. Blake had a large long closet on the same wall he shared with Ellie. Up against that closet wall were two large dressers. Both had drawers on one side and a door on the other, hiding shelves for stacking clothes. The hidden door to Ellie's room was on the back wall of his closet.

Before they began unpacking further and organizing, they decided to check on something familiar they smelled drifting upstairs. They scampered down to the kitchen, almost running through the huge house. They also found a new game: who could make it to the landing first. Ellie went down the left stairwell, Luke the right, Blake, in the middle, was far away from both, so he had to be fast to win. The dining room was so big they caught each other there. At the back, they jumped down to the lower floor of the kitchen, not even touching the three stairs descending to the stone floor of the attached kitchen, which stretched the entirety of the back. Grandmom was in the middle of a bunch of boxes, with men hooking up the refrigerator and making sure the stove worked. This they did with a sheet cake Grandmom made to ensure the stove was operational. She was now whipping up a creamy topping. It seemed the workers wanted to stay in the kitchen hooking up machines just to stay near the food.

There was still much to do: the house, the yard, the barn, the boathouse, the little cottage, and they could not forget the caves. Would they ever find all the secrets the house held? As far as the house was concerned, it was ready yet again for another war. It was in the perfect position to be of help. There would be hours spent on the third floor, looking out to the sea and reporting what they saw. This was a part they had not anticipated.

From the kitchen, they went to the barn. They positioned the chests near the stalls and stopped by the new pasture to say hello to the cow and five horses, who seemed to be content chewing nothing. They carried the barn equipment from the front to the particular stalls intended for each horse. Ellie had her special trunk, just outside Blue's stall, beside his chest for blankets. They nailed hooks on the walls for each horse's bridle and strapping, organized each saddle near the appropriate stall, and went back to the kitchen, hoping the cake was ready. It was, and they joined the men helping Grandmom and Nett for an afternoon snack. Milk: it was cold. How'd that happen? Tommy, Capt'n Charlie's son who managed Pop's store in Buxton, had delivered ice. There was also a bushel of blue crabs, bubbling and spitting as they sat in the shade on the back porch. Things were looking up.

After the snack of milk and cake, they retired to their rooms again and began unpacking. They had shelves and drawers to fill. Ellie was anxious to find a place for her dolls to live. She had a huge closet and was so proud to hang her dresses in a way to hide the ladder she had discovered on the back wall. This was the same kind of ladder as in Luke's room, leading to the secret attic of trunks. She could read the Magic Book any time she wanted to. And the passageway to Blake's room, that was special. So she only put small books on the part that moved. She wanted the case to move easily, not with so much weight that she had to struggle. This was truly a magical house, and she loved her room and her big bed. Already it had tons of blankets and puffy quilts on top. She also loved it because it was so close to her grandparents. They had a sitting room off the big bedroom with a fireplace.

The windows looked out over the front yard, and she could see the road coming in from the village. Mom and Aunt Nett had already whipped the dust from her beautiful, rich-looking drapes. They were from a bolt of cloth Uncle Jabez had been given by Captain Johns, the privateer, when he raided the Red Sea merchant ship. The cloth from India and China was hard to sell, so the captain gave it to his friend, whom he knew was building a house. Aunt Rhetta had finished all the windows with the bolts of heavy fabric. The colors were rich and plush, and each set matched the furniture in the room where they hung. The rods they were attached to were gold colored and ornate. This was a beautiful place.

Blake was having a hard time finding places for his clothes, as most of his available space, and there was a lot of it, was already taken up by the necessities that enhanced Blake's life: his knife, his hatchet, small figurines carved by the Indians, his deerskin hide outfit, his boots, the Jade Dragon he intended to bring in to occupy one whole shelf, the statuettes of pirates he would ask Grandpop for—and he intended to move some of the things he found in the trunks in the attic to his room, adding more precious items to his collection. For the first time in a long time, he took the leather bag from his pocket that carried his flint. He put it on a small table by the door in order not to forget it when he left.

A double bed! Big enough for the three of them to sit on cross-legged to hatch ideas. The window of his room looked out over the front yard. He could also see who was coming up the road from the village. There was something else he observed. The pitch of the roof over the front veranda was slight. It could easily be walked on, or one could sit out there. There was no end to the opportunities he saw for himself.

Luke had the largest room. It shared a wall with his mother's apartment, which stretched front to back, taking up the right side of the third floor. Grandpop and Grandmom had an identical apartment, on the opposite end, and both had fireplaces. Each actually was two rooms: a sitting area and a bedroom area. Nett's room had been the one where Ellie had met her real mother's ghost and the apparitions of Weroansqua and Aunt Rhetta. Also, it was from Luke's room they had accessed the attic. He already had things in his room that Uncle Jabez had left. The books and some brass items brought no bids, so both the pirates and Captain Johns had given the items to Jabez, in appreciation for handling their business and to unclutter their ships. The heavy draperies held a fresh air scent, since they had been hung outside so long. The house had lost its musty odor. Now all the windows and doors were open. The breeze was whipping through, making everything smell fresh. They could even smell the ocean air, as both huge apartment/bedrooms had windows facing the sea, and they were flung open. The third-floor windows were sending breezes from sound and sea down to the floors below.

Most of the activity was now taking place on the second floor with Nett, Ellie, Luke, and Blake. Grandmom had not yet left the kitchen, and Grandpop was hiding in his study. It set the mood for what would be going on in that house most every day from now on.

Grandpop had finished his rest, never more than twenty minutes, and was now organizing his many sets of papers. There was a section for school, one for government, one as notary public, and sections for each subject. His petition for public roads, electric lights, consolidation of the island schools, not to mention his new obligation as advisor to the navy—all were now catalogued. He was a busy man who had no time to dwell on his previous job. He had so many duties to take its place. Most of all, he was happy his family was away from the expected carnage of sub warfare between the warring sides of World War II.

They continued settling in until almost dark. All the helpers and extra vehicles had long gone home. Grandmom covered the long dining room table with thick cloth and newspaper from packing. She boiled the crabs, dumped them on the middle of the table, and called "Supper!" This she did by banging on a pot.

As the family gathered at one end of the table to crack and eat the crabs, sent over by "someone," they discussed the grand size of the table. Grandpop suggested he ask Mr. Conn to make some tall seats for eating in the kitchen around the long, tall counter that ran down the middle.

Grandmom requested a small kitchen table, as there was room. Ellie reminded them of the one in the small cottage, and on and on it went.

The chatter was nonstop. Everybody had something to tell about their special space. Nobody mentioned anything about secret passages.

The children were excused to take care of the horses, while the grown-ups lingered to continue to talk, and eventually clean up.

Chores over, the kids returned to what seemed to be an empty house. Voices on the veranda solved the mystery. Grandpop, Grandmom, and Nett were in rocking chairs, Grandpop smoking, Grandmom crocheting, and Nett just resting. The swing was empty. Not for long. The nightbirds and woodland sounds were unusual. It was something they would learn to love. In full view of the entire porch, the wolves lounged at the edge of the clearing. Nobody seemed surprised.

That night, each member of the family retired to their own private quarters to finish readying their rooms for a more welcome and comfortable existence. The kids arranged and rearranged clothes, books, personal treasures, and then they began to miss each other. No matter what they did, something was missing. For Luke and Blake, it was each other. Luke pulled the book on his bookcase, and as it opened, he was surprised to see the passageway between his and Blake's bedroom was open. He stuck in his head and walked through. As he emerged out the door of the open bookcase, he saw Blake sitting in the middle of his bed, looking down-trodden. He flashed the biggest grin when he saw Luke and bounded off the bed and gave him a big hug, his head pressed into Luke's chest. They both smiled and jumped on Blake's bed.

"I'm sleeping here tonight," Luke said. "Okay with you?"

"Let's get Ellie," and Blake was off the bed again. He opened the door of his closet and walked through to the door leading to Ellie's room. He tapped lightly on the wall behind. Almost immediately, the bookcase swung open, and Ellie walked through to the closet. She must have been standing right there.

They all laughed at the closeness they still could have. As they sat on the floor of Blake's closet and talked quietly of feelings, happiness, sadness, and closeness, they talked so long, they began to get sleepy. Luke found a stack of puffy quilts in Blake's closet. He knew they were there, as he had some stacked on the floor of his closet also. The bed coverings had also been thrown over the outside clothesline for the sun to burn off the must and replace it with fresh air. They smelled good. He threw each one a quilt, and they all stretched out and continued to talk until they fell asleep and ended up spending the night on the floor of Blake's closet.

★ 19 ★

They're Here!

At breakfast the next morning, everybody looked a little tired. They had probably stayed up much too late, arranging things in their private quarters. The children looked rested, despite having talked late into the night, and raring to go. They could hardly wait to be excused from the table to start their day. Grandmom had already been out to the new chicken coop and gathered eggs. Grandpop was going back to the keeper's quarters for one last go-through, and Nett was going with him. The kids asked for permission to take the horses for a morning stretch. They promised to be back by dinner.

Luke helped both Ellie and Blake with their saddle. Blake protested, as he wanted to only use the blanket.

"There's no way I'm going to let you fall off that horse. What if we want to run? How you gonna stay on if he wants to stretch his legs?" He had seen Blake with his not yet grown-up legs trying to straddle the horse to stay upright. His knees hit so high up, there was hardly a grip. Also, he was really worried about Ellie not having the safety of a saddle. She would never live through a fall. Once she broke something,

269

she would probably bleed to death. Everybody was always anxious when Ellie got a scratch. She had inherited a rare disorder that caused her blood to clot slower than normal, and it was hard to stop, even a scratch. Ellie was careful, but she was also determined to do what everyone else did, so Luke was going to make sure they all rode safely. Grandpop had already promised him a saddle also. Luke really wanted to be rugged, but he was not yet old enough. Pop had convinced him he needed one, with the simple statement, "If you ever want to race your horse, you both have to get used to a saddle. There will be no going fast unless there's something to hang on to." So he slid Blake's saddle from the balustrade over to the horse, by the ropes and pulleys that lifted the weight. When Blake got on his horse, he loosened the clips that held the saddle to the ropes, and they swung away. The same had been made for Ellie's saddle. One of the Coast Guard boys was from Texas, and he invented the way to lift the saddles with ropes.

They were lucky. It was low tide, and they walked abreast on the hard sand, until Blake gave Spirit a nudge and he was off. Not to be outdone, Luke urged Gus forward and was in hot pursuit. Blue was making a sound, snorting as though being left behind did not please him. Ellie leaned forward, gave him a slight kick with her heel, and proceeded to catch up. It was a race, with all kids hanging on for dear life. Ellie's hands were wrapped tightly in the bridle, and she was holding on with her knees. She was glad she had the saddle. Even with the saddle, Blake almost slid off, and as he caught himself slipping, he slowed down. Luke was right on him and passed just a little ways, and then slowed for Ellie to catch them. When she did, she urged Blue to pass them all. She was giving him a psychological win. It was a beautiful day, and by now they were nearing The Point, so they cut across to get to the other side.

Just abreast of the lighthouse they stopped, tied the horses behind the dunes to the small scrub oaks, walked over to the dry shore, and let the sun put them to sleep. They couldn't help it. They had talked almost all night the night before and probably didn't get much real sleep on the floor of Blake's closet, and it was warm today. The ocean was calm, and they could hear each wave as it tumbled onto the shore in a soft roll.

They awakened to darkness, and they were startled by it. Surely they had not slept all day long. As they opened their eyes, they saw the blue hulk of Poseidon blocking out the sun. He was waist deep, with one arm at his side, his hand and wrist on the water. Water and sargassum vines poured down his body like a waterfall. In the other hand he held his trident. The sunlight lit up the three prongs and caused them to emit what looked like electric sparks. Something silver hung from the prongs. Poseidon's trident was his weapon, given to him as the earth was divided into three rulers, this according to Greek mythology. Zeus was given the lightning bolt, Hades the helmet of invisibility, and Poseidon the trident. The trident, when struck on earth, caused an earthquake. It also called forth tsunamis, controlled storms, and could calm the sea. Wrapped around his lower waist was the curl of an enormous fish tail, only a portion visible, the forked tail somewhere out in the ocean. As he thrust the staff toward them, dripping from the mighty spear were three silver threads, with a crystal hanging from each. The icy-looking old man dipped his weapon toward the three youngsters and let the strings drop in front of them.

Poseidon reached over and picked up the crystal meant for Ellie. As gently as he could, with his massive size, he moved closer to her, and in a language only she could understand, he told her that her beloved Moira had met with a tragic misfortune that had taken her life. Ellie was shocked, and it registered on her face. Moira dead? She could not imagine. Why? Did they not live forever? Her head dropped, and Poseidon waved his hand over the sea. The boys just looked at the strange sight of the mighty Poseidon, half in, half out of the water, leaning over, staring into the eyes of their cousin. She in turn was staring back, but her eyes were filling with tears. They sat mesmerized at the two seemingly communicating. Later they would learn that Moira had mysteriously been struck by something unfamiliar to the sea creatures, and it had taken her life. It would make sense, but only later.

Poseidon lightly placed the crystal around Ellie's neck and motioned again toward the sea. Through her tears, Ellie saw the most fantastic sight. Shooting straight up and making a twirl was a young dolphin. The most amazing thing about the new mammal was that it changed colors as it spun, sort of like the Dorado and sailfish did when they breached. But these colors were not as dark as those two fish. They were like a rainbow, and they rippled around the young dolphin like music. Ellie immediately understood from the look Poseidon gave her that this dolphin was hers. The word "Iris" kept whirling around in Ellie's mind. It must have been the name of the dolphin. Poseidon looked pleased. The boys looked puzzled, and Ellie smiled.

With that, he leaned forward and to the side and, using his unoccupied hand, reached out over his head and slipped head first quietly into the sea. His blue hair spread over the sea, as his trident was the last thing they saw slip beneath the smooth ocean. As the patron of horses, his blue foam horses were not to be seen, nor did he seem to be in his chariot. It seemed to be a special visit.

They were now all sitting up, and as they reached over for their necklace, they heard the squealing of the dolphins as they appeared above the water, dancing on their tails. They were all here! The children hastily stood as the thread wove a familiar suit around them, making their goggles, helmet, and flippers. The rings of sargassum washed on the shore. They waded out, threw the grassy matts over the backs of their respective dolphins, and as the dolphins dove under them, the children straddled the mammals while the silver thread fastened them to the saddle being woven to the matts. As the dolphins rose above the water, they carried three extra bodies, all wrapped in silver and melded to their slick backs.

Each spoke familiarly to their mounts and gave one last look toward shore as their horses waited patiently beyond the dune. What must they have thought seeing Poseidon—they must have a connection, an inner awe. He, after all, was their spiritual protector. Willi took off first. He and Luke headed to sea, with the wind blowing against them to the east, and every once in a while dipping under for a fresh splash of the tasty salt water. Iris, the rainbow dolphin, glistened and changed as her skin reflected the silver rider she carried. Blake and James were following Willi. Ellie began to communicate. She concentrated on her message and, with her knees, led Iris to the right, toward The Point. Ellie found that Iris was indeed a younger version of her beautiful white friend, and in her mind she "understood" that this was the daughter, and equally as impressive as her mother, and stronger. They left the other two, but Ellie was not worried, as dolphins seemed to possess a radar that did not allow them to get lost. As she nudged Iris ahead, it was obvious they were going very close to The Point. There was a trough between the landmass of The Point and the first shoal that rose to create what they called the Hatteras Shoal. Ships could not make it through the trough, but whales knew about it, and they could easily maneuver between the two sand hills. Evidently dolphins knew the paths of the ocean floor also.

Ellie was taking Iris to a point off the shore opposite the house on the hill. She wanted to show her exactly where they would be on the beach. They navigated the trough and rounded The Point. When Ellie thought she saw the familiar dune, she leaned over and wrapped her arms around the neck of the dolphin and rested her head on the fin. She guided the dolphin with her knees, back and forth, back and forth in front of the area where they now lived. And in her mind, she indicated to Iris she would be here. Iris made a series of rhythmic clicks and ducked under the ocean. In Ellie's heart, she knew her new friend was familiar with her mind. She had gained confidence in her powers to communicate with nonhuman creatures. Ellie nudged the dolphin around and went back toward The Point. Going around The Point the same way they came they ducked between what Ellie could only describe as two sand mountains and came out to deep sea again. At last, they arrived at their starting point and headed out to sea. Mission accomplished!

Luke and Willi seemed to be headed straight out to sea. Luke hoped they were going to the shipwrecks. Now that he had learned so much about them, he wanted to see if he could find some of the ones whose bones lay at the bottom *of the sea. There had been 2,300 documented wrecks on the shoals since the year 1500. There was no estimate of those lost undocumented. Luke, not as clairvoyant as Ellie, however, was given gifts by Powwaw, and that added to the strength of Poseidon, who claimed his dolphin as the most intelligent species in the ocean. There was a thread that connected them all: Poseidon, the dolphin, and the child. He was familiar with the connection he and the dolphin held through the silver thread of Poseidon. Willi understood what Luke wanted to do, and he veered in the direction of a concentration of wrecks deep under the ocean. They found the rusted and salt-eroded parts of ships within a few minutes. They began to ride in and out among the openings of huge sailing ships, their masts lying on the sand straight out from the body of the vessel, in a manner, if one should see them from above, that the ship would look complete. Some were broken apart, with the parts were so scattered and piled on each other, one could not tell which part belonged to which ship.*

*James and Blake joined them, and the two went in and out, inspecting the things they could recognize. They were also joined by sharks, but the predators did not appear to be interested in them. The dolphins held a bit of respect from the mighty teeth of the sea. Sharks usually did not confront them. Luke thought maybe Poseidon had a hand in causing the sharks to leave them alone. The ocean floor was thick with growth creeping over the parts of the ship. The algae was so thick it looked like a green mossy compilation of forms and structures that at one time formed a mighty ship. There were former wooden schooners, some three-, four-, five-masted originally, as long as 100 yards or more—the big and the small, some merchant ships, some freighters, all having lost their battle with the sea. Only a few times could they actually recognize a particular part, such as the huge anchors or old iron ship's wheels and heavy ballast stones now released from their cages. They swam past a huge iron vessel. It took them such a long time to cover the area. Luke read the sign on the side. From what letters were left, he pieced together what he thought to be, "*DIAMOND SHOAL*" and a number that looked like "11." He would later find out it was "71."*

They saw again the rounded top of the ship that was the Monitor, looking for all the world like Grandmom's sewing box, here, sunk in a storm, as it was being towed south. It too was large, as they swam around the circular upper structure. The schools of fish that lived among these wrecks numbered in the thousands. Their colors likened to the pictures of exotic fish in the encyclopedia. Their fins were comparable to bird feathers, colors that could not be duplicated. Willi moved away from the shoals, farther out to sea, and here they found more merchant ships, huge sailing ships, and rubble of indistinguishable shapes and forms of the many victims of storms.

Blake and James kept close to the larger Willi, and when the big dolphin refused a nudge by Luke to go in a certain direction. Luke looked at what Willi was trying to avoid. It was something on the ocean floor that was very thick and fuzzy, and didn't look threatening, but it was a thing that Willi knew and of which he wanted no part. Luke was well read, and in his mind, it could have been an unexploded mine resting on the floor. Maybe it was, maybe it wasn't. He would find it in his grandfather's encyclopedia.

Many of the ships he saw were laying on their sides, like ships asleep. He and Blake knew they were far from shore, and it had been a while since they saw Ellie, so they connected with their rides to turn around. The dolphins responded and began their ride across the smooth ocean.

Suddenly the water changed, and the dolphins dove under something as they continued underwater. Something dark and long was moving through the water above them. Its dark form traveled just over their heads, but the kids could not see just what it was. Luke was thinking it was a whale. As the dolphins continued toward shore, they were going in the opposite direction of the dark form. Luke motioned Blake to get close as they sped steadily toward the beach, hoping to find Ellie. The thing came close. It was powerful enough to displace the water around them, and the dolphins struggled not to get sucked closer. Both Luke and Blake looked up as the dark form passed overhead. It had a portion protruding above the top, with spikes sticking up from that. Luke's heart stopped! It was shaped like a bullet, and it looked like *the size of the lighthouse, as water distorts shape. The last thing he saw was a huge round propeller churning up the inner ocean. Luke knew what it was.*

Like a horse, Luke nudged Willi to go faster. He motioned for Blake to do the same, but James was ahead of them, and keeping close to Willi.

Their ride was over. He needed to get home. They sped toward the lighthouse, and almost there, they saw Ellie and the beautiful Iris, playing around nearer the shore. Luke did his best to communicate with her. They mentally connected, and Ellie knew her ride was coming to an end. She didn't mind. They were supposed to be home by dinner, and she had accomplished what she started out to do. She had shown the dolphin where she lived. She was also anxious to tell Luke and Blake about Iris. Surely they must be wondering what happened to Moira. She was sad and happy all at the same time. She wondered if Moira was old and had died a natural death. And she couldn't believe that this younger version was as special and beautiful as the white dolphin. Ellie had seen Iris change colors as she changed directions, as if her coloring had something to do with energy. Ellie needed to get someplace quiet and say good-bye to Moira.

Near shore, they felt something like a pulse reverberating through the water. It was a forceful wallop that moved under the sea like thunder. It moved the three, and the dolphin squealed, the kids dismounted, and Luke leaned down to Willi and cautioned him to be careful. He was happy the dolphins were not farther out to sea, as underwater sound could damage their inner sonar. He imagined the beautiful fish he had seen. Were they damaged? When the three gained the beach, their suits fell away.

Luke awakened with a start. He sat up and shook his head to clear it, and then remembered the underwater blast that shook the earth. The others were beginning to stir, sit up, and rub the sleep from their eyes. He needed to get out of there. They were confused as to why it was all cut short. But Luke, being the oldest, when he said hurry, they did. He grabbed Ellie by the arm and reached out for Blake. The three of them half ran, half were pulled across the sand to the dunes where the horses waited. When they got to the horses, everybody was talking, Blake was protesting, and Ellie was just confused.

Ellie kept protesting, though, too. "I have something to tell you both. Can we stop a minute?"

"They're here! They're here!" Luke said in a halting sputter of fear and excitement.

"What?" Ellie and Blake both asked at once, their confused faces wondering what Luke was doing. He had almost yanked Ellie's arm off.

"Blake, did you see that dark thing we passed out there? It was a submarine! A submarine!" He was almost yelling as he reached to help Ellie mount her horse.

Blake showed the shock and fear he felt as he heard the words. It was something he never thought he would hear. His actions reflected his fear, as he tried to jump and get his foot in the stirrup. Luke came to his rescue and cupped his hands to allow his little brother to mount.

"Luke, I'm scared!" Blake said in a shaky voice as it broke in almost a sob.

"C'mon, we got to hurry. Don't worry, they didn't see us. But we got to go tell Pop, now!" and he hurriedly jumped on Gus. "Look, I'm scared, too, but we can't be until we get home. You okay, Ellie? Don't worry, they are headed out to sea, and I think they fired a bomb at something. I felt explosion travel through the ocean."

"Is that what that was? I felt it, too," said Ellie.

"Me, too." Blake was shaking.

"Blake, don't be scared. Just be careful. Nothing is going to happen to us, but we have to go tell Grandpop. We can't afford to be afraid. Remember, we learned a lot from Manteo, so now we have to be the kids he thought we were." Luke was also shaking a little, but from anxiety, not fear.

Blake sat on his horse and calmed himself. He remembered being brave, and he tried to remember that feeling. A calm washed over him, and as he looked at Ellie, her eyes were closed. She was sending her calm to him. He could feel it. She moved Blue next to Spirit and held out her hand. She motioned with the other one for Luke to stand beside the two of them. Luke and Gus sidled up to her, and the three held hands and closed their eyes. They sat there until each of them stopped shaking. Then, with a sweet smile, Ellie let go.

They were all in a better place and started south to The Point and home. They began to quicken their pace, and by the time they got to The Point, their horses were in a comfortable gallop.

"Not too fast," Luke said. "We have plenty of time. I think it just fired, so it will take time for it to come around again. I don't want anybody falling off. Let's just get going." They kept a steady pace till they got to the path where they would turn up.

As they trotted down the beach, Ellie did her best to tell her cousins about her communications with Poseidon. Her mouth quivered a little as she told them about Moira, and they all wondered if maybe there had been another explosion, and it had taken Moira's life. They wanted to talk to a grown-up, but that was not possible. Ellie knew she would dream of Weroansqua that night and get answers then. Also, for some reason, she smiled inside thinking that Iris belonged to her, and Poseidon had once again chosen a special part of his family for her.

They arrived a little after the time that Grandmom wanted, and Pop was sitting on a stool in the kitchen getting ready to dig into some fried fish. When he looked up, he knew something was terribly wrong, and on instinct he stood up and came to the children. He gathered them to him and asked what had caused them to be so white and flushed at the same time.

Luke blurted out what he had seen. Blake blurted out what he had felt. The part Pop couldn't understand was how they could know that kind of thing. Was the sub close to shore? What did it look like? The three looked at each other and allowed Luke to do all the talking.

"Pop, I saw it. It came to the surface. There wasn't enough for a ship. It was small, but by the wake, there was so much more of it below the water. It was moving so fast out to sea, I only saw it for a little bit. It had big spikes on the top. Then, after it disappeared the ground shook, and thunder came from the water. It made the beach under us move. That thing fired something at somebody, I just know it. Pop, what are we going to do?" He looked straight into his grandfather's blue eyes and waited for an answer.

"C'mon," he said, and they all followed him, leaving Grandmom and Nett standing by the stove, having not moved a muscle nor said a word. Grandmom was clutching her apron to her heart, and Nett was covering her mouth.

Grandpop went to the study and got the car keys. He motioned for the three to come with him, and he tore out of the yard, leaving divots in the dirt as he raced down the two-track road to the village, on his way to the Coast Guard station.

The horses remained where they were left, saddle and everything.

When they returned, it was late afternoon. They carried with them a short wave radio, the Navy had insisted he take it home, and connect it immediately. They knew he had as good a vantage point on his third floor as they had on top of the Coast Guard station. The boys at the station had been all through the house and could see the advantages. He would figure out how to hook it up in the morning. Too much time was lost today in the drive. He needed to be able to contact the base with information as soon as he got it.

Finally, the children worked off their energy by tending to the patient steeds. They put a little extra energy in grooming them. They needed a distraction.

The supper table was quiet. Grandpop did not see the need in alarming everyone, even though his stomach was in knots. He tried to keep the conversation light. He knew how Grandmom felt, and he worried about Nett. No matter what was said, he knew she was thinking about Bill, just as he was thinking about his sons Jack, Wallace, Curtis, and Fay. If truth be known, even he, like Blake, did not really believe what was going to happen, and as far as he was concerned, the worst was getting ready to play out.

That night the ground shook under the house. Luke rushed out of his room and encountered Grandpop as he hurried from his room to the stairs leading to the lookout on the third floor. They stood at the window looking into the black sky—black, except for the glow of fire off in the distance, far out to sea.

Grandpop put his arm around his grandson and pulled him to him.

Yes! They were here.

EPILOGUE

The accounts of shipwrecks and the heroism of surfmen have been a pleasure to research. In writing, I recognized men whom I met while stuck to my grandfather's leg. I watched as he left the house and begged to go. On those trips I met David Stick, the author of so many books on this subject. Mr. Stick was the recipient of the journals and logs from the various stations, set to be destroyed as they were found in the attic of a building scheduled for demolition.

I met Levene Midgett, captain of the Coast Guard at the Rodanthe (then Chicamacomico) station, on whose DUCW I took a ride. Captain Bernice Ballance, whose presence in my grandfather's house at supper-time was a welcome visit, came with local conversation and information. Uncle Baxter Miller was recipient of not one but two Lifesaving Medals. I watched Dick Burrus play baseball against my uncle Tommy, and Burrus, who wiped the field with his opponents, was always the victor. Men like Guy Quidley; Stockey Midgett; Anderson Midgett; Frazier Peele; Clarence Brady; Charlie Williams II; Rocky Rollinson; Gibb Gray; Ben Dixon MacNeil; E. S. White and his wife, Maude, two of my grandfather's friends; the Farrows, Odens, Burruses, Barnetts, Scarboroughs, Hoopers, Fulchers, Austins, and Willises—all were movers and shakers of progress on the island. These are only a few of the men and women who put their education and common sense to the benefit of society as it existed on this island. For those who have wondered what we did, the answer, "Same as you."

No matter how small the place, there are always those who make it better, the same happened here. We had heroes, inventors, innovators of all categories, strong Christian values, strong discipline, good teachers, and statesmen. The island was always self-sufficient. We lacked nothing. We found most answers inside ourselves and in the land, sea, and sky around us. In story form, I have tried to present this way of life. To tell you the truth, it was fun!

This was a remarkable time in the history of this island, but not nearly as remarkable as its existence as the buffer between two world wars and the sacred shores of the homeland. The next volume—the last of the five chronicling life on the island when it was totally separated from the mainland, without bridge or paved road or strangers—tells of the battle for a strip of land that stood between the hoards of people living mainland, and the enemy that wanted to conquer.

The Island at War, the title of the final volume, offers looks at the Revolutionary War, War of 1812, Spanish-American War, World War I, and finally, the sacrifice made by island people in World War II. Not until World War II ended were the citizens of the mainland informed of how close they had come to being invaded by the German Empire. Authorities feared the knowledge would create panic from New York to Florida, so they quietly worked with islanders to contain the knowledge of carnage that washed up on the beaches.

Every inhabitant on this island became involved in that war, those who enlisted and participated on the battlefields of sea and ground and those who were left behind. Heroism was not limited to the battlefield. It was displayed by ordinary citizens who recognized the need.

Join me as I honor my ancestors on this island you have also adopted. You have chosen a wonderful place to visit or live. I mean to tell you just how wonderful it is.

APPENDIX

A Partial List of the Shipwrecks of the
Areas Covered in *Surfmen and Shipwrecks*

AREA AROUND PRESENT-DAY OREGON INLET

J. F. Becker, 1903
Sarah J., 1961
June, 1899
Voucher, 1817
Eagle, 1870
Waltham, 1874
Montana, 1904
*Five smaller sailing ships, unnamed**

PEA ISLAND

Charles J. Dumas, 1911
Flambeau, 1867
C. C. Thorn, 1846
Isabella Parmenter, 1925
Annie E. Blackman, 1889
B. T. Martin, 1861
*Four smaller sailing ships, unnamed **

NEW INLET (SOUTH OF PEA ISLAND, AT INLET)

James Woodall, 1896

Sue Williams, 1890

John Maxwell, 1912

Tamarack, 1921

Three smaller sailing ships unnamed *

CHICAMACOMICO (PRESENT-DAY RODANTHE)**

George L. Fessenden, 1898

Mirlo (British), 1918

Josie Troop (Canadian), 1889

America (Italian), 1876

Milledgeville, 1839

San Delfino (British), 1942 (Torpedo)

Marore, 1942 (Torpedo)

Henry Norwell, 1896

Alfred Brabrook, 1899

Seven smaller sailing ships, unnamed *

GULL SHOAL (SOUTH OF SALVO AT DAY AREA)

Raymond T. Maull, 1906

General S. F. Merwell, 1912 (Torpedo)

Elm City, 1912 (Torpedo)

G. A. Kohler, 1933

Louise, 1942 (Panamanian)

Saxon, 1907

Priscilla, 1899

Blaisdell, 1875

S. G. Hart, 1898

Ciltvaira, 1942 (Torpedo)

City of Atlanta, 1942 (Torpedo)

Six other smaller sailing vessels, unnamed *

LITTLE KINNAKEET (VISIBLE FROM HIGHWAY 12, NORTH OF AVON)

Robert W. Dasey, 1899

Hettie J. Dorman, 1900

Annie E. Pierce, 1892

L. Warren, 1876

Leroy, 1842

Chester Sun, 1942 (Torpedo)

*One other smaller sailing ship, unnamed**

BIG KINNAKEET (JUST SOUTH OF AVON)

Mary S. Eskridge, 1911 (Torpedo)

Islington, 1830

John Shay, 1889

Thames (British), 1869

*Six other smaller sailing vessels, unnamed**

CAPE HATTERAS

Monitor, 1862

Martha, 1893

Congress, 1842

Carroll A. Deering, 1921

*Twenty-eight other ships lost in the area of Diamond Shoals, most unnamed**
This is the closest to Diamond Shoals. The lighthouse warns ships off. Most ships tried to anticipate this area as they steered for sea. Rescues here were usually oars and surfboat, not much from shore.

CREEDS HILL (NORTH OF FRISCO)

Australia, 1942 (Torpedo)

Six other ships lost before the station was put in place.
Most of the Creeds Hill surfmen also went to the rescue of ships also cited off the Cape Hatteras station, as in the Carroll A. Deering. The stations of both Cape Hatteras and Creeds Hill went out to that ship several times before it was finally boarded by the keeper of the Cape Hatteras station. This ship was caught deep in the sand of the Diamond Shoals.

HATTERAS INLET

John N. Parker, 1884
City of New York (Federal), 1862
Governor (Federal), 1861
William Rockefeller, 1942 (Torpedo)
Five other ships lost in that area, unnamed.
Nineteen named ships wrecked off the coast of Ocracoke, and eight unnamed.

OTHER NOTES

In 1918 the Diamond Shoals Lightship LV 71 was torpedoed by a German sub after the keeper, Walter Barnett of Buxton, the officer in charge, radioed the sub to land. When the sub intercepted the contact, it messaged the lightship it had only minutes before it also would be hit. The officer in charge and his men quickly manned the lifeboat and rowed to safety as the ship was blasted off by U-140. During that same attack, the German sub sent torpedoes toward the USS *Merak,* an American cargo ship. The crewman on watch on the *Merak* saw the wake of the torpedo and took evasive measures to avoid a hit. In so doing, the ship ran aground on the Diamond Shoals. The submarine surfaced and began to strafe the deck of the *Merak.* The crew escaped and were picked up by the *Lightship.* They were then given the warning, and all escaped once again in lifeboats. All of this happened within twelve miles of shore. The heavy artillery broke windows in some Hatteras residences.

* *Most of the ships aground were barks, wrecked before the lifesaving stations were in full operation. The ships, their passengers, and the cargo washed up on the beach, up and down the forty-two miles that make up the island.*
** *The only station left in the United States that demonstrates the old lifesaving method of breeches buoy rescues. Once a week at the old Chicamacomico Station in Rodanthe, the drill is performed for spectators.*

CPSIA information can be obtained
at www.ICGtesting.com
Printed in the USA
LVHW08s1828090718
583168LV00001B/77/P